KISS TO Shatter

ANNA B. DOE

Text copyright © 2022 Anna B. Doe
All Rights Reserved
Copyediting by Once Upon a Typo
Proofreading by Once Upon a Typo
Cover Design by Najla Qamber Designs
Cover Photography by by Braadyn
ISBN: 9798363802577

This is a work of fiction. Names, characters, places, and incidents are the products of the author's imagination or are used fictitiously and are not to be construed as real. Any resemblance to actual events, locales, organizations or persons, living or dead, is entirely coincidental.

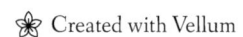

❧ Created with Vellum

Dance with me.
Bring my demons to their knees.
- Nicole Lyons

CONTENT WARNING

While *Shattered & Salvaged Duet* isn't a dark romance, the duet contains mature content and dark themes appropriate for readers 18+.

I've decided to include a list of trigger warnings to help readers decide if this book is for you. The list contains some major spoilers, so to avoid disappointing readers who want to go in blind, I've posted the full list of trigger warnings for this duet, but also my other books, on my webpage and you can find it here: https://www.annabdoe.com/trigger-warnings

BLURB

Prescott Wentworth is my brother's best friend and teammate. We hate each other. But we also can't keep our hands off each other.

The day I met the star wide receiver, he was acting like a grumpy ass, and I was so over big, bulky men messing with my life. He was gorgeous, with wide shoulders, a chiseled jaw hidden behind a week's worth of scruff, and the meanest glare I've seen in my life. So what if he was injured during a game? At least he's alive, not that he appreciates it.

Now it's a new school year, but some things never change.

Like the sizzling tension between Prescott and me every time we're in the same room. But the more we fight, the more I want to shut him up. With my mouth.

Then he sees me on a date with someone else, and something in him snaps.

The deal is simple: it's just sex, and nobody can ever find out. Especially not my brother.

But then the demons from my past come back to haunt me. The darker they become, the more I need Prescott. And I'm beginning to feel like he needs me too.

NOTE: Kiss To Shatter is book one in Shattered & Salvaged Duet. It ends on a cliffhanger. Shattered & Salvaged Duet contains dark and mature themes appropriate for readers 18+. For the full list of trigger warnings please visit www.annabdoe.com/trigger-warnings.

Prologue

JADE

People always say that one moment can change your life forever.

For me, it wasn't a moment as much as it was the words that were said.

Four words, to be exact.

Four simple words that shattered my life as I knew it.

The cancer is back.

After that, nothing was ever the same again.

Chapter 1

PRESCOTT

I mindlessly scroll through my social media, my leg bouncing up and down with nerves. I've been sitting here waiting for the better part of the last half an hour. Like seriously, why is this a thing? Aren't appointments made to avoid this insanity? Apparently, the answer would be no.

I slide my finger over the screen, and dozens of photos of my friends during the summer break fill my feed. Beaches, mountains, parks, parties... You name it; they've done it.

The familiar image of Central Park pops up on my screen, I almost scrolled past it, but then I see her. Her back is to the camera, but it's her. That dark hair is pulled up in a high ponytail revealing the graceful line of her neck. I trace my finger over the image, the temptation to click on her name almost overwhelming.

"Prescott Wentworth?"

My head snaps up instantly at the sound of my name. An older woman is looking around the waiting room at the handful of people sitting there. Locking my phone, I stand up.

"That's me."

The nurse smiles. "You can enter. The doctor will see you shortly."

"Thanks," I say, just as the deep voice behind me mutters: "It is about fucking time."

Great, just what I needed.

The nurse's smile falls instantly because, of course, he wasn't trying to hide his disdain. Oh, no. Henry Wentworth wants everybody to know when he isn't happy. Why should anybody else have a good day when he's an unhappy son of a bitch.

The chair next to me creaks as he gets to his feet.

With an apologetic smile in the direction of the nurse, I make my way to the office. The moment the door closes behind us, I turn around to glare at my father. "Was that really necessary?"

"Of course it was!" Dad scowls at me, the vein in his forehead throbbing. "We've been waiting here for the past forty minutes."

I pull out my chair. "Nobody asked you to come."

That was not the right thing to say because his face turned beet red. "The last I checked, I'm still paying for your insurance, and you better remember that."

Because how could I forget?

My fingers clench by my sides as I try to regain my composure and not blurt out what's on the tip of my tongue. Thankfully, the door opens just then, and Dr. Stevens steps in.

"Hello, Prescott. It's good to see you again."

"It'd have been better if we were received thirty minutes ago," Dad says, sitting down in his chair. "You know when our appointment was actually scheduled?"

Seriously? I glare at my dad, but he's too busy scrolling through his phone.

Dr. Stevens, the best freaking orthopedic surgeon on the east coast, shifts his attention from Dad to me and back.

"I'm sorry for the wait, but there was an emergency they needed my assistance with..."

"Of course, there was." Dad rolls his eyes. "Can we get along with this? Some of us try not to be late to their meetings."

The doctor's jaw clenches, and I'm not sure which one of us wants to deck him more at this moment. "Of course. Let's get to business, shall we?"

The doctor opens the file and pulls out some papers along with an x-ray.

"Hmm..."

I shift in my seat, my foot tapping furiously against the floor as I watch my doctor from across the table. His lips are pursed as he looks at the latest scan of my knee.

This was it, the final verdict.

Mid-season last year, my ACL tore during a game, and I had to have surgery to repair it. After months of pain and healing and PT, it all comes down to this very moment, and I'm not sure if I'm ready.

My palms are sweaty with nerves. I brush them against the side of my leg, letting my fingers wrap around the armrest.

Why is this taking so long?

An elbow connects with my side, snapping me out of my thoughts. I turn my attention to my father, who just glares at me. It's easy for him to be calm; it's not like his whole life is on the line.

No, mine is.

My football career.

My future.

My promise.

"Can we cut to the chase already?" Dad asks impatiently. "Will he or won't he be able to play?"

I'm not sure why he insisted on coming with me. It's not like I'm five and need him here, and God knows he doesn't fucking care, one way or the other.

"The scan looks good. It seems like everything has healed well." The doctor turns toward me, pushing his glasses up his nose. "How do you feel, Prescott? Any pain?"

I flex my knee, feeling slight resistance that's been there ever since the surgery, but the pain that's been a part of my daily life for the last few months isn't there. Then again, I haven't been to the gym today, so I'm not even lying when I say: "It feels good. No pain."

Not technically.

The doctor hums once again, his eyes going over my chart. "Based on the notes from Dr. Snow, she thinks you're ready to get back on the field."

My heart does a little flip in my chest. "So, I can play again?"

"I don't see why not. The last few weeks, you've been progressively working on getting your muscles back, and while you're still not at a hundred percent, I believe once you're back to your normal training regimen, you'll bounce back in no time."

His words ring in my mind, but it takes a while for them to really register.

I can actually play again.

Really, truly play again.

I close my eyes and let out a shaky breath, trying my best to compose myself. After months of healing and rehab, I'm cleared to return to the field.

Cleared to *play*.

And just in time for my senior year to start.

"Thanks, Doc," I say, my voice tight.

"Don't thank me. Thank yourself. I know this took longer

than originally planned, but you've worked really hard to get back to where you were before. You should be proud, Prescott."

Dad looks up from his phone. "Are we done here?"

I turn to my father, but not even his asshole behavior will be able to dull my excitement. I've just gotten the best news possible, the news I've been waiting on for months, and nobody will destroy this for me. Especially not him.

Doc nods. "Just let me write you a clearance letter, and you're all good to go."

Dad didn't even bother waiting for the doctor to finish before getting up and leaving, which was completely fine by me. After I'm done at the hospital, I get in my car and go straight to campus. The weight that's been sitting on my shoulders since I entered the hospital last November is finally lifted, and I'm not about to spend another damn minute sitting on my ass and twirling my fingers when I have work to do if I want to make this season count.

There is no if, I remind myself. *You have to make it count. You promised.*

The parking lot is almost full when I pull my mustang into a parking spot in front of the football facilities. It's early afternoon, and since we have a few more days before classes start, Coach is pushing the team to work harder than ever. My fingers itch to put on my jersey and join my team out on the field.

Nine months.

It's been nine long months since I've been able to play.

Grabbing the doctor's note, I get out of the car and pull out my duffle bag from the trunk where it's been all this time. At this point, after all the years of playing, keeping my bag around has become second nature. I throw the duffle bag over my shoulder and head into the building, the AC hitting me straight in the face as I make my way toward the field.

The first things I hear are the noises—the grunting and panting, whistle blowing, Coach yelling. The corner of my mouth tips upward as I slowly step onto the field and let myself take it all in—the smell of the grass, and the feel of the sun burning my skin, making the sweat drip down my face. I tilt my head back, looking up at the stands. Stands that can hold thousands of people on a game night. Watching, chanting...

"Sullivan! What the fuck did I say?" Coach bellows, snapping me out of my thoughts.

The sophomore clenches his fingers by his sides, his face beet red. "Right."

"Exactly, *right*. Then why the fuck did you go left? Who the fuck is supposed to catch the ball? Your opponents? Let's do this again, and this time try to remember your right from your left."

"Okay, Coach."

"Again!"

As my teammates line up, I make my way to the sidelines where the coaching staff is standing and clear my throat, "Coach."

The older man slowly turns toward me, his dark eyes meeting mine. "Wentworth, fancy seeing you here."

"Well, I guess that's good since you'll be seeing more of me starting now."

I hand him the doctor's note, turning my attention to the field. I watch as Nixon calls the play; players start moving as Nixon pulls back into the pocket. My brain is processing the whole thing almost as if it's in slow motion. Nixon's hand pulls back as he gets ready to throw. That Sullivan guy barely makes his way through the defensive line but is not fast enough to be at the right place at the right time. The defense intercepts the ball and runs it into the end zone.

Coach mutters something under his breath, his hand running over his face and through his hair in frustration.

"Go suit up, Wentworth." I blink, unsure if I heard him correctly. He turns toward me and glares. "What are you waiting for? A special invitation?"

"No, Coach."

"Then why the fuck are you still standing here? Go, you have two minutes, or I'm making everybody run drills."

I glance toward the field, a smile slowly making its way to my lips. "Based on what I've seen, Coach, maybe more drills aren't such a bad thing."

Before I can react, his hand slaps me over the head. "If I wanted to hear your opinion, I would have asked for it. Two minutes."

"Yes, Coach."

I hoist my bag higher and turn on the balls of my feet when Coach calls my name.

"Yeah?" I glance over my shoulder, but his attention is already on the field, looking for his next victim to yell at.

"It's good to have you back, Wentworth."

I let myself take in the field one more time. "It's good to be back."

Chapter 2

PRESCOTT

"Why the fuck didn't you tell me you were coming?" Nixon asks when we get back into the locker room. "That you're *playing*?"

I plop onto the bench in front of my locker. My legs feel like jelly from exertion, and a jab of pain spreads through my knee and into my muscles.

Fucking hell, this was harsh.

I guess I shouldn't have expected anything else. I haven't been properly conditioning in months. It'll take some time to get back in my pre-injury shape.

You don't have time for that.

"When were you cleared, dude?" Jamie, our running back, asks as more of my teammates enter the locker room.

"This morning. I came straight from the doctor's appointment to tell you assholes the good news." I press my hand against my thigh, my fingers gripping the tense muscles. "Not that you seem to appreciate it."

"You had your doctor's appointment today?" Nixon crosses his arms over his chest. "What the fuck, dude? Why didn't you say anything?"

"Because I didn't want you to hover over me like a fucking hen, Cole." I push to my feet, gritting my teeth to brace for any possible pain. "Now, will you give me some space to change, or are you waiting for me to whip my dick out so you can all appreciate that bad boy?"

Harry, one of our kickers, shakes his head. "One would think you'd be happy to be back."

"I would," I glare at my teammates. "If you all weren't as nosey as women."

Manni bursts into laughter, slapping me none too gently over the shoulder. "It's good to have you back, Wentworth."

I straighten, rubbing at my sore shoulder to match my throbbing knee, my eyes falling on the sophomore wide receiver who took my spot last year.

Joshua Sullivan.

He's watching me silently from the bench on the other side of the room, his lips pressed into a tight line.

"It's good to be back."

Finally, my teammates go about their own goddamn business, leaving me alone. Not my best friend, though.

"What?" I ask Nixon, pulling my shirt over my head and tossing it on the bench. I was sweating so badly from the workout the coach put us through; the damn thing was clinging to my skin.

"Seriously, why didn't you say anything? I could have gone with you."

And have my best friend, who's set to enter the draft next year, be there in case the doctors tell me that I'll never be able to play again? Fuck that.

"It's fine. It's not the first nor will it be the last appointment I do on my own. Besides, you had practice."

Nixon's eyes narrow at me, silently calling out my bullshit.

"Seriously, dude. It's fine." I turn to my locker, put my

combination in, and pull out my duffle. "I'm fine." *Just feeling the consequences of not practicing for months.* "I'm back on the field, so it's all good."

Nixon turns to his locker. *Fucking finally.* "I still think you're an asshole for not telling anybody what's going on." He looks at me over his shoulder. "Not like that's something new, but still..."

No, it's not. I've been a grumpy asshole these last few months ever since I got injured, and even more when the injury took its sweet time to heal.

As if it's completely healed now, a little voice in the back of my head taunts me just as another jab of pain goes through my leg as I shift my weight. Grinding my teeth, I push it back.

"It was good to have you back, though."

"Aww..." I force out a grin. "Did you miss me, Cole?"

A sweaty shirt hits me in the head. "In your dreams, you idiot." I pull the shirt off and toss it back at him, but he manages to catch it. "I'm off to shower."

"Need me to come and hold your hand?"

Nixon shakes his head. "Forget I ever said anything."

Laughing, I turn my attention to my duffle bag and start pulling out my stuff. As I'm tugging out my shirt, my palm wraps around a plastic bottle. I look down, my fingers tightening around it as I realize what I'm holding—my pain meds. They probably got lost in all the other bullshit I've been carrying in this bag from the time when I was going to my PT. I totally forgot I had them.

I suck in a breath, my heart racing faster as I just stare at the bottle as if I'm transfixed. The pain I've been in just after the surgery flashes in my mind, and then there was the sweet oblivion after I gave in and took the pill.

Almost on autopilot, I pop open the lid, staring at the last few remaining pills inside, and the promise of that sweet, sweet oblivion grows stronger than ever.

I could take one. Hell, even just half of the pill would make this pain go away. Just...

"Dude, why didn't you go and shower?" the sudden question snaps me back to reality, all the noises filling the locker room coming back to me.

I quickly snap the lid back in place and drop the bottle into my bag before turning to face Nixon.

"I was just checking my phone," I lie, grabbing my towel and gel as Nixon pulls his own phone out of the bag. "You wanna go and grab something to eat after we're done?"

"Actually... How about you join me?"

I narrow my eyes at him. He was all easy smiles, but there was something about his tone that made me suspicious. "Whatever for?"

If he wanted me to come to his place to watch him and his new wife fawn over each other, he didn't know me for shit. Nobody in their right mind would force themselves to endure that torture, although Yasmin was a pretty good cook.

"I just need your help with something. So, you coming or what?"

He's evading, and that can never be good.

"Am I going to regret this?"

Nixon thinks about it for a moment before nodding. "Most likely. So, you in or what?"

That was what I was afraid of.

"Fine." I rub my hand over my face. "I'm in. But you owe me."

"Yeah, yeah. How about you wash off the stink and meet me at Emmett's in half an hour?"

Emmett's, but that's...

"Nixon..." I turn around, but my best friend's already walking out of the locker room.

Closing the door of my mustang, I look up at Emmett's building. Well, technically, it's my building complex, too, since earlier this summer, I moved here with one of my hockey buddies, Spencer.

I still have no idea what we're doing here since Emmett graduated last spring, but it better be good, or I might strangle Nixon.

I'm just about to call him to see what the hell's going on when I see a nice ass peeking from the back of the trunk in one of the tiniest pairs of shorts I've seen. I give it an appreciative look—it's a fine ass, sue me—and my gaze drops down those toned legs before slowly making my way up just as the girl steps back from the car, her face coming into view.

Fucking hell.

Of course, it had to be *her*.

Because that's just my luck.

Jade Cole.

My best friend's little sister and the bane of my existence.

I have barely seen her since we returned from Hawaii, where we spent spring break with our friends. A spring break where on the last day, when everybody else was asleep, she snuck out to the beach to skinny dip and challenged me to join her. A challenge I couldn't ignore, although I knew better.

But now she's here, and the image of her naked body illuminated by the moonlight and that silky skin of hers brushing against mine underwater pops back in my mind, more vivid than ever. My whole body stiffens at the memory, my cock growing painfully hard.

For the ever-loving God. She's your best friend's little sister! Get a grip, Wentworth.

Why couldn't we continue with the pattern from last spring? Where I barely would catch glimpses of her in passing. The less I saw her, the less tempted I'd be to do anything about these... feelings she evoked in me. A weird mix between wanting to strangle her and wanting to kiss the hell out of her. Neither of which I can do anything about.

I almost—*almost*—got her out of my head, but now she's back, and, of course, my life couldn't be that easy.

I watch as a strand of that lush dark hair slips from the confines of her ponytail and falls into her face. She puffs it away; her cheeks pink from the work as she hauls a big-ass armchair out of the trunk of the truck.

"Give me that." Crossing the distance, I grab the armchair out of her grasp. Not so much because I want to help but because I need something to help hide the boner in my workout shorts.

"What the..." Jade turns around, those stormy, blue-gray eyes sending daggers my way. "What are *you* doing here?"

"Trying to help?"

Jade puts her hands on the chair and tugs it toward her. "Well, I don't remember asking for your help."

"Seriously?"

"Yes, seriously." Her eyes narrow. "Now, let go of my chair."

"I'm not letting go." I tug the chair toward me. "The damn thing is probably twice as heavy as you. Now, will you let it go before you fall on your ass?"

"I'm not letting it go," she grits, the color rising in her cheeks. "Besides, I don't see how that's your problem."

"It apparently is my problem since Nixon told me to come here."

If possible, those stormy eyes turn even darker.

"Of course he did," she mutters. "Well, your services aren't necessary, so off you go."

Off you go? Is she serious right now? Once again, I tug the damn chair toward me. "You shouldn't chase off people who are trying to help you."

She pulls the chair toward her. "I didn't *ask* for your help."

I tug it back harder. "Why do you always have to be so difficult, doll?"

"Don't call me that!"

Jade stomps her foot and pulls once again. Only this time, the armchair actually slips from my grasp. Her eyes turn wide as she loses her balance and starts falling back. I try to grab it before it falls on her, but I lose my footing in the process.

Fucking hell.

Shoving the chair out of the way, I slip my hand around her waist and pull her to me. There's just enough time for me to shift our positions as we both fall to the ground.

The air is kicked out of my lungs, and I swear every bone in my body feels rearranged from the force of the impact. I close my eyes and breathe in a shaky breath as I try to compose myself and just... breathe.

This is so not *what I needed.*

A hand presses against my chest, and a warm breath touches my face.

"Are you crazy?!" Jade hisses.

I blink my eyes open, her face coming into view. My vision is slightly blurry, so it takes me a few tries until that familiar scowl comes into focus. Not like I couldn't have lived without it.

Jade jabs her finger into my chest, drawing my attention. "Do you have a death wish?"

"I could ask you the same thing." I try to shift, but a jolt of pain spreads through my leg. I bite back a hiss, forcing the words out, "If you weren't so stubborn..."

"Me?" she shifts on top of me, her palm pressing against my chest as she sits upright, her pelvis rubbing against mine. "I'm the stubborn one?"

"Yes, you," I groan loudly and grab her hips. "Will you stop moving already? Wasn't it enough that you beat me..."

"Beat you?"

"Yes, beat me. I'm pretty sure I have bruises since you aren't exactly light."

Her lips parted, those stormy eyes widening in outrage. I expect her to rip me a new one in three, two, o—

"What do you two think you're doing?"

We both look up only to find a very pissed Nixon standing above us, his arms crossed over his chest as he glares at us. Or, well, more precisely, me. "Well?"

"Hey, don't look at me!" I protest. "She fell on top of me, not the other way around."

"Of course, it's my fault!" Jade grumbles, slamming her clenched fist against me.

"It is! If it weren't for your stubborn ass, the ass still sitting on top of me, by the way, none of this would have happened."

"Wha—" Jade sucks in a breath, her cheeks heating as she realizes I'm right. Or maybe she can just feel my boner poking her, not that there is anything that I can do about that. "Ugh, I hate you," she mutters and quickly scrambles to her feet.

"Of course you do," I roll my eyes exaggeratedly, just because I know it'll piss her off even more. "I was just trying to do a good deed and help you so this very thing wouldn't happen. But did you listen?" I lean against my elbows, my muscles protesting the movement. Tomorrow's practice will be a bitch. "Of-fucking-course not. Damn woman."

With some effort, I manage to push to my feet only for Jade to jab her finger into my chest with every word she says: "I. Don't. Remember. Asking. For. Your. Help."

I grab her wrist to stop her from poking me. "Will you stop it already?"

"Okay, okay, okay, will you both stop it?" Nixon gets in between us; his face turned toward his sister.

See? I'm not the only one who realizes she's the problematic one out of the two of us.

Jade glares at me over her brother's shoulder. "I'll stop it when he admits he's the one in the wrong."

"I invited him, Smalls. Will you chill already?"

"And who gave you permission to do that?" Jade tilts her head to the side and crosses her arms over her chest.

"I didn't realize I needed fucking permission." Nixon says without missing a beat. "I figured you wanted this done as soon as possible."

"I do, but between you, Zane, and Mason, we have more than enough help. You didn't have to invite *him*."

The way she says him, you'd think I'm the devil reincarnated.

I dust off my pants. "Trust me, doll, if I knew he was asking me to come and help *you*, I'd have found a reason to stay away."

Jade presses her lips in a tight line and grinds her teeth. "And that's exactly what I've been trying to tell you all along." She grabs that damn chair off the ground. "Now that we've got that figured out. Go to hell, Wentworth."

With that, she marches toward the building without a backward glance.

Nixon shakes his head and turns toward me. "Was that really necessary?"

"What? She started it. I just tried to be *nice* and help."

"I seriously don't understand you two."

"What's there to understand? She's a spoiled brat, and, for whatever reason, she hates my guts."

"Hate might be too strong of a..." Nixon starts, but I give

him a pointed look which has him reconsidering. "Okay, yes, she pretty much hates your guts."

She didn't hate your guts when you were in Hawaii last spring, a little voice reminds me, but I push it back.

I'll most definitely *not* think about that fiasco.

"Besides, it was your idea to invite me without telling me shit. So thanks for that, dude."

"Oh, come on! Would you have come if I told you?"

I narrow my eyes at him.

"That's what I thought," Nixon grins. He starts toward the truck where Jade picked up the chair earlier. "Although seriously, you should be thanking me. What else would you have done this fine afternoon?"

"Oh, I don't know, gone to Moore's to celebrate the fact that I'm back on the field?"

"And we'll do that. Once we haul all this shit up into Jade's apartment."

I look skeptically at the trunk, where a few boxes are still inside. "How much of it is there?" *Maybe they're close to being done?* "That it?"

If so, I can do this good deed, not that the lady in question will appreciate it, Nixon will be happy, and I can go about my afternoon as planned. Moore's, a few drinks, maybe a lady to help me forget the throbbing in my knee and... other parts.

Help me forget *her.*

"Umm..." Nixon rubs the back of his neck. "There might be more at Maddox's."

More?

"How much more are we talking about?"

Nixon turns his back to me, grabbing a couple of boxes and shoving them into my hands.

"Nixon? How much more?" He keeps his mouth firmly shut. "Goddammit. How much stuff can one girl have?"

"It's technically three girls. But you're doing a good deed. Think of it as extra practice; only you'll get a beer afterward, too."

I tighten my hands around the boxes, shifting the weight. "I feel like a beer ain't gonna cut it."

"Just carry the boxes, Prescott. The faster you do it, the faster we'll be done."

Chapter 3

JADE

"Dammit!" I mutter as I place the chair in the living room. My back hurts, and my arms hurt. Everything hurts. But it's worth it because there's no way I'd have let *him* carry that damn chair upstairs if for nothing else than to show him he's wrong. "Freaking idiot."

"Who's an idiot?" Yasmin asks as she comes into the living room.

"My stupid brother, aka your husband."

Yasmin chuckles, "What did he do now?"

"Did you know he invited Wentworth?" I prop my hands against my hips.

Yasmin's brows rise. "I didn't realize that, no."

"Of all the people! I swear if I don't strangle him, nobody will."

"Strangle who?" Grace asks, popping her head from her room. She looks from me to Yasmin and back, tucking a strand of her auburn hair behind her ear. "What's going on?"

Yasmin leans against the doorway. "Jade's pissed because Nixon invited Prescott over."

Penny turns toward us, eyes wide. "He did not."

If somebody knows about our weird dynamic, it would be Penny. After all, she had a front-row seat to our fights during the spring break week we spent in Hawaii.

Henry, her guide dog, lifts his head from his paws and looks at his mistress. It's like the dog has a keen awareness when she's distressed or might need him.

"He damn well did. He deserves to suffer."

Yasmin shakes her head. "Just leave him in one piece? I love my husband."

I roll my eyes at Yasmin and her mushiness. "Don't remind me. You're lucky I love you, otherwise..."

Some days it was still hard for me to grasp that my twenty-one-year-old brother was married. And it's not from their lack of PDA. I swear, one of these days, I really might puke from their sweetness. But I'm happy for them. If anybody deserves to be happy after everything that has happened over the last few years, it's my brother.

"What's your deal with him anyway?" Grace's question breaks me out of my thoughts.

"What do you mean?" I ask carefully.

"I second that." Yasmin pushes off the doorway and grabs one of the boxes from the floor to take it to the kitchen, joining Penny. "Why don't you like the guy? I mean, your bickering..."

My nose scrunches. "We don't bicker."

"...is entertaining to watch, but still. What gives?" Yasmin finishes, completely ignoring my interruption. She opens the box, her eyes still on me. "Is there a particular reason you don't like him?"

"My brother?" I pull my brows together. "He's just annoying, but I guess it goes along with big brother territory, although..."

"I'm not talking about Nixon," Yasmin gives me her you'll-have-to-try-harder-than-that-to-fool-me look. "What's your deal with Prescott?"

"Wentworth?" Tingles run down my spine at the mention of his name. I pull my brows together. I should most definitely not feel *tingly* at the thought of that man.

"Yes, Wentworth. What's the deal between you two? Why are you always fighting like cats and dogs?"

Not always.

We didn't fight that last night in Hawaii. Far from it. But then we got back home, and I haven't seen him since. Not that I wanted to see him. The guy is stubborn, infuriating, and so damn broody. He's been acting like injuring his leg and sitting out half the season is the end of the world. He's been biting everybody's head off at the slightest comment for months when so many worse things could have happened.

"Because he's irritating?" I suggest sweetly.

"That's bullshit, and you know it."

"I don't know, Yas. Seems good enough to me." I shrug. "There's a bunch of reasons why I don't like him. Starting with the fact that he's a self-centered, broody asshole. Is that better?"

Yasmin opens her mouth as if she's about to contradict me. I raise my brow, waiting, but no words come out.

"Okay, you might be right. But he's not that bad."

I go toward the fridge, grabbing a bottle of water. "Like herpes isn't bad, it's just annoying?"

"Now you're just being mean. He's been dealing with a lot since his injury. Maybe if you met him before..."

"And that excuses his behavior; how again?"

"It doesn't. I just think you should cut him some slack." Yasmin gives me a pointed look. "Somebody could say the same thing about you, you know."

"You saying I'm a shitty friend, Yas?"

"No, of course not, but you've been edgy lately. What's going on with you?"

I press my mouth together. The last things I want to talk about are me and my demons. God knows there are so many of them that if we open that particular box, I'd be overwhelmed by it all, drowned in my own darkness. Can't blame a girl for wanting to keep it all tightly locked.

"I'm fine," I shrug.

"Don't trust her," Grace says. "That's what she's been telling me for weeks now."

I shoot a dirty look at my best friend. Of course, she'd go and spill my secrets. "Maybe because it's true. Ever thought of that?"

"No, you've definitely been off," Penny chimes in.

"What's this today? Everybody against Jade day?"

"See? Everybody can see it. If I didn't know better, maybe I'd trust you." Grace shakes her head. "And don't go scowling at me like that. The only thing you'll accomplish is getting wrinkles."

"Why are you not with your boyfriend again?"

Along with my brother and Yasmin, both Rei and Grace invited their boyfriends to come and help us move into our apartment.

"He and Matteo are putting together my bed, or at least they're trying to," she shrugs. "I figured it's best for me to stay out of their way."

The three of us exchange a look before bursting into laughter. "Boys..."

"What boys?"

I turn around to find Nixon standing at the door, a couple of boxes in his hands.

"You, who else?" I glance over his shoulder. Prescott is standing behind him, carrying more boxes.

"I'll have you know. There are no boys here, only men, little sister."

"Mhmm... Of course, you are."

Nixon's eyes narrow on me. "Where do you want me to put these?"

"What does it say on the box?"

"No idea, Smalls. I didn't check."

I roll my eyes. Of course, he didn't. "Just put it wherever, and we'll sort through it."

"Wherever it is." Nixon drops the boxes next to the coffee table, dusting off his hands on the side of his legs.

"You done?" Yasmin asks him, pulling the plates out of the box and taking them to the cupboard.

"Almost." Nixon goes to her, wrapping his arms around her middle and pulling her to him, his lips brushing against the top of her head. "There's still stuff at Maddox's, so we'll go and grab them."

I watch as Yasmin turns in my brother's arms and smiles up at him. An ache spreads through my chest, making my lungs squeeze. I turn around, only to come face to face with Prescott. He drops the boxes on the floor before straightening to his full height. And damn, the man is tall enough I have to tilt my head back to be able to look him in the eyes.

Our gazes meet, and I swear I can feel his arms wrapped around my waist, feel his body heat enveloping me. A shudder runs through me.

As if he can read my mind, he quirks one of his brows at me, amusement dancing in his dark brown eyes. The corner of his mouth lifts in a smug smirk. The only kind of smile he has these days. But I remember that one time, three years ago, when he had a genuine smile that made my heart stop.

Before he was pissed at the world because of his injury.

Before I was broken and jaded after witnessing my mom's death.

Before, when we were just two kids who knew nothing about life.

"C'mon, Wentworth, let's get rolling."

My brother's voice snaps me out of my thoughts. I blink, taking a step back. Prescott looks at me for a second longer before shifting his attention to my brother. "Let's go."

I turn around, grabbing one of the boxes. When I look up, I find Grace watching me silently.

"I'm going to put these away," I say to nobody in particular and dash for the bathroom.

Closing the door behind me, I drop the box on the counter and lean against it, letting out a long breath.

This is ridiculous.

My phone vibrates, drawing my attention. Grateful for the distraction from the certain somebody who shall not be named, I pull the phone out of my back pocket. I'm expecting Nixon's message about one thing or another like he's sent me so far, but it's not my brother.

Unknown: Where are you? I stopped by the house, but it was empty.

Unknown: We need to talk.

Unknown: I miss you.

My fingers clench around the phone as I reread the messages. This is so not the kind of distraction I had in mind. Swallowing the lump in my throat, I exit the app and lock my phone before sliding it back in place. Shoving all the unwanted thoughts to the back of my mind, I leave the bathroom and join my friends.

"So I told her, babe, either you stop that shit, or there won't be anything left for the second round," Matteo, best friend of Grace's boyfriend Mason, shakes his head as everybody starts laughing. "I swear to you, some chicks are crazy."

He joined us a couple of hours ago, slightly traumatized from his most recent hookup. No one could blame him if the story he told us was true.

"Dude, you have to stop using dating apps. There are a hundred shades of crazy over there."

My back stiffens at Prescott's dark chuckle.

I open my mouth to tell him exactly what I think, but my brother's faster.

"As if you're the one to talk. Did you forget that chick that was legit *mewing* when she was all hot and bothered?" Yasmin slaps Nixon over the head. "*Ouch!*" He looks down at her, pouting exaggeratedly. "What was that for?"

"Do you really have to be so crass?"

Nixon rubs the back of his head. "Is it really crass if it's true?"

Prescott lets out a loud groan, "You did not just remind me of that."

"Mewing?" Mason asks.

"So there was this chick..." Nixon starts, just as Prescott pushes to his feet.

"No, nope, not listening."

"Oh, come on! You can't leave us hanging like this now," Matteo protests. "I shared my crazy dating story with you."

"I can, and I will. I'm off to take a piss while he tells you the story."

That dark gaze meets mine, so I roll my eyes. "So charming."

The muscle in his jaw twitches. "We can't all be princesses like you."

I grit my teeth, but before I can say anything, he slips through the glass door and into the apartment.

We finished moving in about an hour ago, just about the time the pizza came, so we sat down on the balcony to chill for a while. It felt like every bone and muscle in my body was hurting, but we were mostly done and just in time for classes to start.

The place was really great. Not only did it have three separate bedrooms, along with two bathrooms, a make-shift kitchen, living, and dining room, but it was also within walking distance from campus, which would make it easy since I didn't bother bringing my car.

"She was legit mewing?" Matteo asks, returning my attention back to the current topic.

"No shit. It was hilarious. Hayden was passing by his room and heard it all. So he called us to come and listen. We almost pissed our pants as we were eavesdropping. Later he told us that he tried to keep his cool and thought it was a one-time deal, but no matter what he tried to do, the result was the same. Kiss? Mew. Touch? Mew."

My body tingles, remembering exactly the feel of those hard hands and calloused fingertips touching my skin. A shiver runs through me at the phantom touch. Prescott Wentworth definitely knew how to touch a woman.

"Shit, that's crazy." Matteo shakes his head. "What did he do?"

"If I hadn't been there, I wouldn't have believed it. The dude practically ran us over as he dashed out of his dorm, half-laughing, half in a panic to get the girl out and away from him."

The guys burst into laughter. And okay, it is a little bit funny. Mewing when you're turned on? Who does that? But the poor girl didn't deserve them making fun of her for it.

Schooling my features, I pinch Nixon's side. "You guys are

such pigs." I roll my eyes. "Maybe the girl was mewing because he was a shitty lay. Ever thought of that?"

"Not particularly, no," my brother muses, rubbing his chin. "But now that you mention it..."

"Of course not." I finish my drink. With the way this night is going, I better bring out the whole bottle. "I'm going to grab more drinks; anybody needs a refill?"

There are a few nods in agreement around the table as I get up and grab the pitcher. I slide into the kitchen. The place is still messy, with a few unopened boxes sitting on the counter waiting to be emptied, but the vast majority are placed on the floor, opened, and ready to be recycled.

I look up and spot Prescott leaning against the doorway.

"Fucking hell. How long have you been standing there?"

He crosses his arms over his chest, completely unfazed. "Shitty lay, Cole? That's the best you've got?"

I'm not sure which I hate more; when he calls me by my last name or doll.

I raise my brow at him. "Eavesdropping, Wentworth?"

He ignores my taunt. "I can assure you; these hands know exactly how to make a woman's body sing."

My stomach clenches at his words, and my mouth goes dry. I curl my fingers, my nails digging into my palms.

Get yourself in order, Jade.

"Or mew as it appears."

I try to say it with a straight face, I really do, but it's so damn hard. I bite the inside of my cheek to prevent myself from laughing out loud, but it's useless. The last thing I see before turning my back on him is Prescott's eyes narrowed at me, a frown appearing between his brows.

Good, that makes two of us.

The cool air hits me in the face as soon as I open the fridge. I grab a stack of beer and place it on the counter before pulling out a bottle of mixed mojito and refilling the pitcher. Once done, I leave it in the sink and turn around, only to collide with a hard chest.

"That chick was crazy," he mutters.

"Mhmm... it's always the girl's fault."

"This doesn't have anything to do with faults. It's just a fact. She was freaking *mewing*. I couldn't invent that shit up even if I tried really hard."

I pat him on the chest, feeling the strong, warm muscles under my fingertips. "Whatever you have to tell yourself to sleep better at night."

In a split second, his fingers wrap around my wrist, and he tugs me closer. I suck in a sharp breath as those dark eyes of his meet mine. "You're playing a dangerous game, Cole."

The corner of my mouth tilts upward. "Why? Are you planning to show me just how right you are?"

The energy sizzles between us from the pent-up tension. His eyes darken, his fingers around my wrist tightening as my heart speeds up a notch, but as soon as it appears, it's all gone.

Prescott drops my hand as if I burned him, taking a step back and putting distance between us. Some much-needed distance.

I turn my back on him and let out a long breath, trying to collect myself. "Didn't think so." I grab the beers and shove them into his hands. "Take those out."

"Seriously?"

I raise my brow. "Do I look like I'm joking?"

"Shouldn't you treat me better? After all, I did help you move and carry your shit up, you know?"

I glance at him over my shoulder. "I'm sure that even if I forget, you'll be there to remind me. Now carry those outside."

He grabs the beers from me and mumbles: "Of course, why appreciate the fact that an injured man is helping you?"

"You're a far cry from an injured man, Wentworth. Get your head out of your ass for once, will ya?" I push him toward the door. "And you better not make me spill mojito, or I might strangle you."

"So disrespectful."

"If I were you, I'd be careful about what you say. You wouldn't want people to find out that a big, bad football player is afraid of a kitty."

"You wouldn't dare."

"Don't mess with my mojito, and you won't have to find out."

He starts to turn around, but I push him out the door. He stumbles over the threshold, drawing attention to us.

"Good," Yasmin tilts her head back to look at us. "We were worried you two killed each other."

"The jury is still out." I smile sweetly as I walk around him to my seat; all the while, I can feel Prescott's eyes on me. It's unnerving the way just being around him can throw me off-kilter. He irritates me, yet I can't help but look at him.

Like you're only looking at him.

I refill my glass and sit back down. The conversation has shifted from Prescott's sex life—thank God 'cause nobody needs to hear that shit. I sip at my drink. Listening to my friends makes me realize how much I missed this. Spending the summer in New York with Grace was fun, but I missed my friends.

A little before midnight, people start to leave. First, Matteo, then Penny goes next door to her apartment, just as I walk Nixon, Yasmin, and Prescott to the door. Rising on the tips of my toes, I press my lips against Nixon's cheek. No matter how annoying he can be, he's still my brother. My only family, really. "Thanks for helping us today."

"Anytime, Smalls. We still on for brunch on Sunday?"

I roll my eyes at him. Nixon got this new idea that we

should have brunch every weekend, making it a tradition of sorts.

"You know that makes you sound like some rich boy, right? Who even has brunch?"

"We do." He tries to pinch my side, but I'm already anticipating it, so I pull back. "So, brunch on Sunday at Macy's?"

"Yeah, yeah." I give a hug to Yas. "I'll see you two."

I look up, my eyes fixed on Prescott standing behind them, watching us silently. My throat bobs as I swallow. "Thanks for the help," I force the words out.

Surprise flashes on his face, but he recovers quickly. "You're welcome."

"Not that we actually asked, but..."

Bitchy? Maybe. But I couldn't help this feeling that he always has the upper hand on me somehow.

Prescott shakes his head. "You couldn't have left it at thank you, could you?"

The corner of my mouth twitches. "What would be the fun in that?"

"Okay, let's go before you two strangle one another." Nixon turns Prescott around and shoves him in the direction of the exit. "I finally got my wide receiver back, and I need him in one piece if we want a chance of getting that title one last time. We'll see you soon, Smalls."

He's cleared to play?

Prescott looks over his shoulder one last time as the door to the elevator opens, and they step inside.

I stand in the doorway a moment longer, just staring at the elevator. I'm not sure why I'm so surprised. He's always been a good player, and if he weren't injured, the Ravens would have most likely won the championship last year too.

Grace's laughter snaps me out of my thoughts. With a shake

of my head, I enter the apartment to find Grace getting out of her boyfriend's lap, giggling.

My heart clenches at her obvious happiness. When we met, Grace was always so sad. Not that it was surprising, considering the guy she'd been in love with just disappeared out of nowhere, leaving her questioning everything.

Grace must hear me because her attention shifts to me. "They gone?"

"Yeah. They just left." I lift my hands over my head, stretching my sore muscles. "I think I'm going to go take a shower and call it a night."

Grace nods. "I have a break tomorrow at two. Lunch?"

Letting my hands drop, I go over the schedule in my head. "I think I can swing that." I turn my attention to Mason. "Thanks for helping today."

Mason smiles, his fingers clasping around Grace's hand. "Of course."

That damn tightening is back as I look at them, making it hard to breathe. Clearing my throat, I wish them goodnight before going down the hallway.

Rei and Zane went to bed early, which isn't unusual considering they were both going to be up before dawn to go to the rink to practice.

I enter my bedroom and look around at the mess. Our main focus today had been putting together furniture and organizing and cleaning the common spaces, so my bedroom is still one big pile of unopened boxes and suitcases. Opening one, I fish inside for a towel and my PJs before going into the bathroom.

Both Grace and Rei agreed I should take the master bedroom since I was the one who found this apartment, and you won't hear me protest about it.

Closing the door behind me, I turn around and face the bathtub, my mouth going dry at the sight.

"Get a grip, Jade. This isn't the same bathtub; even if it was, you're better." My fingers dig into the counter as I repeat more firmly. "You're better."

Maybe if I say it enough times, I'll make it true.

Turning on the hot water, I turn my back on the bathtub and quickly take off my clothes before slowly looking at the tub again.

It's different than the one I have back at home. When we were remodeling, I convinced my parents to get me one of those freestanding tubs because I loved the way it looked. This one is a shower and tub combo with a glass door.

It's different.

You're different.

Chanting those words to myself, I slip inside the shower. My whole body aches, my skin sticky from sweat and dust clinging to it from all the hard work.

The first touch of warm water on my skin is pure heaven. I tilt my head back, letting the water wash away all the stress of the day, along with the dirt, before grabbing my shampoo. The familiar scent of lavender and rosemary fills the space as I shampoo and rinse my hair before applying the conditioner. While I wait for it to process, I take the body wash and spread it over my fingers, gently rubbing it into my sore muscles.

For a while there, showers were a necessity. I got in, quickly scrubbed myself, and got out because I never knew when my mom would need me. Oh, she said she didn't, but I knew better than to believe her. But since her passing, they have turned therapeutic in a way. Whenever I felt tired or lonely, I'd hop in and let the water wash away the bad memories.

I close my eyes, letting my soapy hands run over my body.

Never a bath, always a shower.

Not after...

The blurry image of the ceiling flashes before my eyes.

The pressure in my chest grew as the air was sucked out of my lungs.

The bubbles all around me as I open my mouth to let out a scream.

My throat grows tight as the memories overwhelm me.

I sink my nails into my skin to ground myself, trying to take a deep breath and then another.

Once I'm calm enough, I finish my shower as quickly as possible and get out.

With a towel safely wrapped around me, I clean off the fog from the mirror and look at my reflection. My face is pale, and I have deep circles under my eyes. The last few weeks have been hard since it's been a two-year anniversary since we found out about mom's cancer. And although overall I've been doing better, there were days when the memories became too much to deal with—the nightmares too hard to shake.

Turning on the faucet, I splash some cold water on my face. As I straighten, the towel holding my hair starts slipping, so I fix it. That's when I notice them.

The bruises.

There are a few scattered over my upper arm and one on my breast.

No, not breast. Underarm. Just under my armpit.

I watch the purple bruises as if transfixed.

Slowly, I raise my hand and trace my fingers over the discoloration.

"I'm telling you; everything was amazing. Theo is just so sweet and perfect and..." I let out a long sigh because, seriously, there are no words to describe just how perfect Theo is. And he's my boyfriend.

My freaking boyfriend!

I never thought I'd have one, but once Nixon went to college and his intimidating, over-the-top shadow wasn't cast over me, people have actually started to notice me.

Boys have started to notice me.

Theo and I had a class together this last semester. We chatted occasionally, but nothing happened until early May when a group of us were studying. We were the last two left alone, and then, out of nowhere, he leaned in and kissed me. We've been dating ever since.

"Yeah, yeah. I know all about how perfect Theo is," Elena, my best friend, comments dryly. "That's all you've been able to talk about lately. Theo-this and Theo-that."

"Elena..." I drawl out as I climb to the second floor. The downstairs was quiet when I got home. Strange, since Mom always makes a point to be there when I get home from my dates.

"Don't Elena-me. You know I'm telling the truth. It's just..."

The light peeking through the gap in the doorway of my parent's room catches my attention, as do the hushed voices.

"Elena, I'll call you back," I say softly. Not waiting for my friend's answer, I hang up before moving closer just to see my dad pacing the room. He runs his fingers through his hair, pushing it back.

"This can't be happening. Not again. Not..."

"You think I want this?" Mom asks, coming into view. "This is the last thing I want. Not now." She extends her hand and grips my dad's arm. "Kevin..."

That's when I see them.

She's wearing one of the sleeveless tops she usually wears for workouts, and there are dark bruises covering her side, just underneath her armpit.

What in the hell... I step forward, pushing the door open. "What's going on?"

I blink, the room coming back into focus, as do the bruises

on my body. Shaking my head to clear my mind, I grab my tee and pull it over my head.

"It's just bruises, Jade. You probably hit yourself carrying all the damn boxes," I chastise myself, but then that damn tub draws my attention again.

The stupid thing brought out the memories that I've worked so hard to keep buried. Between that and it being the two-year anniversary of when mom told us about her cancer, it's no wonder my head is all messed up.

"It's just bruises," I repeat. "Just bruises. Nothing else."

Still, no matter how many times I repeat it, that night, I don't fall asleep.

Chapter 4

JADE

I nibble at my nail, my attention to the front of the auditorium, only half listening to my English lit teacher go on and on about one dead poet or another.

Like seriously? Who cares? I highly doubt any of them were as clever and deep as we were trying to make them out to be. Just because he used dark colors in his poems doesn't mean he was depressed or heartbroken, Margaret. Maybe he just liked dark colors.

Letting out a sigh, I move the word document to the side, not that I actually wrote any notes in it whatsoever, the open browser behind it coming into focus. My throat grows tight as I read over the words on the screen—early breast cancer signs and symptoms.

I tried to let it go, tried to push it out of my head, but it was impossible. A part of me—a big part of me—didn't want to know the answer to my questions, but the other part of me couldn't let go of it either. It was a vicious cycle that had me up at night, my brain conjuring all the possible scenarios.

But the thing about the internet? It was a rabbit hole, and

once you opened it, there was no coming back, just one long dark spiral into a bottomless abyss.

Did it stop me?

Nope.

I click on one of the links, wait for the page to upload, and then read. Page after page, article after article, until my heart starts to race faster, and my vision blurs with all the information.

"Jade?" A hand lands on my elbow, snapping me out of my thoughts. "Jade!"

I turn to Penny. Her head is tilted to the side, and her brows are pulled together. "Sorry, Pens. I got lost in my thoughts for a little bit."

And not just for a little bit, either. People are collecting their laptops and books as they get out of their seats. I was out long enough to miss the rest of the class.

"I can't really blame you," she pulls her hand back and closes her laptop and braille keyboard, putting them into her bag, so I do the same. "This was really boring. Is it bad if I just want to go back to one of my music classes?"

"You're reading my mind. Whoever thought we should attend gen-ed classes in college was an idiot. Are you done with classes for today?"

"Yes. You ready to go?" she asks, her fingers curling around the harness.

"Ready when you are."

I wait as Penny gives Henry the command, letting them leave in front of me. The class had emptied out a bit, but there were still some people mingling around. A few of them gave Penny curious looks as she made her way to the door. I glance up at the hallway entrance and see a group of girls standing by the door, their eyes on Penny as they giggle. Or not so curious. I scowl at them.

"Seriously, don't they have something better to do?" I mutter to myself, but of course, the comment doesn't go unnoticed.

"Just ignore them."

I shift my attention to Penelope. "How do you even know what I'm talking about?"

She rolls her eyes, not bothering to stop. "I can't see, but that doesn't mean I don't feel their stares on me or hear them for that matter."

I guess there is that. Penny might be blind, but she's not deaf and definitely not stupid. No, she's kind, independent, and so freaking smart. Like seriously, I can see, and I get lost more often than not. Penny? No way. It's like she has some inner GPS or something.

Moving forward, I push the door open and hold it so Penelope and Henry can get out. "You'd think we left petty bullshit back in high school."

"You'd think that," Penelope agrees, grabbing onto the railing and making her way down the stairs. "You have any plans for tonight?"

I pull out my phone and check the group chat. "Rei and Grace are home, and they ordered Mexican. You in?"

"Sounds like a plan."

"It's like they knew." I quickly type back, so they know to wait for us.

"Knew what? That we're coming home?"

Message sent, I shove the phone into my pocket. "No," I chuckle. "Knew that tacos would go well with the tequila I found yesterday when I finished unpacking my room."

"Alexei will kill me tomorrow," Rei groans.

"Whatever for?" I finish pouring tequila into our glasses before looking up. "Enjoying your life?"

"For stuffing myself with unhealthy food and alcohol so close to qualifications for the Winter Games?" she slides her hand under her tee, rubbing her abs. Because, yes, the girl has abs. That's how hard she works.

"Tacos have veggies inside; I'd hardly call that unhealthy. Besides, you had *one* taco."

"One giant ass taco," Rei chimes in as I offer her a drink. "And how many shots?"

"Stop it!" Grace chides. "One taco night won't kill you. You probably burn through double the calories with just one practice."

Rei sighs, but she takes a drink. "True. The practices have been extra grueling lately."

"You need me to go and kick Alexei's ass?"

Alexei is Rei's figure skating coach. He might be one of the best figure skaters of his time, but he's also an entitled asshole who's pushing Rei too hard more often than not.

"Nah, we both know what's on the line, and if I plan to succeed, there is no more messing around."

"Do you think you're ready?" Penny asks softly.

There is a beat of silence before Rei shrugs. "I don't know. There is so much that could go wrong, so much that can't be predicted. Quad jumps are extremely hard on the body, and I have to keep working out and building my strength in order to get through that four-minute program the best I can."

"So, no more tacos and tequila?" Grace pouts.

Rei looks longingly at the table. "No more tacos and tequila. At least not until I get back from Japan."

I pick up my shot. "One last drink?"

Rei rolls her eyes. "One last drink."

Penny and Grace lift their own shot glasses, and we clink them together.

"To an amazing year."

"And to Rei kicking some serious ass on the ice."

Soft *clinks* chime in the room as our glasses connect, and we down the drinks. The liquid burns its way down my throat, warming my belly.

"How does Zane feel about you spending all your time practicing?" Grace asks, pulling her legs underneath her.

A smile spreads over our friend's mouth at the mention of her boyfriend.

Over the last year, most of my friends have paired up, and then my brother got married this past spring. I was so glad for them and loved to see people I love happy, but there was this other part of me, dark and jaded, that was growing more and more unsettled.

Which made no sense. I'm not interested in love. Not in that way, anyway. I'm content with loving my friends and family. They're the only people I allowed myself to care about. Because as I've learned in the last few years, love is a bitch, and the only thing it brings you is heartache. And there was only so much heartache a person could survive. I'd reached my limit the day I watched my mom take her last breath after fighting with cancer for months.

My phone vibrates, snapping me from my thoughts. I grab it from the coffee table and check the message.

Marcus: Hey, what are you up to?

Me: Just hanging out with the girls.

Marcus: Sweet.

Marcus: You ladies wanna go out? There's a party at the hockey house.

"Who's that? One of your boy toys?"

I look up to find all my friends watching me.

"Hell no. The last one traumatized me for life."

The guy was obsessed. We went out on a couple of dates, and he genuinely thought that we were dating, even asking me to go visit his family for the holidays. After *two* dates and some lousy sex. Like, who does that?

I shake my head. "It's Marcus."

"Oh, I only saw him in passing on my way to class. How is he?" Grace asks just as another message pops up on my screen.

Marcus: C'mon? This year is going to be INSANE, and this might be my only chance to kick back and enjoy. Pretty please?

"Moaning about classes. He wants to go to some party. You guys game?"

Even before I finish asking the question, I see Rei shake her head. "5 am practice."

"I think I'll skip this one. I scheduled a dance class at the community center at nine." Grace gives me an apologetic smile. "Rain check?"

"Penny?" I ask sweetly. "You're my last hope. These two became boring when they started dating."

Penny shakes her head. "Sorry, parties are just not my thing. Too loud and overwhelming. Plus, Henry isn't really a fan either, if I'm being completely honest."

"You three are no fun at all," I pout.

"If you feel like it, you should go."

"Alone?"

It doesn't sound fun at all. Last year, we went out to one party or another almost every weekend, but this year, things were changing.

"Didn't you just say Marcus will be there? You won't be alone."

"He's not you."

"Aww," Grace throws her arm over me and pulls me into her side. "Hear that, girls? She misses us."

I shove her away. "I don't miss you; I just want to hang out with my friends. *Girls* only." I give them a pointed look.

"And we will." Grace pulls back, a smile on her lips. "The school year has barely started." I reach for the bottle of tequila, pouring myself another shot. "We have time."

But do we? The question pops into my head, leaving me breathless in its intensity.

"We should make it a monthly thing. Just us girls, no boys allowed."

Rei nods her head. "I'll try my best. You know, to have fun sans drinking."

"We'll need a DD," I say absentmindedly, my fingers wrapping around the shot glass.

"Seriously, you should go. Have fun." Grace wiggles her brows. "Who knows? Maybe you'll meet someone interesting."

I roll my eyes at her. My friends have been hinting that I should try dating more seriously. "Just because you two are in a committed relationship doesn't mean everybody wants the same. A hookup, on the other hand..."

My phone buzzes, drawing my attention and reminding me I still haven't answered Marcus.

Marcus: Jade?

Me: Girls have other plans early tomorrow, but I'm game.

Marcus: Great. Pick you up in an hour?

Me: Sounds good.

"I guess I should shower before Marcus gets here." I get up and lift my hands in the air to stretch.

"That would be go—" Grace's eyes narrow at me. "Hey, what's that under your arm?"

I look down at my armpit to see the bruise I'd noticed last week has grown bigger, darker. I just stare at it for a moment, unblinking.

"Jade?" Grace gets up to check it out up close.

"Is that a bruise?" Rei asks, joining us to get a better look. "Why do you have a bruise?"

"Did you bump into something?"

"And get a bruise under her arm?" Rei asks skeptically.

"Maybe? I'm not sure. But it's fine." I drop my hands by my sides and take a step back, needing some space. "Maybe I bumped into something in my sleep." *If I was sleeping more than a few restless hours every night.* "It'll go away."

Penny shifts in her seat. "Does it hurt?"

"Not really." I force out a smile. "I should really go shower."

Before any of my friends can say anything, I turn around and go down the hallway, not stopping until I'm in the bathroom, the door firmly closed behind me. I lean against it, my breathing ragged. Running my hand over my face, I look up at the mirror. I gulp down and push myself from the door to move closer, raising my hand to look at the bruise covering the underside of my arm.

My stomach rolls uncomfortably, my dinner threatening to make a reappearance as I watch the dark mark. I tug my shirt over my head, noticing that the ones on my side have also grown bigger. I touch the sensitive flesh, feeling a slight sting.

I trace the skin around the area, and that's when I notice it. The slight thickening in the hollow of my armpit. Not a bump, but definitely... something.

My throat bobs as I swallow the bile rising, feeling the bitter taste in my mouth.

So much for ignoring it.

Chapter 5

PRESCOTT

"Dude, what are you still doing here?" Spencer asks, stepping into my view.

I grit my teeth, my leg muscles protesting as I push the weights up, a bead of sweat falling into my eyes. I blink, my vision coming into focus, as my fingers tighten around the grip handles until my legs are completely extended.

One.

Two.

Thr—

I curse as my legs give out on me, and I return to the starting position, panting hard.

Spencer shakes his head and throws a towel at me. "Don't you think you've had enough?"

Slowly, I unclench my fingers and wrap them around the towel, wiping the sweat off my face.

"I don't see why you're bitching. I'm cleared to play."

And if I want to get back into shape and keep up with the rest of my teammates—you know, the ones that have been playing and practicing for the last nine months while I was sitting on the bench twiddling my thumbs—I have to put in the work.

"And where exactly are your teammates?" Spencer asks, raising his eyebrows at me.

"They left after we were done with the conditioning, not that it's any of your business." Sliding my legs to the side, I sit upright but don't even try to get up because my legs feel like jelly. Grabbing the water bottle from the floor, I down it in one breath. "What are you doing here?"

"We were just finishing with our workout when I spotted you. I thought you were long gone. You know, because the football team usually uses the gym for conditioning from five to seven, and now it's almost eight-thirty."

"Well, I'm here," I grunt, pushing to my feet. My knee protests the movement, a jab of pain spreading through the joint and into my muscles, but I grit my teeth and suck it up as I get to my full height.

Son-of-a-bitch.

Maybe Spencer was right, and I actually overdid it, but it was hard not to. If I don't get back to my pre-injury shape, even the doctor's clearance to play won't help me keep my spot on the team. "Where are your hockey buddies?"

Taking a moment to brace myself, I throw my towel over my shoulder and start for the locker room, Spencer hot on my heels.

"Gone. They wanted to get back home and set everything up for the party. I was actually planning to text you to see if you wanna come with me when I saw that your grumpy ass was still here."

"My only goal this year is to help my team win the championship." I push the locker room door open. "Where else would I be?"

"You won't win the championship if you push yourself too hard and end up reinjuring yourself."

"I'm fine," I grit just as another jab of pain goes through my leg. Or at least I would be after I get some rest. But who has time for that?

Doing my best to hide the pain, I slowly make my way to my locker, sitting down on the bench in front of it.

"You're a sweaty mess."

"That's because I've been exercising for the better part of the last three hours."

"And you're walking funny."

I glare at him over my shoulder. "I repeat, I've been working out for the last three hours. Some of us don't have extra padding to save our asses from bruising when somebody tackles us."

"Whatever, dude, I'm off to take a shower."

I watch as he grabs his stuff and goes into the bathroom. Thankfully, the locker room is blissfully quiet. In a few weeks, once different sports seasons kick off, that won't be the case.

Running my hand over my face, I let out a long sigh. I enter my locker combination and pull the door open, grabbing my bag from the inside. I shove my hand into the bag, tapping around the bottom until my fingers wrap around the plastic bottle. Glancing over my shoulder to ensure Spencer's still in the bathroom, I slide the lid open and turn it upside down.

Two lone tablets fall into my palm. I watch them for a moment, feeling my heart speed up as I weigh my options. My tongue darts out, sliding over my lower lip. The sound of footsteps nearing snaps me into action. Not giving myself a chance to overthink it, I tilt my head back and throw them into my mouth, swallowing them both in one go.

The pain in my knee wasn't as intense as it was when I first injured it, but the moment I got back to conditioning, the agonizing pain came back. Some days I can deal with it; others, it's just too much.

And now there aren't any left.

I stare at the empty bottle, willing it to fill once again, but of course, it doesn't happen. I shouldn't even be taking these any longer. If you ask my doctors, they'd tell you I don't.

"So?" Spencer asks, breaking me out of my thoughts.

I quickly close the bottle and throw it back into the duffle before turning toward my friend. I was so lost in my own head; I didn't even hear the shower stop.

"So what?"

He looks at me like I'm crazy. "So, are you coming to the party?"

JADE

"Damn girl, you're on a roll tonight!" Marcus grins at me as I down another shot of tequila. I'd been on a roll even before we got to the party, and I wasn't planning to stop anytime soon.

The warm liquid slides down my throat with ease, warming my belly. I've drank so much; I've lost count, and, at this point, I'm so numb I don't even flinch at the mix of the bitter and sour taste on my tongue.

"You wanted to party, so we're partying."

Clinking my shot glass with his, I place it on the counter with more force than necessary. The impact makes the world sway a little bit. I grip the counter and close my eyes for a moment before blinking them open, but it's no use.

Maybe it's not the world that's shaking; maybe it's me.

Hands fall on my shoulders, their reassuring weight steadying me. "Hey, are you okay?"

"Sure." I look up, only to find two Marcuses looking at me, matching worried expressions on their faces. "I'm great."

"You sure?" he lifts his brows, assessing me. "You seem a bit unsteady on your feet."

I wave him off. "The world's moving."

"Is it now?" he chuckles.

I glare at him. "Don't tease." I grab his hand and tug him toward the door. "Let's go dancing."

Marcus doesn't move an inch. "Are you sure you can dance?"

"Positive." I give him another tug. "C'mon, we're partying."

He runs his palm over his face. "Okay, let's go."

Together, we move through the throng. My hips are swaying to the hard beat of the music pulsing through the house as we join the group of people dancing in the living room. When I find an empty spot, I turn around, only to collide with Marcus's hard chest.

He grips my shoulders and pushes me at arm's length. "You planning to knock me over?"

"Sorry, didn't realize you were *that* close." I wrap my arms around his neck as we start to dance. "Hopefully, James won't mind."

James is Marcus's boyfriend. They were both on Blairwood's track team and started dating last spring. I have to admit, at first, I was surprised. Not because Marcus is dating a guy, love is love, after all, but the only people I've ever seen him flirting with since orientation were girls, so I was surprised when he brought James to one of our gatherings. They were a cute couple, though. I could totally see why he was into him.

"He'll be thankful you brought me here," Marcus laughs. "He isn't one for parties."

"Good thing I'm here then." I winked at him, or at least I *think* I winked at him. Just then, the song changes to one of my favorites. It must be somebody else's favorite, too, because the volume increases to an ear-piercing level, but I don't care. Instead, I raise one hand in the air as Marcus and I dance.

I let the music take over. The only important thing is getting lost in the beat that's loud enough to dull the demons yelling in my head.

Not tonight.

I'm not sure how long we dance; it could be minutes, or it could be hours. My cheeks are flushed from the heat. Sweat trickles down my spine as the songs blend together.

Slowly rolling my hips, I turn around and blink my eyes open to come face to face with a guy. He watches me dance unashamedly, a Solo cup clasped in his hands. He's handsome—a few inches taller than me, his dark hair disheveled like he ran his fingers through it. A guy next to him says something that makes the corner of his mouth lift.

Yup, definitely handsome.

Marcus leans over my shoulder, his lips brushing the shell of my ear. "James just texted. He's outside. Want us to walk you home?"

I shake my head, my eyes still on the guy across the room. "Nah, you go."

He turns around to check out who I'm watching. "You sure? I don't want to leave you here all on your own."

"I'm not alone." I tilt my head to the side. "I'll have company."

He looks over my head, his brows pulling together. "I don't know, Jade."

"I'll be fine." I place my hand on his and gently push him back. "Go. Have fun with your boyfriend. At least one of us should."

"From what I see, I'm not the only one who's about to have fun."

Fun? No, more like oblivion. But that's okay. As long as I can forget, I'll be okay.

"Right, so you better not cock block me." I force out a smile and take a step back. "Say hello to James for me."

Marcus grins and shakes his head. "Call me if you need me to walk you home."

"You know it."

Not wanting to give him a chance to protest anymore, I smile at him before turning around. Sliding between the moving bodies, I go back to the kitchen, where I pour myself a new shot of tequila.

The effects of the alcohol were starting to wear off after all the dancing I just did, making my thoughts grow louder. I down the drink in one go, and just as I'm about to pour myself a new one, a hand grabs the bottle. When I turn around, I come face to face with the guy from earlier; only he's brought a friend too.

"Share a drink with us?"

I observe him for a moment before tilting my glass in his direction in silent invitation. "Why not?"

Chapter 6

PRESCOTT

"Wentworth!" Xander slaps me on the shoulder as he joins us in the kitchen. "Long time no see, man. How are you doing? How's the leg? Will we see you on the field soon?"

With his ginger hair and bushy beard, the tall dude looks like he stepped out of the Scottish Highlands. Last year he transferred to Blairwood. He is playing for the hockey team along with Spencer and Zane, so we've hung out a few times. And since most of my football buddies have suddenly become domesticated, I had to find a new crew to party with.

"Let's hope so," I say, ignoring the first part of the question. I tip my chin at him. "You know the playoffs are over, right?"

Xander shrugs. "I could say the same about you."

I rub at my stubbled jaw. Okay, it might be a little more than stubble, but who has time to shave? "Hey, I have my reasons…"

"He's been brooding ever since his injury," Spencer interrupts me as he joins us, a bottle in hand and a big grin on his face. "Found the good stuff."

"I'm not brooding," I protest, crossing my arms over my chest.

Have I been in a mood for the last few months? Maybe. But

seriously, none of my friends can tell me they wouldn't feel exactly the same way if the tables were turned and one of them had been the injured one.

"Some days, you're worse than a girl on their period, Wentworth." Xander narrows his eyes at the bottle. "Is that..."

"High West Whiskey," Spencer wiggles his brows, his grin widening.

"Damn, where did you get it?"

"Theo's room."

Xander shakes his head. "Dude, he's going to kill you."

Theo was another one of the hockey players, Spencer's freshman-year roommate, and considering we're currently in his house, I think Xander is pretty accurate.

"You better have a will set for when he offs you because I don't wanna go through the hassle of finding a new roommate."

"Hey, it's not my problem the sucker keeps it hidden under his bed," Spencer shrugs, opening the lid and pouring some of the whiskey into our cups. "He should have found a better hiding spot in the last three years."

"I don't think that'll go over well with Theo, but it's your funeral, Monroe." Xander turns his attention back to me. "But seriously, dude, how are you doing?"

"Fine." I take a long sip of the whiskey, letting it burn its way down my throat. "I'm back on the field, working on getting back those muscles."

"And by that, he means killing himself working out to the point he'll get injured again if he doesn't slow down."

I glare at my roommate. "Are you turning into Cole? Because seriously, I don't need that shit in my life."

"I'm just saying it as I see it. I saw you flinch when you were getting off the leg press machine." He raises his brows, challenging me to contradict him.

I shift my weight, feeling the muscle in my jaw tick. "I'm

fine."

I'm not even lying much. The meds started to kick in, and the pain dulled into an ache. It was still there—it's always there—that distant throb in the middle of my knee, like a needle poking in my flesh every time I move.

"What you are is full of shit."

I open my mouth to tell him to fuck off when obnoxiously loud laughter comes from the living room. We all turn toward a group of baseball players sitting on the couches.

"Well, at least you're working hard to get back in shape," Xander mutters.

I turn toward him, not sure where he's going with this. "Why?"

He looks around, making sure that nobody's listening, before leaning closer. "That guy," he tilts his chin almost imperceptibly in the direction of the baseball team and, more importantly, their pitcher. "Heard he had some issues with his shoulder last season."

My heart slows, and I lean closer, trying to hear him better. He can't mean what I think he...

"You don't think he..." Spencer asks, his eyes wide.

"Used some extra juice to help him get out on the diamond?" Xander shrugs. "It's just a rumor."

I swallow the lump in my throat, remembering the bitter taste of the pills on my tongue as the guilt slams into me.

It's not the same. I try to reason with myself.

Using supplements and steroids for college athletes, hell, even high school athletes at this point, isn't unheard of. Some people have a lot riding on their ability to play. Scholarships, going pro, and making a better life for themselves, but damn, the risks...

If you were caught, you were done.

There is no going back from something like that. And even

if a team does pick you up, nobody will ever look at you the same way.

My gaze darts to the pitcher. He tilts his head back and laughs like he doesn't have a care in the world, his arms shifting around the girl sitting on his lap. My stomach twists as I watch him, mulling over what I just found out. That damn throb is still persistent in my knee, reminding me of what I did, reminding me of my new normal.

How long will I be able to play without pain meds to help me manage the worst of the pain?

"Whatever, it's his funeral." Spencer downs his drink and pours us each a new round just as a group of giggling girls enters the kitchen. A brunette looks up, her eyes meeting mine before they shift to the bottle in Spencer's hand, and a smile curls her red lips.

"Have some of that whiskey to share, boys?" she asks in that sultry voice girls love to use, her gaze straying back to mine.

From the corner of my eye, I see Spencer turn toward them, taking the group in. "I don't see any boys here, love. But if you wanna hang with real men, we can figure something out."

"Oh, really?" I watch as her tongue sweeps out, sliding over her plump bottom lip. Bringing the cup to my mouth, I down the contents in one go. "And what do real men do?"

Spencer smirks, "Drink whiskey after a hard day of practice."

I grab the bottle out of his hand and pour myself another round, but before I can take a sip the brunette wraps her hand around mine and brings the cup to her lips. My eyes fall to her mouth as it wraps around the edge of the cup, and her throat bobs as she swallows.

"That was my drink," I say dryly. Not just that, it was the only means of pain relief at the moment.

What are you going to do tomorrow? Or the day after? a little voice at the back of my head taunts me. *Drown yourself in alcohol to dull the pain? Hard to play football when you can't stand on your feet.*

I shove it back, irritated with myself for letting it get to me.

"I was thirsty." One brow rises in a silent challenge. "I'm Mindy, by the way."

"Prescott," I grumble.

"It's nice to meet you, Prescott." Her fingers brush against my palm as she pulls her hand back.

"How about we take this outside?" Spencer asks.

There are murmurs of agreement coming from the girls, and we make our way to the backyard. Loud music blasts through open windows, and while the house is full, there are quite a few people outside, both in the hot tub and pool, enjoying the warm, late August night.

As we take our seats in some pool chairs, Xander gives the girls some cups, and I fill them with alcohol. I nurse my drink, only half listening to the conversation as they chat about the summer and the beginning of classes, my thoughts still on the pitcher.

A hand falls on my forearm, making me flinch.

"Mr. Football Player, huh?"

I look to find the brunette watching me. I shake my head, trying to regain my composure. I was so lost in my head; it took me a moment to realize she was waiting for an answer.

As if she didn't know.

"Yeah," I clear my throat. "You a fan?"

"Of football players?" Her gaze drops to my biceps. "I'm partial to them. You score a lot?"

When I was playing. I slide my phone back into my pocket. "Occasionally."

"How about I help you score tonight?" the brunette asks, moving closer.

What was her name again? Mira? Martha? Mary? The fuck if I remember. Her firm tits brush against my chest, her lips sliding down the side of my neck, nipping at my skin.

"Ye—" Before I can finish, I see a familiar figure coming out of the house behind her shoulder. I watch as the blond pitcher shoves his hands into his pockets and, with a quick, almost imperceptible glance around, slides down the few stairs and makes his way to the dark side of the house.

"Prescott?" the girl, *Mindy*—that's her name—urges, her fingers sliding under my chin and turning my attention back on her.

"Another time."

"What?" An unhappy frown appears on her face as she glares at me. "You can't be serious."

Or not.

Not bothering to answer her question, I get up.

"I'm off to take a piss," I say to nobody in particular, but thankfully both Spencer and Xander are focused on their own girls to pay me much attention.

I move through the crowd since apparently more people have come after we got here. Students are enjoying the final moments of freedom before classes start in earnest.

Somebody shoves me, making me stumble. My knee protests the movement, and I hiss as the stab of pain spreads through my leg. I grab for the doorway, trying to steady myself.

Dammit.

Closing my eyes, I push back the black spots that appear in front of my eyes. Maybe drinking wasn't such a good idea after all.

Keeping my head low, I make my way to the house but then beeline to the dark corner, where I saw the pitcher disappear.

I blink a few times, letting my eyes get used to the darkness as I slowly walk further away from the party when I hear voices.

"You've got the money?"

There's a loud snort, "As if you don't know me."

My heart starts beating harder as I move closer, listening intently. They're standing in the woods, between the trees, just two shadows lost in the night.

"I know you. That's why I'm asking," the guy doesn't sound the least bit amused.

Pitcher groans. "It was just that one time." There is soft rustling, and then, "Here. Happy now?"

The other guy counts the money before shoving it into his pocket and pulling out a baggie.

What the hell am I doing here? This was such a bad idea.

I'm about to turn around to get out of there before either of them notices me, but I barely make a step before a soft *snap* echoes in the night.

Shit.

Both heads turn in my direction. Even though the dealer has a black hoodie pulled over his head, I can feel his eyes zero in on me. "What the fuck did I tell you about bringing company?"

"Hey, don't look at me. I didn't invite anybody."

Maybe I can still leave without them noti—

I take one step when his voice stops me.

"Prescott Wentworth." My whole body stiffens at the amusement in the pitcher's voice. "Fancy seeing you here."

Slowly, I turn around. I have already been caught sneaking around, so it's not like it'll make any difference.

The pitcher knowingly smirks as he takes me in, his gaze stopping pointedly at my leg. "Then again, is it really? How's that leg of yours doing these days?"

"Fine," I bite out.

He raises his brows. "That why you're here?"

"I got here by mistake."

"Yeah." That annoying smirk grows bigger. "That's what we

all say."

I press my lips together, my fingers curling into fists by my sides as he walks closer to me, that grin still on his lips. "Don't worry. I won't tell if you won't," he makes a motion of zipping his lips. "But between you and me, Manolo has the good stuff."

The pitcher looks over his shoulder. "Hook up our friend here, will ya? The football team depends on him to deliver this season."

With that, he walks away, leaving me alone with the dude standing in the shadows.

Manolo.

I expect him to bolt immediately, but he just leans against the tree and crosses his ankles.

"So?" He tilts his chin toward me. "What do you need?"

I can't see the guy's face but based on his voice, he sounds young. Probably around our age or even younger.

"I don't..."

He interrupts me before I can finish. "Weed? Molly? Something harder like coke? Or are you looking for performance enhancers?"

I shake my head. Is this guy for freaking real? He's acting like we're at a town fair, bargaining for apples. "I'm not..."

"Pain meds?"

My heart stops, my mouth hanging open. The corner of his mouth twitches in amusement. He finally found something to grab my attention, and he knows it.

"Can't be easy going back to practice after hurting your leg. Heard you smashed your knee. That shit's gotta hurt like a bitch."

It does, but I keep my mouth shut. I should turn around and get my ass out of here, but no matter how much I try to make my legs move, I can't. It's like they're glued to the spot.

"How about this?"

Before I can react, he throws something at me. Instinctively, I raise my hand, my fingers wrapping around a plastic bag.

I look down to see it's filled with pills, along with a little black card with a number on it.

"I told you, I'm not here for this," I grit through clenched teeth.

"Then it's a good thing this time's on me, right?" He pushes from the tree and sinks his hands in the pocket of his hoodie. "But if you change your mind and ever need a refill," he points at the bag in my hand. "That's my number. Texts only."

With that, he turns around.

"Hey! I told you..." I try to protest, but he's already walking away. "Fucking hell."

I look down at my hand and the bag sitting in my palm. Even in the darkness, I recognize the little pills. They're the exact match for the ones I've been taking so far.

Whoever the Manolo guy is, he knows his shit.

My fingers clasp around the bag. I should get rid of it. If somebody finds it...

It's just pain meds, chill.

I run my free hand over my face, rubbing at the stubble on my jaw. The corner of the bag peeks from between my fingers, taunting me. I unclasp my fingers and stare at the pills, my throat growing tight.

Besides, what will happen now that you're back on the team? Now that you're practicing full-time? You can barely get over the session in the gym on your own without feeling the jab in your knee. What about practices? What about drills? What about the games?

My palms turn sweaty from all the possible scenarios going through my head.

Would it be so bad if I kept them?

Just in case.

As a backup.

I swallow the lump in my throat and before I can think more about it, I shove the baggie into my back pocket.

Just a backup.

I quickly make my way back to the party, still in a daze from what had just happened to the point I almost miss Spencer waving at me.

"Dude, did you fall into the toilet or something?" He looks over my shoulder. "What were you doing behind the house?"

Toilet, right.

"The line was long, and I didn't want to wait, so I took care of it outside," I shrug, the lie coming easily.

Considering the number of times I've lied to my friends in the last year, it's not even surprising.

Spencer nods. "You coming back or what? Mindy has been asking about you."

The image of the needy brunette pops into my mind.

"I'm not really feeling it. I think I'll go home."

"You? Not feeling chicks?" Spencer's mouth falls open. "Are you sick or something?"

He tries to reach for my forehead, but I push him back. "Yeah, I'm sick of you hovering. I'll see you at home."

Spencer laughs, "Maybe, maybe not."

Well, at least one of us will have fun tonight.

I lift my hand in a wave and turn toward the back door. The inside of the house is packed almost as much as the outside; only it's excruciatingly hot.

I'm pushing through the people, trying to get out of there, when I catch a glimpse of dark hair at the bottom of the stairs.

Jade Cole.

She's walking up the stairs with two guys. Not even walking, more like being carried. Their hands are under her armpits, holding her upright as she stumbles over the steps.

Jade's head falls back as she laughs at something one of them said, but it's clear that she's drunk. I narrow my eyes at them just as they hit the top stair. No, not even drunk. Downright intoxicated.

My fingers ball by my sides, my nails digging into my skin. I look around, trying to find any of her friends, Nixon, anybody, but just as my luck would have it, there's nobody.

"Fucking hell."

I glance at the door.

Go home. This is none of your goddamn business. For all you know, she's into those guys and completely fine with what's about to go down.

Yet, no matter how much I try to convince myself that that's true, I can't look away.

That's why they have to carry her up the stairs?

Jade's wicked smile and those blue eyes of hers shining brightly in the moonlight on the Hawaiian beach flash in my mind. The feel of her body as she fell on top of me just the other day, her scent surrounding me.

What if she wants this?

But what if she doesn't?

Muttering curses, I push a guy out of my way and take the stairs two at a time. The ache in my leg intensifies, and I'm breathing hard by the time I'm at the top. The hallway is empty, and all the doors are closed.

"Brilliant."

The moment I get my hands on her, I'm going to strangle her.

Walking down the hallway, I open one door after the other. People curse me for interrupting them, but I don't give a damn as I move to the next room. You'd think people would be smarter and lock the damn door behind themselves if they don't want to be interrupted.

Three rooms later, I find her.

One of the preppy boys is lying on top of her while the other is standing by the side, wanking his small dick.

For a split second, all I can do is stare, seeing red. My breathing is ragged, fingers curling around the door handle, and I'm surprised I didn't pull it out.

Jade's body moves underneath him. In want or in protest? I can hear her murmuring something, but her voice is so soft I can't decipher the words.

"Don't play coy now," the guy on top of her snickers, his fingers wrapping around her wrists and pinning them over her head.

"You sure as hell weren't coy downstairs when you were rubbing all over our dicks," the other one says, grabbing one of her exposed breasts.

Jade flitches from his touch as she struggles under the other guy who's pinning her to the bed. "N-no."

Good enough for me.

They're so into it that they don't even notice me there until I cross the room and grab the asshole lying on top of her off. His legs fly, trying to find some footing, but I pull him high enough so I can connect my fist with his face.

"The lady said no, asshole," I hiss in his face before letting him drop on the ground and turning my attention to the other dude who's now trying to zip his pants in a frenzy. His movements are so fast he pinches his dick with the zipper letting out a loud howl in pain. Any other day I might feel sorry for him, but not today. Not after what he was about to do.

In a few strides, I cross the room and have him pinned by the wall. "How does that feel, you jackass?"

"D-dude, it was just a j-joke," the guy stutters. "She was a-asking for it."

"A joke, huh?" I push him harder. "Asking for it? The only

thing I heard was her saying, "no." That doesn't seem like she was asking for it to me."

Pulling my hand back, I connect my fist with his gut. He sucks in a breath, doubling over. I lean down so I can whisper in his ear. "Remember this feeling the next time a girl tells you no."

"W-what...?" Jade's soft question snaps me out of my rage slightly. I glance at her, seeing her try to brace her hand against the mattress so she can get up, but she's either so drunk she can't, or they roofied her drink. Fucking brilliant.

The guy tries to stand straighter, but I kick him in the balls for good measure. "This is your final warning. If I see you bringing another unconscious girl upstairs, you'll see what it means to have a Raven at your throat, capiche?"

"Y-y-yes."

"Good." Spitting on the floor next to him, I turn around and face the woman who got me into this mess in the first place.

My heart tightens as I watch her still, half-naked form on the bed. I rub against my chest, trying to push away the feeling rising in my chest and suffocating me, but it's useless. I look around the floor for her shirt and find it torn in the corner. "Fucking great."

Sliding my hand to the back of my neck, I grab my hoodie and pull it over my head.

"Wentworth?" she asks, her eyes narrowing on me.

"It's me." My throat feels so tight it's hard to push the words out. "Let's get you out of here, okay?"

The mattress dips as I lean against it, helping Jade get into a sitting position. I do my best to keep my eyes on her face and ignore her naked chest. I might be a lot of things, but I'm not an asshole. At least not this level of asshole-ness.

"W-what..."

I slide my hoodie over her head, letting the material fall. "Hands."

She tries to lift her arms, but the attempt is so weak I give up and help slide her hands into the sleeves. Once I get her to her feet, the hoodie slides down completely, engulfing her short form, and that tight feeling in my chest only grows stronger.

"What are you doing?" she asks groggily.

"Getting you the hell out of here. What does it look like I'm doing?"

I slip my hand around her waist because she looks like the next strong breeze will kick her on her ass and turn us toward the door. The assholes that took her are nowhere to be found. They probably shit their pants and scurried away in fear.

My fingers tighten around her waist. The itch to find them and finish what I'd started is growing bigger by the second, but at the first step, Jade sways on her feet.

"How much did you have to drink?"

"Enough."

"Is anybody here with you?"

I can deposit her with her friends and get out of here. That's what I need to do. Get the hell out of here before I do something crazy. Something I'm damn sure I'll regret.

"Eager to get rid of me, Wentworth?" she slurs. Her head lolls back, those damn stormy eyes meeting mine. They're blurry from the effect of whatever she put in her system but no less intense.

"Hell, yes. Now, did you come with somebody, or do I need to take you home?"

"Marcus."

Marcus? Who the hell is Marcus?

She rubs her hand over her face, smudging her makeup. "But I think he left? Not sure."

Great, just... great.

"Okay, let's get you out of here."

I try to pull her closer to me so I have a better grip on her, but she presses her hand against my chest, pushing me back. "I can walk on my own."

"No, doll, I don't think you can. And while I think it would be fun to let you try, I don't have time for that shit. So either you let me help you, or I'll throw you over my shoulder and carry you out of here. It's your choice."

Her eyes narrow, lips pressing in a stubborn line. She should look ridiculous, with her hair messy like that and the black smudges under her eyes, but she doesn't. She's breathtakingly gorgeous, like always.

And you shouldn't notice the way she looks. As a matter of fact, you shouldn't notice her at all.

"You wouldn't do that."

I quirk my brow at her. "Do you want to try me?"

She opens her mouth as if she's about to protest but changes her mind.

"I thought so."

"God, I hate you."

"The feeling's mutual, doll." I tug her across the hallway and down the stairs. The music is still blasting, and if it's even possible more people have joined the party. Which is good since the last thing I need is for somebody to spot me leaving the party with Jade Cole and Nixon somehow finding out about it.

My leg throbs even stronger than before, jolts of pain spreading through my limb at the extra weight I'm carrying. For all the bravado back in the room, there was no way I'd be able to carry anybody with my leg hurting like that. Not that Jade needs to know that, so I bite the inside of my cheek, suck it up, and carry on.

A few people are standing on the front porch, talking, but none of them pay us any attention as I help Jade to my Mustang. By the time she's in the passenger's seat, I'm sweating like crazy, and my jaw is clenched so tight I'm surprised it didn't snap.

I slowly make my way around the car, each step sending another blast of pain through my leg. Sliding my hand into my pocket, I open the bag inside of it and pull two pills out.

Not letting myself think about it, I toss them into my mouth and swallow. I've been taking so many painkillers ever since the accident that I barely notice them sliding down my throat.

Holding in the wince, I pull open the door and slide inside my car.

My attention darts to Jade. She's leaning against the window, her hand covering her face. She must feel my eyes on her because she blinks, her gaze focusing on me.

"You didn't have to save me, you know. I'd have figured it out."

Yeah, because it looked just like she could deal with those two assholes all on her own.

"I'm no savior, doll" I turn on the key, starting the car. "Don't go making me into something I'm not."

Jade lets out a snort, "As if that's possible."

Shifting my attention forward, I maneuver my car onto the street. The radio is playing softly in the background as I navigate the streets to one of the buildings closer to campus.

"Do you have a ke—" I turn to Jade only to find her asleep next to me. "You're shitting me, right?"

Her cheek is pressed against the window, lips slightly parted.

"Cole?" I call out, gently jabbing my finger in her side. But there's nothing. No reaction whatsoever. "Doll?" I tried again, harder this time, but still, no result.

"Fucking hell." I throw my head back and look at the ceiling, my curled fingers punching the steering wheel. Turning my head to the side, I watch a strand of hair fall on her face. Unable to resist it, I reach across the console and push it behind her ear. "What the hell should I do with you now?"

Chapter 7

JADE

An annoying ringing snaps me out of my dreams. I moan in protest, turning to my other side, and pulling the cover over my face to stifle the noise that is making my head throb so hard it's about to explode.

Damn, what the hell did I do last night?

My mouth feels so dry, my eyes itch, and the pounding... That damn pounding in my skull will be the death of me.

The ringing stops, only to start immediately once again. I'm about to push the covers down so I can find the source of all that noise and crush it when there's a loud groan, and a body—one very large, very hard, very *male* body—rolls over me, crushing me to the mattress and making the ringing stop.

Fucking finally.

I don't even have it in me to be mad at the guy for sleeping over at my place since he had the decency to turn off that horrendous noise, and now I can go back to sle—

"Fucking hell," he mutters, making the bed squeak as he gets off.

But it's not the God-awful noise that has my whole body freezing.

It's the sound of his voice—one I recognize.

My eyes snap open instantly. I shove the covers down and sit upright abruptly, a jolt of pain shooting through my skull at the sudden movement.

Shit, that fucking hurts.

I grab my head, rubbing against my throbbing temples.

Maybe this is all just one really bad dre—

"Oh, good, you're awake."

Or not.

Prying my eyelids open, I stare at the man sitting next to me, his hands rubbing over his face and stubbled jaw.

And not just any man.

Prescott-fucking-Wentworth.

"What the hell are you doing in my bed?" I ask, pulling the covers higher as I just stare at his gorgeously infuriating face.

His fingers splay open, those dark eyes fixing on me. He lets his hands fall to his lap, and I don't miss the fact that he's shirtless.

And damn, he looks even better than he did this past spring. He's got some muscle on him since the last time I saw him, and it looks good on him, as does the new ink on his chest.

Too damn good.

You don't even like him, a little voice at the back of my head reminds me.

Doesn't mean I can't appreciate the eye candy.

Not that I'd ever admit that to the scowling man in front of me.

"Your bed?" He scoffs, that frown that seems to be etched between his brows deepening. "You're in *my* bed, doll. In case you missed it."

My fingers clench around the covers as I slowly take in the room around me, ready to point out how wrong he is, only to realize he's right. I'm not in my room.

Shit, shit, shit.

My gaze drops down to my body, and my muscles stiffen when I notice the hoodie that I'm wearing. Definitely not what I had on last night, that much I can remember. The rest of it though? Pain spreads through my head as I try to clear the cobwebs clouding my memory.

What the hell happened last night?

I rub my fingers through my messy hair, pushing it out of my face, before looking at the man sitting in front of me. Prescott is observing me quietly, but I don't miss that trace of amusement in his eyes.

He's really going to make me ask it, isn't he? Asshole.

"Did we…" I start, my voice feeling raw from all the alcohol I had last night. "Umm… Did we have…"

"Fuck no." That amusement is gone in a blink of an eye. "I don't have the tendency to sleep with girls so drunk they don't know their own name."

Something about the way he says it makes my back stiffen as one word rings in my mind loud and clear.

No.

I hold onto it until blurry snippets from last night start appearing in my mind.

The party. Drinking. Dancing with Marcus. More drinking. Marcus said he'd take me home, but I refused him. Drinking and dancing with some guys.

After that, it's all kind of hazy. But I remember the guys telling me we should take it somewhere private. And we did.

The image of the guy looming over me flashes in my mind. His hands were on my body, roaming and groping.

No.

A cold sweat washes over me. My throat bobs as I try to swallow the knot that's formed, but it's stuck.

A big, warm hand lands on my knee, making me jump in surprise. "Do you remember what happened last night?"

"A little," I mutter. Turning my back to him, I slide my legs over the edge of the bed. I'm still wearing the shorts I had on last night. I get to my feet, the hoodie falling down, the soft material brushing against my naked breasts, the friction making my nipples harden.

"Jade…"

"What time is it?" I ask, glancing at him over my shoulder.

"Five thirty."

That gets my attention. "In the morning? Why the hell would you get up that early? On the weekend too."

"It's Friday, hardly the weekend."

I wave him off. "Close enough."

Prescott crosses his arms over his naked torso. "How about I've got shit to do. Not all of us can party all night and sleep all day long, doll."

My fingers clench into fists. "Fuck off. And stop calling me that."

I look around until I spot my chucks on the floor.

"Is that a thank you for saving your ass last night?" he asks as I slip my shoes on.

"I don't remember asking you to save me." I glance around his room pointedly. "Or to bring me to your place, for that matter."

"You think this was my first choice?" He snorts. "Don't flatter yourself, doll. I couldn't get you off my hands fast enough…"

"Then why am I still here?" I challenge.

"But your drunken ass had to pass out on me so I could either leave you out in the parking lot, take you to your brother's, or bring you here," he continues as if I didn't say anything.

"And I was in no mood to explain to your brother how you ended up in this situation in the first place."

"Next time, don't try to save me, so you won't have that problem." With one last glance at him, I turn on the balls of my feet and get out of his room. Or I would have if his fingers didn't wrap around my wrist and pulled me back. A zap of electricity goes through my arm, all the way to the pit of my belly.

"Where do you think you're going?"

"Home." I look down at where his hand is connected to mine before raising my gaze. "Now, if you'll excuse me..."

"I'll walk you."

He'll walk me? How about hell to the no?

"No, thanks." I tug my hand out of his grasp. "The walk of shame will be bad enough on my own. I guess at least one good thing came out of your stupid-ass alarm."

Done with this conversation, I grab my bag from his desk and go toward the door. This time he doesn't try to stop me.

His apartment is quiet when I make my way out of the door, taking two steps at a time until I'm out in the open. The morning is chilly, so I tuck the sleeves of the hoodie over my hands as I look around.

The buildings surrounding me are similar to the one I'm living in, making me realize we are living in the same neighborhood. I look around, my eyes narrowing slightly at the number hanging on the wall of the building as my heart starts to speed up.

Not just the same neighborhood.

The building next door.

Why does the idea of it make my stomach tighten? And not in revulsion either.

This is getting ridiculous.

Rubbing at my forehead, I shake my head and march to my own building.

I'm quiet as I make my way to the first floor and slide my key in the door, but before I can turn it, I can hear the soft *clink* from the other side as the door opens, and I come face to face with Rei.

My friend stops in her tracks, her eyes taking me in. "Long night?"

"You could say that," I respond, running my hand over my face.

"Did you have a good time?"

You sure as hell weren't coy downstairs when you were rubbing all over our dicks.

A shudder runs through me as the ugly words ring in my head, and I remember the weight of his body pressing me into the mattress. His fingers wrapped around my wrists while the other guy went for my chest.

I rub the side of my breast, feeling a little sting even through the thick cotton.

"It was okay." My gaze drops to her duffle. The bag is almost as big as her. "You going to the rink?"

Rei smiles. "Zane's picking me up. How about we grab lunch later, and you can tell us all about it?"

No way in hell am I bringing up last night if I can help myself.

"Yeah, maybe. I have to check my schedule. Text you later?"

"Sounds good." She pulls her phone out of her side pocket. "That's Zane. I better get going."

Talk about close.

"Have a good skate," I say as I slip into the silent apartment.

I walk down the hallway and go straight to my room, not stopping until I'm in the bathroom. Flipping the switch on, I'm faced with my reflection in the mirror.

God, I look like a mess. My hair is one big bird's nest, my eyes bloodshot, and there are dark smudges under my eyes from the makeup. I don't bother with wiping it off before taking off my clothes. I leave the hoodie for last, my fingers holding onto it for a heartbeat longer than necessary before letting it drop to the floor and facing my reflection.

The knot is still visible in my armpit, as are the bruises, but now they're accompanied by the dark, fingertip-shaped bruises on my breast. Most likely, from where the guy grabbed it, his mark imprinted into my skin.

With a shake of my head, I turn my back on the reflection and turn the water on to the highest temperature possible. I wait until it's warm enough before climbing into the tub and standing under the spray.

I let the water wash last night off me. If only it would be as easy to wash away the memories.

PRESCOTT

"Somebody's cutting it close," Scotty says in the way of a greeting as I enter the buzzing locker room. I bypass my teammates, most of which are already in full gear, and go straight to my spot, dropping my duffle bag on the bench and pulling open my locker.

"Dude, where were you?" Nixon hisses.

"I overslept," I mutter, pulling the shirt over my head. All thanks to a certain brunette that shall not be named, I only woke up when my third alarm went off—with a raging boner no less since she spent the whole night snuggled against me—and then she had to be difficult on top of everything.

Freaking girls and their stubbornness.

But I can't say any of that out loud if I want to keep my dick intact. Not that there is any reason for it to be in danger either way. Nothing happened. I just did a good deed. That's all. A freaking good deed, and that's how she reacted?

Not sure Nixon will see it that way if he finds out his little sister spent the night in your bed, good intentions or not.

"Seriously? You overslept?" I can see why he'd be skeptical about it.

Ever since I'd been cleared to play this past week, I've been one of the first players to come to practice. I was eager to be back on the field, eager to play, and show the world there is more to the Wentworth name than a washed-out player retiring from the game because of an injury.

"The old man's been warming the bench for so long he forgot what it means to put in the work."

My back stiffens as the words echo in the room. All the clamor dies at once, leaving the room deadly quiet, and I can feel everyone's eyes watching me.

I clench my jaw, my fingers tightening around the jersey in my hand as I slowly look over my shoulder to glare at the guy in question.

Sullivan.

There's a smirk on the sophomore's face as he looks at me, all fake bravado.

"Forgot how to put in the work?" I ask softly, almost too softly. The guys lean in, exchanging silent looks as the tension sizzles in the room between us, so strong I can almost feel it crackle. "You think *I* forgot how to put in the work?"

"Wentworth..." Nixon starts, his fingers wrapping around my forearm. I tug my wrist out of his reach, not in the mood to be placated.

"Oh no, let's hear what Sullivan has to say since he's the only one putting in all the work, apparently."

The smirk falls off his face, color rising on his cheeks. "That's not..."

"Isn't it? Isn't that what you said?" I jab my finger into his chest, feeling the anger brewing inside me. "I've been busting my ass the last few months in rehab so I could play again. Yet, you have the audacity to talk to me about hard work? You, a guy who, after months, still doesn't know how to read plays and differentiate left from right?"

Somebody curses quietly in the background, and Sullivan's cheeks turn beet red in embarrassment.

I raise my brows, waiting for him to say something else, but just as he opens his mouth, Coach enters the locker room.

"Gentleman." He takes in the room, his eyes stopping on Sullivan and me. "Do we have a problem here?"

There is a beat of silence as I stare at Sullivan, waiting to see if he'll bitch to Coach, but he just presses his lips together tighter.

Of course, he won't say anything in front of him. He wouldn't risk stepping on his toes.

"No," he clips. "No problem."

Coach turns to me, one bushy eyebrow raised. "Wentworth?"

"No," I shake my head and take a step back, but there is no hiding the sarcasm dripping from my voice. "It's all good."

Coach's eyes narrow slightly. "Then why are you all standing around chatting like a bunch of ladies gathering for an afternoon tea?" He shakes his head. "Get your asses out on the field. We've got work to do. Week zero is just around the corner, and you know what that means."

It's like he said the magical words because the next moment, people start scurrying off either out to the field or to finish dressing, and I'm no different.

Week zero.

The beginning of the season.

And the announcement of the starting lineup.

Chapter 8

JADE

"I need coffee," I say as a way of greeting. Sliding into one of the bar stools, I prop my elbows against the counter and drop my chin onto my palms, letting out a long sigh.

"A long day?" Yasmin asks, brows raised.

"Something like that. Do you have coffee in IV? I think that might be the best option at this point."

My sister-in-law chuckles, "Afraid not, but I can hook you up with a double shot of espresso."

I let out a sigh, "I guess that'll have to do."

The door to the kitchen opens, and a familiar redhead pops out. "What will have to do?"

Yasmin picks up one of the cups and goes to the coffee machine. "Somebody partied hard last night and needs caffeine."

"I never mentioned anything about partying."

"You're telling me you stayed up studying the first week of classes?" Yasmin gives me a pointed look over her shoulder.

"No, definitely not."

She chuckles, returning her attention to my coffee. "Didn't think so."

"But that doesn't mean I was out partying." Although, that was exactly what I'd been doing. "Maybe we had a girl's night and stayed up until five in the morning."

"Did you?"

"I mean, we did hang out..."

Yasmin places a lid over my cup and hands it to me, raising one of her perfectly shaped eyebrows.

"Before I went out," I finish, grabbing the cup and taking a long sip.

My eyes fall shut as I practically inhale the black gold, waiting for that first jolt of energy to kick in.

"Damn, she's even worse than you, Yas." Alyssa shakes her head, her wide blue eyes on me. "Maybe even worse than Callie."

I guess if I was worse than Callie, things must be really serious.

"I assume it's not the right time to mention I'll require a refill?" Yasmin bursts into laughter. "What? I still have one more class to go to, and I don't think I slept more than five hours."

Once I got home, I felt too jittery to be able to fall asleep. As if that was as easy as simply shutting your eyes. But nothing was that easy. More flashes of the evening started to come back to me. It's all still pretty fuzzy, but I could connect the important bits, like having too much to drink, dancing, and the guys.

A shudder runs through me at the mere thought.

I definitely remembered the guys.

Worried, almost terrified, dark eyes flash in my mind. A deep line between his brows. Hard lips pressed in a tight line.

"Jade?"

I blink, returning my attention to my friends, who are both looking at me expectantly. "Sorry, I got lost in my head for a little bit."

Yasmin's smile falls. "Are you okay? You look a bit pale."

"I'm fine," I wave her off, forcing a smile out. "Just tired. What I need is another coffee or two and ten hours of uninterrupted sleep. Not necessarily in that order."

"Try having a baby. It's like that, only every day."

"Where is your baby?" I ask, grateful to be able to change the subject to something other than me.

Although Alyssa and I weren't necessarily close, occasionally, we hung out in the same group, so I knew she had been pregnant. Hell, everybody knew she had been pregnant. It's not something that goes unnoticed on a campus the size of Blairwood's.

"She's home with her daddy." Just the mention of her daughter and boyfriend has a smile spreading over her face.

"How is she doing?"

"Good, fussy," Alyssa rolls her eyes and gives a pointed look at Yas. "I swear you all spoil her too much, and she's using every bit of it."

"She's *four months* old!" Yasmin protests.

"Exactly!"

"Hey, don't look at me." Yasmin raises her hands defensively. "It's all Maddox."

"Especially him, but none of you are any better." Alyssa shakes her head. "Always demanding to hold her. It's not even strange that she doesn't want to sleep if somebody's not holding her."

"I don't see where the problem is."

"Of course you don't. The next time Edie wakes up in the middle of the night or startles every time I try to put her in her crib, I'll bring her to you."

"I thought we already established I'm the fun aunt. We're here to help her wreak havoc."

"Oh, really?" Aly narrows her eyes. "Well, you just wait, 'cause payback is a bitch."

I'm lucky that I didn't take a sip of my coffee because it would be all over the counter by now because of the look of utter shock and astonishment on Yasmin's face.

"You're pregnant?!"

"God, no!" Yasmin protests, turning her attention to Aly. "Bite your tongue. I love Edie, but damn, I'm not ready for a baby. Not anytime soon."

Aly shrugs as she opens the dishwasher and starts to empty it. "I didn't exactly plan it either, but sometimes the best things that come in life are unexpected."

My smile falls as her words ring in my mind. She's right, occasionally, the unexpected becomes the best thing in your life, but more often than not, it'll wreck you from the inside out.

"Nixon would be a good daddy, right Jade?" Alyssa wiggles her brows playfully.

"Oh, no, don't get me in the middle of this. Besides, you know my thoughts on discussing my brother's sex life. Not interested."

"Oh, he'll be an amazing dad. I'm not worried about that. Some time far, far, *far* in the future."

Yas's right about that. Nixon will be an amazing dad. He adores Yasmin with all he's got, and I've seen him with Edie a few times. He's smitten with her. All the guys are. Although, was that really ever a question? I'm half-convinced he wouldn't mind that much if a baby came a little earlier, either.

Will I ever be able to meet it? Shaking my head, I push the thoughts away.

Noticing the time, I finish the last of my coffee. "Make me another one to go? I should really head to my next class, or I'll be late."

Yasmin grabs my cup. "You coming to the first game?"

"I wouldn't miss it."

I might not be into sports, but there is no way I'll miss a football game as long as my brother is playing. This is his senior year, after all.

Prescott's broody face flashes in my mind.

Seriously, Jade? You don't even like the guy.

Shaking my head, I grab my fresh drink and hand Yasmin the money. "See you, girls, later."

Contrary to the required general ed classes I have to take, my photography and graphic design classes pass in a blink of an eye, and by the time the professor concludes the lesson, I'm still eagerly sitting at the edge of my seat, wanting more.

Writing down a note to read the assigned chapters, I close my books and shove them into my bag. I pull my phone out as I head out of the auditorium, checking my messages.

Grace: Drinks and dinner at Moore's? I went by the cafeteria, and the food was crappy.

Penny: I have the studio booked for two hours. Rain check?

Rei: I'm still at the rink, but I can join you once I'm done.

Grace: Sounds good.

"Dude, it's not the end of the world," somebody says loud enough to draw my attention.

I look around to find one of my classmates, Joshua Sullivan, talking to another guy who looks vaguely familiar, although I'm not sure where to place him.

"Of course, you'd say that. It's not like you were benched."

"That's not what I meant," the guy groans. "You should probably wait until your coach gives the final list of starters."

"That was the final list of starters for this season." Sullivan kicks a rock with his foot, the little pebble flying in my direction. He looks up, his gaze meeting mine.

Damn, I'm so caught. Biting the inside of my cheek, I lift my hand and wave—it's not like he didn't see me anyhow—before turning around and continuing on my way. My phone vibrates, reminding me I haven't answered my friends.

Grace: Jade?

Me: Just got out of class, can meet you there in ten.

Grace: I'll hurry up. I might have stopped to watch Mason play ball with his friends.

I roll my eyes at her message. Of course she somehow ended up watching her boyfriend play basketball between the cafeteria and Moore's. It's been their thing since they were teens. She used to sneak into the gym at the community center they both attended and watched him play, but she never did anything until he finally asked her out. I guess some things never change.

"Hey, Jade, wait!"

I look up at the sound of my name to see Joshua Sullivan jogging after me. I slow down, letting him catch up to me.

"Sorry, it wasn't my intention to eavesdrop," I say lamely.

Sullivan and I are both minoring in graphic design and have had a few classes together in the past, including Digital Illustration. I've seen his work, and the guy is really talented both on the computer, but also with pen and paper.

"It's fine. We weren't really quiet about it." Sullivan shakes his head as if he wants to push those thoughts away and change the subject. "What are you up to?"

He runs his fingers through his light brown strands, mussing his perfectly styled hair, those blue eyes fixing on me. He's handsome. I'll give him that. Tall, with wide shoulders and just the right amount of muscles for a football player.

"Meeting some friends at Moore's. You?"

"I'm going there myself. Cole called for a football meeting."

I raise my brow as I start walking, Sullivan following after me. "Did he now?"

"Something about creating bonds."

That sounded like something my brother would say. As one of the team captains, it was on him to keep the guys in order, and he took his role seriously.

"There is nothing like alcohol and food to help you guys bond."

"Don't forget about the chicks." His eyes widen as he realizes what he said. "Shit, that's not... I didn't mean Nixon..."

"Don't sweat it." I wave him off. "After all, my brother is one of the football players, so I've heard it all in the past. Besides, there is no way he'd fuck around on Yasmin."

I've seen how much my brother loves his wife, including that first moment he brought her to our home. They weren't even dating then, but I could see Yasmin as somebody he could fall for. And fall for her, he did. Hard.

Pushing the door to Moore's open, I duck inside. Although it's still relatively early, the place is buzzing with activity.

I look around, taking in the familiar space. The dark wooden bar spreads over the one side of the room, big TVs placed over it showing different games going on at the moment. The place is decorated with different sports memorabilia featuring Blairwood alumni.

"I don't see any of the football players," I comment, shifting my attention to Sullivan. "Or my friend. Wanna grab a drink while we wait?"

"Yeah, sounds good."

"So, how is football going?" I tentatively ask as we make our way to the bar.

Sullivan is one of the wide receivers on the Ravens' team. He stepped into Prescott's place after he was injured last year. Looking back, it was probably a lot of pressure on a freshman. Sullivan is a good player, but he isn't Prescott. He is still too green, and more importantly, he doesn't have the same connection Nixon shares with Prescott and Hayden since the three played together from their freshman year on.

Sullivan's smile falls, a frown appearing between his brows. "You heard my conversation earlier." He shrugs, trying to play it off, but I hear the frustration in his voice. "Coach put me back on the bench."

"I'm so sorry, Sullivan. You were good last season, I..."

"Just not good enough?" he chuckles humorlessly. "It's fine. I guess it was to be expected now that Wentworth's back on the team."

Before I can comment, the bartender turns to us, and we place our order before resuming the conversation. "I don't know what to say."

"There is nothing to say." He shrugs nonchalantly. "We all knew he'd eventually come back. We've gotten quite a few new additions to the team this year, and the transition hasn't been going exactly smooth, so..."

"So, the team bonding?"

"Yeah." He rubs the back of his neck. "Not sure it'll help, but whatever... We've got to do something."

"It's going to be fine." I place my hand on Sullivan's shoulder, giving it a firm squeeze. "Every team needs some adjustment period. I'm sure you guys are going to do great. I meant what I said; you played well last season. And just because Coach didn't put you as a starter doesn't mean you'll be on the bench the whole season."

"Thanks." If possible, his expression darkens even further. "I guess we'll see, huh?"

"Yea—"

"What the fuck do you think you're doing?"

The hair at the back of my neck rises at the sound of *his* voice. Low and kind of growly.

Slowly, I turn around and come face to face with no one other than Prescott Wentworth.

Next to his hulking height, Sullivan looks small in comparison. Prescott's eyes are fixed on my hand on Sullivan's arm, his lips pressed in a tight line.

What the hell's his deal?

"What am I doing? What the hell are *you* doing?"

Slowly, he lifts his gaze to meet mine, those dark brown eyes glaring at me. If looks could kill...

"I didn't ask you." He shifts his attention to Sullivan, completely dismissing me. "Seriously, dude?"

Sullivan rolls his eyes before turning to look at Prescott. "What?"

"What the fuck do you think you're doing with Cole's little sister?"

Sullivan's muscles tense at the accusation. He glares right back at him. "We're just talking. Chill."

"Not that it's any of your business," I mutter, letting my hand slowly make its way down Sullivan's arm before pulling it away.

Prescott's eyes follow my every move, his jaw clenching. The moment my hand falls from Sullivan's, his head snaps up, his eyes narrowing even further.

Playing with fire? Maybe, but it's so much fun to see the vein in Wentworth's forehead tick.

"It is my business."

I cross my arms over my chest, lifting my chin up. "Oh yeah? And how exactly is it your business?"

Wentworth grits his teeth, and the corner of my mouth tilts in amusement. It is so fun to rile him up.

"Hey, did you..." Nixon stops in his tracks when he sees me standing in front of Prescott. He looks from me to his teammates and back. "What's going on here?"

Prescott tilts his head to the side, his brow rising as if to say, let's see how you'll get out of this mess.

Silly, silly boy.

"Just talking to the guys," I smile at my brother. "I heard you're having a boy's night?"

"It's not *boy's* night." Nixon frowns. "It's team bonding."

"Tomato, tomahto." I wave him off, noticing more football players going toward the back. "I guess you should go. Team captain can't be late."

That crease between his brows deepens, his gaze shifting to the drink that the bartender just placed in front of me. "Do not think I don't know what you're trying to do."

"And what would that be?" I grab it, taking a sip of the sweet drink. "Having a drink while I wait for my friend to arrive?"

Nixon just shakes his head and turns his attention to the bartender to place his order before looking at me once again. "We'll talk about this later. C'mon, boys."

Sullivan grabs his beer. "I'll see you in class, Jade."

"See you in class."

Nixon pushes a silent Prescott toward the rest of his teammates. His eyes hold mine as he moves backward, that square jaw clenched tightly. Of course, he doesn't have anything smart to say now.

"Don't cause any trouble, Smalls." He points at his eyes and then at me, which has me rolling my eyes.

"Yeah, yeah." I take a sip of my drink as I watch them go toward the back. "Have fun at your boy's night."

Nixon looks over his shoulder. "It's team bonding!"

"It better be good *bonding* 'cause I expect you to win your first game," I yell after him.

"Expect who to win?" I turn around to see a slightly winded and flushed Grace standing in front of me. "What did I miss?"

Once again, my eyes dart to the back of the room where the football players have occupied most of the space and drawn the attention of half of the people sitting in the bar.

"Nixon being Nixon."

"Your brother's here?" Grace looks around.

"These days, he's everywhere I go." Turning my back on them, I catch the eye of the bartender and wave him over. "So, where's the lover boy? You left him to play with the guys?"

"Well..." Grace tucks a strand of hair behind her ear and gives me a sheepish smile. "About that..."

Chapter 9

PRESCOTT

"We should go in strong. Show them that we're not messing around."

Grunts of agreement follow the statement of one of our running backs.

"While I agree to some point, it might come to bite us in the ass if they manage to regroup in the second half, and we're already tired."

I nod in acknowledgment. There was something in that theory too. Taking a sip of beer, my eyes scan the space.

Moore's is filled with people, not that it's strange. Thursday through Sunday, most of the students come here to pregame before hitting one party or another. And then there were the game nights when either football or hockey teams played, and it's like half the campus crammed into this space afterward.

A shimmer of dark hair draws my attention. It shouldn't be this visible, this taunting, not in a dimly lit room, but it is.

Why did she *have to be here?*

First, she went on my vacation. Then she moved into my building complex. Then she snuck her way into my bed. And now, she's occupying my bar.

Laughter booms at the table. I return my attention to the conversation at hand and my teammates. Especially a certain teammate.

What was her deal with Sullivan?

I narrow my eyes at the guy in question. As if he can feel my gaze on him, Sullivan looks up, our eyes meeting for a split second before I look away.

Look at Jade.

Because that's a good option.

Not.

But seriously, what is their deal?

Okay, so they have a class together. It still doesn't explain what they were doing here, her hand on him, her fingers slowly grazing their way down his arm as if they belonged there.

My fingers curl around the bottle in my hand, imagining it's his neck.

"Yo, Wentworth!"

"What?" I turn to the table to find my teammates watching me expectantly. *Fuck, what were we talking about?*

"You with us?" Gregory, one of our kickers, smirks at me. "Or are you looking for some hot pussy?"

Nixon throws a balled-up napkin at him. "Don't be crass, dude."

"Hey, don't you go throwing shade on me, Cole. Just because your lazy ass got domesticated..."

"Domesticated," Nixon snorts. "It's called growing up. Maybe you should try it sometime?"

Gregory sprawls back in his seat. "And where would the fun be in that?"

"Somebody's gotta take care of all the ladies of Blairwood that are still mourning the loss. With their QB1 officially off the market and one of their favorite wide receivers off to the pros, somebody has to console them."

"I think Wentworth has been doing quite a good job with keeping the ladies occupied these last few months with all the free time he had," Sullivan says.

I raise my brows. "Jealous, Sully?"

"Of what?" he snorts. "You? Sorry to disappoint, Wentworth, but not everybody wants to be you."

I grit my teeth, trying to keep my cool. It won't do me any good if I jump across the table and punch the smug bastard in the face. "They just want to play, like me," I mutter, taking a swig of my beer.

The silence that settles over the table is almost deafening. But seriously, I've had it with him and his snark. He might think he's the top dog because he's the guy who got to start his freshman year, but the only reason that happened was because I was out for the season. That's all. He isn't the shit he thinks he is.

A leg kicks me under the table. I look away, only to find Nixon glaring at me, so I glare right back.

"Okay, boys, we're not here to talk shit about each other," he gives me a pointed look before doing the same with Sullivan. "Tonight is about talking strategy."

"I thought we were here for team bonding," somebody throws from down the table.

"That too, but mostly to strategize. You can think about chicks after we've won our first game of the season. Or better yet, leave the chicks out of your heads until *after* the season is done. We don't need all the girl drama when we're having the most important season of our lives."

Somebody coughs. "Says a married man."

Nixon looks around the table, meeting the eyes of every player sitting there, but whoever said it smartly keeps his mouth shut.

"As I was saying," Nixon says slowly. "On Saturday, we play

against Columbia. Last season we lost to two teams, and they're one of them, so we have to make sure to wipe the floor with them. Thankfully," he slaps me on the shoulder, "this dumbass here is finally cleared to play because we'll need all the seasoned players we can get."

Hurt flashes on Sullivan's face, but he schools his features immediately.

I lift my brow at him. *Not so smug any longer, are we?*

Sullivan's jaw tightens, but he doesn't say a word.

"I know this is a reconstructive year," Nixon continues, his eyes taking in every player sitting around the table, "and we're still learning how to mesh together, but there are some really talented people here, and I have faith that we can bring the title back home once again. So work hard, keep your head straight, and eyes on the end game."

A chant of Ravens spreads through the group, and the rest of the people seated in the bar soon join in.

I grab my beer, taking a pull before facing Nixon. "You sound just like him."

"Just like who?" he asks, looking at me confused.

"Coach. Who else?"

"I guess it comes with banging the coach's daughter," Phillip, our running back, says.

Nixon slaps him over the head. "She's not just the coach's daughter. She's also my wife, so you better watch your mouth."

Phillip shrugs. "Hey, I'm just saying."

"Well, phrase it better. Besides, this doesn't have shit to do with Coach but with my role as a team captain."

"Who knows? Maybe one day, when you hang your cleats up for good, you'll come back and continue the tradition. Keep it in the family and all."

"Well, even *if* that does happen, you assholes won't be

around to witness it one way or the other." Nixon shakes his head. "Can we get back to the topic we came here to discuss?"

After a few more jabs at Nixon, the conversation thankfully returns to our first game and the opponents we'll play this season. I try to keep my attention on the conversation, but eventually, my gaze wanders off and finds its way back to the bar.

There is a jab of disappointment mixing with relief when I don't find Jade there. I start to turn back around when I see her. She's standing at one of the high tables along with Grace and her boyfriend, and what looks to be half the basketball team huddled around.

A tall dude with wild, curly hair leans down and whispers something in Jade's ear that makes her laugh. Her body brushes against the guy as she whispers something back.

A foot taps mine under the table, drawing my attention. "You've been awfully quiet tonight."

I run my fingers through my hair. "Just tired."

"You've been working a lot since you were cleared."

I tilt my bottle to the side, noticing that the corner of the tag had started to peel off thanks to the condensation. "Hard not to when I have to compete with all the new guys."

"You don't have to compete with anybody."

"Yeah, right," I snort. It was easy for Nixon to say that. He wasn't the one who warmed the bench for the better part of last year.

"I'm serious. Do you think Coach would just hand over your spot to some rookie?" Nixon asks, keeping his voice quiet.

"If he's good? In a heartbeat."

"Then it's a good thing that there is nobody better than you, is there?"

I raise my brows at him.

"I mean it. There are some good guys on the team. There is

some real potential here, but potential will carry us only so far. You've seen them play in the pre-season games."

I did, and it was a disaster. Makes me wonder if we were that bad our rookie year. Most likely.

Coach liked to try a few new things in the pre-season and mix things up a little to see if they'd work. He likes to give newbies some playing time so they can get used to being on the field in case something unexpected happens mid-season and he has to put them in the game.

I flex my leg under the table, feeling that familiar tug in my knee.

"It'll all work out okay. You'll see." He checks his phone as he finishes the rest of his beer. "You plan on staying?"

"Yeah, I think I'll have another beer."

It's not like I have anybody waiting for me at home.

Nixon nods. "I'm off. Yas is finishing with her shift at the café, so I figured I'd pick her up."

"Leaving us already, Cole?" Phillip smirks knowingly.

"Some of us have better things to do than to party all night."

"Admit it, you're just getting up in age," Gregory says, always the helpful one.

"We'll see who's the one getting up in age when I wipe the floor with you in the gym tomorrow." Nixon looks around the table, always the team captain. "Don't stay up too long, and for all that's holy, don't get wasted. If Coach sniffs it on you, and trust me, he will, he'll make us all pay."

"Yeah, yeah, dad."

More choruses of agreement come from down the table, making Nixon shake his head. He looks over his shoulder.

"Keep an eye on her, will you?" He whispers so only I can hear him. "She's been..." He rubs his chin, his voice trailing off. "Off."

Off?

My eyes narrow. "What do you mean?"

"I don't know. She's just been acting weird lately. Maybe it's Mom's birthday that's coming up. I don't know. Just... keep an eye out for her? She's my little sister."

As if I needed a reminder.

"Yeah, sure," I agree reluctantly.

"Thanks," he slaps me on the shoulder. "You're the best."

His words are like a punch to my gut. I wonder what he'd have said if he knew what happened in Hawaii. If he knew the thoughts that sometimes slip into my mind. Completely and utterly inappropriate thoughts. If he'd think I'm still the best if he found out.

Doubtfully.

I watch as Nixon says goodbye and walks out of the bar before turning my attention to Jade, who's still talking to the basketball player. Nixon's words still ring in my head.

Is there something to it, or is he just exaggerating with his big-brother protectiveness? She seems fine. Like she usually is. Probably more perky than when she's around me, but for all that I know, her smart-ass comments can be reserved especially for me.

I watch her finish off her drink and signal the waiter for another one. Which one was it? Second? Third?

The image of her being dragged up those stairs flashes in my head.

No, that wasn't normal.

Sure, I've seen her drink before, but I never saw her blackout drunk like she was last evening.

The guy leans closer, way too close, his lips brushing against the shell of her ear as he whispers something to her. Jade throws her head back and laughs loud enough so I can hear it over the sound of music and the chatter of people.

Get a grip, Wentworth. She's your best friend's little sister.

Grabbing my beer, I take a pull from the bottle, only to find it empty.

Great, just my luck.

I look around but don't find any waiters, so I push to my feet.

"You guys need anything? I'm going to the bar to grab a drink."

I'm only half listening as they throw in their orders. Pushing through the crowd, I make my way to the bar. The girl behind the bar notices me instantly, the recognition flashing on her face as she makes her way toward me, making other people grumble in protest.

"What can I getcha, handsome?" She flashes me a megawatt smile and leans her elbows on the counter, the motion making her tits press together and show off her cleavage. But even that can't keep my interest when laughter rings through the room.

I rattle off our order, my attention already going over my shoulder just in time to see Jade shoving the tall dude away playfully before slipping from the table and going to the back of the room where the bathrooms are.

Fingers brush against the back of my hand. "Anything else?"

"Huh?" I turn around to find the girl watching me expectantly. "No, that's it. Can you take it back to the football table?"

"Yeah. You sure you—"

"Thanks." Pulling out the money, I place the bill on the counter. "That should be able to cover it," with a flash of a smile, I push away from the bar and go toward the bathrooms.

I should join the guys before they start asking questions. The idiots are nosier than a group of old ladies, but there's this pull I can't resist that's driving me forward.

I'm just rounding the corner when I bump into somebody. My hands go to the person's shoulders, steadying them.

"I'm so—"

The words die on my lips as her scent hits me first. Lavender and something more, I'm not sure what exactly. Then she tilts her head back, and those blue eyes are fixed on mine.

"What are you doing here?"

"I think the better question is, what are you doing?"

Jade watches me for a moment before shoving my hand away. "Excuse me? What gives you the right—"

"I have all the right in the world if you're flirting with one of my teammates..."

"This is about..." she lets out a loud groan. "Oh, for fuck's sake! We were *talking*. Not flirting. Not that it's any of *your* business either way."

"You can't go around messing with my teammate's heads. He needs to be concentrating on the game."

"Well, the only football player I see around is *you*." She jabs her finger into my chest. "And as far as I remember, I haven't invited you here, so why don't you go somewhere where they want you? Like maybe that bartender *you've* been flirting with." She pokes me again, that arrogant brow rising.

"Jealous, Cole?"

She snorts, "Of what?"

"I don't know." I wrap my fingers around her wrist, stopping her from poking me any further. "You tell me."

Jade tilts her head back, those blue eyes of hers burning brightly.

"In your dreams," she lets out a soft chuckle. "It seems to me like you're the jealous one here, Wentworth."

I suck in a sharp breath, noticing for the first time how close we're standing to one another. That sweet scent of hers fills my lungs, and I can feel her warm breath tickle my skin, making the hair on my nape stand at attention. Our joined hands are the only barrier separating my body from hers.

So close.

Too damn close.

Before I can react, she pulls her hand out of my grasp and glares at me. That's when I see it. The glassy haze of her irises.

"Jade…"

"You're not the boss of me, so go and boss somebody else."

With that, she slips around me and goes for the door. I let out a shaky breath, running my fingers through my hair and tugging at the strands. My heart was galloping in my chest, and I could swear I still felt that lavender scent around me.

"Fuck you, Nixon."

It's all his damn fault. If he didn't say shit, I wouldn't have gone after her.

Liar, liar.

Taking a few minutes to compose myself, I make my way back to the table.

"What took you so long?" Phillip asks as I slide into my seat.

"Keeping tabs on me?" I grab the beer sitting in front of me and take a long pull wishing it was something stronger.

It seems to me like you're the jealous one here, Wentworth.

She's crazy. That's what she is. Jealous of what exactly? Her flirting with some boys? As if. Besides, she's Nixon's little sister, for fuck's sake.

The little sister you can't stop thinking about.

"Just making observations," Phillip chimes. "No need to get all broody about it."

"I'm not broody," I mutter, my gaze darting toward Jade's table once again. My teeth grit together. Her hand is around the guy's shoulder as she talks to him. The guy says something, and she leans closer, her tongue darting out and sliding over her wet lips.

Not flirting my ass.

The little wench is doing it on purpose.

I drink the rest of my beer and signal the waitress who's just passing by. "Double scotch on the rocks."

"What happened to not getting drunk?" Sullivan asks.

"Hey, I'm not your captain."

"No, you're just an asshole who thinks he's better than the rest of us," he bites out and pushes his chair back as he jumps to his feet.

Thankfully, just then, the waitress comes back with my drink. I take it from her hand, downing it in one go, my attention going to Jade's table just in time to catch them grabbing their things and leaving. That dude is still plastered around her.

Is she going to take him home? Take him to her bed? Or go to his? Will she curl around him like she did when she was in my bed like she can't get close enough?

I wrap my fingers around the armrests of the chair; it's the only way I can make sure not to go after them and rip his hand from her body.

"Bring me another one."

Chapter 10

JADE

"So..."

"So?" I pull open the fridge, grabbing the creamer, and add a generous amount to my gigantic cup of coffee. Leaning against the counter, I stir the contents before taking a sip and letting the hot liquid warm me.

Grace leans her elbows on the counter, placing her head on her clasped hands as she gives me a small smile, and I know what's coming even before she says the words. "What did you think about Michael?"

Dead center.

"He seems fun," I say non-committedly.

Michael was nice. He was flirty and funny, but most importantly, he was available.

If you're flirting with one of my teammates...

Flirting with one of his teammates, my ass. Wentworth didn't care one bit that I was flirting with his teammate. Okay, maybe he did, but his panties got all twisted up later on.

Seriously, who did he think he was? To trap me in a dark corner like that and start bossing me around? I have one big brother; I don't need another one.

"Date-worthy kind of fun?" Grace asks, snapping me out of my thoughts. There is a note of hopefulness in her voice that's not hard to miss.

I give her a pointed look. "Just because you're happy and in a relationship doesn't mean everybody else has to be, you know?"

"You know what?" Rei asks as she closes the door behind herself. Her hair is pulled in a top knot, a few stubborn strands curling around her flushed cheeks.

"That Grace can't expect us all to be happily in a relationship. Hell, I don't even want a relationship."

Like ever. But I don't add that last tidbit.

Rei drops her duffle bag by the door with a loud *thud*. I'll never understand how she carries that thing that's twice her size. "I didn't realize you were dating."

"I'm not. I went out for drinks." I give Grace a pointed look. "Drinks that were supposed to be with my bestie, but she showed up with a group of guys."

Rei gasps, "She did not!"

I glare at my friend. "Don't encourage her."

Rei lifts her arms in defense. "I'm just joking. But seriously, what's the problem? If he's hot enough…"

"See?" Grace gives me a pointed look before turning her attention to Rei. "Oh, trust me. He's hot enough—tall, dark, and handsome."

"That seems like a good start." Rei nods her head. "You like them tall, dark, and handsome."

"I also like them not connected with my life or friend group. You know, fewer chances of running into him once I throw him out of my bed."

Rei rolls her eyes as she opens the fridge, pulling out some of the fruit and veggies for her smoothie. "Wait, who's the guy again?"

"One of Mason's teammates. We were at Moore's last night."

Rei's brows pull together in confusion.

"You know when you ditched us, so Grace figured she'd invite her boyfriend and his friends? That day?"

Grace takes a towel from the counter and tosses it at me. "Hey, you had fun!"

"That's not the point."

"But it seemed like you guys had a good time the other day!"

"I'm not denying that, but just because we had fun doesn't mean that I want to date the guy."

"How about *one* date? For me?" She bats her eyelashes. "Pretty, please?"

I rub my forehead, feeling the headache looming. "I'm not caffeinated enough to deal with this."

I'm still sleeping for shit, tossing and turning for the better part of the night until my body finally gives in as the sun starts to creep through the curtains.

"Just think about it. I heard from a reliable source that Michael would be interested if you're game. It could be a double date!"

"A reliable source, huh?" I take a sip of my coffee. "I bet you did."

"I mean, what would be the harm in that?" Rei asks.

"How about giving him false hope?"

Grace raises her brows. "By going on one date with him?" I open my mouth to protest, but she stops me. "No, think about it. You don't have to say anything now."

There was nothing to think about, but I wasn't about to continue this discussion. "I'm off to change since I have a class to get to. Meet you guys later for the football game?"

"You know it." Grace grins. "I'm so ready for the season to start. Mason is also..."

I narrow my eyes at her.

"... coming with us. *Alone*. Geez."

"He better be."

PRESCOTT

The strong beat of the music is blasting in my ears as I secure my shoulder pads. I grab the black jersey and pull it over my head. I concentrate on the rock blaring in my ears, trying to empty my mind of everything that's not football and our next opponent.

An elbow connects with my side. Pulling my headphones down, I turn around to see the coaches enter the locker room.

"Okay, boys. It's game time." Coach claps his hands, demanding our attention. There's a beat of silence as everybody stops what they've been doing and focuses on Coach's words. "I know the pre-season has been a bit rocky, but I have complete trust in the team we're building." He scans the room, making sure to meet the eyes of every player. "I've chosen every single man in here for a reason. This year, all the eyes are already turned our way to see if we can make the impossible and bring the title of national champions back home. I know you have it in you. Now, I need you to go out there and prove it to the rest of the country."

Heads nod in agreement at Coach's words. His eyes fall on Nixon, who tips his chin at him before taking a sweep of the room.

"You heard the man. They want to see us fail, but we won't make it easy, now, will we?"

Soft murmurs of agreement spread through the room.

"I asked, will we?" Nixon yells, this time louder.

"No!" everybody chants as somebody turns up the music.

Nixon nods, the veins in his neck bulging as he yells. "Who are we?"

"Ravens!"

"Who are we?" Nixon bellows louder, a leader turning to face his team.

"Ravens!" The chant spreads through the room, increasing in volume.

"Fucking yeah." He lifts his hand in the air. "Now let's go show them they've underestimated us."

Nixon turns to me, and we bump fists, grabbing our helmets from the bench before making our way out on the field.

There's nothing quite like playing that first game of the season on the home field. The roar of the crowd as we head out is almost deafening. I let it guide me as the offense takes to the turf. Stormy gray eyes meet mine for a split second before we fall in formation. I bend forward, facing the player on the other team.

"You're done, pretty boy," he spits. "You're leaving this field with your tails tucked between your legs."

"Not sure about you, buddy, but my dick's too big to do that," I smirk as his eyes turn into tiny slits.

Nixon calls out the play, and the moment the ball is snapped into his awaiting hands, I'm already moving down the field. The ball lands safely in my arms. My feet pound against the grass, each step sending a little stab of pain through my knee, but I grit my teeth, pushing through it.

One of the players is catching up to me, so I throw a lateral to Collin, our tight end, who catches it and continues sprinting toward the end zone until he's tackled. First and ten, with twenty yards to go.

It's good to be back.

Chapter 11

PRESCOTT

Forcing a smile, I nod at the reporter as I slowly leave. It takes all of me to hide the slight limp as I make my way to the locker room.

As soon as I push the door, I'm greeted with a madhouse. My teammates cheer as I enter, some patting me on the back and congratulating me on a good first game back over the blasting music. Everybody is running on a high after the win. Hell, even Coach was smiling as he left the locker room after our post-game talk, and the guy never smiled.

Finally, I reach my spot, easing down on the bench in front of it and let out a shaky breath.

"That was one pretty sweet catch in the fourth, Wentworth," Nixon says, slapping me on the shoulder. I'm grateful to be sitting because I'm not sure my legs wouldn't give out on me.

"It's good to be back."

It's the truth, but damn, I can feel the last three hours in every freaking bone in my body.

"Hell, yeah, it is. This is going to be our year, man. I just know it."

I want his words to be true, desperately, but right now, just the idea of doing this again anytime soon makes me want to puke my guts out. It was only by pure determination and adrenaline that I'd made it to the end of the game.

Pain meds.

I look down at my shaky hands. I curl and uncurl my fingers a few times, trying to get myself under control.

I can't. I know I can't, and yet...

An ear-piercing whistle spreads through the room.

"Yo!" Gregory yells, looking around to make sure he has everybody's attention. "There's a party at our house. I'll see you all there." His gaze stops on Nixon. "That goes for you too, Cap."

"Yeah, yeah, I'll be there. Somebody has to make sure you assholes make it to our next practice in one piece. Today was a good day, a good *game*, but remember, this is just game one."

Phillip lets out a groan. "Can we not? We just got off the field. Let us enjoy it for a bit."

Nixon lifts his hands in surrender. "Fine. Have at it."

"Thank you!"

The conversation resumes around us. Nixon turns toward the locker, shaking his head. "I swear they're going to be the death of me. We weren't like that."

I let out a snort, "No, we were worse."

Ripping my jersey over my head, I toss it in the laundry bin before pushing to my feet and doing the same with my pants. I bite the inside of my cheek as the pain grows stronger in my knee as I balance my weight on one foot. Just as I think I'll make it, my freaking pants get stuck on my foot, and I stumble.

Nixon's fingers wrap around my forearm, steadying me before I can fall down face first. "Hey, you okay?"

"Yeah," I croak out, my voice tight. "Just lost my balance there for a bit."

Shrugging his hand off, I grab my towel. "I'm going to take a shower."

I nod at a few people leaving the locker room when Nixon's voice stops me. "You coming later, right?"

"Of course. I'll see you guys there."

Thankfully, the bathroom has emptied out, so I slide into the first open stall and turn on the water before stepping under the spray. Bracing my palms against the wall, I bite back the hiss at the touch of cold water over my skin.

I'm not sure how long I stay like that, but by the time my muscles loosen enough that the pain isn't unbearable and I can make it back into the locker room without drawing unwanted attention to myself, most of my teammates have already left.

I quickly put on some clothes and make my way out to the parking lot. Tossing the duffle bag onto the passenger's seat, I slide into the car.

My fingers grip around the steering wheel as I watch the darkness ahead. Every so often, my gaze falls back on that damn bag.

It's like it's a living, breathing thing. I swear I can hear it calling my name. Giving me promises I so desperately need to hear.

Tempting.

So damn tempting.

"Fuck." Ripping my hands from the steering wheel, I clench my fingers into a fist and pound them against the leather.

Then, I finally give in and open the zipper. Pulling out that familiar plastic bottle, I take the pill, letting it dull the pain.

"I figured you'd have been here by now," I say, walking around the hood of my car to meet Nixon and the girls.

"Had to make a pit stop first."

"Is that what you call picking up your wife?" Yasmin asks, poking him in the side as she joins us. "A pit stop?"

Nixon throws his arm around Yas's shoulders, pulling her in. "Don't get all fussy about it, Yas. I had to be here, so I figured I might as well bring my beautiful wife. I need somebody to save me from growing bored out of my mind while I babysit my teammates."

"What's my role here, then?" Callie asks as we make our way through the cars parked around the front porch and toward the house.

"You're the package deal."

"A pit stop and a packaged deal? Wow, Nix," Callie rolls her eyes. "You had a way better game before you were married."

"I don't need any game, at least not off the football field, since I have the only person I want, and she ain't getting rid of me that easily."

I slap him over the shoulder as we climb onto the front porch. "Good luck getting yourself out of that one."

The party is in full swing as we enter the house. Heads start to turn in our direction instantly, people cheering the moment they notice their star quarterback has finally joined the party.

A few of our teammates rented a house on the outskirts of Blairwood, just near the forest, but the best part is the big-ass backyard. The music was blasting loudly, and somebody pulled out the table and brought a few kegs as well as enough alcohol to get us all drunk. The bonfire is lit in the middle of the clearing, burning brightly. The smell of burnt wood filled the air.

Zane waves us over to the beer keg, handing us each a solo cup as we join him.

"I have to admit, I was worried there for a second since you were struggling with your physical therapy, but it's good to see you back on the field," Zane says, clinking his cup against mine.

"Even better to play next to him," Nixon grins.

Guilt spreads through my stomach, making the bile rise in my throat for lying to my friends. But there was no way in hell I could tell them the truth.

Fake it till you make it, right?

It wasn't a secret that I've been struggling with my recovery. I was pissed off at the whole world for robbing me of the last season and winning the championship.

And then the injury wasn't healing right. The whole process was slow and painful as fuck, and things weren't much better after the cast was off. My leg felt off, but no matter how much therapy I went through, the pain never went away, at least not entirely. I knew what would happen if I told them the truth. They would tell me I shouldn't continue playing, but that wasn't an option. I have one year. One more year left, one chance to win that championship before it was over, and I turned all my focus to med school.

Shifting my weight, I feel my muscles tighten, the pain in my leg not as strong, thanks to the painkillers I took earlier, but still there. Always there.

"You're just happy you have at least one player who's used to your shitty throws and can make you look good," I say, plastering a smirk on my face.

"My throws are perfect," Nixon protests.

I snort, "Only in your dreams, Cole."

"Oh, please, admit it. You missed playing."

He can't even imagine. Not being able to play for the last nine months has been extreme torture. Football has been an essential part of my life since I could walk. If I'm not a football player, then who the fuck am I?

Just the idea of having to give it up before I can win it, *actually* win it, makes me want to punch something.

"I want us to win the national championship. Together."

"One day. One day, we'll win it together."

My throat grows tight as I push the memories back in the box where they belong.

"I missed the game, you on the other hand..."

"Screw you."

"Hey, if you're fishing for compliments, you better look for them elsewhere."

"Good to see you two are still the same," Zane shakes his head.

"Where's your girlfriend?" Callie asks.

"She's..." Zane turns around, looking over the crowd of people. "There."

I look up toward where he's pointing to where Rei and Spencer are standing close to the bonfire and talking with Grace and her boyfriend, drinks in their hands.

Spencer looks up the moment we join the group, clinking his cup against mine. "That was some game."

"Thanks."

Spencer nods, taking a sip of his drink. "Hopefully, now that you're back in the game, you'll stop bitching as much."

"I wasn't bitching..."

Before I can even finish, there's a loud chorus of: "Yes, you did."

I glare at my friends, who are laughing their asses off. "Whatever. Not one of you had to sit on the sidelines for the past nine months, so you can all suck my dick."

"That tiny thing in your pants?" Spencer smirks. "Thanks, but no thanks."

"Screw you, Monroe."

"Same to you, Wentworth."

Zane removes his attention from his girlfriend long enough to narrow his eyes at us. "I still don't get how you two live together and not kill each other."

"My thoughts exactly," Nixon says, joining the conversation. Then, as if it's an afterthought, he takes in our group. "Hey, where's Jade? Didn't you say she'd come?"

Yasmin purses her lips. "She's probably around here somewhere."

My whole body stiffens at the mention of her name, every muscle taut. I didn't realize she would have been out there in the stands. Then again, I'm not sure why I'm surprised.

I vaguely remember the scrawny girl coming to a few of Nixon's games back when we were freshmen. Not that I paid her much attention then.

Just like you shouldn't do it now if you don't want to lose your head.

Does it stop me from looking for her? No, it doesn't.

"She went to get a drink," Rei says, joining in the conversation.

"Of course she did," Nixon mutters, his jaw clenching. "I swear, that girl will be the death of me."

"Oh, hush." Yasmin slaps him on the chest. "Like you were any better just a few years ago."

"But..." Nixon starts to protest, only Yasmin puts her finger over his lips to shut him up.

"No buts. Don't be a patronizing dick, and let the girl enjoy her college years."

Finishing what's left in my cup, I wrap my fingers around the plastic.

"I'm going to grab a drink," I say to no one in particular.

"Grab me one, will ya?" Spencer asks.

Nodding, I slip through the crowd, making my way to the terrace where I saw the kegs earlier. It feels like there are even more people than just moments earlier. Some are dancing, some are talking, and some are playing games.

There are so many people that even though we're outside,

the air is stifling. I try to catch a glimpse of that familiar stubborn face, but since it's dark, it's hard for me to decipher one person from another. A few guys stop me as I refill my glass, wanting to congratulate me on being back on the team.

I turn around, ready to get back to my friends, when I see her. All thoughts leave my mind the moment my eyes fall on her.

Jade Cole.

And she's not alone.

Oh, no. No one other than fucking Joshua Sullivan is standing next to her.

They're standing in the shadows, closer to the trees. Jade throws her head back, laughing at whatever that idiot said to her, all that thick, dark hair swaying with the movement.

My fingers ball into fists by my sides, jaw clenching as I just stand there and stare.

Does he have a death wish or something?

I gave him a friendly warning because if Nixon were to see it, the warning wouldn't be so kind. No, he'd probably break the guy's nose first and then start asking questions.

Jade reaches forward, her fingers brushing against his forearm casually.

Not flirting, my ass.

What the hell does she even see in the idiot?

Before I know what I'm doing, I slip between the group of girls and move toward them.

"Seriously, Sully?" I grit, trying my best to keep my cool.

They turn to me, a flash of unease passing over his face until he realizes that it's me, not Nixon, and then it changes to anger. Jade, on the other hand, just crosses her arms over her chest and gives me her death glare.

"What the hell, Wentworth?" Sullivan's head snaps to me. "Where did you come from?"

That's what he's worried about? He's even a bigger idiot than I thought.

"That's not important. What's important is, what the hell are you doing flirting with Cole's little sister?" I cross my arms over my chest, my whole attention on my teammate.

"Are you shitting me?" Jade huffs.

"You stay out of this," I growl, not bothering to look at her.

He runs his hand over his face. "We were just talking. Chill, dude."

"Talking my ass." I glare at him because we both know this is a load of bullshit. "Do you want me to call Cole? I'm sure he'd be more than happy to talk to you."

Sullivan's jaw clenches as he glares at me. "Screw you, Wentworth." Then he turns to Jade. "I'll see you in class."

With that, he leaves. Freaking finally.

Jade marches to me and jabs her finger into my chest. Her lips are pressed tight, fire blazing in her blue irises. "What the hell's wrong with you?"

"Wrong with me?" She can't be serious, can she? "What's wrong with you? I already told you. You should know better than to flirt with your brother's teammates, doll."

"Stop. Calling. Me. That. Asshole." With each word, her finger probes at my chest.

"Stop poking me." Irritated more than anything else, I wrap my fingers around her wrist and tug her toward the trees, away from prying eyes.

The moment we're out of sight, she tugs her hand out of my grasp, those blazing eyes sending daggers my way. "I'll stop poking you the moment you stop messing with my life. Who do you think you are? My prince charming?"

I let out a humorless chuckle, "I'm sorry to inform you, doll, but I'm no prince charming."

"As if you'd ever be able to be one," she snorts. "There's not a drop of charm in your black heart to save your life."

She starts to turn around, but I grab her hand once again and tug her back.

"I mean it, doll. Stop flirting with the football players. The team doesn't need that shit right now."

She lifts one brow. "Jealous, Wentworth?"

Jealous?

"You're insane. Why would I be jealous?"

"Oh, I don't know. You tell me."

"You're being ridiculous," I shake my head. "Seriously, just stay away from the footba—"

"Football players. Yeah, yeah, I heard you." Jade rolls her eyes at me. "Just tell me one more thing. Does that include you?"

I blink, unsure if I heard her correctly. "What..."

She takes a step closer. "Because if I remember correctly, you had no issues going skinny dipping with me last spring." She presses her finger against my chest, slowly lowering it down, tingles rising in the wake of her touch. "Or does that not count as flirting, so you think Nixon would be okay with it? Because let me tell you, he would not appreciate one of his best friends rubbing all over his..."

I grab her hand, stopping her from continuing further. "I know that."

Fuck, I know that.

But did it stop you from doing it? a little voice taunts me.

Jade grazes her finger over my chin, her voice dropping lower. "Do you?"

"Don't play with me," I hiss, grabbing her other hand to stop her from touching me before I do something stupid. Something I'd probably regret.

Her brow arches up. "Or what?" She moves closer, her

warm breath touching my skin. "What are you going to do, Wentworth?"

"You're playing with fire," I whisper, my fingers tightening around her wrists. "You do realize that?"

Those blue eyes turn molten. Her gaze drops down to my lips. My throat turns dry as I watch her tongue slide out and trace the curve of that full lower lip as she slowly, oh so slowly, turns her gaze back to me. "Maybe I like the burn."

Before I know what I'm doing, I have her pressed against the nearest tree, her arms pinned above her head. She lets out a breath of air before my mouth crashes over hers.

This is bad, bad, bad.

But does it stop me from kissing her?

Fuck no.

Jade lets out a moan, her back arching toward me, her tits brushing against my chest as we devour one another. She tries to take control of the kiss, but I nip at her lower lip in warning before dipping my tongue into her mouth.

She tastes like coke, whiskey, and bad, bad decisions, but I can't seem to get enough of her. A loud rumble comes from my chest as I switch her wrists to one of my hands, sliding the other one at the small of her back and pulling her closer to me. She's soft to my hard, fire to my ice, each curve of her pressing just at the right place like she belongs there.

My cock twitches as she rubs her hips against mine. I slide my hand to her waist, digging my fingers into her flesh as I pin her against the tree once again before moving my hand lower and sliding it under the hem of her skirt.

I can hear her low moan as my fingers find her lace-clad pussy. She's so soaked I have trouble moving her panties to the side, but once I do, my fingers slide inside her easily.

Mine.

I tease her, running my fingers up and down her slit, circling her clit with every pass, matching the rhythm to my tongue swirling inside her mouth, taunting, teasing.

She moans once again, this time in protest, her teeth sinking into my lip and drawing blood. We break the kiss, both of us panting hard.

"Freaking vicious creature," I mutter, licking the blood from my lip.

"Don't play with me, Wentworth."

"Fine. Is this what you want?" I slide my fingers down and thrust two inside her. Jade whimpers, her pussy clenching around me tightly.

"Yes," she whispers.

Although it's dark, I can clearly see her pupils are dilated, a dusting of pink covering her cheeks. Smirking, I bury my head into her neck, licking and nibbling at the sensitive skin as I continue fucking her with my fingers.

"Went—" she starts to protest, but I bite into the column of her neck, repaying her for biting me earlier as I fasten my movements.

I pull my fingers all the way out before sinking them deeper than before, so deep my palm presses against her clit. I rotate my wrist, making sure to keep the pressure on her clit as I suck on her neck.

Fuck, she's so tight. So fucking perfect.

Jade's lips part, but before she can make a sound, I capture her mouth with mine, swallowing any noise she might make as I plunge my fingers into her until she comes so hard on my hand, her pussy squeezing me to the point I swear I can't feel my fingers.

My cock is pressing against my zipper, and I'm so hard it's painful. I swear if I don't feel—

"Dude!" The sound of a familiar voice snaps me out of the haze. And I'm not the only one. Jade's wide eyes are staring at mine with what I can only assume is a matching look of horror and panic at the sound of her brother's voice. "Have you seen Wentworth?"

Shit, shit, shit.

We're both impossibly still as we listen to the conversation happening not that far from here. The hard-on that's been bugging me just seconds earlier is now completely gone.

"Not recently, but knowing him, he's probably somewhere around here fucking around. You know how he is."

"Yeah, I guess you're right. Thanks."

We hold our breaths until we finally hear them walk away. Slowly, I unwrap my fingers from around Jade's wrists, pulling my hand out from under her skirt. I can still feel her slickness on my fingers and taste her on my tongue.

This is bad. So freaking bad.

Taking a step back, I clear my throat. "You should go back. He's been looking for you."

"Apparently, he's been looking for *you*, too."

"Well, he was looking for you *first*," I bite out. Does she really have to be this stubborn? "Just clean up and get out of here. I'll stay here a while longer before walking to the other side. The last thing we need is for somebody to see us come from the same place and for word to get back to your brother."

Jade runs her fingers through her hair, letting the wavy strands fall this way and that. "We wouldn't want that to happen. After all, he's well aware of your track record with girls."

Before I can open my mouth, Jade turns on the balls of her feet and marches toward the party.

Letting out a frustrated breath, I lean against the nearest tree, running my hand over my face.

What the fuck just happened?

One moment we were fighting, and the next...

The image of Jade pressed against the tree flashes in my mind. The sounds she made when I slid my fingers inside her echoed in my eardrums.

I lift my hand, the one that was moments earlier buried inside her, to my face, inhaling her musky scent, and my dick springs to life once again.

Cursing silently, I drop my hand and readjust myself.

That woman is going to be the end of me.

What just happened was bad enough, but this shit can't keep happening. If Nixon appearing out of nowhere and almost catching us wasn't a sign, I don't know what is. I almost fucked my best friend's little sister against a freaking tree. If he found out... he would kill me. Plain and simple. And he would have every right to, too.

No, I have to steer clear of Jade-freaking-Cole. For both of our sakes. No matter how tempting she might be.

I'm not sure how long I stay in the woods. Long enough for my boner to go down, at least slightly, and that familiar ache to return to my knee. Sliding my hand inside my pocket, I pull out the bag and grab two pills, throwing them into my mouth before pushing away and finding my way back to the party.

Stopping by the drinks table, I make myself a drink, washing away the bitter taste in my mouth. I turn around, ready to find some of my teammates when my eyes fall on Nixon's.

"Look who's here!" He's standing with a few guys from the team, his arm thrown over Yasmin's shoulder. A wide grin on his face makes my stomach clench uncomfortably. The guilt is eating at me. "Where the hell were you? We were just looking for you."

Well, if you found me, you'd have gotten an eyeful.

"Around," I shrug, joining them. "What's up?"

"We were just talking about the game, but you found a

better way to celebrate," he smirks, tipping his chin in my direction. "You still have something on your mouth, dude."

I swipe my thumb over my lower lip. Looking down, I notice the dark red stain on the tip of my finger. *Fucking hell.* "Yeah, I guess you could say so," I mutter, rubbing harder at my mouth.

"Where's your friend? Don't tell me you already ditched her?" Spencer throws his arm over my shoulders as he joins the conversation.

"You know Wentworth," Robert, a senior kicker, chuckles. "He's a one-and-done kind of deal."

A movement over his shoulder catches my attention. I look up and see Jade's eyes fixed on me across the distance. For a heartbeat, we just stare at one another, all the other things, all the other people, falling into the background.

But then Rei leans closer, telling her something. Jade's the first to break eye contact.

My fingers clench around the cup in my hand as I bring it closer to my mouth, taking a sip of the vodka and letting it burn down my throat.

Maybe if I drink long enough, it'll burn away the taste of Jade Cole from my memory too.

Because there is no way, this can happen again.

Ever.

Chapter 12

JADE

I groan loudly as the insistent buzzing wakes me from my sleep. And it was a sweet dream. I bury my head into the pillow, trying to cling to the remnants of it as long as possible, hoping whoever's calling will get the memo and leave me alone. But then, the man in my dreams looks up, and a pair of dark brown eyes fixed on me, the mouth surrounded by weeks' worth of stubble curling upward in a mocking smile.

Fucking hell.

Blindly I tap the mattress until my fingers curl around my phone, and I answer the call.

"What?!"

"Good. You're awake," my brother says, way too chipper for this early in the morning.

"What do you want, Nixon?" I croak, rolling to my back and rubbing my fingers over my pulsing temples.

Damn, how much did I have to drink last night?

I think I stopped counting after the fifth drink or was it the sixth?

But it's not like I had an option.

I kissed Prescott Wentworth. Well, if we want to be technical about it, he kissed me.

But I liked it.

I liked it a lot.

The image of Prescott is still fresh in my mind. The way his body pressed into mine. The feel of his hands on my skin as they roamed my body. The way his mouth was pressed against mine as if he'd die if he didn't kiss me. And boy, did he know how to kiss a girl properly. I swear I could still feel his fingers wrapped around my wrists, pinning them against the tree as his mouth worked its way down my neck.

Just thinking about it has a shiver running down my spine.

It unsettled me, the way my body reacted to him, the way *I* reacted to him. It was unlike anything I'd ever felt with anybody else.

It scared me.

"Jade?" Nixon asks, breaking me out of my thoughts. "You listening?"

"I-I'm listening."

"Good, I thought you might have fallen asleep on me, considering all the drinks you had last night."

"Nixon..." I groan. "Was there a point to this call, or do you just take pleasure in torturing me?"

"I just wanted to make sure you haven't forgotten about our brunch."

Brunch? My brows furrow. "What brunch?"

"The one that starts in the next ten minutes." There's a small pause, and I can hear Yasmin talking in the background. "Please, tell me you didn't forget."

Shit! He was serious about that?

"Of course not," I lie and throw the blanket to the side, forcing myself to get up. "Why are we having brunch this early again?"

Nixon lets out a sigh, "You totally forgot, didn't you?"

"Not at all."

"You did. I knew I should have reminded you last night before leaving. Then again, I'm not sure you'd have remembered this morning anyway."

Yeah, I guess there was that tidbit.

Plus, I was doing my best to avoid Nixon for the better part of the night and forced Grace and Rei to dance with me instead. I hated avoiding my brother, but after he almost caught Prescott and me and everything that had happened, I kind of made a point of staying away. The last thing I needed was for my brother to start asking questions.

"I'll be there, don't get your panties in a twist."

"You better. You missed it last time."

"Because you're having brunch early. On a *Sunday*," I protest, pulling open my closet and grabbing the first shirt I can get my hands on.

"It's eleven in the morning. I hardly think that constitutes as early."

"Well, it's my only day to sleep in."

"You don't have any classes before ten. Ever."

"That's because I don't do well in the mornings," I let out a sigh. "I've gotta go. I'll see you in a few."

Before he can say anything else, I hang up. Tossing the phone on the bed, I grab a bra, slide it on, and fasten the clasp. My boobs feel tender, but I don't let myself think too much about it before tugging the tee over my head just as the phone buzzes once again.

"What now?" I mutter, grabbing the phone only to find a text message waiting for me.

Nixon: Just so you're not tempted to go back to

bed, you have a driver waiting so you better hurry up.

I roll my eyes.

Me: I don't need a babysitter.
Nixon: Hurry up.

Oh, now he's went and done it.

As slowly as possible, I pull on my leggings, 'cause nobody should have to suffer through pants on a Sunday after being awoken way too early before going to the bathroom to finish getting somewhat presentable. It's a good fifteen minutes before I get out of the apartment.

I look around the parking lot, searching for the familiar black BMW, when my phone vibrates. Lowering my gaze, my brows pull together when I notice the unfamiliar number on the screen. I'm about to answer it when the phone call ends as quickly as it started, and that's when I hear it. The low purr of the engine.

My head snaps up, and I do a double take as a black Mustang pulls from one of the parking spots and approaches me. I suck in a breath, and I swear my heart does a little flip in my chest.

What the hell's he doing here?

Before I can process what's going on—or, you know, run inside—the car comes to a stop in front of me. I just stare at it, unsure of what to do, but before I can decide, Prescott leans over the passenger's seat and opens the door for me.

"Do you plan to get in today or what?" he asks in that irritating tone of his that has me crossing my arms over my chest defensively.

"*You* are my ride?"

"No, the little green people will come to fetch you in a bit," he deadpans. "Yes, I'm your ride. Now, can you get your ass in the car, or do you need me to do it for you?"

I don't budge an inch. "I thought Nixon was waiting for me."

"He probably remembered that I live in the building next door, so he texted me to pick you up and gave me your number in case you don't show up. So, are you coming or what?"

I roll my eyes at him and slide into the car. "Why are you so grumpy?" I give him a side eye as I pull on my seatbelt. "I thought you were a morning person."

Prescott runs his hand over his face and pulls on the road. "I'm still hungover, and today was my sleep-in day."

He looks almost as bad as I feel. Hair disheveled, that damn scruff that at this point is practically a beard, the dark circles under his eyes. Makes you wonder what keeps a star wide receiver, who just got back from an injury and is on top of his game, up at night.

Prescott glances at me, those brown eyes of his meeting mine.

"Well, it's good to know that he didn't just interrupt my dream."

Prescott quirks his brow, the corner of his mouth twitching. "Having interesting dreams, are you, Cole?"

Those heated eyes watching me, the feel of his hands and his mouth on me, making the hair at the back of my neck rise.

"Shut up, and drive. Will ya?" I mutter, turning my head to look out the window.

Prescott smirks. "Whatever you say, doll."

I give him a side eye, which only makes him chuckle.

Asshole.

The rest of the ride goes smoothly, and in no time, we're parked in front of Macy's.

"Well, thanks..." I start just as Prescott says: "About yesterday..."

"We're not talking about yesterday," I mutter, unbuckling the seatbelt and getting out of the car.

Prescott curses behind me, but I'm already walking toward the local diner. The smell of grease, sugar, and coffee hits me the moment I step inside, and I let it wash away the scent of Prescott from my mind.

Taking a sweep of the space, I find Nixon and our friends seated in the corner booth. Before the door fully closes, Prescott slides behind me, his tall frame looming over me.

"Jade..."

"Not talking," I grit through clenched teeth as I make my way to our friends.

"Look who's finally here!" Nixon says as soon as we join the group.

"Yeah, yeah," I muttered, sliding into the booth across from him and Yasmin. "Don't get your panties in a twist. I told you I'd be here, didn't I?"

"Granted, that's what you said last weekend, but you fell right back to sleep," Yasmin chuckles.

"That's why I called in the reinforcements this time around," Nixon grins just as Prescott mutters a hello.

"Make some room for me, will ya?"

I look up, my eyes narrowed. Does he really have to sit next to me?

"What?" He raises his brows as if he can read my mind. "Should I sit on the floor?"

Huffing, I slide closer to Alyssa. "It's not my problem you have a big ass."

"You checking out my ass, doll?"

"In case you forgot, there is a baby at the table," Maddox's warning is followed by a stream of unrecognizable noises coming from the little girl lying in the crook of his arm.

At four months, Edie Mae is the little princess everybody knew she'd be, and she has everybody wrapped around her little fingers, but nobody nearly as much as her daddy.

"You know that she can't actually understand what we're saying, right?" Prescott asks, leaning over the table.

The motion has him getting all in my face, and not even the smells of the diner can obscure the spicy scent of his cologne.

Did he really need to sit here?

"She has ears; therefore, she can listen just fine. And sooner rather than later, she'll start to talk. I'm not going to let my daughter's first words be some kind of profanity."

Edie lets out more noises, moving her little fists as if she knows what her dad just said and is agreeing with him.

My stomach tightens at the sight of the two of them, unease spreading under my skin as I watch Maddox lean down and brush his mouth against the top of her ginger head. He murmurs something softly to Edie, his hand securely wrapped around her middle. If you didn't know, you'd never realize that Maddox isn't Edie's biological father because that man would die before he ever let anything happen to her.

"Maddox, can I please have her now?" Yas leans closer, tickling Edie's sock-clad foot and pouting exaggeratedly.

"Not happening," Maddox says, not even dignifying her with his attention. Nope, that boy only has eyes for his two girls.

"But I barely get to see her!" Yasmin turns to Alyssa. "Tell him, Aly. I swear she's grown so much since the last time I saw her."

Aly gives her a pointed look. "You saw her yesterday when you were picking up Callie for the football game."

"She has you there," Callie says, her fingers typing away on her phone. Since her boyfriend started playing in the NFL and moved, she's been constantly texting him.

"It was just for a few minutes. So, that doesn't count."

I glance at my brother. "You should seriously give her one of these before she steals a baby from somebody."

Nixon's eyes turn into saucers, mouth falling open, but before he can say anything, Yasmin whips her head toward me and kicks me under the table. "Bite your tongue!"

"What?" I lean down, rubbing at my leg. "Maybe then you wouldn't give Maddox those heart eyes every time he's holding the baby."

"I'm giving heart eyes to Edie, not Maddox. And that's because she's cute. Not because I want one of my own." Yasmin looks up at my brother, and I swear I can see stars in her eyes. The way they're so in love with each other is equally cute and disgusting. "Not yet, anyway."

Nixon smirks. "We can always practice, though. You know, for when the time is right?"

I groan, grabbing the menu from the middle of the table. "And I think I just threw up in my mouth."

Tucking my hair behind my ear, I check out the selection. Eggs and bacon, blueberry pancakes, chocolate pancakes, waffles...

"You're just... What the heck is on your neck?" Nixon asks, his tone suddenly very cold.

I look up from the menu. Why I bother looking at it when every time I come, I order exactly the same thing? I'll never understand. "What?"

Nixon is staring at me; his eyes narrowed, lips pressed in a tight line. "That," he points at my neck.

Everybody at the table turns in my direction, suddenly interested in the conversation.

Self-consciously, I raise my hand and touch the side of my neck. The skin feels a little tender, but...

Yasmin leans closer. "Is that a... hickey?"

"What?!" my hand covers my neck to where I suppose the bruise is. How did I not see it? Then is it really strange, considering I put a towel over the mirror so I wouldn't have to face my other bruises? Because I was good at ignoring my problems like that.

He did not...

A very vivid image of Prescott's mouth on my neck flashes in my mind. I turn to the man in question, who has a look of utter horror on his face that I'm pretty sure matches mine.

"It is!" Yasmin chuckles. "Oh my God, I didn't realize hickeys were still a thing!"

"It's not funny, Yas," Nixon and I say in unison.

My brother glares at his wife before turning his attention to me. "What the fuck, Jade? Who gave you a hickey?"

"I don't see how that's any of your business." I tug my hair to the side to cover the bruise.

Seriously, a freaking hickey!

If we weren't surrounded by people, I'd strangle him.

"Because some asshole thought it would be wise to mark my sister like she's some kind of property or some shit."

Thankfully, I wasn't drinking because I'm pretty sure if I were, I'd spit it all over the table.

If you only knew, buddy. If you only knew.

And apparently, I'm not the only one because Prescott suddenly starts coughing. Hard.

Nixon frowns, and I duck my head and bite into my lower lip so I don't burst into hysterical laughter.

"Are you okay?"

Prescott murmurs something, still coughing.

I run my fingers through my hair, looking at the man in question. "He looks a little blue."

Yasmin glances at me. "Kind of like that hickey of yours."

If possible, Prescott starts coughing even harder.

"All good, Wentworth?" I ask sweetly, batting my eyelashes at him. He glares at me, but it doesn't look half as funny when he's struggling to breathe.

Pity.

"F-fine," he wheezes, trying to suck in a breath.

"You sure?"

His eyes narrow at me. "Just got something stuck in my throat."

"I know the feeling very well," I mutter, the sensation of his mouth pressed against mine still fresh in my mind.

Prescott holds my gaze for a few heartbeats longer before his eyes drop down to my neck, and I swear I can feel my skin prickle to attention from his hard glare.

"This isn't something to joke about!" Nixon protests, breaking us out of our staring contest.

"It's a hickey, Nix." I roll my eyes, turning my attention to my brother. "Chill. It's not like the guy tattooed his name on me."

My body goes still as Prescott shifts in his seat, his arm brushing against mine.

"I'm not going to chill. Tell me who it was."

I let out a huff, "No."

If possible, my brother's face darkens even further. "No?"

"No," I repeat. "I don't need my big brother to go and fight my battles for me. I'm quite capable of doing it myself."

His gaze drops down to my neck. "I see you've been doing very well so far."

"I was, and I don't remember asking for your opinion."

Nixon grabs his coffee and takes a sip. "Why you have the need to meddle in my sex life..."

The coffee spurts out of his mouth. "Sex life?"

"Yes, Nixon. *Sex life*. I'm allowed to have one of those, in case you've been wondering."

Nixon wipes his mouth with the back of his hand. "I..."

"No," I shake my head. "Do I have to remind you that I went to high school with you, and I know exactly how big of a player you were?" That makes him shut up. "So, no, Nixon, I don't want to hear another word of this. As I told you, I'm a big girl, and I can take care of myself. And if I want to let a guy sink his teeth in my neck, I have every right to do so." I glance toward my sister-in-law. "No offense, Yas."

"Oh, none taken." She elbows Nixon in the side. "I know very well what a player he was before."

"*Before*," he grunts. Turning to her, he grabs her hand and brings it to his lips. "Before you. Before us."

A knot forms in my throat at the sight of the two of them. I'm happy for Nixon. I really am. He deserves all the love he can have. But there is this other part of me, an envious part, that's jealous that he's moving on when I can't seem to run away from my past. From my demons.

"Well, there's no before for me. Just now. So kindly stay out of my freaking business and concentrate on your wife. And you know, maybe giving me some nieces and nephews." I turn to the server, who finally comes, placing the trays with food our friends ordered on the table.

"What?" Prescott asks. "You guys are trying for..."

"I think the word you're looking for is kids, Wentworth," I say cheerily and take a moment to watch his eyes grow wide before turning my attention to the server. "I'll have a blueberry pancake, please."

"Jade's joking," Yasmin scolds, digging into her omelet.

"We're not trying for anything. Now, if only Maddox would share..."

"Nope." Just then, the baby starts fussing. Aly reaches for her, but Maddox shakes his head and gets up, turning Edie, so she's snuggled into the crook of his neck and gently patting her back. "You eat. I've got her."

My gaze drops from Maddox to the man sitting next to me. "At least there's one man here who's not afraid of commitments."

"This doesn't have anything to do with commitment. College is supposed to be fun, and babies are..." his words trail off as he watches Maddox. "Babies."

I burst into laughter, "Babies are babies? That's the best you can come up with?"

"Hey, don't look at me. I'm not good with kids."

"Why does that not surprise me?"

Yasmin laughs, "Pot meet kettle."

"What?"

"You haven't even held her once!"

"Between you and Callie, it's not like I had a chance."

"Excuses, excuses."

At the mention of her name, the blonde finally looks up from her phone. "Callie what?"

Thankfully, my and Prescott's food arrives shortly, and we change the subject to classes and football as we finish our breakfast. I'm only half listening because Prescott's arm is brushing against mine the whole time as we eat, making me a nervous wreck. I keep expecting somebody to say... something, but nobody does.

As we're leaving Macy's, Nixon throws his arm around me and pulls me into his side. "I didn't mean to piss you off earlier. I just worry about you."

"And while I appreciate it, you really need to stop. I'm a big girl."

"I know, but you'll always be my little sister."

I roll my eyes at him. "Don't be corny."

"It's the truth." Nixon looks over his shoulder. "Hey, Wentworth! You good with dropping Jade off at her place?"

"Nixon!" I chide.

The last thing I want is to be cooped up in a car with Prescott after spending the last hour pressed against the hard line of his body. Or have any possible conversation that might take place.

"Sure thing."

"I can walk just fine." I glare at Nixon before turning my attention to Prescott. "I don't need you two to micromanage me."

"Are you going back to your place?"

"Well, yeah b—"

"Me too, so why would you walk back?"

I open my mouth to protest but close it swiftly. I hate it when he's being so... rational.

"See? Problem solved." Nixon presses his mouth against the top of my head. "I'll see you later, Smalls."

"Later," I say and hug Yas goodbye before the two of them go to their car.

Letting out a sigh, I follow after Prescott, mentally preparing myself for the drive back. I expect him to mention the kiss again, but he doesn't, so I play with the radio until I find the station I like before settling back in my seat and clasping my hands in my lap.

Maybe he won't say anything.

Maybe he already forgot about it.

Maybe—

"We should seriously talk about what happened last night,"

Prescott says finally as he pulls into a parking space in front of our building complex, breaking the silence.

Or maybe not.

"Oh, you mean like the fact that you gave me a freaking hickey?" I look at him, my brows raised. "Or the fact that my brother wants to kill you without knowing he wants to kill you? Is that what you'd like to talk about?"

Prescott runs his hand over his face. "What happened last night was a mistake, okay? I'm sorry. It was totally out of place. It should have never happened. It *will* never happen again. You're my best friend's little sister, for fuck's sake!"

His words are like a blow.

Mistake.

That's what I'm to him—a freaking mistake.

I let out a humorless chuckle.

"Well, you didn't think I was little when you saw me flirting with other guys and got jealous, and you definitely didn't think I was little when you had me pressed against that tree and buried your fingers inside me." I shake my head and fiddle with the seatbelt until it finally unclasps.

Out.

I need to get out.

"Jade..." Prescott tries to grab my hand, but I'm already pushing the door and sliding out of the car. "Don't—"

"No, you said what you meant." I press my palms against the roof of the car as I lean down to face him. "There are guys who want me, Wentworth. You don't get to act like a jealous asshole when it suits you."

Then I close the door in his face and march into my building.

Chapter 13

PRESCOTT

"Read chapters thirteen through eighteen. We'll be working on those during our next lab," the professor says as she wraps up the class. "I'll see you on Thursday."

I quickly jot down the note before closing my books and shoving them into my bag. I push to my feet. My leg protests the movement, my muscles stiff from sitting down for so long, or maybe it's the beating I took yesterday. I'm not sure if the first game was a fluke or if our recent opponents were stronger, but the team was struggling. The second game was a blood bath, and I could feel it in every bone of my body.

My phone beeps as I exit the building. I pull it out, my whole body tensing when I read the name on my screen. For a moment, I'm tempted to let it go to voicemail, but I know it won't help one bit, quite the contrary.

Pressing the answer button, I put the phone to my ear. "Hey, Dad."

"Prescott, is there a reason why you haven't answered your phone?"

"I was in class before. It just finished."

"Oh, yeah, that poor excuse for your education."

Nobody else, only my father, would think being pre-med is a "poor excuse for an education."

"Did you need something?"

"Your next game is a home game?"

"It is."

"Good. I have a meeting in Boston the day before, so I'll be stopping by that day."

So, a convenient intervention. God forbid, he'd make some time to come and visit his son at college. Not that I want him to. I'd be the happiest if he'd just leave me alone, but who'd he complain to then? I guess I should be happy that he announced himself so I can mentally prepare for it.

"Hopefully, you'll play better than you did yesterday. That was pathetic, Prescott. If this is how you plan to play this season, it would have been better if you gave up when you were ahead instead of sullying our family's name."

I grit my teeth, trying to hold back my anger. It's not like he cares what I think one bit, anyway.

"Anything else, Father?"

"No, that's all. We'll have dinner next week after the game, so don't go scurrying off with your friends partying and drinking."

"Whatever you say."

There's some kind of noise in the background before he says: "Next week."

That's it. No goodbye or have a nice day. Next week.

"Fucking hell," I mutter.

"Who pissed in your cereal?"

I look up only to find Spencer watching me expectantly.

"Nobody," I say, shoving my phone back into my pocket. "What's up with you?"

"I'm going to the cafeteria to grab lunch. You coming?"

"Sure thing."

I have a couple of hours free, just enough to grab some lunch and maybe dig into the mountain of homework and reading material my professors gave me this week—and it was only Tuesday—before I had to make it to the gym for conditioning.

I listen to Spencer talk about some girl he met at the party last weekend as we make our way to the cafeteria and grab lunch, my mind still on my conversation with my father.

It shouldn't bug me. He's been like this with me my whole life. Nothing I did was ever good enough. Not like…

Shaking my head, I push those thoughts back into the box they belong to and scan the cafeteria. I spot Nixon sitting with a few guys from the team, so we go ahead and join them.

"You look like something ran you over," Nixon says as I take the chair opposite him.

"He's more grumpy than usual," Spencer adds helpfully. "I think somebody pissed him off. Or maybe he just needs to get laid. I don't think I've—"

I look up and glare at my friends, not that I know why I hang out with them anyway. "I don't need to get laid."

Spencer leans in toward Nixon and whispers conspiratorially: "He definitely needs to get laid. It would put him in a better mood."

"He can hear you just fine. And I have more important things to worry about than sex."

Like keeping my spot on the team, finishing this year, and taking the MCATs—real-life problems.

My gaze zeroes in on the group sitting a few tables behind Nixon. More importantly, on a certain brunette.

Seriously? Did she really have to be here today of all days?

After the debacle at the brunch, I did my best to avoid Jade. We had completely different majors, so our paths didn't often cross on campus, and since I usually left my apartment early and returned late, I didn't see her there either.

Until today.

My throat goes dry as I watch her laugh with her friends at the table. I know I should look away, but I can't seem to do that. It's like my mind is trying to drink her in as much as possible.

But then my line of vision is interrupted when a group of guys stops in front of them—the basketball players. I watch as they chat before the guys take the available seats, that guy from the bar sliding in next to Jade with a grin on his face.

I press my lips together, the food I just ate leaving a bitter taste in my mouth.

She's your best friend's little sister.

But even if she wasn't, she's too good for you.

"Wentworth?"

I shake my head at the sound of my name, forcing myself to move my gaze from her.

Nixon raises his brow. "You listening to us?"

"What did I tell you?" Spencer asks. "He's all off. Even more than usual."

"Shut up, Monroe. It's just been a shitty day. A shitty *week*."

"Tell me about it," Phillip groans. "Coach's been riding our asses more than usual."

"I don't know what's his problem," Sullivan comments. "It was just one loss."

I tried to ignore the guy up until now. What was he even doing sitting here? I have no idea.

"Just one loss?" I turn to him, my eyes narrowing. "It was more than just one loss. It was a clusterfuck of a game against the team that shouldn't have given us any problems. It's not even surprising that he's pissed. We should be equally angry at ourselves."

"Hey, don't look at me. It's not like it's my fault. I was just sitting there."

"You're saying it's my fault?" I ask, happy to finally have somebody to turn my anger toward. I've been looking for a fight ever since I finished my conversation with my dad, and Sullivan seems like the perfect choice.

"It was everybody's fault," Nixon says, giving me a warning glare. "Now, will you two stop? You're fighting like cats and dogs. We're a team, for fuck's sake. Teammates don't turn on their teammates."

The silence falls over the table at Nixon's harsh words. The guy rarely ever yells, so it's not even surprising.

"I have a class to get to," Sullivan mutters, breaking the quiet. "I'll see you later."

He grabs his things and leaves. I watch him walk through the room, but instead of going straight to the door, he stops at Jade's table. They talk for a little bit before she, too, grabs her things, and together they leave.

I tip my chin in their direction. "You not going to say anything about that?"

Nixon glances over his shoulder to look in the direction I pointed.

"Don't they have a class together? I think he's a graphic design major like her."

The way Sullivan looks at her has nothing to do with them being classmates and everything with him wanting more. How couldn't he see that? For all his talk about keeping her protected, he's blind to some things.

You should be grateful for it because if he finds out what you did...

He won't find out because it was a one-time thing. It won't happen again. It can't. I won't let it.

"What's your deal with Sullivan, anyway?" Nixon asks,

breaking me out of my thoughts.

I look down at my plate, shoving some of the veggies and rice from one side of my plate to the other. "I don't know what you mean."

"Bullshit."

My head snaps up at the sharp tone of his voice. "There's been something going on between you two since the day you returned. Is it the fact that he took your spot?"

"You're imagining things."

But, of course, Nixon continues as if I haven't said a word. "It was just until you came back. You know that? The guy's decent but nowhere near as good as you. Hell, if you were interested in going pro, you could totally do that."

"I'm not interested in going pro. What I'm interested in is winning this season, and if we don't get our shit in order, that's not going to happen." I look down at my half-eaten plate. "I'm going to the library."

"You barely ate anything."

"Not hungry."

"Can I have those?"

Spencer points at the chocolate chip cookies still on my plate. I'll never understand how he managed to keep his mouth shut this whole time. They're my favorite, and the ladies in the cafeteria know it, so they always sneak me one extra.

I glare at him. "I'm taking those for later."

My roommate pouts, "I thought you were not hungry."

"That's why they're for later. Get your own damn cookies, Spence."

"Asshole."

"Dickhead."

Nixon shakes his head. "You two are weird."

"Takes one to know one." I wave at them over my shoulder. "Later."

Chapter 14

JADE

"Thank God you're still here!"

I look over my shoulder to find Vicky, one of my classmates, standing in the doorway of the dark room, panting.

Letting go of the negative I've been working on, I grab a towel to clean my hands as I turn to face her. "What's up?"

"Can you please, please, please help me?" she asks, still breathing hard.

"Sure." I give her a concerned look; she looks like she's ready to pass out. "Is everything alright? You should take a few deep breaths."

Vicky shakes her head. "No time."

"Well, you won't tell me anything if you pass out." I give her a pointed look. Vicky nods and leans her hands against her thighs, sucking in a long breath. I watch her as she repeats the motion a few times until her breathing is steadier before she straightens.

"I need you to step in for me."

"Step in for what?"

"You know how I work for the college newspaper?"

"Yeah," I nod. "I think I've heard it mentioned before."

"Well, I was supposed to take photos for one of the articles we've been working on, but I just got a call from my daughter's school. She's not feeling well, and they need me to pick her up. Can you please do it?" She clasps her hands. "Pretty please? I'd postpone it, but I've left it for the last minute to begin with, so…"

"Yeah, sure. I can do it." I glance toward the wall. "I have to finish those first, though."

"That's not a problem. Wait…" Vicky pulls out her phone, and a few moments later, my own phone vibrates on the desk. "I just sent you his info. The team has practice every afternoon at five? Six? I can't remember exactly. Either way, you should have a few more hours to wrap this up. Just text him, so he knows you're coming."

"Okay, what kind of photos are we talking about?"

"Him practicing with the team and then a few shots of him by himself should do just fine. I'll never know why they just didn't pull some from the archive."

"Sure, no problem."

Before I can react, Vicky pulls me into a hug. "Thanks, Jade."

"Who's the—" Her phone rings, interrupting me. Vicky lets go of me and looks down at the screen.

"Shoot, I really have to go." She turns around and opens the door, yelling over her shoulder: "I owe you!"

"Not a…" Before I can finish, the door behind her closes. "Problem," I finish, shaking my head.

I can't really blame her, though. Although, I wouldn't really call us friends. Since our photography class is small, I've gotten to know her and discovered she's a single mom, on top of being a part-time college student and working two different jobs. Why she thought joining the school paper was a good idea on top of all her obligations, I'll never understand. Either way, I don't mind helping. It's not like I have anything better to do.

I open Vicky's message and look at the number she sent me. It looks slightly familiar, but why... I copy the number and enter it into my phone. Only there is no need to save it because it's already in there. Not that there was actually a reason for me to have it since I don't talk to him.

A mistake.

"Are you shitting me?"

The sound of the whistle is the first thing I hear as I make my way toward the field. I haul my bag higher as I walk closer to the fifty-yard line where the team is currently facing off. Shielding my eyes from the setting sun, I watch as the players move almost effortlessly over the grass. The ball is tossed to Nixon, his red practice jersey clinging to his skin as he pulls his hand back, his eyes scanning the space for his players before he lets the ball fly.

My heart tightens as I watch him play, remembering the last time I came to one of the team's practices, back when I was a sophomore in high school. I didn't want to go. Instead, I wanted to hang out with my friends, but Mom insisted we should go and support Nixon.

Shaking my head to push away the memories, I lift my camera and scan the space through the lens, waiting for the perfect moment.

The running back carrying the ball is tackled to the ground. The whistle blows once again, and Coach starts yelling something as the players pull apart, everybody lining up on the thirty-yard line. Nixon calls out the play, and the ball is tossed to him. He holds onto it, moving into the pocket as the players shift around him, an intense look on his face. I snap a photo, and then the ball is flying. I follow its trajectory, my lens settling on the number eighty-eight, with a big golden Wentworth written in bold on his back.

I swallow the lump in my throat as I watch him take off from the ground, his arms wrapping around the ball and pulling it tight to his chest.

My finger presses the shutter, capturing the moment as he's in mid-air. I lower the camera just as he starts running toward the end zone. The defense gets in his way, but he ducks to the side, changing the course to try and ditch the guy.

I move closer just as Prescott breaks away and runs toward the end zone. I try my best to avoid the action, but one of the coaches notices me. His brows furrow as he glares at the camera. "You can't be here."

Is he for real?

I look pointedly at the stands where girls are standing and cheering. "It's an open practice. Besides, I'm with—"

"Smalls?" I turn around only to find Nixon jogging toward me. "What are you doing here?" He frowns. "Did something happen? Are you okay? Is Yas..."

"Everything's fine," I reassure him and lift my camera. "I'm just jumping in for one of the girls working for the newspaper. She was supposed to shoot..."

"Cole, are you planning to get your ass to the field so we can finish this game, or do we have to do all the work?"

Tingles go down my spine at the sound of his voice. I bite the inside of my cheek, my gaze moving to the man jogging toward us. He pulls the helmet off, and damn, he shouldn't look this good all sweaty like that, but somehow, he does.

I watch as he lifts his free hand and runs it through his hair, messing the blond strands. Seriously, it's annoying how good he looks.

"Dude, I did *all* the work. Who do you think makes you look good out on the field?"

"I don't remember it that way." Prescott lifts his shirt and wipes away the sweat from his forehead, his defined abs glistening under the late afternoon sun. One, two, three, *four* pairs of squares appear from beneath the dark cotton.

"Of course you don't." Nixon rolls his eyes and points his finger at him. "He'd be the one."

You hate sweat. I remind myself. He lets the jersey drop back in place, but it clings to his body, leaving a patch of skin out in the open.

Doesn't mean I would mind licking it off his skin.

"Jade?"

I blink, looking up to find two pairs of eyes, one dark, one light, watching me. "What?"

"The one you need to shoot?" Nixon reminds me. "They're doing a comeback piece on Prescott. There's also the fact that he's just been named co-captain," Nixon snorts. "As if he needed more reason to be full of himself."

"Shut up, Cole."

"Of course they are," I mutter, glancing at the man in question because that's just my luck.

Surprise flashes on his face. "You work for the newspaper?"

"No, one of my classmates does, but she had an emergency and asked me to cover for her. Trust me. If I knew it was you, I would have told her to ask somebody else."

"Cole! Wentworth!"

At the sound of their names, both guys turn around almost instantly, standing at attention. Coach has his hands crossed over his chest as he glares in our direction, the rest of the team standing behind him and giving us curious looks.

"Are you here to play football or chat up the ladies?" Coach yells from his spot on the field.

"Play football, Coach," they both say in unison.

"Then why the fuck are my two star players standing on the sidelines? Get your asses out here."

They run toward the field, joining their team. I snap a few more photos of the team as I watch them work until Coach blows the whistle and calls off practice.

The guys chat as they get off the field, grabbing their stuff from the sidelines. I scroll through the photos, making sure Vicky will have something to use when Nixon and Prescott join me once again.

"All done?"

"I just have to get a few of Prescott on his own, and I think it should be good."

Prescott groans, "Seriously?"

Nixon slaps him over the shoulders. "Good luck, mate."

"You're leaving?"

"Yup." Nixon turns around but doesn't slow down. "Yas is having a special surprise for me when I get home. Can't disappoint the missus."

"Of course not."

Nixon laughs, "Don't be a sore loser, Wentworth." He turns to me. "Go easy on him, Smalls."

"Yeah, yeah. Say hi to Yas for me," I call after him before turning my attention to Prescott. "Now..."

"Is this really necessary? I've got places to be."

He's got places to be?

"What do you think? That I was waiting in line for an opportunity to shoot your smug ass? If you want to blame somebody, blame yourself for agreeing to do the article. I just got stuck with it since Vicky had to leave."

"I didn't agree to anything. Coach wanted me to do it. He talked about a good image for the team and shit." He runs his hand over his face. "Whatever, let's just get this done."

"Fine."

I spot a football somebody left on the sidelines and go to grab it. When I turn around, I find Prescott watching me, brows raised.

"You'll throw it? I thought you were here to take photos."

Smirking, I curl my fingers around the leather. It's been a while since I played catch with Nixon. When we were kids, he'd bully me into playing, and he would go on for *hours* until I wanted to strangle him.

"I'm here to take photos."

I pull my hand back and throw him a perfect spiral. His eyes widen in surprise, but he manages to catch the ball before it falls on the ground.

"Hidden talents, Cole?"

"I figured you better than anyone knows who my brother is."

Although said gently, the words sober him up. His jaw clenches as he stares at me, fingers curling around the ball. "Are we doing this or not?"

What are we really doing?

The words are on the tip of my tongue, but I push them back.

I give my head a shake. "Sure thing."

I coach him through different positions and snap the photos. His muscles flex as he grips the ball, that intense glare of his directed right at me the whole time. My tummy clenches almost involuntarily as I press my shaky finger against the shutter. I'm grateful for the barrier between us, even if it's just a lens.

I pull the camera away and check the photos, making sure there is enough for Vicky to choose.

"I think we're done," I say, shutting off my camera and letting it fall against my stomach. "I'll send the photos to Vicky when I get back home."

"Okay," he rubs the back of his neck. "I guess that's it."

"That's it." My eyes fall down to his lips. Soft and so tempting. I swear I can feel them pressed against mine. I bite the inside of my cheek. *Get a grip, girl.* "I'll see you later."

Before he can say anything, I turn on the balls of my feet and walk away.

What was that?

Heat spreads through my cheeks. I hurry my steps, my eyes glued to the ground so I don't trip over my own feet.

It's crazy.

He shouldn't unnerve me like that.

We kissed once.

Okay, we did a little bit more than that.

And then he called it all a mistake.

A freaking mistake.

Granted, was it the best decision I've ever made? Far from it. But I didn't think kissing him was a mistake. It felt too good, too right, too...

"What are you doing?"

I jump in surprise, my hand flying to cover my rapidly beating heart as I turn around to see Prescott leaning over the console, those brown eyes glaring at me through the open window of the passenger door.

"Will you stop doing this shit?"

"What?"

"Coming out of nowhere and scaring the fuck out of me? Like, seriously."

He grits his teeth, the vein in his forehead throbbing. "Maybe if you paid more attention to your surroundings, I wouldn't be able to surprise you."

Maybe if you didn't mess with my head, I would. I bite my tongue. "I'm paying enough attention to my surroundings. Thank you very much."

Not in the mood to continue this discussion, I start walking, but before I can make five steps, the black Mustang is slowly rolling after me, an irritated growl coming from the inside of the car.

"Get in the car."

I keep my gaze forward, refusing to engage with him and his asshole attitude. He can go and find somebody else to boss around because it ain't gonna be me.

Does he get the memo?

Of course not.

"Get in the car, Jade," he growls.

"Didn't you say you have places to be?" I ask, ignoring his demand. "You better hurry up, wouldn't want you to be late."

"Get in the damn car, Jade."

I turn around to glare at him. "Make me."

Chapter 15

PRESCOTT

Make me.

My cock stirs at the fire burning in those big, blue eyes. She raises one brow, daring me to do it. Daring me to get my ass out of the car and make good on my threat.

My fingers curl around the steering wheel as I try to calm my rapid breathing and racing heart.

Make me.

Her words echo in the space between us as we just stare at one another for what feels like forever.

The corner of her mouth lifts. "Thought so."

With a flip of her hair over her shoulder, she sashays away without a backward glance.

Make me.

Not giving myself time to think, I put my car in park and push the door open with more force than necessary, my focus solely on Jade. Ignoring the jab in my knee, I run after her. My fingers curl around her wrist, pulling her toward me. Her body crashes into mine, all those lush curves pressing against me as I tug her closer.

"It was your choice, doll," I whisper, leaning down, so my

lips brush against the shell of her ear. I inhale her sweet scent—lavender mixed with sun and grass from hours spent out on the field.

Home.

She smells like home.

A lump forms in my throat, but I push it back, my voice coming out tight and raspy. "Don't forget that."

She sucks in a breath, those pretty eyes widening slightly.

Sliding my hands around her waist, I pull her flush against me, lifting her feet off the ground.

"What are you doing?" Jade asks, her fingers gripping my shoulders. "Put me down!"

"I asked you nicely..."

"What you did was boss me around," she protests. "Put me down, Prescott. Now."

"But you wanted to do it the hard way," I mutter, ignoring her interruption as I walk her to my car. I pull open the passenger side door and put her down. Her body brushes against mine as she gets to her feet, leaving tingles in its wake. "Now, do I need to put you inside, or do you want to do it on your own?"

Jade tilts her head back, glaring right at me. "I don't remember it that way."

"Of course you don't." She rolls her eyes and tries to walk around me, but I place my hands on the roof of my car, caging her in. "Get that stubborn ass inside my car, Jade. I won't repeat it again."

"You're acting like a neanderthal, Wentworth. It doesn't look good on you."

"Well, you're acting like a spoiled brat, so I guess we're even." I tilt my head to the side and pointedly look at her. I'm not below putting her ass into the car myself.

After what seems like forever, she finally grits: "Fine."

Lifting her chin a notch in defiance, she turns around and slides into the car.

I shift in my place. "Was that so hard?"

She slowly turns toward me. "Do you really want me to kick your ass?"

A chuckle breaks out of my lungs. "Only in your dreams, doll."

"Don't ca—"

I close the door before she can finish. Suddenly in a way better mood, I make my way around the car and slide into the driver's seat.

"That was rude."

"So is threatening people, doll." I start the car, checking my rearview mirror before taking off. "Where is your car anyway?"

She shouldn't be walking home alone at night. This is a relatively peaceful campus, but you can never be too sure.

The image of Jade being dragged upstairs at that party flashes in my mind.

My fingers tighten around the steering wheel. *Definitely never too sure.*

"Back home."

I turn toward her, my eyes narrowing. "Home home?"

"Do you know any other home?"

"Why the fuck for?" How is she going from her apartment to campus every day? *Every night?*

"Because I didn't need it? Both Nixon and Yasmin drove, and Grace has a car," she shrugs. "It seemed pointless since I can get one of theirs if I really need it."

"Like you borrowed it tonight?"

She rolls her eyes. "I was *fine*. Until you jumped out of the bush like Ted Bundy."

"I was driving," I point out, taking a turn toward our neighborhood.

"Do you think that gives you less of a serial killer potential?"

I shake my head as I park my car in the first open space in front of our building. "You're crazy."

She leans her head against the headrest. "Says the guy who's following unsuspecting girls in his car."

I turn to her, taking her in. Her hair is tossed over one shoulder, leaving the line of her neck exposed. My eyes trail down all that silky skin, the bruise long gone.

The memory of that night flashes in my mind. Her soft lips pressed against mine, the smell of lavender enveloping my senses and making me dizzy as I burrowed my head into her neck. Her sharp intake of breath when my lips pressed against her skin, hard enough to bruise.

My mark.

Her throat bobs. I slowly raise my eyes to meet hers. Her irises are dilated, lips slightly parted as she watches me.

Is she remembering that day too? Does she remember the feel of my mouth pressed against hers?

Her teeth sink into her lower lip, drawing my attention to her lush mouth. My stomach clenches as she grazes her teeth over her lip, letting it pop.

"Jade," I groan, my fingers tightening around the steering wheel as I fight for control.

This was such a bad idea.

Driving her home. Thinking about her. Letting myself have that one taste of her.

It's not enough.

I should have known it wouldn't be enough.

Because having Jade that one time is like drinking a drop of water when there is a whole ocean in front of you.

"Prescott?"

She's not yours to have.

I shake my head. "We can't."

"I know. What did you call it?" She taps her finger against her chin. "Right, *a mistake*."

She spits the words out, that fire blazing brighter in her irises.

"You're my best friend's little sister," I whisper to remind her, to remind myself, to remind us *both* why this is such a bad idea.

A strand of hair slips from behind her ear. Before I can think better of it, I reach forward, brushing it away. My fingers skim over her cheek, feeling her soft skin.

She sucks in a breath at the touch, a shudder running through her body.

Yet, do I move my hand from her?

No.

As if my fingers have a mind of their own, they slide down the column of her neck, clasping around her nape.

"And you're an irritating asshole," she huffs.

"An irritating asshole you want to kiss," I whisper, pressing my forehead against hers.

Such a bad idea.

I suck in a breath, hoping to clear my head, but it does the complete opposite. It fills my lungs with her sweet scent, making me want her more. My fingers clench around her neck, pulling her closer to me.

"Did we ever have any good ideas?" Jade asks softly, making me realize I've spoken out loud. "You and I, Wentworth?" She raises her hand, the tip of her finger tracing my jaw. "We're the two sides of the same coin. We're both damaged and jaded. Hell, I don't even like you, and yet, it doesn't mean I want you any less."

"You shouldn't want me at all. And I sure as hell shouldn't even be thinking about you twice. Your brother would kill me if he ever found out what I did. What I want to do to you."

"But you won't."

Is there regret I hear in her voice? Longing? The fuck if I know.

"No, I won't."

Jade nods, and with one last swipe of her finger, she lets her hand drop and pulls away.

And I let her.

The loss of her touch is like a blow, making me ache for her touch almost instantly.

"Thanks for the ride," Jade mutters. Fiddling with the door handle, she finally opens the door. I watch her as she gets out of the car and rushes toward her apartment building. My fingers curl against the steering wheel as I watch her walk inside, the only thing that's keeping me from getting the fuck out and going after her.

It's better this way.

She's not just any girl. She's your best friend's little sister.

Besides, you don't deserve her.

Then why the fuck doesn't it feel better at all?

Only once the door is shut behind her do I let go. Curling my fingers into fists, I pound them against the steering wheel. "Fuck."

I shift in my seat, feeling that familiar jab in my knee. I grit my teeth and press my hand against my leg, rubbing at the aching muscle, but even that doesn't help. Biting the inside of my cheek, I lean against the console, popping open the glove compartment, and grab the bottle stashed inside. Opening the lid, I turn the bottle upside down, one pill falling into my palm. I shake it and peek inside, but there is nothing.

Empty, once again.

I throw the pill in my mouth and swallow it.

Now what?

I toss the empty bottle back into the compartment, but it

hits against something, making things scatter on the ground. Cursing at myself, I bend down and start collecting different papers to shove them all back inside when I notice the little black card with a number written on it.

My mouth goes dry as I just stare at it, holding my breath as the memory of that night flashes in my mind. The pitcher meeting with the dealer at the party. The pills.

If you change your mind and ever need a refill... That's my number—texts only.

"No," I shake my head. My fingers wrap around the card, crumbling it in my fist. "I was cleared. I don't need pain meds. I can do this."

Shoving the papers back into the compartment, I close the door and get out of the car.

I can do this.

Chapter 16

JADE

The door closes behind me, and instead of waiting for the elevator to arrive, I take two steps at a time, with Prescott's words still ringing in my head.

"And I sure as hell shouldn't even be thinking about you twice. Your brother would kill me if he ever found out what I did. What I want to do to you."

"But you won't."

"No, I won't."

Stubborn, irritating asshole. Pulling the keys out of my bag, I shove them into the lock and turn it. I'm going to send these photos to Vicky, and then I'm going out. I'll find a bar, get a few drinks, hell, get drunk, and—

"Jade? Is that you?"

"It's me," I call out just as Grace peeks her head out of her room.

"Hey, I'm just—" She stops in her tracks and gives me a once-over. "Is everything okay?"

No, everything is not okay, but I can't tell her that because it'll lead to more questions. Questions I don't have answers for. At least not any that'll make sense because there's no sense whatsoever in all these feelings that he stirs inside me.

"Perfect. What were you saying?"

"I'm going over to Mason's. You wanna come?"

"And be a third wheel to the two of you? I think I'll ski—"

"His roommates are also home. They're playing some video games."

I narrow my eyes at her. "And who exactly is all there?"

"Oh, you know, the usual crowd. Matteo, Quinn, Nate," She rubs the back of her neck and looks away. "Michael…"

"Mhmm… Why am I not surprised?" I give her my I-know-what-you're-trying-to-do look.

"What? We're just hanging out. That's all. And I figured since Rei's not home tonight, you'd like to join us, but if you'd rather stay here…"

She turns around and goes back to her room.

"Is there booze?"

Grace looks over her shoulder with her brows pulled together. "I guess so?"

"And you're not going to try and hook me up with any of your boyfriend's teammates?"

"As if you'd let me." she rolls her eyes. "So? You coming or what?"

"Fine. But I have to send some photos to one of my classmates first."

I press my fingers against the controller, each one landing a kick at my opponent on the screen.

"C'mon, c'mon, c'mon!" Grace chants by my side, jumping in her seat. "You can do this. Kick his butt."

"I'm trying," I say, my eyes on the screen as I press my

fingers against the winning combination that has my character reaching out for her sword and jabbing it into my opponent, making him fall on the ground.

Grace jumps up, her arms in the air. "And that's how you do it, boys!"

She lifts her hand for me to high-five, and I comply. The guys had been playing some kind of war game when we got here, but Grace convinced them we should switch to Tekken. It's been us against the boys, and so far, we've been kicking their asses.

"This isn't fair," Matteo groans from his place. "Did you hijack it in some way or something? You can't be winning this much."

Grace pokes her tongue at him. "Don't be a sore loser."

"Yeah, Matteo," Mason grins, pulling Grace onto his lap. "You shouldn't be a sore loser."

His best friend glares at him. "Don't even get me started. You let her win."

"Did not."

"Did so."

"You both are acting like sore losers." Quinn slaps Matteo over the head. "What are you, five? Gimmie that. I'll show you how to play it."

I hand the other controller to Grace. "Your turn. I'm going to grab another drink."

Grabbing my cup from the table, I lift my arms in the air to stretch my sore muscles.

"The drinks are in the fridge," Mason calls after me, his attention on his girlfriend as she picks her character.

"Thanks."

I walk out of the living room and toward the kitchen. The lamp over the sink is turned on, illuminating the room in a dim light. A few pizza boxes are stacked on the counter from our dinner earlier.

"Hey, you."

I turn around to see Michael stop and lean against the doorway. "Hey."

"Need help?"

I lift my cup. "Just grabbing a refill. Mason said it's okay."

"Of course." He pushes from the doorway and walks toward me, taking my cup. "Whiskey and coke, right?"

"Right."

He pulls open the fridge and grabs the bottles. I lean against the counter and watch him make my drink before pulling a beer bottle from the fridge and popping it open.

"To more nights like this?"

He lifts his bottle, and I press my glass against his. "To more nights like this."

Although I was a little bit skeptical at the beginning, I had to admit I was having a good time. The boys were funny, and it helped that we were beating them at the game. Plus, Grace stuck to her end of the bargain and didn't mention anything about double dates or whatnot.

As if on cue, groaning spreads from the living room, making me chuckle.

"You're playing this at home, right?"

"Maybe a little bit." I take a sip of my drink. "Grace has a PlayStation back home, and we might have spent a better part of the summer playing it."

"It shows."

"Keep it a secret?"

I push from the counter, ready to get back to the living room, but Michael grabs my hand pulling me back.

My body stiffens, surprised at his touch. I zero in my gaze

on his hand wrapped around mine before lifting to meet his dark eyes, forcing myself to relax.

This is just Michael.

"What will I get for keeping your secret?" He quirks one of his brows at me, the corner of his mouth twitching.

"Satisfaction of watching your friends get beaten by a couple of girls?"

Michael hums, his full lips pursing as he pretends to think about it. "How about something else?"

"And what do you want?"

"You know what I want."

I did. Michael offered to walk us back home with Mason that night after Moore's and asked me if I'd go out with him. I said no.

I shake my head. "Michael..."

"C'mon, Jade. It's just one date. What can it hurt?"

"I don't date."

"Okay, so *dinner*. You do eat those, don't you?"

"I eat dinner, yes."

"See? We can go and have dinner."

"It's not that easy."

"It's just that easy," he counters right back. "I like you, and I'm pretty sure you like me. We go out, grab dinner, and have fun. It doesn't have to be more complicated than that."

"You're a roommate and teammate of my best friend's boyfriend. It's more complicated than that. I'm not joking when I say I don't date."

"Ever?"

"Not since high school, at least. And I don't want to date. I like you; I really do, but I can't mess this up for Grace."

"Is that it, or is there somebody else?"

It was a mistake.

"No," I shake my head. "There is nobody else. Nobody that matters anyway."

Michael watches me for a moment before nodding.

"Okay, then go on a date with me."

I open my mouth to protest, but he lifts his hand and presses his finger against my lips to quiet me. "Just one date. One chance. I promise not to make it weird afterward if it doesn't work out. What do you say, Jade?"

He flashes me that grin of his. Completely open and sweet. In another world, I could totally see myself falling for that grin.

In another world...

Chapter 17

PRESCOTT

"Shit!" I mutter, but it's already too late. The linebacker's arms are already around me, and before I can even attempt to do anything, he's pulling me to the ground. All the air is kicked out of my lungs from the impact, making it hard to breathe.

The whistle blows, but I can barely hear it from the ringing in my ears.

"G-get your ass off me," I wheeze, pushing Stevens away from me.

"Sorry, dude."

He jumps to his feet, but the best I can do is roll to my back and look up at the sky as I try to breathe.

Damn, that hurts.

It wouldn't even be so bad if it was the first time. But nope, this was the fifth time I've been tackled. Today.

Gregory offers me his hand, and I take it, leaning on him way too much for my liking as he helps me to my feet.

"You okay?" Nixon asks as he joins us, his worried eyes taking me in.

"Yeah, fine," I bite out, irritated with myself.

I take a step, ready to get back to my spot, but my leg buckles underneath me, making me stumble.

Fucking hell.

I try to conceal it, but apparently, I'm not doing a good job because I find Coach watching me. He tilts his chin toward the bench. "Wentworth, get your ass out. Sullivan, you're in."

"What? Why?"

"You're done for today, Wentworth."

I glare at the man, but he just scowls right back, not in the least bit fazed by my animosity.

"Fine," I grit. Pulling off my helmet, I stomp—okay, limp—toward the tunnel that leads to the locker room.

The place is completely quiet since the rest of my teammates are out on the field where I should be—playing right alongside them. Not Sullivan.

"Fuck!" I throw my helmet at the locker. There's a loud *bang* as it hits the metal and bounces to the floor.

I run my fingers through my hair and hobble to the bench. Putting in my combination, I rip the locker open and grab my bag, the pulsing pain in my leg growing stronger. I've been working without pain meds for the last few days, and each day I've gotten worse. Slower and clumsier.

Me: I need more.

My fingers grip the phone as I stare at the screen. I'm not sure what the protocol for this kind of thing is. The dude said to text. But should I tell him what I need? Should I tell him my name? Should I have even texted him from my regular phone?

"Shit. This is such a bad idea."

But what other choice do I have? If I don't start playing like usual, people are going to start asking questions. Not Coach, though. He'll put my ass on the bench faster than I can say touchdown while putting somebody else on the field.

Somebody like fucking Sullivan.

Over my dead body.

My phone buzzes in my hand, and I can feel my heart speed up in anticipation as I open the message.

Unknown: ???

Seriously? That's the best he's got?

Me: Pain meds?

Unknown: Oh… Mr. Football player.

Unknown: No worries I've gotcha, mate.

Me: When?

Unknown: In a hurry?

Fuck this shit.

I'm about to text him that I've changed my mind when a new message comes through.

Unknown: Don't worry. I'll get them to you tonight. Can't have you losing that game tomorrow.

My throat tightens at the mention of the game. What if Coach decides to pull me out of the starting lineup after the debacle that this week has been? My dad will have a field day.

Unknown: Give me an hour.

Just then, I hear voices coming from the hallway. Apparently, the practice finally wrapped up. I toss my phone back into my bag and turn my back to the door just as it opens and my teammates haul in. Their voices are quiet, and I can feel some of them giving me wary glances, but I ignore them as I take off my equipment.

"What the hell was that?" Nixon asks as he stops by my side.

"Nothing."

"It was clearly something. Is it your leg? Is it hurting you?"

Grabbing my things, I close my locker. "My leg's fine," I

mutter. The last thing I need is for people to start questioning if I should be here at all. "I'm going to take a shower."

Before Nixon can say another word, I turn on my feet and march into the bathroom. It takes all that's in me to do it, but I somehow manage it without showing a smidge of pain. The moment I enter the bathroom, I let my body sag against the wall. Just for a moment.

Soon.

Everything will be better soon.

As I hear the laughter nearing, I push from the wall and turn on the water, putting my game face on. I quickly wash up so I can get out of there.

Putting on my clothes, I grab my duffle bag and head for my car. I check my phone on the way, but there isn't a new message from Manolo.

Should I just wait?

He said an hour but hasn't given me a location where to meet.

What now?

I toss my duffle bag into my backseat.

"Prescott, wait!"

My back stiffens at the sound of my best friend's voice.

I look at him over my shoulder as I pull open the door. "If you're here to lecture me..."

"I'm not here to lecture you," Nixon stops me. "I'm here as your best friend. Not that I know why since you've been acting like a grumpy asshat."

"I'm not in the mood, Cole. Go home to your wife."

I slide into my car, but before I can close the door, Nixon presses his hands against the door and the car, stopping me from closing it in his face.

"But I want to go and have a drink with my friend."

I stare ahead, not sure if this is a good idea.

"You in or what?"

"Fine," I finally agree. "Just stop pestering."

"I don't pester," he chuckles. "I'll meet you at Moore's."

"What about that chick? She's pretty."

"Should Yas be worried?" I walk around the pool table, weighing my options. I could go for the red stripe, but it's too close to two of Nixon's balls.

Hmm...

"Hell no. I'm not checking her out for me. I'm checking her out for you."

"I'm quite capable of finding my own hookups, Cole."

Taking a sip of my whiskey, I observe the position of the balls for a while longer. I place the glass out of the way before leaning down over the pool table and placing the cue against my knuckles.

"You sure about that? Because I haven't seen you with anybody recently."

"Keeping tabs on me, Cole?" I do a few test shots. My tongue darts out as I narrow my gaze on the ball.

"No, I'm just wondering if you're keeping somebody hidden from me, that's all."

And I miss.

"Fuck."

So much for keeping my cool.

"That was pitiful," Nixon laughs and shoves me away. "Let me show you how it's done."

He gets to the table and quickly pockets three of his balls before he finally misses one.

"Showoff," I mutter, downing the rest of my drink. My gaze falls on my phone, willing it to buzz, but no luck so far.

Where the hell is he?

"Sore loser."

"As if," I huff, going back to the table. "I'd have to lose first, and we have yet to finish the game."

"We'll see about that."

We both go around the table, pocketing the balls until there's only the black one left.

"But seriously, it makes me wonder if I am right."

Are we back to this? Can't he just let it go?

"Right about what?" I ask, playing dumb.

"About a girl, Wentworth. I've never seen you not flirt with a girl, especially when she's so obviously trying to get your attention since the moment we've walked into the bar."

"Maybe I'm just trying to focus on football this year."

"Maybe." He takes his shot, the black ball smoothly going into the pocket as he straightens and turns to face me. "But why do I feel like that's not the whole truth?"

I shake my head, making sure not to show anything on my face. "You're delusional."

"Maybe."

"I'm going to grab another drink. You want one?"

Nixon shakes his head no. "I think I'm going home. You good?"

"Fine." I look toward the girl that's been checking me out. She was sitting with her friend a few tables away, and I felt her gaze on me for the better part of the night. She's pretty. A little on the shorter side, with shoulder-length dark hair and dark eyes. Our gazes meet, and she looks away, giggling. Maybe they're right. Maybe I should just find a willing girl and have some fun.

"You sure?"

"I don't need a babysitter, Cole," I groan. "Go home."

"Call me if you need me."

What I need is another drink and for that damn text message to arrive.

"Sure thing." I slap him over the shoulder as we make our way to the front of the bar. "Now, go before I call your wife and tell her how you're checking out other girls."

"For you!" he calls out as he goes for the door.

"Yeah, yeah." I prop myself against the bar, signaling for the bartender to get me another drink. He nods and grabs the bottle of whisky, pouring me another two fingers, and slides it over the bar. I place the bill on the table, grab my glass, and move to one of the high tables in the corner of the room. The last thing I want is company.

Downing half of my drink, I place it on the table, my hand going to the side of my leg and rubbing against the sore muscle. The alcohol has dulled the ache somewhat in my leg, but it's a far cry from the real thing.

I pull out my phone, ready to text Manolo, and ask what the hell he is up to when a figure joins me in the dark.

"You know that mixing the two isn't the best idea, right?" the man I've been waiting for asks.

I look around, but nobody's watching us. Still, I lean forward and hiss so only he can hear me. "Are you insane?"

"Chill, it's a slow night. Plus, I made sure your buddy left first," he flashes me a smile.

"Do you have it?"

"So eager. Of course, I do. Manolo always delivers." He winks at me. *Actually, winks at me.*

"How much?"

He grabs my drink and finishes it. When he places it back on the table, I notice another one of his black cards. The dude really loves theatrics. I'll give him that.

"Have you ever considered being a drama major?" I ask, pulling out the sum and placing it on the table.

"I'd be pretty good at it, I think." He nods at me. "If you need more, you know where to find me."

"But what about..." I start to ask, but he's already walking away toward the back.

I slide my hand into the pocket of my hoodie to grab my phone and ask him where the hell my pills are, but my fingers wrap around the plastic bottle instead.

Chapter 18

JADE

I stare at my reflection in the mirror and see a few new bumps that have appeared in my armpit next to the original one. I trace my finger over the small, hard buds feeling the tightness of the skin and a dull ache behind them.

My throat bobs as I swallow.

You can't keep on pushing this back, a little voice warns me. As if I don't know. As if I haven't been down this path before. *Put on your big girl panties, and just do it.*

Maybe it's just my lymph nodes. I've had those inflamed in the past, but it got better.

But what if...

I let my hand trace down my side, over the small bruises covering my side and breast. I cup my breast, feeling the weight of it in my palm, the aching flesh...

"Jade?" Grace yells loudly, snapping me out of my thoughts. I let my hand drop down as if I was just caught doing something I shouldn't have. "Mind if I borrow that black dress of yours?"

It's just Grace, for God's sake.

Running my hand over my face, I grab the silky black robe from the hook on my door and slip it on, making sure I've tied it securely around my waist before getting out of the bathroom. "Which one?"

"The sleeveless one?" She pulls the hanger from my closet to show it to me. "I mean, it's a bit chilly, so I'll have to wear a jacket, but still."

"Yeah, sure, go for it."

"Great, thanks." She slips the dress from the hanger and pulls it over her head. "I still can't believe you agreed to the double date."

It's not like I'll be wearing that anytime soon. I walk past her and go through the hangers until I find a tight dress with sleeves that come to my elbows. It's a bit on the longer side, but the back dips pretty low, leaving the whole upper part of my back open, showing off the delicate flower design of my tattoo.

I never thought much about getting a tattoo, but then I saw this design, and I knew I had to have it. The tattoo went from my neck, across my spine, all the way to my lower back; a thin ribbon was intertwined between the lilies and some greenery, a perfect tribute to my mother.

"Can we not make a fuss about it?" I groan and go to the window, cracking it open to let in some fresh air. "It's just a group of friends going out for dinner. Nothing more, nothing less."

"Mhmm... keep telling yourself that."

"I don't have to keep telling myself anything. That's the way it is." She opens her mouth, but I lift my finger and point it at her. "And if you don't stop talking about it, this is going to be the first, and the last time anything like this happens."

Grace rolls her eyes but starts toward the door. "Fine. I'm going to finish my makeup. The guys should be here in thirty."

"Sounds like a plan."

Just as she's at the door, Grace slows down and looks back. "Hey, how did the game go?"

"We won, but it was a tough game."

"That sucks. Although a win is a win."

It was, but I'm not sure Nixon or any of his teammates will look at it that way. It's not realistic to think they'll beat every single team without any difficulty, but some teams should be easier to win over others.

I wait for her to leave and close the door behind her, but even then, I don't risk getting changed in the bedroom.

Grabbing some underwear and my dress, I go to the bathroom and close the door before dropping my robe, my back to the mirror.

Only then do I change.

"You look beautiful," Michael says as he holds my door—seriously, do people still do that?—to help me slide into his car.

Grace insisted that although we're going to the same restaurant, we should take two separate cars since she's planning to go to Mason's after their date. When I asked why we don't just meet the guys at the restaurant so I could get back with her car, she gave me a death glare of all the death glares before leaving the room. So like the good friend I am, I waited for my ride and let her have it.

So what? It was one date. It's not like it's going to change anything.

"Thanks, you clean up nice too."

He's wearing a white dress shirt that makes his skin look even more golden than usual. The first two buttons are left undone, revealing a patch of skin and firm muscle beneath it. His dark hair is perfectly styled, jaw clean-shaven. Any girl would feel lucky to be on Michael's arm.

So why do I not feel even a twinge of excitement?

Closing the door behind me, I watch him walk around the car and slide into the driver's seat, giving me a curious glance as he starts the car.

"I didn't take you for a tattoo girl."

"And why not?"

"I don't know," he shrugs, giving me an apologetic smile. "I guess I just didn't think about it? I'm making a mess of this, aren't I? I haven't been out on a date in way too long."

"Hey, don't look at me. I'm not dating, remember?"

"Right. You eat dinner."

"Exactly." I let out a small chuckle, "In your defense, I got it a few months ago. The tattoo."

"A spur-of-the-moment decision?"

The night I got it flashes in my mind. It was the anniversary of the day my life changed forever, the day I found out my mom had cancer.

It was weird.

I woke up, and something just felt off. I was lying in bed, trying to figure out what was wrong when it hit me.

Some days I wake up, and it's just a normal day like any other, but others? On other days, she's the only thing I can think about. The pain and loss are so real; it's like it all happened yesterday.

I don't think I'll ever get used to it. Not entirely, anyway.

So I got up, woke up Grace, and went to the tattoo shop I'd been looking at online for a few weeks, ever since I saw a similar design to this one and started playing with the idea of getting a tattoo myself.

"You can say that," I say slowly, pushing back the memories. "What about you? Got any tats?" I ask, changing the subject.

Thankfully he goes with it and tells me all about the tattoo covering his leg that he got as a junior in high school and how his mom flipped when she saw it.

"She was running after me around the house with her wooden spoon clasped tightly in her hand."

"She did not," I laugh.

"Oh, yes, she did. I still think if there was a way for her to make me return it, she would have done it."

"That's hilarious. Did she end up catching you?"

Michael glances at me, a big grin on his face. "What do you think? She cornered me and pulled at my ear so hard the damage is permanent."

"Poor baby."

"What can I say?" He looks around the parking lot, a fond smile on his lips. "As the youngest of five brothers and sisters, I might have caused the most mischief."

"Wow, five brothers and sisters?"

"Yes, I had to get my family's attention somehow." He kills the ignition and turns to me. "It's just you and Nixon?"

"It's just Nixon and me," I confirm. "Well, and now his wife."

"That's cool too." He looks at the restaurant. "Ready?"

"Yeah, sure."

I unbuckle my seatbelt and open the door just as Michael gets around the hood, his brows raised.

"I could have done that."

"You could have, but I'm quite capable of opening my own door."

"Afraid it'll look too much like a date?"

"Maybe?"

"At least you're honest," Michael chuckles. "C'mon, let's get inside before Grace starts worrying that I kidnapped you."

We make our way inside the restaurant. A pretty girl around our age is standing at the hostess's table. She smiles at us, and Michael tells her that our friends are waiting for us. With a nod, she grabs two menus and leads us toward our table. Michael lets me walk in first, his fingers skimming over my back as I pass by.

"Ten bucks they comment on how long it took us to get here."

I glance over my shoulder, the corner of my mouth curling upward. "I'm not taking a bet I'm going to lose."

"Damn."

Turning my attention forward, I look for the familiar red hair. I expect Grace to be smiling, but instead, there is a serious expression on her face.

My brows pull together in confusion, and that's when I see him.

A few tables away from ours, no one other than Prescott Wentworth is sitting with an older couple, and the way he glares at me sends tingles running down my spine.

Chapter 19

PRESCOTT

What the hell is she doing here?

My gaze is glued to Jade as she enters the restaurant in a little black dress that hugs her every curve, causing my throat to grow tighter by the second.

She hasn't noticed me yet, so I take my time drinking her in. The way she moves, the severe lines on her face, that little frown between her brows as she scans the space.

And then he walks in, and I know exactly what's happening.

Jade's on a date.

Here.

With the basketball douche.

The guy places his hand at the small of her back, and my fingers grip the fork in my hand until the metal digs into my skin.

There are guys who want me, Wentworth. Jade's words ring in my mind as I watch her follow the hostess to her table. *You don't get to act like a jealous asshole when it suits you.*

I know that dammit. I don't need her to tell me. I see the way guys look at her. And I hate it. I hate every lingering gaze directed her way. I hate every smile she gives in their direction. They don't know her. They don't understand her. Not the way I do.

And I hate myself for wanting her when I have no right to do so.

She's your best friend's little sister.

Only there is nothing little about her now.

Nothing little about her at all.

The guy leans down and whispers something in her ear. Jade looks over her shoulder, and I can see her mouth curl and hear that soft laughter of hers. She gives her head a shake, his mouth moving as she says something before turning forward.

I suck in a breath as she continues her perusal of the restaurant, brows pulling together, and then her gaze lands on mine and locks.

We just stare at one another across the room, all the other noises falling into the background. It's like there's just her and me, closed off in our own bubble.

My heart thunders in my chest like I've been running without pause for miles. Her eyes widen in surprise, lips parting. She didn't expect to see me here. Good. That makes the two of us.

"Prescott?"

"Huh?" Reluctantly, I shift my attention from Jade to my father, who's scowling at me across the table.

"The least you can do since we went out of our way to visit you is listen when somebody's talking to you!"

Went out of his way, my ass. The whole point of him stopping here is because it was *on* his way. Not out of it. Besides, nobody forced him to do shit. I'd actually prefer it if he didn't come at all, but if I say that, he'll do the exact opposite, which is the only reason why I keep my mouth shut.

"I just thought I saw somebody."

"One of your groupies?" Dad shakes his head disapprovingly. "You should seriously stop messing around and focus on what matters."

"And what exactly matters, Dad?" I ask, gritting my teeth to try and keep my voice low. "You think my career choice sucks, and you just spent the last half an hour complaining about how bad my game is."

"You'll watch your mouth, boy. I'm still your father and the only reason why you're where you are."

And here we go again. Dropping my fork on the plate, I grab the glass of Jack and coke, taking a sip from it.

Dad's mouth twists in distaste. "You shouldn't be drinking that."

I look pointedly at his glass of whiskey. "Hypocritical much?"

"You shouldn't be talking to your father like that." Mom's words are so soft it takes me a moment to grasp that she spoke out loud.

I turn to look at her, but her gaze is pointed at her still-full plate. She shifts her food from one side to the other. There is an ache in my chest as I watch her. She's lost some weight since the last time I saw her. She's always been slender and petite, but now she's all skin and bones. Her blonde hair is lifeless, and her skin is dry. There is nothing of the woman that I remember from my childhood.

Look at me, I urge her silently. *Just once. Look at me.*

It's useless, though. Even if I said it out loud, it wouldn't make any difference. It's been years, *years* since she looked at me.

Really looked at me.

Nine years to be exact.

Even in those rare moments when her eyes meet mine, it's

like she's looking through me, not at me. Not that I can blame her. Not after what I've done. What I've cost her.

"Oh, no, Molly, let the boy talk. I'm sure he has a lot to say. He always thinks he knows the best. That he's better than us."

His words are like a blow, and I take every single one he throws at me.

"I never thought I was better than you."

"Your actions have proven otherwise.

My fingers ball into fists under the table.

"Nothing to say now, Prescott?" He leans closer, his voice dropping low. "That's because you know I'm telling the truth. Because you know how reckless you are. You know that it's *your* fault. You kill everyone you love."

If he wanted to punish me, he knew exactly the right way to do it. The worst part is he's right. What happened seven years ago was my fault. And I'll have to carry it with me for the rest of my life.

You kill everyone you love.

I grab my drink and down the rest of it in one go, wishing it was pure whiskey instead. "I'm done here."

I push to my feet, my chair screeching over the floor, and make my way out of the room. My dad's words still ring in my head, loud and clear, as I make my way out of the restaurant and toward my car. Pulling the keys out of my pocket, I unlock the car just when I hear footsteps coming after me.

"Prescott! Wait."

My hand freezes on the handle at the sound of her words. She's the last person I expected to go after me. "You should get back to your date."

"What happened inside? You just stormed out—"

"Jade..." Her name comes out like a growl. "Get back inside. Now."

"Like hell I am." Soft fingers wrap around my arm, and she

tugs me toward her. Those stormy blue eyes fix on mine, and I can feel my throat tighten. "What happened—"

"What happened is none of your business."

"It is my business since you're clearly upset, and you're about to get in your car and drive, God only knows where."

"Worried about me, doll?"

That familiar fire blazes in her irises. "Fine." She shoves me away. "Be a dick about it. I was just trying to be nice. But apparently, it's wasted on you."

She turns on her heels, ready to march off, but at the last second, I grab her wrist and tug her to me. Her body collides with mine, and I can feel a zap of electricity course through me at the touch.

"Don't you know already?" With my free hand, I tuck a strand of her hair behind her ear. My fingers graze her cheek, and I swear I can feel her tremble under my touch. I lean closer, my voice lowering as I whisper, "There is nothing nice about me."

"You're—"

Before she can say anything else, my fingers slide to the nape of her neck, and I pull her to me.

My mouth crashes against hers in a hard kiss. I'm angry. At my parents, at her, at myself, and she's here, so I lay it all out on her. Jade sucks in a breath, giving me an opening to slide my tongue into her mouth. Our tongues tangle in a battle of wills, sucking and swirling. Jade presses her hand against my chest, and for a moment, I think she'll push me away, slap me, something, but her fingers tighten around me as she pulls me closer, returning every swipe of my mouth over hers with one of her own.

Fuck.

Breaking the kiss, I pull back. My breathing is ragged as I open my eyes and find her watching me, eyes wide, cheeks pink.

"We shouldn't be doing this," I pant but don't make an attempt to take a step back.

Hurt dances in her eyes at my words, but she clenches her jaw. Closing the distance between us, so close her lips brush against mine, she whispers, the challenge clear in her voice: "Then don't do it. Don't kiss me."

Do I back down?

Fuck to the no.

I turn us around, so she's caged against my car and kiss her once again. My body presses against her, feeling all those lush curves as I devour her mouth with mine like I'll die if I don't kiss her. Like she's the air I need to breathe. Like she's mine.

Mine.

The word echoes in my mind, loud and damning.

Cursing, I pull back as quickly as possible, leaving a healthy distance between us.

My tongue darts out, sliding over my lower lip.

What the hell am I doing?

I grab her hand and push her toward the restaurant.

"Prescott..."

Plastering a smile on my face, I open my car. "Something to remember when you go back inside to your perfect little date. Can he make you feel like I do, doll?"

Sliding inside the driver's seat, I close the door behind me. The last thing I see before I speed away is those stormy eyes glaring after me.

Chapter 20

JADE

"What happened with Wentworth?" Michael asks, his words snapping me out of my thoughts.

"What?" I look up, realizing we've arrived at my apartment while I'd been lost in my own head.

"You went after him, and then when you came back, you just seemed off."

Prescott, right.

He's asking about Prescott and how I ran after him like some foolish little girl.

There is nothing nice about me.

He was right about that one. There isn't anything nice about him. Oh no, Prescott Wentworth is one giant asshole. That's what he is. And the next time I see him, I'll show him exactly what I think about him and his assholish ways.

"I'm sorry," I give him an apologetic smile. "My head is just all over the place."

"Is there something going on between you two?"

"What? No!" My heart starts beating faster at his question. Did he see what happened earlier? Is that why he asked? I went to the bathroom to make sure I looked presentable before joining the table, but maybe I missed something. "He's my brother's best friend, and after he stormed out like that... Well, I just wanted to check on him and make sure he was okay."

Michael watches me for a moment as if he's weighing my words. "You sure it's just that?"

"Trust me. I can't stand him, and the feeling is mutual, but regardless he is Nixon's best friend."

Except when he's kissing me.

Something to remember when you go back inside to your perfect little date. Can he make you feel like I do, doll?

I swear I could still feel the burn from when his mouth was pressed against mine. He was angry, and he wanted to punish somebody, and that somebody was me. I didn't mind it because I wanted to do the same. I wanted to get out this anger and frustration and fear on somebody. And Prescott? He could take it. He could take on my demons and come out swinging.

Don't think about him.

"I'm sorry for storming off like that. It wasn't fair to you."

"It's fine, really. Let me walk you to the door?"

Nodding, I slide my bag over my shoulder and get out of the car. The night air is chilly as I meet Michael at the front of his car.

"You really should let me do that."

"It's not a date thing. I can get out of the car alone, so what's the point in waiting?"

"So you can let the guy feel useful?"

"I'm sure there are better ways to do that," I let out a soft chuckle as we get to the door. "I did have fun tonight, though."

The corner of Michael's mouth curls up. "Enough for you to give me a chance for an actual date?"

"I..." I open my mouth, but no words come out.

Understanding flashes on his face. "I see."

"No, you don't. You're really a great guy, and I did have fun, but..."

"Not enough to give me a chance? I get it." He tries to walk around me, but I step in his way.

"I'm not in a good place right now, Michael," I admit softly. It's the first time I've said the words out loud and to a virtual stranger, no less. "That's why I said no in the first place. I can't be dating or in a relationship right now, and you deserve a girl who'll be all in. I'm not that girl. I'm not sure I'll ever be that girl again."

Michael takes a moment to consider my words before nodding. "Okay. Don't be a stranger, and come next time with Grace. We need to have a rematch."

"You can try." Rising on the tips of my toes, I wrap my arms around him. "Thanks for tonight, Michael."

"You know it."

Pulling back, I unlock the door and slide inside the building, and make my way to my apartment. With Rei traveling, and Grace at Mason's, the place is quiet as I walk down the hallway. I enter my room, closing the door behind me, but before I can flip the switch, the light turns on.

My heart stops, and it takes my brain a while to process what's just happened. I turn on the balls of my feet, ready to scream when I see the person sitting on my bed, arms crossed over his chest as he glares at me from across the room.

"Are you insane?" I lift my hand, pressing it against my wildly beating heart. "You just gave me a heart attack!"

"You really shouldn't leave your window open when you leave your house," he says calmly.

Win— My eyes dart to the window, and sure enough, it's still open. "You *climbed* in here? Through a window? Are you freaking insane?"

"You already asked me that." Prescott leisurely slides his legs off the mattress and stands up.

"Well, you didn't answer me! Because to me, it seems like you are. Who the fuck climbs through the window into somebody's room? I'll tell you, only insane people. You could have broken your neck."

Prescott makes his way to me, his face completely blank.

"Would it have mattered?"

"What?"

"If I broke my neck? Would it have mattered?"

There is something about the way he moves, almost an eerie calm around him, like a predator circling on his prey. Do I step back? No. I take a step forward and jab my finger in his chest.

"What it would have been is a freaking inconvenience. That's what it would have been." I let out a sigh, "Why are you even here?"

"I came home ready to get drunk, so I could forget what happened earlier, but I couldn't get you out of my head. I couldn't stop thinking about you in that restaurant. With him. Did he kiss you?"

Another step closer. There's barely any space left between us. He's there, all I can see, all I can smell, all that is. He's everywhere, and it's making it hard for me to *breathe*.

"What?!" I shake my head. "Is that why you're here? I already told you; you don't get to do this. You don't—"

The words are stifled as his mouth captures mine. Prescott slides his hands into my hair and pulls me closer to him as his tongue enters my mouth, swirling with mine. He tastes like whiskey and coke, sweet and bitter, and all Prescott.

Every swipe of his mouth over mine is hard and bruising. His hands tighten in my hair, pulling my head back; his mouth ravages mine, but I meet him there. Swipe for swipe. I give as good as I get.

He's trying to punish me for tonight.

For going out with Michael.

Well, two can play this game.

He's not the only one who's angry.

I'm angry too.

At the world.

At *him*.

I grab his shirt, pulling him closer as my hand slides lower, my fingers touching the naked skin of his abs. Prescott shivers under my touch, *actually shivers*, as I push his shirt out of my way, revealing all that glorious skin. His hands slide down my body, grabbing the hem of my dress and pulling it over my head. I can hear material tear, but the sound is lost to the frantic beat of my heart and our loud breathing.

Prescott bends down, his arms wrapping around my middle and pulling me into his arms. Our naked skin touches, and I swear I'm burning from the inside. His mouth slides over mine as my legs wrap around him.

"Fuck," I hiss as my pussy connects to the bulge in his pants, and I can feel it clench in need. My hips roll of their own violation, needing to reveal this ache inside me, fill this emptiness.

"That's the plan, doll."

Running my fingers through his hair, I tug his head back. "Don't. Call. Me. That," I say slowly before kissing him again.

Fingers dig into my ass, pulling me closer. My hands roam over his broad shoulders, feeling the hard, taut muscles under my palms until I'm suddenly tossed on the bed.

The air is kicked out of my lungs, leaving me breathless. But then the mattress dips, and Prescott is over me. I wrap my hands around his shoulders as he starts kissing me, down my neck, and over my chest. His expert fingers unhook the clasp of my bra, my breasts spilling out of the lacy material. He cups my boobs and sucks one of my nipples into his mouth.

A jolt goes through me, my body arching off the mattress, fingers digging into his back as he switches from one breast to the other.

Fingers skim over my side where the bruises are still visible, and I freeze as his eyes meet mine. "What's this?"

Shit.

There is a beat of silence as the panic spreads through me.

"Accident," I mutter quickly, pulling him back to me. "No talking."

I press my mouth against his, trying to get him back where I want him—with his mouth firmly occupied with mine, and thankfully he doesn't protest.

My hand slides between our bodies, working on the button of his pants, but the damn thing doesn't budge. I let out a groan in frustration which only makes Prescott chuckle.

"Impatient much?"

"I want you inside me." I brush my hand over the hard length of him. "And based on this, your dick agrees."

"My dick would need to be dead not to agree."

Pushing my hands away, Prescott gets to his feet. He watches me watch him, his hand slipping into his back pocket, and tosses something to the bed. A wallet. Then, in a few swift movements, his pants are unbuttoned, and he shoves down his jeans and underwear, his dick springing free.

My mouth goes dry at the sight of him, long and hard. Perfect, just like the rest of him.

Prescott wraps his hand around his base, giving his cock a few slow strokes, his eyes still glued to me. My tongue darts out, sliding over my lower lip as he moves closer.

"Take off the panties," His voice is rough, his words leaving no room for argument. Not that I'd want to fight, not about this.

I slide my hand over my belly and onto the lace material. Slowly. Inch by tantalizing inch. Teasing. Taunting.

Prescott's eyes grow darker as he follows my hand as I gently rub my clit. My pussy is so wet that the material clings to me as I rub the small bud, desire burning inside my belly.

I let out a soft moan as the lace moves, and my finger slips between my lips, teasing my opening.

Prescott swears loudly, and the next thing I know, my hand is shoved away, and Prescott is looming over me. His lips are pressed in a thin line as if he's barely holding back.

"No more teasing, doll," he all but growls before his mouth is on mine.

I let my hands trail over his naked chest, tracing the defined muscles as we kiss. Then I feel him shift over me. Prescott pulls back, grabbing the wallet from the bed and pulling out a condom. He rips the foil package open and puts the condom on before his body joins mine once again.

The heat radiates off of him as he traces kisses over my skin, his hand working his way down my body, moving my panties to the side all the way, those long fingers of his teasing me.

"So freaking wet," he murmurs, his finger dipping inside me just enough to make me squirm. "Are you always this wet, or is this just for me?"

My fingers dig into his shoulders as I try to stay still. "Wentworth..." I groan, done with playing this game.

"Yes?"

"Stop being a tease and just fu—"

The words die on my lips as he removes his hand and settles between my spread thighs, sliding inside me in one long thrust. I let out a shaky breath as my body gets used to his length.

"*Shit...*" His biceps quake as he holds back. Those brown eyes of his are so dark they seem black.

I roll my hips against his, pulling him deeper inside me. And it feels good. Too damn good.

My fingers skim over the hard muscles of his back. "Hard," I whisper. "I need you to fuck me harder."

He doesn't need any more encouragement. Prescott pulls out of me, leaving just the tip teasing my entrance, and he slides back inside. I tighten my legs around him, my fingers holding onto his shoulders for dear life as he thrusts in harder, deeper.

I grip the back of his neck, pulling his mouth on mine. The kiss is sloppy as he continues fucking me, and I meet him thrust for thrust. The pressure builds inside me, my pussy tightening around his cock, and then he hits just the right spot, and I fall. My whole body tenses as the orgasm slams through me, rocking me to my very bones with its intensity.

"Shit," Prescott mutters. He buries his head into the crook of my neck. His movements turn faster, more frantic, as he chases his own release. I clench my legs around him, my fingers running through his hair as I graze my teeth over his neck. "Come for me."

He grunts and I pull his head up, my mouth meeting his as he slides into me. Once, twice, and then his muscles tense as he comes inside me.

His body falls over mine, and we just stay like that, completely spent. I can still feel ringing in my ears as I try to catch my breath.

I'm not sure how long we stay just like that before Prescott rolls off me.

"That was..." I let out a shaky breath, still at a loss for words.

I've had some good sex before, but this was off the charts. I'm not sure why I'm surprised. I don't like the guy. He irritates me more often than not, but the sexual attraction was always there, so strong I could have sworn it was palpable.

"We shouldn't have done this," Prescott says softly.

My body freezes as his words register in my mind, and it feels like I've been slapped.

We shouldn't have done this.

The first thing he could tell me after sex, and he chooses this?

"Screw you, Wentworth."

My voice is calm and collected; when inside I feel anything but. Pulling the blanket with me, I get off the bed.

Out.

I need to get out of here.

"Jade, wait." I hear something fall behind me, but my attention is firmly set on the bathroom door. "*Dammit*! Just wait."

A hand grabs mine, and I'm pulled back.

"If you tell me one more time what a big mistake this was, I'm going to…"

His mouth crashes over mine once again, but I shove against his chest. "Stop it! You can't keep on doing shit like this, and then say how wrong it is."

"I didn't say it was wrong. I said we shouldn't have done it."

"And that is different, how?"

"You don't even like me!"

"You don't like me either! And yet you want me." I raise my brow, challenging him to deny it, but he keeps his mouth shut. We both know I'm right. "We don't have to like each other for this thing between us to work. It's just sex. Nothing more and nothing less."

He frowns at me in confusion. "Just sex?"

"Just sex," I repeat. "I know you think you're irresistible, and girls are falling over their feet to get to you, but let's get real."

"You hadn't exactly been running in the other direction earlier," he throws right back.

"That's because I'm apparently an idiot who's a sucker for punishment."

Prescott runs his fingers through his hair. "So, just sex? That's what you want?"

"That's what I want." *Seriously, how many times does a girl have to say it?* "I don't want flowers, or dates, or whatever. I'm not in the market for happily-ever-afters. Hot, sweaty sex, on the other hand? Sign me up for it."

"Since when?"

I pinch the bridge of my nose, growing irritated by the second. "Since when, what?"

"Since when do you not believe in happily-ever-afters?"

Since my dad left my mom when he found out she had cancer.

Since my dad and my brother left me to deal with everything on my own.

Since I found my boyfriend cheating on me with my best friend when I needed them the most.

Since my mom died.

But I don't say any of those out loud.

"Since the only thing love brings you is heartache."

Prescott just watches me for a minute as if he isn't sure what to do. Finally, he nods. "Okay."

"Great."

"Great." He looks around my room. "What now?"

What now?

I tighten the grip I have on the blanket and tip my chin toward the window. "Now you can get your ass out of here."

"You're joking, right?"

His stupefied face makes me want to burst into laughter. You'd think I asked him to do something outrageous, like dance naked in the middle of the school cafeteria.

I raise my brow at him. "Do I look like I'm joking?"

"Jade…"

I turn my back on him and go toward the bathroom. "Don't fall on your ass on your way out. I'm not calling the paramedics or explaining what you were trying to do."

"Seriously? That's the only thing you have to say?"

"Yes, seriously, Wentworth. We just agreed, sex only." I look over my shoulder. "You can't go breaking our agreement on the first night. Which one is it, window or door?"

I'm about to push the door open, but before I can slip inside, Prescott's fingers wrap around my wrist, and he pulls me back.

"Fine, have at it."

I let out a snort. "As if I need your permission."

"I'm leaving but let's make one thing clear first. You're mine, Jade. *Mine*." He presses his mouth against mine in a fierce kiss before quickly pulling back. "And I don't like sharing."

With that, he walks away, leaving me breathless as he climbs out my window and disappears into the night.

Chapter 21

PRESCOTT

"Do I smell bacon?" Spencer asks as he enters the kitchen. He drops his duffle bag and goes straight for the pan, reaching for my bacon. Before he can take it, I slap him over the hand with the wooden spoon. "*Ouch.* What was that for?"

"Get your own breakfast," I grumble, taking a sip of my coffee before adding the eggs to the pan.

"Why? You're clearly making enough for both of us."

"Correction. I'm making enough for myself 'cause I'm hungry."

Once again, I woke up at the crack of dawn and couldn't fall asleep, so instead of tossing and turning, I went to the gym. I'd probably still be there if my stomach didn't start growling. It was so loud that one of the coaches noticed and kicked me out until I got some food.

"You're an asshole. You know that?"

"A hangry asshole. So if I were you, I'd be careful who you're trying to steal food from."

"It's not stealing," Spencer mutters as he opens the fridge and looks inside. "It's called sharing. You should look it up."

You're mine, Jade. Mine. And I don't like sharing.

The hair at the back of my neck raises as those words ring in my head. I could still see the way those blue eyes darkened, the shade of the sky just before the storm before I pulled her in for a kiss.

My cock twitches at the memory.

Seriously? I shake my head, my hand falling down to rearrange myself while my roommate is busy looking for food. "If you wanted to share, you should have found a different roommate."

"I picked you because I thought you'd be fun, but of course, I got the shorter end of the stick. Besides, shouldn't you be in a better mood?"

I give him the side eye. "And why would I be in a better mood?"

"I figured if you finally got laid, you'd feel more like yourself, but maybe I was wrong."

Got laid? My palms start to turn sweaty. *How the hell does he know I got laid?*

Did he see me leaving Jade's place? He couldn't have. I made sure to double-check that the coast was clear before making my way out of her room—which was way more difficult than climbing inside the room.

"And what makes you think I got laid?" I ask, trying to keep my voice as calm as possible.

Spencer pops out of the fridge, a container of leftover Chinese in his hand. "Dude, have you seen your back?"

My back?

I try to look over my shoulder, but I don't see shit. Now that I think about it, it did feel a little bit tender, but I figured it was probably because of all the workout hours I'd put in.

"What's wrong with my back?"

"Dude, it's all messed up and full of scratches," he barks out a laugh and plops down on one of the bar stools. "You didn't know?"

"Hell, no."

I didn't know that Jade had scratched me. I was too freaking lost in her to notice. Too lost in her smell, in her kisses, in that tight pussy of hers, to think about the damage she was causing. Too lost...

The smell of burnt food spreads through the room.

"Shit." I grab the pan from the stove, turning it off.

She left marks on me, and now, she cost me my breakfast. I should have known better than to mess with Jade-freaking-Cole. That girl has trouble written all over her.

I look over my breakfast, noticing that most of it is still edible, so I put it on my plate and take the seat next to Spencer.

"So," Spencer wiggles his brows. "Who's the hellcat?"

I glare at him. "It doesn't matter."

"What? Was she that bad in bed? Is that the problem?"

Bad in bed? Ha! If only that was my problem. Maybe then, I wouldn't be thinking about it, about her, or thinking about when I can sneak in her bed once again and find a creative way to make her pay for scratching me.

"I'm not talking about her," I mutter, shifting my attention to my breakfast. I shove a piece of bacon into my mouth, but all the while, I can feel Spencer's eyes on me. "What?"

"You don't want to talk about her? You always talk about your hookups."

"Do not."

"Do too. Like, seriously. All the freaking time. Which makes me wonder even more, who's the hellcat?"

"You're delusional, and you're starting to get on my nerves. She's just a hookup. That's all."

"Mhmm... Just a hookup."

I grab my plate and get to my feet. "I'm going to my room. I have some reading to do before my class."

Spencer gives me a knowing smirk. "And maybe give those scratches a look. You don't want them to get infected, do you?"

"Freaking asshole," I mutter as I get into my bedroom and walk straight to the mirror that's hanging on the closet door. I turn my back to it and look over my shoulder. There are six bright red scratches on my back, surrounded by a few paler ones.

"I'm going to fucking kill her."

Chapter 22

JADE

"Why do I feel like you're trying to avoid me?"

I look over the edge of my laptop to find my friends standing in front of my table.

"I'm not trying to avoid you."

Rei slips into the seat next to me. "Was the date that bad?"

I shift from Grace to Rei. "What date?"

"Umm… the one you went on the other day?"

Shit.

My date with Michael, *right*.

The one I forgot all about because Prescott wiped it out of my mind with his very talented… hands. And mouth. Okay, and dick. His very talented and very big dick. Not that I'll ever admit it out loud.

"Oh, that date."

"How many dates are you going on?" Penny asks as she takes a sip of her coffee.

"It was bad," Rei shakes her head. "I knew it."

"It wasn't bad. I just don't date."

"You don't date, but you went out on a *double date* with Grace and Mason?"

"I went out to *dinner* with a group of friends," I correct, shifting my attention to Grace. "And I'm not avoiding you. You haven't been home all weekend." I give a pointed look to Rei. "Neither have you."

"I was home, but I didn't hear you stopping by," Penny chimes in. "So how was your none-date-date?"

"Just so you know, I'm rolling my eyes really hard right now," I mutter, grabbing my cup, only to find it empty. Great. Now I don't have coffee either.

This time, Penny's the one rolling her eyes. "Duly noted. But tell us."

"It was *fine*. Michael is a really great guy."

"Why don't you sound more excited then?"

"Because there is a but coming, that's why." Grace lifts her brow, daring me to tell her otherwise.

"But I'm not looking for a guy to date. And before you say anything, I'm just not cut out for dating. Besides, I have other things to worry about."

"Like what?" this comes from Rei.

Like those bumps and bruises growing under my arm.

But of course, I don't say that out loud. The last thing I need is for my friends to find out and freak out. I'm doing enough of it all on my own, thank you very much.

"Like finishing this degree and having fun along the way. Like you know, going out to clubs, partying with my friends, getting silly drunk?"

"Mhmm... What I really find funny is the way you stormed out after Prescott."

My lips part as I stare at my best friend. My *ex*-best friend. Did she really just go there? The corner of Grace's mouth twitches as she watches me across the table.

Of course, she did.

Rei's brows pull together in a frown. "Prescott, as in your Prescott?"

My Prescott?

I want to laugh at the absurdity of it, but the words he said before he left the other night ring in my head, making my stomach clench.

You're mine, Jade. Mine. And I don't like sharing.

It's just words, I chastise. He most likely didn't like that I threw him out, so he wanted to have the final say.

Nothing more, nothing less.

"More like a pain in my ass; that's what he is," I mutter.

"So why did you follow after him?" Grace asks.

"Wait, he was at the same place you guys were on your date?" Rei's eyes widen.

"The very same. He was with an older couple, probably his parents. And then he just up and left, and Jade here went after him."

Rei whips her head toward me. "I thought you couldn't stand him."

"I can't."

"Then why go after him?"

"I don't know!" I lift my arms and let them fall by my sides. "He seemed upset, so I went to check if he was okay. I seriously don't see what all the fuss is about. Next time I'll let him be, so he can do something stupid. Would that be better?"

"I just find it strange, that's all. You usually do your best to avoid the guy."

Not usually, just when he pisses me off.

It was strange. I don't know how to explain it even to myself, much less to my friends. I don't like Prescott. I find him irritating and infuriating all at once, but at the same time, a part of me likes him. Physically, I'm attracted to him. Although, seriously, there isn't a sane woman alive who wouldn't be attracted to him, but there is also something else. Something I can't quite pinpoint, and it's driving me crazy.

Completely and utterly crazy.

"Can't really avoid him considering he's my brother's best friend and teammate, now can I?"

"I guess not."

"Can you imagine Wentworth and Jade getting stuck in a cabin somewhere? Damn, I'd pay to watch that show play out."

"They'd either kill each other or..."

I launch across the desk and cover Grace's mouth with my hand. "Don't you even dare say it."

Grace mumbles something incoherently, but my hand over her mouth stifles the noise.

"No. I'm not listening. I'm grabbing my things now, and then I'll order a refill before going to the library. I don't want to hear one word about this. The next time I accept only a girls' night out. With drinks. A *lot* of drinks. Clear?"

Grace nods her head.

"Good." I pull my hand back. "Now that's settled. I'll see you guys later."

I start to pick up my things, ready to get out of here.

"I need to grab some books in the library too," Penny says, her fingers tightening around Henry's harness as she picks up her bag. "Mind if I join you?"

"As long as you don't mention you know who."

Penny lets out a chuckle, "It sounds like you're talking about Lord Voldemort or something."

"Or something," I mutter. "Let me just grab a refill."

I get in line, which thankfully isn't that long, and ask the guy working the counter for another mocha. Grabbing my drink, I make my way outside, where Penny is waiting for me. A chill runs down my spine as a light breeze whizzes by. Autumn is in full swing, and I'm not sure I am ready for it.

"Ready to go?"

"Sure." Penny gives Henry a command, and I walk in step with the two of them. "For what's it worth, I think you and Prescott would be good together."

I can't help myself. I burst into laughter. *Good together? Yeah, right.* "Good at killing each other, maybe."

"No, I really mean it. You two bicker like an old married couple, but it's not the end of the world. You kind of remind me of Miguel and Becky."

"Miguel and Becky?" I ask, the names sounding slightly familiar, although I'm not sure from where.

"Emmett and Kate's best man and maid of honor."

"Oh, right. They're together?"

"Well, they're working on it." Penny's brows furrow. "I think? With the two of them, you can never really know. But they've always been fighting over one thing or another."

"That sounds promising," I comment dryly. "Also, I thought we agreed not to talk about this."

She gives me a sheepish smile. "Yeah, well. I was with you guys in Hawaii."

I give her a side glance. "What does that have to do with anything?"

"I might be blind, but I'm not stupid, you know. There is..."

My phone buzzes, and I pull it out, grateful for the interruption. "Sorry, I have to take this." Hitting the answer button, I bring the phone to my ear. "Yeah?"

There is a beat of silence on the other end to the point I wonder if the other person hung up. But just as I'm about to pull the phone away to check if the call is still connected, I hear a raspy: "Jade?"

My whole body freezes at the sound of the voice I haven't heard in over a year, ever since he walked away from me without a backward glance. For the second time no less.

Fool me once. Shame on you.

Fool me twice. Shame on me.

"Why are..."

"No," I say, my voice pure ice as my fingers grip the phone harder. "You don't get to call me. We have nothing to talk about."

"Ja—"

He tries again, but I hang up before he can get anything else out.

"Jade?" A hand touches my shoulder, making me snap out of my thoughts to find Penny standing in front of me, a worried expression on her face. "Are you okay?"

"I..." I run my hand over my face, pushing my hair back. "Yeah, I'm fine."

"You sure?"

"Yes. It was a wrong number."

If Penny thinks I'm lying, she doesn't call me on it.

"Let's go," I add quickly, not wanting to give her a chance to ask anything about this again. "I really need to start working on that essay for our English Lit class."

"Start?" Penny's brows shoot up. "On the one that's due tomorrow?"

"The very one."

"How much do you have done?"

"Zero."

At the look of horror on Penny's face, I can't help but laugh out loud. My whole body relaxes, and for the first time since I answered the phone, I can inhale deeply.

"It's not that bad. I'll get it done before the due date."

"You have like a few hours left!"

"It's not like I need more. If I start too early, I usually overthink it for too long. Don't worry."

"Don't worry she says. You're crazy, Jade."

"What can I say? I like living on the edge. What are you working on?" I ask, pulling open the door to the library so Penny and Henry can enter before me.

"I'm working on an essay for my music history class."

The librarian looks up from the table as we enter the main space, her eyes falling on Henry. Just then, my phone starts to vibrate loudly, and that hawk's gaze turns to me, her lips twisting in a disapproving scowl.

Turning my back on her, I pull my phone out, shifting it to silent, when the message on top of the screen catches my attention.

Unknown: You can't keep ignoring me, Jade.

Oh, I damn well could and am planning to. There is nothing that I want to say to him and nothing that he can say to me that'll change my mind.

After all, he was the one who walked away *twice*, not the other way around.

"Jade?" Penny places her hand over mine. "Wanna go and grab a table?"

PRESCOTT

"Why are you frowning like that?" I ask Nixon as we leave the training facilities. The coach had us watching our next opponent's tapes for the past two hours. Next week, we'll be facing one of our biggest rivals, and everybody has been on edge.

"It's this damn game," Nixon mutters, running his hand through his hair. "It's messing with my head."

"If it's messing with your head, then we're screwed."

"You're not helping."

"Well, if you wanted me to hold your hand and tell you all's going to be okay, you came to the wrong person."

"Fuck off, Wentworth."

"Gladly, I have some studying to do anyway."

"Good luck. I'm off to class. See you at practice?"

With a nod, I slam my fist against his and make my way across the campus. The library is quiet as I make my way inside—the smell of books and dust permeates the air.

I look around the room, searching for an open spot so I can get some work done when I spot her sitting at the table by the window along with Kate's sister.

For a moment, I just stand there and watch her type away at her keyboard. There's a frown between her brows as, every now and then, she shifts her attention to the book that's standing open by her laptop.

A hand touches my arm. I turn around to find a cute blonde watching me with a smile on her lips. "Can you please move?"

"Sure, sorry."

Rubbing the back of my head, I get out of her way. She follows me with her gaze as she goes to the shelf I was blocking and looks over the selection before rising to her toes. Her shirt lifts, revealing a patch of skin on her midriff as she reaches for the book.

My phone buzzes in my pocket, so I pull it out.

Doll: Enjoying the view?

My head snaps up, my eyes meeting hers over the edge of her laptop—the corner of my mouth lifts.

Me: Jealous, doll?

Doll: It was you who wanted to be exclusive, hotshot. Not me. I'm fine with looking for my fun elsewhere.

My fingers grip the phone in my hand as the idea of Jade

going to that basketball dude, or anyone else, for that matter, flashes in my mind.

Me: Like hell you are.
Doll: Touchy, are we?
Me: I'm not touchy.

I look up, expecting to find her reading the message, but she puts her phone to the side and turns back to her computer.

Seriously?

Me: I'm not.
Me: I'll just keep texting you until you answer, you know that right?
Me: I'm persistent like that.
Me: Besides, we have a score to settle anyhow.

My gaze is fixed on her as my fingers keep typing. Finally, she looks up, but only to lean in and whisper something to Penny. The blonde nods and Jade gets up.

Jade glances at me for a split second before disappearing between the bookshelves. I wait a moment, weighing my options.

I could stay here, do the work I was planning to do, or go after her.

It was as easy as that.

"Screw this."

Pushing from the table, I get to my feet. Giving a quick glance around, I make sure nobody is watching me before following her.

There are a few people looking for books, but none of them pay me any attention as I pass by, diving deeper between the bookshelves until I catch a glimpse of dark hair.

Hurrying up, I grab her wrist and pull her deeper into the library. I press her against the shelf, bracing my hands against it to make sure even if somebody comes around the corner, they won't get a good look at her.

Jade raises her brows. "Following me now, Wentworth? Don't you think it's slightly creepy?"

"If you didn't want me to follow you, you could have answered my message."

"Some of us have work to do."

"So that's why you're hiding out here? Because you have work to do?"

She pokes me in the chest. "I'll let you know; I was looking for a book."

"And where is that book?"

Those blue eyes narrow at me. "I don't see how that's your problem. Was there something you needed, or do you just like to annoy me?"

"Well, the feeling is mutual."

"Good together, my ass."

"What?"

Jade shakes her head. "Nothing."

"It didn't sound like nothing."

"If you don't need anything. I'm going to get back to my paper."

Jade tries to walk around me, but I don't let her slip away.

"Damn it, doll."

My hand cups the back of her neck, pulling her to me, my mouth crashing against hers. Jade sucks in a breath as our lips collide, tongues gliding together. Her fingers sink into my hair as that electrifying feeling spreads through my body.

Moving closer, I deepen the kiss. Jade lets out a soft moan as her fingers tug at my strands, dragging me to her. Our bodies brush together, every soft curve of hers sliding against me.

She's driving me insane— mentally and physically—yet, I can't get enough of it.

I can't get enough of her.

My dick throbs in need. Sliding my hand to the small of her back, I pull her to me, my pelvis brushing against her soft belly. I'm pretty sure a book fell somewhere as I press her against the bookshelf, but we don't slow down.

"Prescott..." Jade's hands run over my shoulders and down my stomach. My muscles tense under her gentle touch. I nip at her lower lip just as her hands slide under my shirt. I grab her hands, stopping them from moving further.

Breaking the kiss, I press my forehead against hers. "Oh, no, you don't."

Our ragged breaths mix together as she slowly blinks her eyes open. "What?"

"You're not adding a matching set of marks on my front too."

"A matching..." She shakes her head as if she's trying to clear her mind. "What are you talking about?"

"I'm talking about the nail marks you left imprinted on my back the other night, for which Spencer has been giving me shit."

"I didn't... Wait, you told Spencer?" Jade hisses, her eyes turning into saucers.

"I didn't tell Spencer shit. He calls you a hellcat." I press my finger against her mouth. "And, yes, you did. I have to be careful when I'm in the locker room because I won't hear the end of it if the guys find out."

Jade shakes her head. "You guys are just a bunch of nosey old ladies."

"Old?" I raise my brow as I pull her to me, my lips brushing against hers. "There is nothing old about me, doll."

Fire lights up in those blue irises, making her eyes seem darker. "How about you stop talking and put your mouth where your money is?"

"And where would that be?"

"On me."

The corner of my mouth curls upward. It's tempting. So damn tempting to do exactly what she asked. To kiss her, right here, right now, slip my hand into her panties, and feel her wetness before I make her come so hard she'll forget her own name. That's exactly why I pull back.

"Another time."

"What?" Jade blinks a few times. She looks cute. All confused like this. "Where are you going?"

I tap my fingers against the shelf. "Back to my table. I have studying to do before practice."

"Studying? You're going back to study?"

"Yup." I nudge her chin up. "Close that pretty mouth. You don't want a fly to get in."

Jade shoves my hand away. "Shut up. You can't be serious."

"I am. I'll see you around."

"You can't leave me like... like this."

I raise my brows, trying my best to keep the smile from spreading over my mouth but failing miserably. "Like what?"

Jade grits her teeth. The frustration is shining in those blue irises as she shifts her weight. I know exactly what she wants, but I want her to say it.

"You know what." Her gaze falls down to my pants and the very prominent bulge in them. "And I'm not the only one."

No, she isn't. But I can't let her call all the shots. She already got what she wanted and had no problem kicking me out of her place before I was done with her. Well, two can play this game of hers.

"I don't know what you're talking about."

"Ugh! What's the point of this if you're of no use to me? I guess I'll just have to find..."

I turn around and press her against that bookshelf before she can finish. "You wouldn't dare."

"You keep testing me, and you'll find out."

"You keep testing me, and I'll get you all worked up every day only to leave you hanging, Cole. Now take your punishment like a good girl."

"Punishment?" She pulls her brows together. "Are you into some kind of kink I didn't know about?"

"Punishment for marking me and then kicking me out of your place."

"You're joking."

"Do I look like I'm joking, doll?"

She presses her palms against my chest and tries to push me away, but I don't budge. "I hate you!"

"The feeling is mutual. But maybe if you're good, you can convince me to stop by later and give you what you need."

"You think I'll be waiting around for you?" Jade huffs. "Think again."

"Jade..."

"I don't need you to take care of my needs, Wentworth. I'm more than capable of doing it on my own." She jabs her finger into my chest. "Think about that when you're running drills on the field later."

Then, with a flip of her hair over her shoulder, she ducks under my arm, her hips swaying as she walks away.

I lean against the bookshelf and run my fingers through my hair before letting my hand drop by my side. My dick aches painfully, cursing me for letting this opportunity slide.

So much for keeping things cool.

Letting out a sigh, I rearrange myself, relieving some of the pressure before pushing from the shelf.

It's time to get back and act like nothing happened.

Getting to the main space, I lift my head, my eyes going instantly to the table where Jade was sitting earlier, only she's nowhere to be found.

Chapter 23

JADE

There's a soft knock on my doorway before Grace peeks her head inside my room. "You busy?"

I click save on the essay I've been working on before lifting my head to look at her. "Just about finished. What's up?"

"Wanna go to a party?"

My brows quirk up as I put my laptop on the bed, giving my full attention to Grace. "Who are you, and what did you do with my best friend?"

"Oh, shut up." Pushing the door open all the way, she hops on the bed next to me. "It's Spencer."

"Spencer?"

"Yes," she rolls her eyes. "He's been going on and on about this party at his place and told me we should come. It's not even a party. Just a small get-together."

I let out a snort. "You know who Spencer is, right? There's no such thing as "small" and "get together" when it comes to those boys."

"I know," she lets out a groan. "But I already told him no the last five or so times he invited me. I can't do it again. It's just going to be for a little while. So he can stop nagging me about it."

I didn't think that was possible, but what the hell. Who was I to say no to a party?

"So what? It's just the two of us?" I ask, leaning over the bed to turn off my laptop.

"Penny agreed to go."

I look at Grace. "She did?"

That was a first. Penny rarely ever went to unfamiliar or overly loud places. They made her uncomfortable, which I guess made sense, considering sound was her best form of orientation and communication, and when it was overly noisy, she couldn't use it.

"I promised we'd keep an eye on her. Plus, Mason should come after he's done with work too."

"See? That's why athletes can never have small get-togethers."

"Oh, shush. He was coming here anyway. Besides, maybe we'll be home by the time he's done with his shift at the bar."

"I guess we'll see about that." I hop off the bed. "Give me a few to change."

"What did I tell you?" I look over my shoulder at Grace and Penny as we enter Spencer's apartment. The door was left unlocked, and the music was blasting loud enough to be heard out in the hallway.

Penny tightens her grip on Grace's hand, and her wide eyes scan the room, probably trying to focus through all the noise.

"Didn't you say this was a small gathering?" Penny asks, her fingers clasping around her white cane tighter.

I stop in my tracks and turn toward her. "Do you want to

leave? Because if you're not comfortable, we'll do just that. No harm done."

For a moment, I think she'll agree, I know I would have if I were in her shoes, but in the end, she surprises me and shakes her head. "No. Let's do it. Just…" Her throat bobs as she swallows. "Just don't leave me alone?"

Grace rubs her arm. "No way. One of us will be with you at all times."

"Thanks," Penny whispers, visibly relaxing. "I know you probably think it's silly but…"

"It's not silly at all," I stop her before she can even finish. "I can see just fine, and these kinds of things can get overwhelming. I don't even want to imagine how it must be to have two senses virtually cut off."

"Not fun at all."

"We've gotcha. Ready?"

Penny nods her head. "As I'll ever be."

I turn around to find a few people watching us. Rolling my eyes at them, I take Penny's hand in mine and help her through the crowd deeper into the apartment. "How about we find something to drink?" I loudly say so she can hear me.

"I don't think alcohol is the best choice right now. I can't be blind, deaf, and drunk."

"I guess not," I chuckle. "Although one drink might help you relax."

"One drink will definitely relax you."

I turn around to find Spencer in front of us, a big grin on his face. "And who do we have here?"

Grace rolls her eyes at him. "Spencer, Penny, our very dear, very sweet friend. Penny, Spencer. Don't fall for his charm. He's a womanizer."

"Hey, is that the best you've got to say about me, Red?"

"All I'm saying is the truth."

"Hardly," he waves her off, taking a pull from his beer. "Don't listen to her. Her taste's questionable at best."

"Questionable?"

"You don't like hockey players! Of course, it's questionable."

Grace jabs him in his chest. "Just because I can see you for who you are, Spencer Monroe does not mean my taste is questionable!"

"Whatever you say, Red." Spencer shakes his head and moves out of the way so a couple can pass by. "What can I getcha to drink? Beer? Vodka?"

We move with him to the kitchen, where a few guys are standing next to the keg.

"Whiskey?" he turns to me and winks. "I've got the good stuff, too."

"Oh, I'll take that. And get one for Pens, too. Grace?"

"I'll have a beer."

Spencer nods. "Coming right up."

"I really don't think that's wis—"

"It's one drink, Penny."

He looks over his shoulder, his eyes narrowing on her. "Why is that name familiar?"

"I'm Kate's sister. I think we met briefly last year?"

"Oh, right!"

Spencer hands Grace a beer and puts two shot glasses in front of us on the counter, filling them with amber liquid.

"Why are you giving away my whiskey, Monroe?"

The hair at the back of my neck rises to attention at the sound of Prescott's low and gravelly voice.

"I'm making our guests feel welcome. Chill."

"Not with my whiskey."

"Didn't you know, Spencer?" I pick up my glass and slowly turn around to face Prescott. "He doesn't like to share."

Prescott's eyes narrow on my mouth as I bring the glass to

my lips and down the drink in one go before grabbing the bottle to refill it.

"What are you doing here?"

The corner of my mouth curls up. "Spencer invited us."

Prescott crosses his arms over his chest. "Did he now?"

"Mhmm…" I take a sip from my drink. "It's good stuff. I can see why you'd like to keep it to yourself."

"If I'm getting drunk, I might as well get drunk on good booze."

Before I can answer, a girl barges into our group and tugs at Spencer's hand. "Spencer! The girls wanna play Never have I ever. You game?"

Spencer's eyes light up. "I've got you one better, Sugar."

I glance at Grace, who just rolls her eyes at the absurdity of it, but Spencer catches her.

"What'd you say, Red? You game?"

"You didn't even say what we're playing."

Spencer wiggles his brows and grabs the whiskey off the counter. "You'll have to come and see."

I grab Penny's drink and hand it to her. "C'mon, Pens. Drink up, and let's see what Spencer's up to."

She tentatively sniffs the cup. "I don't think I'll like that. You drink it."

"Fine." Letting out a sigh, I down her drink, too, the warmth spreading through my belly. "Let's go."

We go to the living room, where a few people are already sitting on the floor.

Spencer claps his hands, drawing the attention to himself. "Okay, people, the rules are simple. We spin the bottle."

"Didn't we just say we're playing truth or dare?" the girl from earlier asks with an annoyingly nasal voice.

Truth or dare?

"What's this, fucking junior high?" Prescott mutters behind me, startling me.

"We are, but here we play it a little bit differently. So, we'll spin the bottle. The one who spins asks the question, and the one who it lands on will choose between truth or dare. If they answer the question or complete the dare, the group has to drink. If the person refuses to do either of those, they have to drink. And if the challenge requires some extra help…" Spencer wiggles his brows. "We'll spin the bottle again to decide who the little helper will be. Any questions?"

"So basically, just a fancy way of getting us all drunk."

Spencer's eyes shine with mischief as they meet mine. "Exactly. I knew you spoke my love language, Cole. Get that sweet ass on the floor, and let's play. Wentworth, you game, too?"

"I just want my whiskey back."

"Well, then sit down and play, so you'll get to drink it."

Prescott curses softly but does as he's told. He walks around the group sitting down all the way on the other side.

I quirk my brow at his grim face as I help Penny down and then do the same.

Once everybody's settled down, Spencer spins the bottle. "Let the games begin."

The first few people the bottle lands on choose truth, so it's pretty tame. Then the bottle lands on one of the hockey players who chooses dare and has to down the whole solo cup of beer as he has his nose pinched. The beer ends up everywhere, and we laugh our asses off at his red face.

"That was pitiful, Montana," Spencer says.

"We'll see you soon, Monroe," the guy says as he spins the bottle, which lands on me. He quirks his brow. "Truth or dare?"

"Dare."

"Take off your panties."

There are a few hoots in approval from the guys sitting around.

Slowly, I get to my feet. I've had a few more shots since we started the game, and my head is positively spinning. I slide my hand under my skirt and pull down the lacy material and let it fall on the ground. I step out of it and lift it in the air, letting it dangle from my finger.

"Wanna keep it as a souvenir, too?" I ask sweetly.

From the corner of my eye, I can feel Prescott's probing gaze on me, but I ignore him, my whole focus on the Montana guy.

"That wouldn't be..."

"What the fuck, Jade?"

I look up to find no one other than my brother standing in the doorway; his eyes shooting daggers at me. When he got here, I have no idea.

"It's just a game, Nixon. Chill." Wrapping my fingers around the lace, I slide it into my back pocket and sit down. "Drink up, assholes."

Everybody has a drink as I grab the bottle and spin it. The bottle lands on Spencer's annoying Sugar babe friend. "Truth or dare?"

The girl giggles like she's five. "Dare."

"Until your next turn, you have to sit in the lap of..." I spin the bottle once again, and it lands on another girl. Some cheer, some groan. "Her."

The girl goes to do as I said, and I down another shot.

"What do you think you're doing?"

I look over my shoulder and glare at my brother. "I was having fun, but you're ruining it. What are you even doing here, Nixon?"

"Prescott told me to come."

I roll my eyes, returning my attention to the game. "Of course he did."

Because why wouldn't he? They're best buds, after all.

"You're drunk."

"Positively buzzed," I counter just as Spencer spins the bottle. I watch the bottle go round and round, making me dizzy until it finally starts to slow down. I blink. On me.

"Truth or dare, Cole?" Spencer smirks at me.

"Dare."

"What?" Grace turns to me. "You can't pick dare again."

"Why not? It's more fun that way."

"Truer words have never been spoken," Spencer says, tapping the corner of his mouth. "Hmm... let's see... How about you drink a shot?"

"That's your famous dare?" The ginger hockey player sitting a few places away from him asks. "You're getting lousier the more you drink, Monroe."

Spencer gives him a who-do-you-think-I-am look as he turns back to me. "Straight from somebody's mouth."

"Be my guest," I shrug. "This one's a win-win for me."

Spencer grabs the bottle and spins it once again. "And the lucky winner is..."

For whatever reason, it feels like forever as the bottle goes around our little circle until it stops.

"You've gotta be shitting me," I mutter, my eyes meeting the dark gaze that's been on me for the past hour.

Spencer rubs his hands together. "This is going to be fun."

We just stare at one another across the room. Anticipation builds inside my stomach. A part of me expects him to back out, but he doesn't.

Spencer grabs a clean shot glass and fills it with whiskey. "C'mon, Wentworth. Lay down and put the shot in your mouth."

"You're an idiot. You know that?"

"But you're having fun."

Prescott grumbles something as he does what he's told, a first. My heart starts beating faster as I move closer to him.

Those eyes find mine instantly and don't back off.

I place my hand over his chest and lean over him, my hair falling down like a curtain, shielding us from the rest of the group.

Prescott's eyes darken as if he, too, just realized that. I lower a few more inches, feeling the heat of his body underneath me, the flexing of his muscles under my fingertips.

"Pull her hair back," Spencer yells, breaking me out of the moment, and reminding me that we aren't alone. Not really. A few people voice their agreement.

"Seriously?" I mutter, my fingers flexing and gripping the material of Prescott's shirt.

"Hell, yes. We can't see for shit."

"Wouldn't want you to miss the show," I roll my eyes, but then Prescott's fingers wrap around my hair, and he pulls it to the side, and any sort of amusement I felt is gone.

What's left is pure, raw need.

Licking my lips, I hold Prescott's gaze as I lower down.

I can feel his body react when my warm breath touches his skin. Our lips brush together as I wrap them around the cup. His fingers tighten in my hair, and I can feel the burning in my scalp. Just a split-second touch, barely long enough to be even considered a touch, but strong enough to send a jolt of electricity through my body as I tilt my head back, letting the shot slide down my throat.

People cheer as I finish the shot, but I can barely hear it from the sound of ringing in my own ears.

Prescott sits up, so I pull back, putting some much-needed distance between us. Turning my back on him, I go back to my spot where Grace is watching me with interest.

"You good?"

"Yeah. Just a bit dizzy," I lie. "I think I'll go to the bathroom."

"Want me to go with you?"

I shake my head, getting to my feet. "You stay with Pens. I'll be back in a bit."

Chapter 24

PRESCOTT

"She's freaking crazy," Nixon mutters as he joins me.

I don't have to ask who he's talking about; his eyes are still locked on the door where Jade disappeared to. "I don't know what's gotten into her."

"Maybe she just wants to have fun."

My best friend turns his head toward me, eyes narrowing. "Don't you start with that bullshit, too."

"It's not bullshit, Nix. Just because you're not interested in parties and drinking doesn't mean other people aren't. Cut her some slack."

Silence stretches between us as he just watches me, and I can feel the hairs at the back of my neck rise under his scrutinizing glare.

"I thought you didn't like Jade."

Fuck.

"I don't."

Did he see something? I tried my best to keep my cool, but it was hard when the girl you want more than your next breath was standing over you, her hands on your body as she leaned in to drink the shot straight out of your mouth, and you just watched her take off her panties in front of a room full of people like it's just any regular day.

I was so tempted to leap across the room and punch Montana in his stupid face for asking something like that from her, but I knew I couldn't. Not if I didn't want people to ask any questions, but maybe I've been wrong, and people could see it regardless.

"I just get where she's coming from," I continued softly. "You've changed. You've figured out your life, and you're happy, and that's great, man, but not all of us did. Some of us are still looking."

"I just hope you're not looking at my little sister." He shakes his head. "What the hell am I thinking? Everybody's looking at her when she's doing shit like she pulled tonight. I should probably go and check in on her, make sure that she's okay and not puking her guts out."

"Go home."

"What?"

"Go home. If you go and look for her, you'll only get into another fight."

I can see Nixon's mind work as he processes my words. I'm right. He knows I'm right. I'm not sure what's happening between the two, but they've been fighting more lately. And it wasn't even one of those silly sibling fights, either.

Finally, Nixon lets out a sigh, "You'll make sure that she gets home okay?"

"Yeah, sure."

"Okay. Thanks, man." He slaps me on the shoulder. "You're the best."

If he only knew the truth, he wouldn't think that. Because if I were the best friend he believes I am, the best friend he deserves, I would have never hooked up with Jade in the first place. If I were the best friend he thinks I am, I would have sent her home this very moment and broken this thing between us off.

The moment Nixon is out of my apartment, I go searching for her.

The door to the bathroom opens, but some guy comes out.

Where the hell is she?

He stumbles toward the living room, leaving the hallway blissfully empty just as the door of my room opens, and she starts to walk outside.

I should have figured as much.

Pushing off the wall, I go toward her.

"What?" She looks up just as I shove her back into my room, closing the door behind us.

Take her home.

But do I do that?

No.

"It's me," The softly growled words are my only warning as I sink my fingers into her hair and pull her to me, sliding my mouth over hers in a vicious kiss.

Fucking finally.

Kissing her has been on my mind since she turned to face me, my whiskey in her hand and on her lips. I wanted to taste that damn whiskey on her mouth, see if it tasted as good as it usually does.

But the joke's on me because it tastes even better, and now I'll never be able to drink the damn thing without thinking of Jade and this kiss.

My tongue dips into her mouth as I push her deeper into the room. Jade's arms wrap around me, fingers sliding under my shirt and making my skin sizzle under her touch.

Her legs touch the back of my bed, and she falls on the mattress. Breaking the kiss, I lower to my knees in front of her. Her breathing is ragged, her chest rising and falling rapidly as I slide my hands over the side of her legs, spreading them wide open for me.

"Still no panties." The words come out rough, my fingers tightening around the soft flesh of her legs.

"I forgot about that," she breathes.

Her hair is a mess, her lips swollen from our kiss, and her cheeks pink.

"You forgot you're not wearing any panties?" I shake my head. "You'll be the death of me, doll."

"What can I say? I'm forgetful like that."

Forgetful, my ass.

"Is that the reason why you didn't answer your phone last night?"

I tried texting her after I was done with practice to see if she wanted to finish what we started in the library, but she never got back to me.

A smile curls her lips. "Oh, I was busy doing other things last night."

"Other things like what?"

She props her leg against the mattress, spreading her legs wider. She traces her finger over the outside of her thigh, moving it up and down, and I can feel my cock twitch in my pants.

"Wouldn't you like to know?"

My tongue darts out, sliding over my dry lips. "Show me."

The little minx pretends to think about it for a moment, but finally, she lets out a sigh. "Fine. It all started when my fuck buddy left me all hot and bothered…"

"What a jackass."

"I know." Those dark blue eyes meet mine. "So I had to take matters into my own hands."

My throat feels tight as the image of Jade lying naked on her bed, playing with herself, pops into my head, so I clear it before asking, "And how did you do that?"

"I'll show you..." She grazes her teeth over her lip. "If you show me."

The corner of my mouth tips upward as I get to my feet, barely feeling the jab going through my knee as I get to my full height. Unbuttoning my pants, I shove them down, pulling my aching cock out.

"That was fast."

"I'm done with playing games, doll."

"So am I."

Jade licks her lips, her pupils dilating at the sight. She slides her hand upward, her fingers going to her bare pussy and gliding through her lower lips. Her breath hitches at the touch, teeth sinking into her bottom lip.

"Fuck."

I tighten my grip around my cock, giving it a few slow tugs as I watch her fingers play with her pussy. They circle around her clit, before her fingers slide lower, disappearing inside her. Jade's hips arch off the mattress, and my dick jolts forward. I slide my thumb over the head of my cock, spreading the precum over the tip as I watch Jade add another finger to the mix.

Her movements grow faster, and I do the same, not once moving my gaze from her.

She's a vision. Her cheeks are pink, her eyes hooded as she stares at me, her chest rapidly rising and falling as she takes what she needs completely unapologetically.

"Come for me, beautiful," I rasp, wanting to see her completely unleashed. *Needing* to see her.

"P-Prescott," she breathes.

Her head falls back, eyes shutting as the orgasm rips through her, making her body shudder.

The familiar pressure builds at the small of my back.

Refusing to give in just yet, I grip my cock tighter and just watch her as she comes off the high. Her body relaxes on the bed, and slowly she pulls her fingers out, blinking her eyes open.

She's still trying to catch her breath, her eyes glassy from the high of the orgasm as she stares at me from the bed.

My bed.

"Did it help?"

"Barely." Her gaze falls down to my hard dick. "You haven't come yet."

"Oh, I'm not planning to come just yet, doll. First, I want to taste you."

Moving closer so my legs are touching the mattress, I grab her hand with my free one and bring it to my lips. I inhale her sweet scent before I wrap my tongue around her fingers and pull them into my mouth.

Jade's eyes grow darker as I suck her fingers clean, slowly savoring the taste of her release before letting them slip from my mouth.

"And then?"

"Then..." I kneel on the mattress, brushing the hair away from her face. "Then I'm going to fuck you so hard you'll forget your own name."

"Give me your worst, hotshot."

The corner of my mouth twitches, "Oh, I plan to, doll."

Moving closer, I pull the condom from the nightstand and put it on. I slide my hand over her thigh, lifting it as I settle between her legs.

My mouth captures hers, tongue sliding between her parted lips and letting her taste herself on my tongue as I teasingly slide my dick through her lips a few times before pulling back all the way and sliding inside her in one long thrust that has us both moaning loudly.

"You have to keep quiet," I pant in her ear as I let her adjust to my length. "You don't want somebody to overhear you and come looking."

"You locked the door."

"What if I haven't?"

Jade goes still in my arms. "Tell me you locked the door."

I slide my hand under her shirt, my fingers wrapping around the lace covering her firm tits as I slowly start to move my hips. I'm about to push the material away, but her hand wraps around my wrist and moves my palm lower.

"Sorry, it wasn't on my mind." I slowly pull out of her, leaving only my tip to graze her entrance. "Then again, you were the one who took your panties off in front of the room full of people, so I figured you wouldn't mind."

With that, I thrust back inside her, deeper this time. Jade sucks in a breath, and I can feel my muscles quake as I try to hold back my release.

"I'm going to kill you if somebody finds out."

"Well, at least I'll die a happy man."

Her walls clasp around me. Groaning, I slide my hand lower, teasing her clit with my fingers as I continue pumping into her.

"It excites you," I whisper. "The idea that somebody might catch us like this." I hurry up my pace. "With my dick so deep inside you, you can feel it all the way to your womb." I trace kisses over her neck. Jade cups my cheek, turning me toward her, her mouth brushing against mine. "Completely at my mercy."

Her teeth sink into my lower lip, and I can feel the coppery taste on my tongue. "Less talking, more fucking."

"You asked for it," I growl, slapping that tight ass of hers.

Then I ravage her. My mouth is on hers, kissing every freaking inch of her body as I plunge into her until I can feel her tighten around me. She starts to call out my name, but I slide my tongue into her mouth to stifle any sound that might come out just as I thrust deeper and harder. That pressure at the back of my spine erupts, and I come inside her.

I roll to the side, not wanting to crush her with my weight. My heart thunders in my chest as I try to catch my breath.

If I thought the last time was a one-off and that the sex couldn't get better, I was utterly wrong.

Running my hand over my face, I look to the side to find Jade watching me. "I kind of like your worst," she whispers, a smile flashing on her face.

Just then, we can hear footsteps outside my room that have us both sobering up.

Jade jumps to her feet and tries to straighten her clothes, although it's pretty useless.

"I need to check the damage in the mirror." With that, she turns around and goes into my bathroom. The moment the light turns on, I can hear a soft yelp.

"You okay?"

"I look like a mess!"

"You look like you just got a good fucking."

Pushing to my feet, I take off the condom and throw it away before grabbing my boxer briefs and sliding them on. Her head peeks through the door, my comb in her hand, detangling the mess on her head. "Don't look so smug about it."

Slipping into my jeans, I go to the bathroom, leaning against the doorway. "Don't know what you're talking about."

"This is the best it'll get." With a sigh, she turns to me. "Grace will totally see through me."

My hand slips to her waist, lowering down to her ass and tugging her to me. "Nah."

Leaning down, I press my mouth against hers in another kiss before pulling back.

"Did you just steal my panties?"

With a smirk, I take a step back. "Don't know what you're talking about."

Those blue eyes narrow on me. "You're lucky I don't have time for this now."

With her eyes still on me, she goes to the door and pulls it open.

"There you are!" Grace says from the hallway. "We've been looking for you."

Fuck.

Jade slips outside just as I move out of the line of sight. "The main bathroom was occupied, so I used the other one," I hear Jade explain, her voice growing softer as she closes the door behind her, and they move down the hallway.

That was fucking close.

Letting out a sigh, I flop down on the bed. My knee's still aching, so I massage the soft flesh. Turning on my stomach, I go for the nightstand and pull out the pain meds. Getting a couple of pills, I swallow them down, my mind still on what just happened. Letting my head drop on the mattress, I smell the faint scent of lavender, and I know there is no way I'll fall asleep tonight.

Chapter 25

JADE

"Okay," Professor Reyes, one of my photography professors, claps her hands. "Now that you've learned the basics, I have a project for you." She takes in our small class, the corner of her mouth lifting in a knowing half-smile. "A friend of mine owns a gallery in Boston."

I shift in my seat, intrigued by where this is going. There's a beat of silence as Professor Reyes looks around the room, amusement clear on her face. She has us, and she knows it.

"I asked her for a favor, and she agreed. In order to put to use what we're going to learn this semester, you'll also have a project of your own you'll be working on. The deadline for this project is the first week in December. I want you to implement all the techniques we'll learn and present me with a portfolio of about five to ten photos. My friend and I will review it and select one student whose work will be displayed in the gallery in January along with some other artists."

"Is there a specific theme you're going for?" I ask, lifting my gaze from my notebook where I was jotting down the notes.

"There is," Professor Reyes shifts her attention to me and nods. "The theme for this project is raw beauty."

Just then, the bell rings, but nobody moves a muscle. A first, but given the topic we're discussing, it's not even surprising. The possibility of this is huge. To have our work displayed at an actual gallery when we're only sophomores? Sign me up.

And Professor Reyes knows it. She gives us a knowing smirk. "If you have any questions, you know where to find me. I'll see you guys next week."

With that, she turns on her heel and returns to her desk.

I quickly grab my things and shove them into my backpack, her words ringing in my mind.

Raw beauty.

What the hell does she even mean by raw beauty?

This class is called *Looking Through the Lens*, which is one of the reasons why I took it. It seemed interesting and *practical*. I didn't want to learn about theory, I just wanted to shoot. That was the point of being a photographer, after all. And so far, I've liked it. We've been learning about focus and colors, how sometimes less is more, and capturing the details that tell the story instead of the broader picture that's pretty but soulless.

Raw beauty could be anything really, which I guess is the point of it, and should give everybody equal chances of winning this competition.

I'm still going over all the possibilities on how to make myself stick out against the rest of my classmates as I walk to Cup It Up.

The local coffee shop is relatively silent, which is surprising since it's the middle of the day, but I'll take it. The bell chimes as I step inside, and Yasmin smiles at me from across the counter.

"Hey, stranger. I haven't seen you since..." She purses her lips as if she's trying to remember it. "The party after the game? That can't be, can it?"

"Well, I'm here every day. Where are you?" I hop onto the bar stool by the counter, letting my backpack drop into my lap.

"Don't even ask me. I had to cut some shifts since this year is kicking my ass."

"Well, if school is kicking your ass, the rest of us are doomed."

"It's not even the classes. It's the internship. There's just so much that has to be done," she lets out a sigh. "Anyhow, what can I getcha?"

"Let's go with mocha. Double shot of espresso, though. I need all the caffeine I can get. Oh, and a chocolate muffin. No, make it two."

Yasmin lets out a chuckle, "A hard day?"

If it were only that easy. It's been a tough few weeks, hell, tough last few *years*. It seems like every time life wants to give me a break, something changes, and *boom*, I'm back at square one.

"Something like that."

Yasmin presses a few buttons on the espresso machine before glancing at me. "What happened?"

"One of my photography professors gave us a project to work on. It's part of our grade, but the best one will also be displayed in a Boston gallery."

Yasmin's mouth falls open. "No way, that's huge, right?"

"What's huge?"

I look up to find Nixon standing behind me, a big smile on his lips as he glances between Yas and me.

"Jade's work will be displayed in a *gallery*," Yasmin says, placing the coffee cup and muffins in front of me.

You'd think my work would hang next to the freaking Mona Lisa, by the way she says it.

"Correction," I grab the cup in my hand, inhaling the sweet

aroma of coffee. "My work will be displayed in a gallery *if* I win this damn competition," I mutter, taking a sip of my coffee.

"What competition?"

The hair at the nape of my neck rises at the sound of his voice, and then I feel my tongue burning. "Shit." I swallow, the coffee burning its way down my throat, so I wave my hand in front of my mouth as if that'll help with the burn.

"Are you okay?" Nixon asks, his hand patting my back.

"Fine," I mutter, my mouth feeling tender. "That damn coffee is just hot."

"Maybe you should try getting a cold one next time."

I turn around and glare at Prescott, who's obviously enjoying this. Asshat. "I don't remember asking for your opinion."

"I'm just saying," he shrugs.

"Well, don—"

Nixon gets in between the two of us. "Okay, you two, can we not?"

Prescott watches me for a moment, before turning to Yas. "Can I get a coffee?"

"Jade." Nixon nudges me with his elbow.

"Whatever." I turn around, grab one of the muffins and peel off the paper.

I haven't talked to Prescott for a few days, since that party at his place. When we hooked up in his room, and the world shattered at my feet. He tried to message me, but I didn't answer any of them. That was my answer to anything I didn't want to do these days.

Avoid. Avoid. Avoid.

This thing between us was too intense. *He* was too intense, and I just needed some time to gather myself and put some much-needed distance between us.

"Oh, and can I have one of those too?"

"I'm sorry, Prescott. We're out of chocolate muffins."

"But Jade has it."

The way his brows pull together, confusion written all over his face, is so adorable I almost burst into laughter.

Prescott? Adorable?

"Yeah, well, Jade just took the last two."

Nixon lets out a groan just as Prescott turns to face me, arms crossed over his chest. "You took my muffin?"

I grin at him, the pain of my burnt tongue long forgotten. "I think what you mean to say is, I'm eating *my* muffin that I got because I was here first." With that, I sink my teeth into the soft chocolatey goodness. Prescott's eyes narrow at me, which makes the pastry taste even more delicious.

"Seriously? You're going to eat both of them?"

"I did buy both of them. So yes, I guess I will."

"How can you even eat two muffins? You're so..." He gives me a once-over that has the heat rising under my skin. "Tiny."

"Oh, trust me, I have more than enough room to put them."

Swallowing the last of my muffin, I lick the crumbs from my fingers. When I look up, I see Prescott staring at my mouth. My stomach tightens at the look of desire flaring in his dark eyes. I shift in my seat, feeling that familiar pulsing between my thighs.

Damn that man and his pretty fuck-me eyes.

The corner of his mouth lifts in the tiniest of smiles as if he can read my mind. I bite the inside of my cheek, my throat bobbing under his intense stare.

"Are you two seriously going to fight over a *muffin*?" Nixon asks, breaking me from my completely inappropriate thoughts.

"Yes," we say in unison, neither of us looking away.

From the corner of my eye, I can see my brother lift his hands in surrender. "Sorry, I asked."

"Look at the bright side. At least they agreed on something," Yas chimes in.

"They agreed over fighting about a muffin, Yas. There is no bright side."

"That's something too."

"Well, don't worry, big brother, there won't be any fight since I bought this muffin fair and square. Therefore, it's mine, and I'm going to eat it right here, right now."

I grab the other muffin from the plate and start peeling the paper off—a look of complete horror flashes on Prescott's face.

"You can't be serious."

"Oh, I'm dead serious."

"Would it be so hard to share?"

I raise my brow. "I thought you didn't like sharing."

His eyes narrow as I throw his own words back at him.

"You're going to pay for this," Prescott whispers, so only I can hear it.

I didn't doubt it for a moment. Hell, a part of me was looking forward to it.

"Bring it on, hotshot. Bring it on." With a smile, I bite into my muffin, making sure to moan extra loudly just to piss him off. If it's to be judged by the death glare Prescott sends my way, he knows it too.

Nixon shakes his head. "I swear if you two don't drive me crazy nobody will."

"Yeah, well, you love us, so..."

A smile appears on my brother's face. "You're lucky I do."

"Here you go," Yasmin places two coffees on the counter. "What are you boys up to?"

"I have another class in twenty, and then practice."

"Let's hope Coach doesn't keep us well into the dead of the night again," Prescott mutters, taking a sip of his coffee.

"It's an important game."

My phone buzzes in my pocket. I pull it out, expecting a message from one of my friends, only to find a familiar stream of numbers written on the screen. My stomach sinks, my heart pounding faster in my chest, the beat of it echoing in my ears and dulling the noises around me.

Dad's been more insistent ever since I answered his call the other day. There was nothing that I wanted to say to him. He apparently didn't share my sentiment. He knew I answered the phone, and now, he was relentless in his pursuit to get me to talk to him.

Unknown: I know you're seeing my messages, Jade.

My anger boils inside me. More than a year, and this is all he has to say?

Why the hell was he even back after all this time, anyway?

He probably needs something. There was no other explanation.

The phone buzzes once again, and another message pops on the screen.

Unknown: I tried giving you time to text me back, but if I don't hear from you soon, I might have to do something you won't like. You don't want me to call Nixon, do you? Call me.

I grit my teeth as I read the message. He thinks he can threaten me? With Nixon, of all people? If my brother were to find out Dad's back, he'd go completely livid.

Shit. That's what he wants.

My fingers tighten around the phone as I type back.

Me: Leave Nixon out of it.

Unknown: You know what's the price for that.

Yeah, I damn well knew.

There was always a price for loving a man like my dad.

Spotting the SUV parked in front of the house, I quickly pull my car into the driveway and rush out.

"Dad?" I yell, looking around the first floor, but there is nobody.

He's here. His car is outside, I chastise, climbing up the stairs.

Although I went to my room, I could still hear Dad and Nixon fighting. It was hard not to when they were screaming at the top of their lungs at each other. Then he stormed out. When he didn't come back, I feared the worst. But he's back.

"Dad?" I call out as I move down the hallway.

When there's no answer, I tentatively push open the door to the guest room where my dad's been staying ever since he came back, only to come to a stop.

"What are you doing?"

Dad looks up from the suitcase propped on the bed, the guilt shining on his face.

"Jade, baby..."

He takes a step closer, but I move back, shaking my head, my eyes still glued to his suitcase.

He was leaving.

Again.

"What. Is. Going. On?" I ask each word coming out clipped.

"You saw what happened. I can't... I can't stay here. Nixon doesn't want me here."

Nixon doesn't want him here?

"What about me, Dad? Huh? What about me? What about what I want? Doesn't that matter?"

"Jade, it's just..."

"What?"

"Too hard. It's just too hard."

The words he told me all those months ago when we found

out Mom's cancer was terminal, and there was nothing that could be done echo in my head.

"I should have known better," I let out an unamused huff as tears threaten to fall. Clenching my fingers, so my nails dig into my skin, I fight them, refusing to let him see me cry over him. Not again. "Nixon was right. Go. Leave. That's what you're best at, after all."

Only this time, I don't let him do it first.

No, turning on the balls of my feet, I leave. The sound of the door slamming follows me as I walk away from my father first and don't look back.

Looking up, I see Nixon standing by the counter and flirting with Yasmin, a big smile on his face.

My big brother is finally getting back to the person he was before our lives crashed down. He's finally happy, and he's been killing it on and off the field. There is no way I'll let our father mess with that.

I didn't doubt Nixon could deal with him, but doing so would mess with his head. I still remember that fight they had just after Mom died, and Dad showed up in our lives, drunk and expecting us to welcome him with open arms. After he'd been gone for months, leaving us to deal with Mom being sick and watching her die before our very eyes.

I wanted to forgive him. I would have done it, too. My mom was gone, and I just wanted that little bit of peace and stability back. I wanted my *dad*. What I hadn't realized was that he was already completely lost to me.

So yeah, while Nixon could do it, I didn't want him to. I wanted him to be happy. He deserved it, dammit. He had his whole life at the tips of his fingers, and knowing Dad's back could put that in jeopardy.

"Jade?" A hand touches my shoulder, making me jump in surprise. My phone falls out of my hand and lands face down on the counter, making all heads turn toward me. Just what I needed, attention.

Nixon frowns as he looks from the phone to me. "Are you okay?"

I shrug Prescott's hand off of me, my heart still beating wildly in my chest. "Fine. I have to go." Grabbing my things, I slide off the chair. "I have work to do."

"Are you going to shoot?" Yasmin asks. "Did you get an idea?"

"I—" I shake my head. "Not yet. I'm still thinking."

"Well, I'm sure you'll come up with something good that will get you that gallery exhibition."

Nixon shakes his head at Yas and gives me a big grin. "Smalls can do way better than good. She's going to kill it. You better mark the calendar for when the exhibition is."

The pride and trust in my brother's eyes—the *love*—are my undoing. There is no way I'll let our father destroy everything that he's been working so hard to get.

"I guess we'll have to wait and see." I glance over the group. "I'll see you guys later?"

"Don't forget about brunch."

I roll my eyes and start for the door. "How could I?"

"I mean it, Smalls."

I lift my hand in a wave, pushing the front door open. "Yeah, yeah."

As soon as the door is closed behind me, I let out a shaky breath and unlock my phone just as another message comes through.

Unknown: What will it be Jade? You or Nixon?

As if there's even a choice.
Me: You'll leave him alone.
Me: Tell me when and where, and I'll meet you.

I push open the door, letting my eyes adjust to the darkness. It took me a while to find the bar Dad suggested, which was good. I knew if I wanted to do this, I couldn't have it anywhere that I might by chance stumble on my brother or anyone else who might recognize me in the process because if Nixon were to find out what I was about to do... Well, he'd probably kill me.

Too late to worry about that now.

I take in the space around me. The high tables, dark wooden bar, barely visible splotches on the floor that could be either from spilled beer, based on the stale smell in the air, or dried blood from some fight. Considering the crowd in here, the jury was still out.

A few older guys who spotted me the moment I entered the bar are still staring at me, making an uncomfortable shiver run down my spine. I make a point of ignoring them, grateful for the jeans and sweater I'm wearing because I don't need any more unsolicited eyes on me. I walk through the bar and quickly scan over the patrons until I find a familiar face seated in one of the booths in the back.

Thank fuck.

He looks up, his dark eyes meeting mine as I make my way to him, sliding into the booth opposite him. He looks just like I remember, and yet, not. The last year hasn't been kind to Dad. His shoulders are slouched forward, wrinkles around his eyes more defined, and the corner of his mouth is cemented in an eternal frown. His golden hair is streaked with more gray than the last time I'd seen him, and there is a week's worth of stubble covering his jaw.

"You came."

I cross my arms over my chest and glare at him. "You didn't leave me much of a choice, now, did you?"

"Jade..." he drawls exasperatedly.

"Father," I reply in the same manner, raising my brow.

His fingers curl around the glass of amber liquid sitting in front of him. Whiskey, most likely. It was always his drink of choice.

"I just want to talk. Is that so much to ask?"

"Considering you didn't find it in you to talk to me for the past..." I tap my finger against my chin, pretending to think. "Eighteen months, was it?" I shrug. "Whatever. Either way, I don't see the reason for your sudden need to change that."

"I've missed you. Can't a father miss his daughter?"

I let out a humorless laugh, "You didn't seem to have the same problem when you turned your back on your kids and walked away. *Twice.*"

Call me petty and bitter all you want, but I refuse to be made a fool all over again. Father or not.

He runs his hand over his face, and it doesn't escape my notice of how tired he looks. How *old*.

Ever since I was born, I was Daddy's little girl. My dad was my whole world, my hero. Until the moment that he walked away from our family when I was eighteen, leaving me alone to help Mom while she was fighting cancer for the second time. For a while, I hoped that it was just a rough patch, and we would get through it. After all, Mom beat it once. I was convinced she would do it again until it became apparent that she couldn't.

I didn't lose just my mother; I lost both my parents in a

matter of months. The only difference was one was taken from me, and the other chose to walk away.

He never looked back, never called, not until she died.

I wanted to forgive him, I was ready to forgive him and take him back, but then he walked out of my life once again.

After that, I swore I would never let anybody else have so much power over me to hurt me over and over again.

Then why are you here, huh?

"You know why I left. I couldn't deal with..."

"You couldn't deal?" I interrupt him, my voice hitching to the point heads start to turn our way. "*You* couldn't deal? Is this a joke now?"

"You know how much I loved your mother. I couldn't watch her die."

"You left before she got her terminal diagnosis!" I hiss. Leaning against the table, I point my finger at him. "Don't you dare talk to me about love. You didn't leave because of anything else but your own selfishness, so don't you dare put this on her."

He extends his hand, placing it over mine. "Jade..."

I flinch back, pulling it out of his reach. "No. You don't get to Jade-me. I'm not a vulnerable little girl who just wants her family back. Not any longer, *Dad*. It was your choice to stay back..."

"Because I wasn't doing well, Jadie. I was in a really bad headspace..."

"Oh, and I wasn't? Do you think my life was all roses and giggles two years ago? I was there with her day in and day out. I watched her *die* before my very eyes, so don't you dare tell me you're the only one who had it bad. Don't you dare tell me you're the only one who loved her. I needed her more than you did."

I still do, but she's gone and not coming back. And there is nobody I can ask for help that'll understand. Not like she did.

Tears prickle my eyes, and my throat tightens as I struggle to breathe. I try to suck in a breath, but I can't.

"Jade..."

"No." I shake my head, pushing the thoughts of Mom out of my head and shoving them back in the little box at the back of my mind. "What do you want? Why are you here?"

After all, that's why we're here. He wants something, and I have to listen so he can go back to wherever the fuck he came from and leave my life in peace.

"Well," Dad lowers his gaze, his fingers gripping the glass so hard his knuckles have turned white. "The last year has been really hard and..."

I snort, "You think you're the only one?"

He looks at me, his lips pressed in a tight line. "The company is bankrupt, Jade. I've lost everything."

I watch him for a moment, the puzzle pieces finally falling into place. "You want money."

"I need help to get to my feet. Just a..."

I shake my head, letting out a humorless chuckle. "You're actually asking for money. You're despicable." Abruptly, I push to my feet. "I'm done here. Don't bother calling or texting again. Because the next time, I will let you call Nixon, and we both know how that'll go once he finds out what you want."

Without another look at my father, I turn my back to him and walk away without an ounce of remorse.

My heart is beating a mile a minute, my chest rising and falling rapidly. The door closes shut behind me with a loud *bang* as I start walking back toward campus. Since I didn't have my car, I took an Uber here, but I was too angry and agitated to wait for a car to get here and risk my father going after me.

Who does he think he is? Coming back out of nowhere and throwing demands at me left and right? Threatening me with

Nixon? Asking for money? *Money,* of all things! Not to reconcile, not to ask how we're doing. He wants money.

Screw him.

I'm so done with allowing men to come into my life and disrupt everything I've worked so hard to rebuild. I'm done.

With the back of my hand, I wipe away the tears from my cheeks.

Just... done.

Bright lights come from my back, the soft purr of an engine coming closer. I expect the car to pass by, but it slows down instead.

This time, my heart starts beating faster, but for a completely different reason as the panic sets in.

I turn around, trying to see who's in the car, but the bright beam of the headlights is blinding me.

The door of the car opens, and I take a step back.

"Jade?"

Chapter 26

PRESCOTT

"Is it just me, or is Coach getting more intense in his old age?" I ask Nixon as I push the front door open. The cool night air hits me in the face, and I welcome the chill that runs down my spine. It's late September, and the nights are coming sooner, temperatures dropping lower. It was a nice reprieve from the intense heat over the summer.

"He knows we can do better, and that's why he's pushing us so vigorously."

"I just think the guy likes to torture us," I mutter, that familiar jab of pain going through my leg with every step I make.

Today's practice was more intense than ever. It's like nothing we did was good enough, and Coach just kept on pushing and pushing until he finally called it quits almost an hour after our usual end time.

"There is that too," Nixon lets out a soft chuckle as we get to our cars.

I throw my bag into the backseat, pulling open the driver's door before glancing at him. He's still just standing there, a contemplative look on his face.

"You not planning to go home tonight?"

Nixon gives his head a shake as if he needs to clear his mind. "No, it's not that. It's just..." He runs his fingers through his hair. "Did Jade seem strange to you?"

My fingers tighten around the metal as I watch my best friend over the hood of my car. "Strange how?" I ask slowly, unsure of where this is going.

Was today strange? Did we somehow mess up? Does he know there is something going on between us? That I slept with his little sister behind his back? Repeatedly.

Sweat coats my palms as the nerves set in.

Get a grip, dude. There is no way for him to know.

"I don't know. She just acted... strange." He lets out a sigh, "Maybe I just worry too much about her. But she isn't making it easy."

"What do you mean?"

We generally don't talk about Jade, but I can see something is worrying him, and the team can't have his attention divided.

Or at least that's what I keep telling myself.

It's not like I want to know more about her.

This isn't what this thing between us is. It's just a hookup—a temporary release with mutual satisfaction.

"She spent the summer partying her way through New York and just continued the same way once she came to campus. For fuck's sake, she took off her underwear in front of a bunch of people and drank a shot from *your* mouth! I'm pretty sure she thinks I don't know the half of it, but when your sister gets back to you only once a week, if that, you learn how to find the answers you need yourself."

"You've been stalking her online?"

Nixon glares at me. "If you had a younger sibling, you'd know what I mean."

His words are like a punch to my gut. They shouldn't be,

but they are. I can feel the ringing in my ears as the memories from different times come surging back, but I push them back as I try to concentrate on what Nixon is telling me.

"I'm not only her big brother but the only family she has left. If I don't worry about her, who will, you know? I asked her to come back home with Yas and me for the summer, but she didn't want to talk about it, just said she was going with Grace to the city. She hasn't been home once since coming to college, and I worry about her. She keeps saying she's fine, but the way she acts…"

"Maybe she just needs time to deal with everything that has happened?"

I remember the funeral. It all came out of nowhere since Nixon didn't tell anybody that his mom was sick, so nobody knew until Hayden sent out a group message with the funeral details. Nixon was livid because his dad showed up drunk, but Jade? It was like she wasn't there at all. She was standing next to her brother and Yasmin, her face pale, those blue eyes lifeless as she stared at nothing, tears streaming down her face.

A ghost.

"That's the thing, when I ask her about it. She says she's fine, but she doesn't want to talk about it. Doesn't want to talk about Mom or what happened."

"People deal with pain in different ways." I should know it better than anyone. Not that I say that out loud. "She'll be fine. Just give her time."

"I guess you're right. Maybe I'm just tired." Nixon lets out a sigh, his fingers drumming over the hood of his car. "I'll see you tomorrow morning?"

"Sure thing."

With a nod, he gets inside his car. I watch him as he pulls on his seatbelt. The worry lines were still etched deep between his brows.

Is he right? Is there something that he's missing? That we're missing?

My phone rings, so I pull it out, my jaw clenching when I see the name on the screen.

Dad.

We haven't talked since that disastrous dinner last week, and I was fine with that. More than fine, actually. But, of course, he had to go and ruin it.

Silencing my phone, I toss it in the car just as Nixon pulls away. I slide into my seat, my leg sighing in relief when I take the pressure off it. Leaning over the console, I open the compartment and grab the pill bottle from inside, shaking two pills into my hand and tossing them into my mouth. My throat bobs as I swallow, the pills leaving a bitter taste in their wake.

The screen of my phone lights up again, drawing my attention.

You kill everyone you love, Dad's accusation echoes in my mind, more vivid than ever since the conversation with Nixon brought back old memories.

Old guilt.

I close my eyes, my head falling back as I try to tune it out.

I should go home, try and get some rest before our away game, or even get some work done since there's a pile of homework and reading material already waiting for me, but as my fingers curl around the steering wheel, I know I won't do either.

I need to get out of here.

I need to forget.

And there's only one place where I can do that.

Turning the key, I listen to that familiar purr of the engine that has my blood start pumping faster in anticipation. The heavy beat of rock fills the cabin as I put the car in drive, and then I press the gas.

I try to keep my speed within the limits while I'm inside the campus, but the moment I'm out, I press my foot harder, watching the hand on my speedometer rise.

My fingers tighten on the steering wheel, the adrenaline coursing through me as I speed down the road.

This.

This is exactly what I need.

The music. The road. The speed.

The only place in which I can lose myself. The only place where nothing else matters. Not football. Not my parents. And definitely not the promise that's haunting me.

I let my mind empty of everything as I take curve after curve until my headlights illuminate on a person walking down the side of the road.

What the hell?

My foot lands on the break, hard, the car slowing down as I come nearer and get a look at the idiot walking by the road in the middle of the night.

And not just any person.

I'd know that stubborn set of shoulders in a leather jacket anywhere.

Fucking hell.

Bringing the car to a complete stop, I unbuckle my seatbelt and open the door. I slide my foot out just as she turns around to face me, a trace of panic flashing in her blue irises as she looks at me.

"What the fuck, Jade?"

Jade blinks, her eyes narrowing as she tries to focus. In hindsight, I should have probably turned off my headlights so that they wouldn't blind her, but I was too stunned to find Jade walking down the side of the road all alone in the middle of the night like the lunatic that she is.

Did Jade seem strange to you? Nixon's earlier words flash in my head, but I push them back, too angry to deal with that now.

"Prescott?"

"Yes, Prescott. Although it could have been some kind of serial killer for all that you know. Are you freaking insane? What were you thinking?"

"It's not..." she tries to protest, but I'm too riled up to listen to her.

Seriously, this fucking girl will be the death of me.

"Do you have a death wish or something?" I grab her shoulder, giving her a shake. "Somebody could have run you over, or God knows what else might have happened. You shouldn't—"

"Fuck you, Wentworth," she hisses, shoving me away. She turns on the balls of her feet, but I grab her wrist before she can take a step, pulling her back to my chest.

Jade tries to struggle out of my hold, but I just tighten my arms around her. I lean down and press my lips to her ear.

"You're not going anywhere," I whisper, a strand of her hair tickling my nose.

Securing my hold on her, I lift her and take her to the passenger's side of my car. My knee protests the extra weight, but I grit my teeth and push through.

"I'm not going anywhere with you," Jade jabs her finger into my chest as soon as I let her down. "I'm so sick of big, overly opinionated men who think they can boss me around."

I pull open the door and place my other hand on the roof of my car, effectively caging her in. "Well, tough luck, doll, 'cause I'm not letting you walk back to campus. So you either get that sweet ass of yours into the car, or I'm going to put you there. Your choice."

Jade grits her teeth, her eyes throwing daggers at me. "I hate you."

I just tilt my head to the side. "The feeling's mutual."

"I'm quite capable of walking back home on my own."

Seriously, does she always have to be so stubborn?

"I. Don't. Fucking. Care," I repeat, this time slower. Maybe if I talk to her like the toddler she's trying to be, she'll finally understand. "Get in the car."

"I don't want to!"

"This isn't some stupid game, Jade. Something could happen to you, and how the fuck could I look your brother in the face knowing I was there, and I left you because you were acting like a stubborn idiot?!" I yell at her, panic and fear making my gut clench as I slam my fisted hand against the metal.

Jade flinches, and a part of me feels bad. A teeny-tiny part that I shove back because the other part? The other part is suffocated by the possibility of everything that could go wrong.

I inhale deeply, trying to calm myself before continuing, my voice softer this time around. "So stop acting like a brat, and let me drive you back to campus."

Something passes over her face, but she schools her features before I can try to decipher it. "Fine."

I watch her slide into the car. She grabs the door handle, and pulls the door out of my grasp, shutting it with way more force than necessary.

Letting out a shaky breath, I run my hand over my face. "How do I get myself in situations like this?"

Shaking my head, I walk around the car and slide into my seat, locking the doors as soon as I'm inside.

Jade turns to me, her eyes narrowed. "Seriously? You put the child's lock on me?"

"I'm not putting it past you to jump out of the car. God knows you're crazy enough to do it," I mutter as I shift the car into drive. "What were you doing here anyway?"

We're on the outskirts of Blairwood, a good thirty minutes by foot from our place, if not more. I usually go driving in this direction since it helps me avoid cops and people, so I can let my baby go without worry. There is no reason for her to be here.

Jade lifts her chin and turns her gaze out the window, clearly ignoring me.

Fine, we can do it her way.

I keep my eyes on the road, my hands gripping the steering wheel so tightly that my knuckles are white as the car accelerates down the road. The music is the only buffer between us.

Every once in a while, my eyes dart toward her. I want to ignore her, but it's hard when she's right there. Her presence, her *scent,* fill the small confines of the car.

"Where are we going?" Jade asks as I pass the turn toward our neighborhood. "You said you were taking me home, and in case you missed it, that's that way."

"I didn't miss it."

She grits her teeth. "Just take me home, Wentworth!"

I glance toward the passenger seat. "Being a brat doesn't look good on you."

Her eyes narrow, and I feel that she'd probably strangle me if I weren't the one driving. Shifting my attention back to the road, I continue driving until I spot the small, familiar sign. I turn the blinker on, slowing the car down so I can shift to a bumpy narrow road, making my way up the hill. It takes us another fifteen minutes, but we finally get to the spot.

Not waiting for Jade, I unlock the car and get out. Running my fingers through my hair, I walk to the front of the car and lean against the hood, taking the first deep breath in what feels like forever.

I'm not sure how long I just stand there all alone when I hear the car door open. Feet touch the gravel, making it crunch, and then Jade slides up next to me.

"What is this place?" she asks, her eyes glued to the bright lights of Blairwood shining in the distance.

"Just somewhere I go when I need to be alone."

Slowly she turns around, those blue eyes fixing on me. My mouth turns dry as she just stares at me. So I stare back, not uttering a word.

"I never heard of this place."

I shrug. "I'm not sure if many people know about it."

The little lookout is hidden from view and is barely big enough to fit one car. I stumbled upon it completely by accident when I got lost my freshman year of college, and ever since, it's been a place I would come to when I needed some space.

"Huh…" With that, she turns around.

"That's all you've got? Huh?"

"What do you want me to say? It's just weird."

"What is?"

"You. Just when I think I'm starting to know you, something else comes up that throws me off guard."

You're not the only one.

The words are on the tip of my tongue, but I bite them back, refusing to voice them out loud. I don't get this. I don't get *us*.

What the hell are we even doing? Sex should be easy, straightforward. At least, it used to be. We get some good old-fashioned exercise, and then we go our separate ways. But there isn't anything easy about this, far from it. If it were any other girl, I would have never brought her here. To my safe place. I know I wouldn't. But this is *Jade*. I didn't even think about it. I just came here. I don't know what to do about it. What to do about her. And it's scary as fuck.

"What were you doing out there tonight?"

Jade raises her brow. "I could ask you the same question."

I press my lips together.

Jade chuckles, "That's what I thought." She moves closer until she's standing between my legs. She raises her hand, her fingers tracing my cheek, my jaw, and my lip. Her gaze falls to my mouth, her pupils dilating. "We suck at talking, Wentworth, but there's one thing we're very good at."

"Oh, and what's that?" I ask, nipping at her finger.

The storm in her eyes turns molten.

"Screwing," she whispers. That one soft word makes goosebumps rise on my skin.

Her mouth is on mine before I can register it. Her hand slides to my nape, her fingers sinking into my hair and tugging at the short strands as her tongue dips into my mouth.

Letting out a loud groan, I push off the hood, my fingers digging into her hair and tugging her head back.

In one swift movement, I turn us around and lift her against the hood of my car, not once breaking the kiss.

Jade's legs fall open, giving me ample space to settle between her thighs. I slide my hand up her leg, my mouth devouring hers as I lower her onto the hood. One lean leg wraps around my waist, pulling me closer to her. Our bodies collide, and she rubs herself against my straining cock.

And *fuck*. I can feel her heat even with two pairs of jeans separating us, which only makes me grow harder.

It makes me crazy, the way I want her, the way *she* makes me want her.

Sliding my hand higher, I grip her ass and hold her closer to me, rubbing myself against her. I tighten my grip on her head, breaking our kiss. I graze my teeth over her raw bottom lip, pulling back just slightly. We're both panting hard, our hot breaths mingling together.

"Prescott," Jade moans in protest, rolling her hips against me.

"Hmm..." I trace my nose over the column of her neck, placing a kiss in the hollow of her shoulder, just where I know she loves it. Her whole body shudders, her fingers digging into my shoulders.

"Don't play and fuck me already."

"Oh, you'd like that wouldn't you?"

Jade tries to pull back, but I ignore her and continue tracing small kisses over her neck and cleavage. "I just said that, didn't I?"

"Mhmm... I'm just not ready to do it." *No, first, I want to have my fun.*

I raise her shirt and place a kiss on the soft skin of her stomach before moving even lower.

"Prescott!"

"What?" I pull back, quirking my brow at her. "I always wanted to do this."

"You did this. Yesterday."

"But I never did it against my car."

I slide my hands down the side of her legs and pull off her boots, then in the same movement, I tug down her jeans and panties, letting them drop to the ground.

"I always wanted to fuck somebody against my Mustang. Guess tonight that fantasy will finally come true. But first..." I rub my hands over her thighs. "But first, I'm going to eat you until you scream my name."

Crouching down, I slide her legs over my shoulders and pull her to the edge of the hood, pressing my mouth against her pussy. My tongue dips between her lower lips, tasting her sweetness. Jade buckles under me at the touch, and a loud moan comes out of her lungs as her hips arch up, feeding me more of her.

That's my girl.

My hands slide to her ass, massaging the soft globes as I hold her closer to me and eat her out like I'm a starving man, and she's my last meal.

"So fucking sweet."

I flick my tongue over her clit, feeling the hard bud tighten at my touch. I continue teasing her like that, a flick here, a lick there, until she's thrashing in my arms, begging me for more. Then I suck her clit into my mouth, slipping two of my fingers inside her.

"God," she hisses, her fingers running through my hair and pulling me closer to her as I fuck her with my fingers. "Harder. I need…"

"I know, doll. I know."

I add another finger, thrusting them inside her. The fit is tight, so freaking tight, but she's dripping for me. I hook my fingers, hitting that sweet spot inside her just as I suck on her clit, hard.

"Shit, Prescott."

She comes so hard and fast I don't see it coming. Her pussy clenches around my fingers, not letting them go, her hands pulling me closer to her.

Slowly, her grip on me releases, and I pull back, placing a kiss on her inner thigh before standing up. My knee protests, but I barely notice it since my dick takes precedence.

I lick my lips as I watch her. She's splayed on my car, her sweater and jacket barely covering her nakedness. Cheeks flushed, lips parted, eyes wide.

Her tongue darts out, sliding over her lower lip. Her chest rises and falls as she struggles for a breath, her eyes meeting mine. "That's the best you've got?"

A grin spreads over my mouth. "Oh, I'm not done with you yet."

I grab her hand and turn her around, her ass sticking in the air, my hand splayed over her stomach as I pulled her back to my chest. "Brace your hands against the hood, baby," I whisper in her ear.

For once, she doesn't protest but does as I say. I slide my

hand into my back pocket and pull out my wallet. I flip it open, ready to grab the condom, only to come up empty.

What the—

"Fuck."

Fuck, fuck, fuck.

Jade looks over her shoulder, those dark eyes staring at me. "What?"

"I don't have a condom. I used the last one..."

When we were together, and I was so lost in her, I never thought to replace it.

Shit.

I start to pull back, the shift making my dick press even harder against the zipper of my jeans. Jade grabs my hand, stopping me.

"I'm on the pill."

I blink, unsure if I heard her correctly. If I understood what she was telling me.

I shake my head. "We shouldn't..."

"I haven't been with anybody else since the summer. And I always make sure to use protection."

It's irrational, this anger that swells inside me at the sound of her words. I know there were other guys for her, just like there were other girls for me. But the last thing I want to think about is another dude's hands, and other parts, on Jade's body when every cell in my body screams *mine*.

"I haven't either, but..."

It's stupid, and I can't even explain it. In the last few weeks, Jade Cole has gotten under my skin. But if we do this, it feels like some invisible line will be crossed. A line we'll never be able to uncross.

Jade's hand slips to the back of my neck. She pulls me closer, her lips brushing against mine as she whispers: "I want to feel you inside me, without anything else between us. I've been thinking about it ever since spring break."

A shudder runs down my spine, and I can feel my cock twitch.

"I thought you hated me."

"I do. You're annoying and infuriating, and you drive me crazy more often than not." She turns around, her other hand brushing against my chest. "But I can't deny that I'm attracted to you. A part of me thinks that hating you makes this all feel ten times better than it would have otherwise been." Her hand slides down all the way to my pants, her fingers quickly undoing the button and pulling the zipper down. Jade slips her hand inside, her fingers wrapping around the hard length of my cock and pulling it out. I hiss softly, my eyes falling shut as her lips brush against mine. "Fuck me, Prescott."

It's like something in me snaps at her words. I turn her around, pressing her hand against the hood, as my leg slips between hers, parting her thighs. My hand goes to her belly as I lean against her back, bending her over the hood of my car, and slip inside her in one swift movement.

We both moan in unison as my cock is enveloped by her wet heat. Completely bare inside her. I grip her hip with my free hand, my fingers digging into her soft skin as I try to brace myself so I don't spill inside her like a twelve-year-old boy watching porn for the very first time.

She feels good.

Too damn good.

Hot and tight, like she was made for me and only me.

"You better hold on tightly, doll."

Jade glances over her shoulder. Her hair is messy, her lips puffy, cheeks flushed. The corner of her mouth tips upward. "Give me your worst, Wentworth."

So I do.

I pull out and slam right back in, sliding deeper than before. I fuck her like I've never fucked anybody else. My hand slides down, fingers finding her clit. I tweak the little bud as I thrust inside her. Her pussy tightens around me, sucking me even deeper as the orgasm builds inside me.

I lean my chin against her shoulder, my lips brushing against the shell of her ear. "Come for me, doll," I whisper, pressing my lips against her neck, my thrusts growing harder, faster.

"F-fuck, I..."

With one final tweak, I feel her suck me in. Her pussy tightens around me, and I swear I can see stars.

Jade's body goes slack in my arms, so I pull her closer to me as my hips jam harder inside her. Burrowing my head in the crook of her neck, I let out a groan as my own orgasm slams into me, and I come inside her.

Chapter 27

JADE

Lifting my camera, I look through the viewfinder and slightly zoom in on the girl lying in the grass and looking up at the sky before I press the shutter. The familiar *click* signals that the photo is saved just as the girl turns to her belly and looks at the guy that's lying next to her. *Click.* A smile spreads over her lips at whatever he says, and she raises her hand to brush away a strand of his hair. *Click.*

Letting my camera drop, I pick up my coffee and continue on my way, my eyes taking in the park around me as I walk through campus.

I still haven't figured out what to do about the theme Professor Reyes wants us to follow when it comes to our project, but I was determined to find it one way or the other. If inspiration wasn't coming, I was not about to twiddle my thumbs and wait for it to slap me over the head.

Tilting my head back, I look at the darkening sky. The sun was starting to set slowly, so want it or not, I was done for today.

Dropping the empty cup into the bin, I snap a few photos of the sunset around campus as I make my way back to the apartment.

Pulling my keys out, I unlock the front door, only to be greeted by the sound of laughter. I stop in the doorway of the living room, finding my friends gathered inside, and I feel a pang of what feels a lot like jealousy.

Which is ridiculous.

I'm not jealous of my friends.

I don't even want what they have.

"Hey, you're home!" Grace smiles at me from Mason's lap. "What were you up to?"

"Just shooting." I look over the group. "What are you guys doing?"

Rei and Zane come from the kitchenette, matching green smoothies in their hands as they sit on the couch, Zane's free hand thrown over Rei's shoulders as he plays with her hair.

"We just ordered takeout. Wanna eat with us?"

"I ate," I lie. "I think I'll just go edit these photos. See if any of them are good enough to submit for that competition."

"Still no luck with figuring it out?" Rei asks, taking a sip of the green stuff. What she puts in that I don't even want to ask.

"It's barely October," I shrug. "There's more than enough time."

"Maybe one of todays will be the winner," Grace says, turning her attention to Mason.

"Maybe." I tap my fingers against the doorway, itching to get out of there. "I'll see you later?"

"If you change your mind about the food, come back out!" Grace calls out as I make my way down the hallway and into my room.

And be their fifth wheel? I think not.

Sliding into my room, I close the door behind me and drop my things on the bed. Grabbing a hoodie and a pair of clean underwear, I take them into the bathroom and start to pull off my shirt when a jab of pain goes through my arm and into my side.

The reflection in the mirror catches my attention, making me stop in my tracks. Two of the bumps under my arm have grown bigger since the last time and are swollen and red. Slowly, I let the shirt drop into the hamper before I unhook the bra, only to be greeted by a purple bruise on my breast.

A knot forms in my throat as I just stare at my reflection.

Maybe it's Prescott—

Even as the words cross my mind, I know they're a load of bullshit. Prescott didn't do this. I barely even let him touch my breasts. Just the idea of it had my stomach rolling. That somebody could touch my breasts... How would they not know? And what would I tell him if he found out?

No, he could never touch them.

Turning my back to the mirror, I step into the shower and quickly wash up, making sure not to look at my reflection before putting on the clothes I had brought earlier.

Grabbing my laptop, I climb onto my bed and get to work.

Shifting my weight, I curl my leg underneath me. My mouse moves over the screen as I work on the latest batch of photos I took this week in preparation of my scheduled dark room time.

Or maybe, I'm just ignoring the fact that I have yet to start reading the next book for my English lit class. The jury is still out.

Nobody could ever confuse me for a geek. I love photography. I love taking photos, trying to figure out the best angle and the perfect light, capture just the right moment to turn a second into eternity. Studying, on the other hand... It's not like I can't do it. I just find it boring as hell. Hence me leaving it for the very last moment.

Point in question...

Sucking at my lower lip, I adjust the lighting on the photo

just the tiniest bit before giving the screen a critical glance. Good, but it still feels like it's missing...

A slight rattling sound breaks me out of my thoughts. I pause, listening. But when there's nothing else, I save the photo only to hear it again.

Not even rattling; more like a skitter.

Clank. Clank. Clank.

Placing the laptop on the bed, I get to my feet and walk slowly to my window. I look around, expecting a bird or something, but there's nothi—

Clank.

I frown at the windowsill.

A stone?

I look down, my eyes widening, when I see the person responsible for the noise. Pushing away the curtain, I open the window.

"What are you doing here?" I whisper yell, looking left and right, but there's nobody around.

Except him.

Prescott is standing just underneath my window, a duffle bag over his shoulder as he lazily throws a pebble in the air before catching it.

"What does it look like I'm doing?"

"That's what I want to know." I look down at my watch. *Almost midnight? Where did the time go?* "Trying to wake up half the building?"

I tilt my head back, praying to all the gods that Grace and Rei didn't hear anything because I'm in no mood to explain what Prescott Wentworth, of all people, is doing standing outside of my bedroom in the middle of the night.

"More like trying to get your attention. Took you long enough, by the way."

"I was working. Hell, for all you know, I could have earbuds in."

He quirks his brow in that I-know-it-all manner I hate. "Did you?"

"No, but that's beside the point. Don't you know about that thing called a phone?"

Prescott pretends to think about it. "Haven't heard of it."

"A magical thing, really." I lean my elbow against the windowsill, propping my chin on my palm. "You type in a number and press call, and it'll connect you directly to the person you want to talk to."

"Smartass."

"I have my moments." I tilt my chin at him. "So what *are* you doing here? Weren't you out of town?"

Shit.

The words slip out of my mouth before I can think them through.

Prescott knows it too. A smug smile tugs at the corner of his mouth as he lifts his brow at me. "Following my schedule, doll?"

"As if," I scoff. "My brother's on your team, in case you forgot."

A shadow falls over his face at the mention of Nixon. "No, I didn't forget."

Then again, if I were screwing my best friend's little sister behind said best friend's back, I'd feel like shit too. Not that Nixon has anything to do with whatever's going on between us.

Fucking. Screwing. Or any other verb you want to use.

Nothing more or nothing less.

Deciding a change of subject is in order, I lift my brow at him. "So, are you planning to give me an answer or what?"

From the looks of it, he probably just came back to campus not that long ago.

"I was walking home when I saw your light was still on."

My stomach does a little flip. It's stupid and completely unreasonable, but it's there. "Want company?"

I graze my teeth over my lower lip, letting it pop out. "I guess so," I shrug, trying not to seem too eager.

Because I'm not.

Eager.

Not at all.

"Catch."

"Wha—"

Before I can blink, he tosses his duffle in the air. I'm so surprised it almost slips my fingers, but I manage to catch the strap at the very last second. The damn thing is heavy as hell too. Tugging it inside, I let it drop on the floor before shoving my head out of the window again, but Prescott isn't down there. Nope, he's holding onto the ladder that's not that far from my window and climbing up.

The ladder creaks under his weight, but he quickly makes his way up.

"What are you doing?"

"What does it look like I'm doing?" he grumbles. "Getting inside."

"You know we have that thing called a door? Another one of those magical things. You push it open and *enter* inside like a normal human being."

He quirks his brows at me. "What about your roommates?"

I open my mouth but close it because, damn, I hate it when he's right.

"Move," he whispers, his arm reaching for the windowsill. There's about half a foot between the stairs and the window, and I watch as he hoists himself inside my room.

His gaze meets mine once he's inside, those dark eyes staring at me as he breathes hard—the material of his shirt shifts with each breath, stretching over the hard muscles and broad shoulders.

I graze my teeth over my lower lip, remembering the feel of those shoulders under my fingertips as he was eating me out on the hood of his car.

Just thinking about it has me all hot and bothered all over again. Because damn...

"Nice shirt."

I blink, my gaze dropping down, only to realize I'm wearing a Raven's hoodie.

His Raven's hoodie.

The one he gave me at the beginning of the semester, and I conveniently never gave it back.

Shit.

I completely forgot about it.

"It's a hoodie," I shrug nonchalantly. I turn around, ready to get back to my laptop when he tugs me back.

"It has my name on it."

"You want it back?" With my free hand, I grab the edge of the hoodie, ready to pull it over my head, when he grabs my hand and stops me.

"Nah, keep it. It looks better on you anyway."

And there it is again. That warm feeling that spreads over in the pit of my stomach.

Feeling uncomfortable, I shift from one foot to the other. "Well, it's big and comfy. That's the only reason why I keep it around."

"You like your things big and comfy, huh?" he smirks.

I glare at him, making my way to my bed. "I seriously don't know why I even let you in."

"Because wanting to admit it or not, you missed me." Flashing me a smile, he grabs the back of his shirt and pulls it over his head, letting it drop on the chair before he bends down and ruffles through his bag.

I lean against my pillows, watching the muscles of his back work. "In your dreams, hotshot."

My fingers itch to grab a camera and take a few shots of him. Shots that are completely different from what I did for the school paper. Something just for me.

Different scenarios go through my head when I see him pull a bottle out of the bag.

My brows pull together as I sit upright. "Are you hurt?"

Prescott looks up, panic flashing in his eyes for a split second before he nods reluctantly. "It was a rough game."

"I caught bits and pieces of it. Congrats on the win."

He drops two pills into his open palm, but before I can offer him a bottle of water he has already thrown them back and swallowed them down, letting the pill bottle drop back into the duffle before he joins me on the bed.

"What were you doing before I got here?"

"You can—"

Before I can finish, he already has the laptop turned toward him, the photo from today that I've been working on is still open on the screen.

I watch him observe it silently for a while, my stomach turning into a knot the longer he keeps quiet.

"This is beautiful, Jade," he says, slowly turning to me.

"They're a cute couple."

"It's not the couple. It's the photo, the moment, and the lighting. I don't even know, but it's all you. And it's perfect."

"Thanks. It's a good one. Not the winner, but a good one nonetheless."

Grabbing the laptop, I put it on my lap and save the photo before pulling a new one and starting the edits.

"That exhibition thing?"

He slides his hand under my shirt, fingers skimming over my naked skin in lazy circles that have goosebumps spreading over my flesh.

"Yeah, I'm still trying to figure out what I want to do."

A shudder runs through me, but I force myself to continue editing as those talented fingers continue their perusal. Up and down, down and up, higher and hi—

I can't help it. My body freezes all on its own as that reflection in the mirror flashes in my mind.

Prescott must feel it, too, because his hand comes to a stop.

I stare at my laptop, unable to look at him, but I can feel him shift on the bed.

"Jade?"

There is a beat of silence, and I'm not sure if he's trying to figure out how to ask about the elephant in the room, or if he's trying to find the safest way to bolt.

"Hey." His finger slips under my chin, and he forces me to turn and look at him. "Is this because of what happened to your mom?"

What? My heart goes into overdrive as my mind zeroes in on his words. *Does he know? Did he figure it out? Did he somehow—*

"Or maybe it's that damn party." Gently, he brushes my hair away, pressing his mouth against the side of my neck.

Wait... "What?"

"What happened at that party? Yes, I came there in time, but what happened? It's messed up. Either way, it's okay if you don't want to talk about it. But I just want to know where we stand. I'm not going to do something that you don't want me to, Jade."

He doesn't know about it.

I let out a shaky breath as the realization hits me.

He doesn't know.

"It's not that, it's just... weird. I guess. I can't explain it."

"So, no touching your boobs." He nods. "Anything else?"

I shake my head. "Everything else is fine."

Better than fine.

"Okay," he whispers, his mouth brushing against mine. "Now, show me how you work your magic."

I let out a soft chuckle, "You seriously want to watch me edit photos?"

"Yeah. It seems fun."

"Okay, it's your funeral."

I get back to my computer, editing a couple more photos before I look down, only to find Prescott passed out.

"So much for that."

I brush my fingers over his scruffy cheek as I watch him sleep. I've never seen him so... soft. So vulnerable.

"I can't very well throw you out now, can I?" Shaking my head, I close my laptop and put it on the nightstand. I lean over him and turn off the light before lying down next to him. "You better not have that godawful alarm turned on because I'll end you, Prescott Wentworth."

With that, I close my eyes and let sleep claim me too.

Chapter 28

PRESCOTT

A loud *clank* followed by a stream of curses snaps me out of my dreams. Groaning, I tighten my arms around the soft body next to mine, cursing Spencer for waking me up as I burrow my head into the crook of her neck, inhaling the sweet scent of lavender and—

My eyes snap open instantly as the smell registers in my mind.

Jade.

The memories of last night come streaming back.

Returning from the away game.

Going home.

Seeing the light in her room on as I was entering my building

Changing the direction and going there instead.

Her.

With all that messy hair and wearing only my hoodie.

My stomach twists like it did when I saw her.

And now I went and fell asleep in her bed, out of all things?

Fuck.

I'm surprised she let me sleep here. I'd have figured she'd

have woken me up and kicked me out. But something changed last night.

I'm not going to do something that you don't want me to, Jade.

I'm not sure what or how exactly, but it did, and I don't know what to think about it.

Giving her one last look, I slowly disentangle my arms from her body, making sure not to wake her up as I get to my feet. My knee groans in protest, but I don't let it stop me as I get up and grab my shirt, slipping it over my head and grabbing my duffle.

Glancing toward the door where I can still hear footsteps in the hallway, I turn toward the window and get the hell out.

"What's wrong with him?"

"He's been in a mood. *Again*. Some days, I swear I live with a fucking hormonal girl."

I lift my gaze from my plate and glare at Spencer, who's sitting across from me with Zane and Xander. The three of them are looking at me like I'm some sort of a weird experiment or something.

Zane's brows pull together. "Is it his leg?"

"More like a middle leg," Spencer smirks. "I think our boy has some girl trouble."

"You know I can hear you just fine, right?" I mutter, grabbing my beer and taking a long pull. "My leg's fine, and I'm not having any kind of trouble, especially not *girl* trouble."

No, my trouble is all woman.

A five-foot-six-inches of infuriating stubbornness and smart mouth kind of trouble.

I kind of expected Jade to text me when she woke up, but

there was nothing. No text messages. No calls. Zero. Null. Nada.

I should be happy about it. After all, she was just sticking to what we decided in the first place. This was just a hookup, nothing more, nothing less. But for whatever reason, it's been bothering me for the last few days ever since I left her and have heard nothing from her.

You don't want to hear from her.

Except for sex.

Which this is all about.

"See? He's back at it. Like a fre—"

I ball the napkin and throw it at Spencer's head. "Still can hear you." I shake my head, pushing the thoughts of Jade out of it. "Seriously, did it ever cross your mind that you're getting on my nerves, and that's the reason why I ignore you?"

Spencer blinks. "No."

"Didn't think so."

"Well, I'm really an interesting person to be around."

The ginger man snorts, "Yeah, only in your head."

"Now, you, I took you under my wing, you should be—"

"Technically, *Zane* took me under his wing. He just invites you for a ride. And it was a smart move since I'm killing it here."

I wasn't sure what exactly his story was, but last year Xander transferred to Blairwood after some shit hit the fan back in Michigan. He didn't talk about it much, and I wasn't one to probe.

Spencer waves him off. "Semantics."

"Pretty big semantics if you ask me. It kind of goes along with your big head."

"Hey, now!" Spencer protests as we all burst into laughter. "The only head that's big is the one in my pants, and I haven't heard anybody protest about it so far."

"That's because your ego is too big to hear it," Zane says, taking a pull from his beer.

I burst into laughter just as Spencer gets into it. Shaking my head, I look for the waiter to order another round, and that's when I see her.

Jade.

She pulls off her jacket and scoots up to one of the bar stools at the other end of the room. Grace is with her, as is a vaguely familiar tall guy. I watched them chat for a bit, my eyes zeroed in on her.

She looks good in a tight-fitting black tee and a pair of jeans.

More than good.

As if she can sense my gaze on her, she looks around the dark room until her gaze lands on me.

My mouth goes dry as we stare at one another, the whole room falling into the background. She's the first one to break our stare, returning her attention to her friends.

"Prescott?"

Forcing myself to turn around, I find Zane watching me with a probing gaze. "You, okay?"

"Yeah, just looking for the waiter, that's all."

Zane looks over my shoulder, and it takes all of me to stay still and not do the same as those green eyes turn to me. "Mhmm... waiter."

It's clear that he doesn't trust me for shit, but I don't bother defending myself. Instead, I look around the table. "Who wants another round?"

Chapter 29

JADE

"No." I shift to the other side, tossing the blanket aside. "No!"

I sit upright, my hand flying to my chest. I can feel the rapid *thump-thump-thump* of my heart as it beats against my chest, my lungs inhaling and exhaling rapidly.

Just a dream. I try to reassure myself as I will my breathing to calm down. *It was just a dream.*

Sliding my hand over my face, I rub at my temples, feeling the aching throbbing behind them. Letting out a sigh, I drop my hand into my lap and look around the space.

My room.

I'm in my room back home.

The anxiety grows inside of me, making my lungs tighten.

I'm home which means... I stumble upright and run out the door. My feet pound against the hardwood floors as I make my way down the hallway and pull open the door to my parent's room.

Bracing my hands against the doorway, breathing hard, I watch the still form lying on the bed. My stomach sinks, my chest tightening as I just stare at it. The room is still, that stale smell of antiseptic and death filling the space.

"No," I shake my head, tears filling my eyes. "No, no, no... This can't be happening. It's too soon. Not yet, just not yet. This isn't real. It can't be real."

Covering my mouth to stop the sobs from coming out, I make myself take a step forward. And then another one and another. Until I'm standing in front of the bed. In front of that immobile body lying there covered with the bedsheet.

I sink my teeth into my cheek until the copper taste of blood fills my mouth.

With a knot in my throat, I move forward. I suck in a long breath as I lean over the bed, my trembling fingers curling around the bedsheet.

"Just do it already," I mutter to myself.

Closing my eyes, I yank the sheet away in one swift movement.

I expect to see my mom's face.

But when I open my eyes, it's not my mom's face I see.

It's mine.

The scream gets stuck in my throat as I sit upright in my bed. Panting, I look around the room. The dark gray bed sheets, my backpack tossed on the floor, camera sitting on the desk.

In my apartment, not back home.

I'm back in my apartment.

I let out a shaky breath and rub my palm over my face as I look around, needing to reassure myself this isn't just another dream. My laptop is still open on the bed, although the screen has long gone black, and a few books are scattered around it. I spot my phone peeking from underneath one of the books, so I pull it out. Two fifty-three AM.

After we'd come home from Moore's, I didn't feel sleepy, so

I decided to get some work done, but I must have fallen asleep at some point only to be woken up by a nightmare. Or is it the premonition of the future?

An uncomfortable shiver runs down my spine, making my whole body shudder.

Shaking my head, I close the laptop and books, taking them to my desk before turning my attention back to the bed. I should try and get some sleep, but there is no way I'd be able to fall asleep.

Not after the dream I just had.

My eyes fall on the photo sitting on my nightstand. Slowly, I make my way there, picking the silver frame and taking in the photo. It was taken at Christmas, Nixon's freshman year of college. Three of us are sitting on the floor in front of the Christmas tree, big smiles on our faces. It's one of the last photos of us together. Just a few months later, Mom's cancer was back.

Another shiver runs through me as I skim my finger over her beautiful face—a face so similar to my own—before I put the frame back on the nightstand and open my closet. I roam around, trying to find a hoodie to slip on so I'm not cold, when I notice the box sitting on the top shelf. I pull it down, unsure of what's inside. The heaviness of it catches me by surprise and makes me fumble back.

"What the..."

The top opens, giving me a glimpse of pink leather. My heart does a flip in my chest as I lower the box on the floor and remove the lid to find two bright pink gloves stacked inside. I pull them out, letting my fingers slide over the sleek leather.

Nixon introduced me to kickboxing when I was sixteen. In his protective, big brother way, he wanted to make sure I knew how to defend myself when he wasn't around to do it, so I humored him, never expecting to love it as much as I did. I was never a sporty girl, but something about it called to me.

Then Mom needed me, and just like all the other things, kickboxing took a backseat to making sure my mom was taken care of.

I never even realized I brought them here.

Letting the gloves fall back into the box, I get up and take off my shirt.

Penny mentioned Emmett loved this building since it had a gym in the basement. I've never been there before, but how hard could it be to find?

From the corner of my eye, I catch my reflection in the mirror. I took off my bra the moment I got home, so I was met with naked skin.

My throat bobs as I see the lump under my arm has grown bigger. Just enough so it can be seen with the naked eye. I skim my fingers over it, sucking in a breath at the tender flesh.

Letting my hand drop, I turn my back to the reflection and grab a sports bra, shirt, and leggings from the closet. I slip on the stretchy material quickly and pick up the gloves.

My door creaks softly when I pull it open, making me cringe. I stop there for a heartbeat and just listen.

The apartment is clouded in darkness, with no sounds coming from any of the bedrooms. I quickly make my way to the front door, softly closing it as I slip into an equally quiet hallway.

When I reach the stairs, I weigh my options but decide to check the basement first since it seems like the most logical choice.

I take two steps at a time, my breathing accelerating as I make it all the way down. The automatic light turns on, blinding me slightly, but then I see the gym sign hanging on the wall next to the double door.

Bingo.

Pushing open the door, I enter the quiet space. The room is

small, but it's well equipped, including the bag hanging from the ceiling in the corner of the room.

The door shuts behind me with a resounding *click*. I glance over my shoulder before returning my attention to the bag, my heart starting to race in excitement.

I slowly slip one hand, then the other, into my gloves. Flexing my fingers, I feel the leather tighten around my palms. There is a familiarity in the movement, in the way the leather envelopes my hands, in the weight of the gloves.

I've missed this, I realize.

Stopping in front of the bag, my legs shoulder-length apart, I bounce on my feet a few times, relaxing my body before I lift my hands, keeping them close to my head.

The first jab I throw is sloppy at best. I can feel the punch bounce back at me, the bag barely moving. I pivot back, trying to keep my stance. Gritting my teeth, I throw another jab and another. With each throw, more of my lessons start coming back to me. I add a cross to the mix.

Jab-jab-cross.
Jab-cross-cross-jab.
Jab-jab-cross.
Jab-cross-hook.

My feet dance over the mat as I move effortlessly. Soon enough, I'm a sweaty, panting mess. My breathing is hard and rugged, and sweat coats my skin. Eventually, my movements grow slow since I haven't done them in forever, but even then, I don't stop. My gaze is zeroed in on the bag as I throw myself into every movement, putting all the frustration I feel, every drop of fear coursing through my body, into punch after punch.

Jab-cross-hook—

A shadow appears out of nowhere in the corner of my eye. I'm so startled, I don't think. I just react. I crouch down, sweeping my leg under the person's feet.

Wide brown eyes meet mine as he hits the mat.

"Holy shit, are you okay?" I ask, pulling off my gloves.

Prescott lets out a loud groan. "Do I look fucking okay? I think you rearranged every freaking bone in my body."

"That's because you snuck up on me." I give him a pointed look. "Again. Seriously, are you hurt?" I take in his body, looking for any sign of injury. He's wearing a loose tee and a pair of shorts, faint red lines marring his leg.

Prescott pushes upright, his face twisting in pain.

"What's wrong? Is it your leg?"

"My leg's fine," he grits through clenched teeth.

"It doesn't look fine. It looks like you're in pain." I look up, noticing the weight bench a few feet behind him. Jumping to my feet, I loop my arm through his. "Let me help you."

"I don't need help."

"Who's a brat now?" I lift my brows pointedly. "Don't be an ass, Wentworth, and let me help you." He tries to pull his arm out of mine, but I tighten my hold on him. "Up."

"So freaking bossy," he mutters, but lets me help him.

"You should be used to it by now."

I lower him to the weight bench. Prescott extends his leg, rubbing his side. He looks up, those dark eyes meeting mine. "I don't think I'll ever get used to you."

My stupid heart tightens at his gruff words.

Get a grip, Jade. You don't even like the guy.

I start to look away just as his hand slips underneath his shirt, revealing a patch of dark blue skin.

I suck in a breath, crouching down in front of him. "What the hell..."

I slip my hand next to his, pushing his shirt up and revealing a massive, nasty-ass bruise; and I just flattened him to the ground.

"What happened?" I ask, my fingers gently trailing the dark

flesh. Goosebumps appear on his skin, and I'm pretty sure he shudders.

"Practice," he shrugs, pulling the shirt down. "It was a hard hit."

"What the hell are you doing here then? Shouldn't you be in bed? Icing this?"

"I could ask you the same thing," Prescott raises his brows in a silent question. "What are you doing in the gym at three in the morning, Jade?"

I raise my chin. "I asked you first."

A frown appears between his brows, and the urge to lean forward and smooth my finger over the wrinkled lines is almost overwhelming.

"Couldn't sleep. I figured I could try to get out some of that energy in the gym."

"At three in the morning with a bruise the size of Texas covering your side?"

Something dark crosses his face, making the hairs at the nape of my neck stand tall. "It's not the first time I've worked out or played through the pain."

No, I imagine it's not. If somebody was used to the pain, it was Prescott.

"Your turn." Prescott's foot taps mine. "What brings you here in the dead of the night?"

The image of my still body lying in bed flashes before my eyes. My stomach tightens, and bile rises in my throat. I swallow it down, pushing to my feet.

"Couldn't sleep," I mutter, turning my back to him.

The dark circles under my eyes.

Crouching down, I grab my gloves and slide them back on my hands. I make my way to the bag, getting back in my stance and throwing a quick jab at the bag, and another, and another, trying to get back the peacefulness I felt as I got lost in the monotony of the familiar motions. But my mind is too restless, the memory of my nightmare too vivid in my mind.

The unnatural hollowness of my cheeks.

Prescott appears in front of me, his hands gripping the bag to steady it. My eyes meet his as I throw another combination. He holds still, steady, taking in punch after punch I deliver without uttering a word. His eyes hold mine, and something that looks a lot like understanding flashes in their depths.

The shaved head.

I throw a right hook at the bag, letting out a frustrated scream.

Another and another and another until the bag is gone, a firm chest appearing in my line of sight. Prescott grabs my wrists, holding strong as I try to tug my hands out of his grip, but he doesn't budge. Instead, he pulls me to his chest, his arms wrapping around my middle.

"It's okay," Prescott whispers softly.

I let him pull me closer, shaking my head. His fingers sprawl over my back, one hand rising to the back of my head and holding me still.

I inhale deeply, his citrusy scent overwhelming my senses. I flex my fingers, curling them around the soft material of his shirt and pulling him closer to me, letting that scent ground me. Letting him ground me.

Familiar, warm, real.

This is real.

"It's all going to be okay."

A hiccup rips out of my lungs—half sob, half manic laugh.

No, it's not.

Nothing is okay.

But I can't say it out loud. I can't admit it. I can't tell him or anybody else about my nightmares because if I do, I'd have to admit what is going on with me. I'd have to say it out loud, and if I do, it'll make it real when it's the last thing I want.

"Jade."

My name is a half groan, half plea. Prescott's palm cups my cheek, tilting my head back. Those dark eyes look at me, his thumb brushing against my cheekbone and erasing one lone tear that escaped.

"Fuck," he mutters, demons dancing in his eyes. Vivid and restless, just like mine.

Two sides of the same coin.

Magnets that can't resist the pull between each other.

That's what we are.

Completely destructive, but unable to stay away from one another.

It's like he understands me. Even when I don't say a word, he *knows*. He knows my storm. The only one who can tame it.

And that's exactly what he does. His fingers grip my face tighter, holding me still as his mouth crashes on mine, his tongue sliding into my mouth. I can taste whiskey on his tongue as it tangles with mine. Whiskey and...

Home.

With a loud groan, I slide my hand at his nape, my fingers tangling in his hair as I pull him closer to me, my lips crushing against his.

Prescott is the first to pull back. He presses his forehead against mine, his warm breath touching my face as he tries to compose himself.

"You should go back to bed. It's late."

Even before he can finish, I'm already shaking my head. "I can't. I can't go back."

Don't make me go back.

Prescott watches me silently with those dark eyes that seem

to see to my very core. I'm not sure what he sees in my expression, but finally, he nods. "Okay. What do you want then?"

What do I want?

I want to not feel.

I want to forget everything that's going on in my life right now.

I want to breathe and not feel like my lungs are going to burst on me.

But instead of saying any of it, I say something I know he can help me with: "Make it go away."

His Adam's apple bobs as he swallows. "Okay."

With one final caress of my cheek, he lets his hand fall down. Our palms meet, fingers intertwining, and then he takes a step back and pulls me along with him.

Neither of us says anything as we exit the gym and climb the stairs to his apartment. He motions for me to be quiet as he pushes the door open, and then we sneak down the hallway to his room.

I hold my breath. My heart is thumping loudly against my ribcage.

The floorboard creaks, and we both come to a stop, listening. If only I could hear anything over the sound of my heartbeat.

There's a soft noise coming from behind one of the doors, but before we can find out if Spencer's awake, Prescott's hand on mine tightens, and he pulls me into his room.

The door closes behind us, and the next thing I know, I'm pressed against hardwood, and Prescott's mouth is on mine.

Neither of us says anything as he does exactly what I asked him—makes it all go away.

Chapter 30

JADE

Snuggling closer into the warmth of the blanket, I inhale deeply, the soft citrusy scent tickling my nose. I rub it against the pillow, trying to stop the itching when the pillow wraps around me.

No. Not a pillow. Arms.

My eyes snap open, and I come face to face with Prescott.

The events of last night flash in my mind.

The nightmare.

The gym.

The sex.

Make it go away.

That's exactly what he did. With his kisses. With his hands. He made me think of him and only him until my body was spent, and my brain stopped thinking about anything but him.

And then I fell asleep.

In his bed.

With him curled around me.

Prescott shifts closer, his arms tightening around me as he burrows his head in the crook of my neck. "I can feel you thinking," he groans, his voice all raspy from sleep.

"You're awake?"

"It was better when you were asleep. Although, did you know you snore?"

I pull back so I can glare at him, not that he can see it because his eyes are firmly shut. "I don't snore."

"Yes, you do. It's all quiet and shit. Kind of cute."

"That's called *breathing*."

"Mhmm... snoring."

"I don't..." I shake my head. "It's too early for this."

"That's what I told you. Go back to sleep. I like you better when you're quietly snoring."

"I don't..."

My words are cut off when the door bursts open, and Spencer appears in the doorway. "Hey, dude, are yo—"

My lips part as horror washes over me. Prescott's eyes widen in surprise. I pull the cover over my head just as the light turns on, my heart beating a hundred miles an hour.

"Shit, I didn't know you had company," Spencer says, clearly amused by the whole situation.

The mattress dips as Prescott rises, so he's covering me from view. "You'd know if you knocked!"

"Sorry, my bad."

"Just get the hell out of here."

"I'm going, I'm going. So much for not having girl trouble," he chuckles. "Hey, is that the hellcat?"

Prescott grabs the pillow from the mattress and tosses it at his friend. "Get out, Monroe!"

"Fine, no need to get your panties in a twist, Wentworth."

The door closes, and I slowly lower the blanket, so my eyes are peeking over the edge of it.

"Is he gone?" I whisper, so only Prescott can hear me.

"He better be." He rolls to his back, his hand covering his face. "Damn, that was close."

"Tell me about it." I let out a soft chuckle, "Hellcat?"

Prescott turns his head toward me. "I told you he gave you that nickname because of the scratch marks."

"Right. I'm sorry, I—"

"Yo, Wentworth!" Spencer yells, but thankfully this time around, the door stays closed. "Are you going to the gym, or do you plan on staying in bed the whole day?"

Prescott curses silently next to me. "I should probably go. If I let him go alone, he'll tell everybody about the girl in my bed."

"He'll probably do it anyway."

"True, but this way, I can do some damage control." He pushes upright, the sheet falling down to his waist and revealing all those glorious muscles. I sink my teeth into my lower lip as I watch him get up, completely naked. His firm ass tightens, and the image of him pounding into me last night flashes in my mind making the heat bloom in my belly.

Prescott looks over his shoulder, a knowing smirk curling his lips. "If you keep watching me like that, I might just stay here instead."

"Didn't you just say you have to go?"

"I changed my mind. Who needs the gym when I have a hellcat in my bed?" he wiggles his brows.

"Stop it!" I throw a pillow at him. "Go to the gym. You know Spencer won't be able to help himself."

"I know." He groans but makes his way to the closet and grabs a pair of boxers.

I watch with regret as he pulls them on and grabs a shirt next. "What will you do?"

"Go home." I shrug. "It's still early enough for me to sneak out, and if you take your roommate with you, I won't even have to use the window."

"You could do that," Prescott nods and grabs his sweats before looking up at me. "Or you could stay. It's early, and I know how much you hate being up at the crack of dawn."

He is right. I hate being woken up, mostly because I barely get any sleep during the night. But last night, I even managed to get a few hours of blissful, uninterrupted sleep. Well, until Spencer showed up and ruined it all.

"Any plans for later?"

"I have that project to work on."

"The gallery thing?"

"Yeah, I still haven't come up with an idea."

Prescott comes to the bed and presses his hand against the headboard as he leans down, his lips brushing against mine. "You'll figure it out."

Straightening, he grabs his keys from the nightstand and takes one off. "So you can lock up before leaving."

"Oh, okay. Do you want me to leave it somewhere?"

Prescott shakes his head. "Just keep it with you. I'll see you later."

"Later?"

"You're coming to the game, right?"

"The game, right." I look at the key in my hand like it's an alien. He can't mean for me to keep it, can he? "Yeah, I'm coming to the game."

"Then I'll see you later."

PRESCOTT

"Well, boys, the unthinkable happened Wentworth has fallen."

I let out a loud groan as I hop onto the treadmill and start the machine. "We haven't been here for even two full minutes."

"What do you mean, fallen?" Nixon asks, glancing at me, but I turn my attention to the display, pressing the button to start the machine.

"He got himself a girl," Spencer explains, always the helpful one.

"I didn't get myself anything," I mutter.

"So, was that a guy you were hiding in your bed this morning?"

"You're hiding a guy in your bed?" Zane asks as he joins us.

I grit my teeth together. "I haven't been hiding a guy anywhere."

"It would be totally cool if you have," Nixon chimes in. "Just saying."

"It wasn't a guy."

"So, it was a girl?"

"Damn, you people are giving me a headache. Can we not talk about it?"

"But how can we not?" Spencer asks. "You were supposed to be my wingman, and now you have a girlfriend?"

"She isn't my girlfriend."

Hookup. A regular hookup, but a hookup nonetheless. A hookup that's currently sleeping in my bed, and I kind of hope that she stays there until I get home. Maybe I could sneak into the bed and wake her up with my to—

"Then why hide her from me?"

"You hid her? Why?"

I glare at my friends. "The girl wanted some privacy. Is that so hard to grasp?"

"The girls you usually date don't care one bit about it."

"Zane's right," Spencer nods. "Remember that one chick who asked me to jo—"

"Okay, I get it. I usually hookup with groupies. Fine. She's not one of them, so can we just let it be and get back to exercise? You know the reason why you assholes pulled me out of bed at the ass crack of dawn in the first place?"

I turn around to find my friends staring at me, completely speechless.

"What?!" I bite out.

Do I have something on my face or some shit?

Spencer is the first to break the silence. "See? I told you he had it bad."

"Well, I'll be damned."

I shake my head, exasperated with this conversation. "I don't have time for this."

"But, it's so fu—"

"No." Shaking my head, I grab my earbuds and tuck them into my ears, turning on the music to the max as I speed up the treadmill going into a run.

I'm done listening to them making this more than it is. More than it can ever be. Not that I want it to be more.

Right?

Right.

The idea alone is preposterous. Jade and I could never be together. Not only would we kill each other, but Nixon would kill me if he were ever to find out I messed with his little sister.

No, we would never work as a couple.

Pushing thoughts of Jade back, I focus on finishing my jog before I switch to the weights. Today it's a leg day, which means I'll be beat once we're done.

And I'm not wrong. Two hours later, sweat is dripping from me, making my shirt cling to my chest as we make our way back to the locker room. My legs are shaking underneath me, but only the fact that I'm still standing is pushing me forward.

Just a little bit more.

Entering my combination, I pull my bag out of the locker and rampage through it until I find the pain meds. Three tablets fall into my palm, and I pop them into my mouth.

"What are those for?"

Nixon's question makes the pills stick in my throat. Swallowing, I force them down as my best friend watches me with interest.

"Umm... my head's killing me." The lie falls easily from my tongue.

I grab my water bottle, washing down the bitter taste lingering in my mouth that I'm not completely sure is only because of the pills.

"A migraine."

"Since when are you having migraines?" Zane asks as he pulls his tee over his head and tosses it on the bench.

"Since, you assholes keep asking all the dumb questions." I tug the shirt off, so it's not plastered to me.

The idea of taking a shower now and dragging myself back home sounds tiring as fuck.

Screw this.

I grab my hoodie and toss it on before shoving my things into the bag. "I'm out of here."

"No shower?"

"Nah, I'll just grab it when I get home."

Nixon's brows rise. "You not coming to breakfast with us?"

After we're done at the gym, we all go and stuff ourselves with food because we're like a pack of hungry lions. Usually, I'd go with them, but...

Or you could stay.

I'm not sure where the words came from. I hated girls in my space. I'd never leave them there all by themselves, too afraid it would be a sign to them this is something more than it is. But this is Jade we're talking about.

"Nah, I'm fine."

"He's going home to get his girl," Spencer smirks and wiggles his brows like the idiot he is.

"Shut up, Monroe." I grab my duffle and toss it over my shoulder. "I'm out of here. You figure out how you'll get home."

"Hey, that's not fair."

"That's for irritating me. I'll see you guys later."

Exiting the locker room, I make my way to the parking lot. Ignoring the pain, I slide inside and turn on the ignition. The drive back to the apartment is fast since most of the campus is still sleeping, and I take the steps instead of the elevator to make it quicker.

My heart is pounding furiously when I pull the door open and go straight to my room, expecting to find Jade sleeping in my bed, but instead, I find it empty.

I sit down on the mattress, my hand running over the cool sheets, the faint scent of lavender and sex still lingering in the air.

She left.

Chapter 31

JADE

My gaze is zeroed in on the key as I twist it this way and that, over and over again.

Or you could stay.

I flip the key between my fingers, over the pointer, under the middle, over the middle, under the pointer.

So you can lock up before leaving.

Seriously, what was he thinking? Leaving me with the key to his place? What if I was some kind of psycho? What would he do then?

Or you could stay.

A shudder runs down my spine as those words ring in my head. It would have been so easy, so freaking easy to stay. I wanted it. I wanted it badly. That's why I forced myself to get out of his comfy, warm bed that smelled just like him, put on my clothes, and got the hell out of there.

Sex.

That's all that we're doing.

Hooking up and getting the edge off.

But damn, it felt good to sleep next to him last night. It was the first night in weeks that I got a few hours of uninterrupted sleep. Well, except that other night when he slept in my bed.

Or you could sta—

The door opens in the hallway, soft footsteps padding over the hardwood floor. I look over my shoulder just in time to see Grace's messy head pop into the living room.

"Mo—" A frown appears between her brows as she sees me sitting at the bar. "Why are you up?"

"Good morning to you too." I tilt my head toward the coffee machine. "Coffee's done."

"How long have you been up?"

"Long enough."

Still looking at me suspiciously, she makes her way to the coffee machine and pours herself a cup. "Are you okay?"

"Yeah, just couldn't sleep." My gaze drops down to the key in my hand. "Do you have a key to Mason's place?"

Grace whips her head in my direction, her wide eyes meeting mine. "Talk about a one-eighty."

I shake my head. "This was a mistake, sorry."

I'm about to push to my feet and get the hell out of here when Grace stops me. "No, it's fine. I'm just surprised, that's all. I do have a key. Why?"

Getting my ass back to the chair, I shrug. "Just wondering, that's all."

"Okay," Grace says slowly, clearly not believing me.

"When did he give it to you?"

"At the beginning of this semester. His roommates agreed although I avoid using it. Feels like I'm invading their privacy in a way. But he still insists I have it since he doesn't want me to wait outside for him when he gets back late from work or from away games, so I humor him."

I clench my fingers, metal digging into my skin. "I guess that makes sense."

Still didn't explain why Prescott gave me the key to his place. Did he give it to all his hookups so they could get themselves out once he was done with them?

Why the hell am I even thinking about it?

"Hey." Grace's hand covers mine, snapping me out of my thoughts. "You sure you're okay?"

"Great. I think I'll go to my room. Get some work done."

"Okay. You planning on going to the game tonight?"

"Of course. Wanna come too?"

"I wish," Grace lets out a sigh. "Mason has a game too."

Getting to my feet, I grab my coffee cup. "Somebody is turning into a hoop bunny."

Grace groans loudly, "Don't say that. It's awful."

"Hey, you picked your guy, don't go crying about it now," I yell as I make my way to my room, still chuckling. Just as I close the door behind me, my phone buzzes in my pocket.

Hotshot: You left.

I bite the inside of my cheek, cursing at my heart for doing a little flip inside my chest.

Me: I told you I have work to do.

Hotshot: And here I was thinking of all the creative ways I could wake you up.

Me: Like what?

Hotshot: As if I'll tell you now.

Hotshot: You'll have to wait and find out.

Wait and find out implied that there would be another night that we'd sleep in the same bed. Wake up in the same bed.

And why doesn't that sound half bad?

Hotshot: I'll see you after the game?

Me: Yeah, I'll be there.

Hotshot: I'd tell you to wear that hoodie you stole but…

But that would never be possible.

Not only is it a completely girlfriend thing to do, and we're definitely not boyfriend and girlfriend, but somebody could see, and word that Jade Cole is hooking up with her brother's best friend and teammate would spread like a wildfire.

And that can't happen.

Ever.

Me: I guess I'll have to find a creative way to congratulate you if you win, Hotshot.

There.

That's what this is about.

Sex.

The only thing it can ever be.

The only thing I *want* it to be.

"C'mon, c'mon, c'mon," I mutter, my fingers holding onto the railing as I watch the game unfold on the field. But just when it seems one of the running backs has found an opening and is about to throw the ball to Prescott, he's tackled to the ground, and the ball's intercepted, and the other team starts running toward the end zone.

"Fucking hell." Yasmin pounds her fisted hand against the side of her leg as the score changes just as the clock runs out, signaling the Ravens have lost.

"Well, that was…" my words trail off as I shake my head.

"Horrible?" Yasmin suggests as we follow the crowd out of the stadium.

"I was going to say bad, but yeah. Horrible works too."

The overall mood is completely somber as the crowd moves at snail's pace. It was painful to watch the game. Ever since the

Ravens stepped onto the field, nothing had gone their way. They lost the coin toss, Hillworth decided to start on the offensive, and scored their first touchdown in two downs. It's like they've read our defense completely, and shattered any possibility of a comeback.

"Nixon will be in a bad mood. He really wanted to beat Hillworth this year."

"True." And he wasn't the only one. "Can you even blame him? That was an epic shitshow, and now the stakes are even higher than ever if the Ravens want to make it to the playoffs this year."

"I know," Yasmin lets out a sigh. "He really wants to win and go out on a high."

"They might still make it," I offer weakly, although we're both aware that their chances were slim.

Slim but not non-existent.

We change the subject as we make our way out of the stadium and go to the back of the building, where the boys will exit once they're done with all the post-game stuff.

I debate about texting Prescott but change my mind. Knowing how he is, he probably won't even bother checking his phone.

"Callie's in Boston?" I ask, noticing that Yasmin's typing something.

Although Callie's boyfriend isn't part of the Ravens team any longer, she's been going to the games with us as long as she was on campus.

"Yeah, they watched the game and wanted to check how Nix is doing." Yas pockets her phone. "Hayden has a home game on Monday, so she wanted to be there for him."

I nod my head, my eyes glued to the damn door. "How's she dealing with all of it?"

"Callie? Surprisingly really good. Although, that might be

due to the fact that if that man's not on the field or in the gym, he's texting her. I swear she's glued to her phone."

"I mean, as long as it's working for them."

Just then, the door opens. The guys slowly start to come out, matching serious expressions on their faces. I bounce on the balls of my feet, nibbling at the inside of my cheek as I wait for Prescott to come. I expect him to be behind my brother, but there's only Sullivan.

I give him a sad smile. Losing out on the field must have sucked, but watching your teammates lose from the sidelines and not being able to help must have been excruciating. He nods at me before disappearing with some of his friends just as Nixon joins us. He wraps his arm around Yasmin's neck, burrowing his head into the crook of her neck, and pulls her into his body.

"I'm so sorry, babe," Yasmin whispers softly.

"Yeah, well, it is what it is."

"You still have a chance," I point out. I hate seeing Nixon disappointed like that. I know how much it would mean for him to win this year. How badly he wants it.

Nixon lets go of Yasmin and throws his hand over my shoulder. "A very slim and complicated one."

"Well, if anybody can do it, I know you guys can."

"Didn't realize you had so much faith in us, Smalls," Nixon says, ruffling my hair.

I swat his hand away, ducking from under his arm. "More like I'm in no mood to listen to you bitch for the next few months."

"I'll give you..." he takes a step toward me, but Yasmin wraps her fingers around Nixon's forearm and tugs him back.

"Hey, why'd you do that?" Nixon protests.

My gaze darts to the door, but there's still no Prescott. I pull out my phone and quickly type him a message.

"Because I know you two, and I don't want you to get in another one of your fights. God, I'm so happy that I'm an only child." She looks over her shoulder. "You coming, Jade?"

"Huh?" I look up from my phone and see Yasmin and Nixon watching me. "Oh, I have to answer a text, and then I think I'll just go back home."

"We can drive you," Nixon shrugs.

"Ummm..." *Shit*, of course, he'd have to suggest that now. "Grace is just going home from the dance studio, so we'll walk together," I lie easily. She actually went out on a date with Mason after his game and won't be coming home tonight, but what he doesn't know won't hurt him.

Nixon runs his fingers through his hair. "Okay, stay safe?"

"Sure."

"I'll see you tomorrow for brunch." He gives me a pointed look. "Try to make it this time around?"

"Yeah, yeah..." I wave him off. "Off with you two."

With a shake of his head, Nixon throws his arm around Yasmin's shoulders and pulls her toward the parking lot and his car. I lean against the wall, scrolling mindlessly through social media as I wait for Prescott to appear. Every once in a while, I look up, but there's no sight of him.

Where is he?

I thought at this point everybody got out, but I hadn't seen him. Did he slip away when I wasn't looking?

No, I'd have felt it. Felt him.

He's inside, but why I have no idea.

A shiver runs through me. I should have probably worn a thicker jacket, but I wasn't ready just yet to part with the leather one.

A few more minutes. If he's not out in a few more minutes, I'll leave.

At least, that's what I keep telling myself.

I'm not sure how long I'm standing in the shadows, waiting, when the door finally opens, and Prescott's tall frame comes out. His duffle bag is hanging off his shoulder, his head ducked.

My throat bobs as I swallow. I was expecting him to be angry, but more than that, he looks defeated, and I'm not sure how to deal with this new version of Prescott.

I'm ready to push from the wall when a man walks toward him and gets in Prescott's way. He looks up, surprise flashing on his face when he sees him, but before he can say anything, the guy lifts his hand and punches him.

What the...

My heart plummets, a knot forming in my throat as Prescott's head snaps to the side. Slowly, he lifts his hand, covering the side of his mouth.

"How did you allow yourself to be tackled like that?" The man shakes his head in disgust. "If not for you, the team would have got that last touchdown and won the game." He spits on the ground. "Despicable."

What the fuck? Is this guy for real?

Prescott's jaw clenches, but he ducks his head. "I know."

He's completely and utterly defeated.

But it's like the man doesn't hear him, or maybe he simply doesn't care. "Gabriel wouldn't have ever allowed something like that to happen."

Gabriel? Who the hell's Gabriel?

"I *know*," Prescott repeats, his shoulders tensing, waiting for another blow or ready to snap himself?

Screw this.

"What the hell's your problem? It wasn't his fault." Pushing off the wall, I move closer and glare at the man. Prescott looks up, surprise flashing on his face when he sees me standing there. "Prescott wasn't the only player out on that field that messed up."

The man's eyes narrow on me. "But he was the one who was supposed to catch the ball when he was tackled."

I cross my arms over my chest. "And where were his teammates that were supposed to be there having his back, so he could catch it?"

The asshole clenches his jaw and sways on his feet. That's right, dude. I'm not about to let you talk nonsense when you and I both know it's just that—a load of bullshit.

"And who do you think you are?"

The man gives me a once-over, so I stare right back. His dark hair, peppered with gray, is a mess, his face washed out, the lines around his mouth and eyes hard. His brown irises are swallowed by his pupils, and his eyes are bloodshot. Drunk. The man is completely drunk.

I open my mouth, but before I can say anything, an ugly smirk spreads over his lips as he sways on his feet once again. "Seriously, Prescott, you should stop playing around with the groupies and concentrate on your studies. Or is that another thing you're planning to fuck up just like you fucked up this game?"

"Fuck off." Prescott's hands ball into fists, and he's about to lunge at the man, but I grab his hand, pulling him back. "She's not a groupie."

The man does another sweep of my body, his scrutinizing stare making the bile rise in my throat. "Could have fooled me. Stop messing around and concentrate on things that matter, instead of wasting both your time and mine."

With that, he turns on the balls of his feet and walks away.

Prescott's body is still tense next to mine as we watch the man get in the car and drive off.

"What an asshole. He shouldn't be driving."

"Welcome to my life."

Wait... "What?" I turn to him, my eyes narrowing. "Is that..."

"You had the dissatisfaction to meet Henry Wentworth in the flesh."

His father.

That was his father.

"I..." My mouth falls open, but no words come out. What is there even to say to what I'd just witnessed?

I notice the blood clinging to the corner of his mouth. Moving closer, I lift up on the tips of my toes and gently brush it away. "I'm so sorry, Prescott. He was wrong, though. It wasn't—"

"He was right." Prescott pulls his arm out of my grasp, turning his back on me. "It was my fault. What are you even doing here, Jade? You should have gone home."

I take a step back, surprised by his sharp voice. For all the fighting we did, he never spoke to me like that. Ever.

"I don't know," I whisper, wrapping my arms around myself.

We stay frozen like that for a moment. I expect him to say something, anything, but when he doesn't, I turn around and walk away.

Chapter 32

PRESCOTT

Gabriel wouldn't have ever allowed something like that to happen.

Of course, he wouldn't because he was freaking perfect. It was supposed to be him. Not me. Never me.

Taking a pull from the bottle, I let my hand drop to my lap as I watch the lights illuminating the small town underneath me. But even this place couldn't give me solace. Not tonight.

Although I feared it had nothing to do with the place, but the woman I brought here not that long ago.

The woman who just saw me at my lowest. I never wanted her to meet my parents. Never wanted her to see me like this. Or anybody else, for that matter. My life before Blairwood and at Blairwood were completely separate.

Until tonight.

What the hell's your problem? It wasn't his fault.

Only Jade... Only Jade would come between two grown men and try to interfere when she just saw me getting punched in the face. And God, was she beautiful.

I didn't deserve her. I didn't deserve her kindness or

support, yet she's given it to me anyway. And then I told her to leave.

I run my hand over my face in frustration.

If she knew the truth, if only she knew the truth, she would have seen how right my father was.

How I wasn't good enough.

Not for that spot on the team.

Not to be a doctor.

Not for her.

Or anybody else.

I take a swig from the bottle.

Never good enough.

Shaking my head, I cap the bottle and toss it to the passenger's side before putting my car in drive and getting the hell out of here.

A quick glance at the console tells me it's well after midnight, and I'm slightly buzzed, so I make sure to drive under the speed limit as I make my way back to campus.

My eyes instantly go to look at her window as I get out of the car. The light's turned off, but the damn window is open.

She always leaves that damn thing open these days.

I should turn around and go back to my place. Get in bed and sleep this whole thing off. I should text her tomorrow, apologize and tell her we should stop this thing between us.

But do I do either of those?

Hell no.

Instead, I go to her building and slowly start to climb. It takes me a while because my head is spinning, but somehow, I manage to get myself inside in one piece.

Pulling my shirt off, I drop it on the floor as I toe off my shoes and get on the mattress.

"Wha—"

"Shh... It's me." I whisper as I brush a strand of her dark hair behind her ear.

"Prescott?"

"You left your window open."

Through the light coming through the crack in the curtains, I can see her blink a few times, chasing away the sleep.

"I did."

"Do you want me to leave?" I ask anyhow, wanting to make sure she's okay with this.

"Do you want to leave?" she counters right back.

I shake my head, unable to voice the words out loud. But I don't have to. Not when it comes to Jade.

She pulls the blanket open, a silent invitation.

And I take it.

"I'm sorry," I whisper, pulling her body against mine. "For yelling at you earlier. I never wanted you to see me like this."

She turns around, her palm cupping my cheek, fingers tracing over the bruise from where Dad punched me earlier. "I'm sorry he treats you that way. You don't deserve it."

She's wrong, though.

I do deserve it, but I don't bother correcting her because it feels good having somebody in my corner. And selfishly, I'll take it, although I know I don't deserve it.

JADE

"Why are you frowning like that?"

I blink, the screen of my camera coming back into focus before I look up, only to find Prescott observing me from across the room. He's sitting at my desk, his dirty blond hair mussed from how he ran his fingers through it, that thick stubble covering his jaw.

The feeling of it scratching my inner thighs as Prescott went down on me this morning flashes in my mind, a shudder running down my spine. Yup, you're not going to hear me complain about that anytime soon. It's safe to say we were late for brunch. Again. But thankfully, we came in just as Edie let out a huge burp, drawing the attention from us slipping into the diner barely a minute apart.

"Just thinking." I shift in my seat, letting the camera drop into my lap.

When we got home earlier, I expected Prescott to go back to his place, but he suggested he'd come after he'd taken a shower and changed so we could study together.

I wasn't sure where that put us, but it was nice having somebody here. Talking with somebody about things that don't include boyfriends and dates and whatnot. I love my friends, and I love spending time with them, but it would be a lie if I said that things haven't changed in this past year because they have.

"About?"

"What the hell I'm going to do for this project."

"Still no idea?"

"Nope."

And I was starting to get irritated by the whole thing. Photography has always come easy to me. And now, this one time I need it to be perfect, I'm struggling.

He lifts his arms in the air, stretching. I watch his muscles flex, the hem of his shirt rising and revealing his defined abs. I nibble at my lip, that ache growing inside me. No matter how much we're together or how many orgasms I have, I can't seem to get enough of him.

Prescott lets his hands fall, the sound snapping me out of my thoughts as his knowing gaze lands on mine. "Maybe you should take a step back."

I give him a pointed look. "Did you ever see me take a step back?"

"I guess there's that," he smirks. "What was the theme again?"

The chair creaks as Prescott gets up. He crosses the room, the mattress dipping under him as he joins me on the bed, lying on his stomach.

"Raw beauty."

His brows furrow. "Raw beauty?"

"My thoughts exactly. It could be anything, really, as long as we use the techniques taught in class this semester. Even you."

"Me?"

"Yes, you."

Before he can say anything further, I lift my camera and point it at him, quickly snapping a photo.

"Women are beautiful." He rubs his jaw. "I'd like to think more about myself as ruggedly handsome."

Lifting my gaze over the edge of the camera, I smirk at him. "So modest of you."

He grins back. "I know, right?"

"No." I roll my eyes. "I don't think there is one modest bone in your body."

"Hey now, I'll let you know. I'm extremely modest."

"Mhmm... in your dreams, maybe." I'm about to raise the camera once again when his strong fingers wrap around my ankle.

"I'll show you exactly what I'm dreaming about," he says, his voice low and raspy as he tugs me down.

"Prescott!"

The camera falls from my hand as he pulls me to him. He

rolls so he's looming over me, but I push him back, throwing my leg over his body and pinning him down to the mattress.

Throwing my head back so my hair is out of my face, I look at him. We're both breathing hard from the exertion. Prescott's cheeks are flushed, eyes dark with desire as his hands grip my hips.

"You were saying?" I lift a brow, a smile slowly making its way to my lips.

"Nothing. You're doing just fine on your own."

"I know." Blindly, I reach for the camera. "Let me take a photo of you."

"Didn't you just do that? Or are you thinking about *those* kinds of photos?" He wiggles his brows suggestively, that sexy smile of his appearing on his lips. "Although, I'd be down for that too."

I slide my hand under his shirt and pinch him. "Get your head out of the gutter, Wentworth."

"*Ouch!* What was that for?"

"To keep your mind on the task at hand." I soothe my palm over his lower stomach. His muscles quiver under my touch, his eyes are growing dark with desire. As I shift my weight, I can feel his hard length pressed against me. Slowly, I pull my hand back. "Now get serious."

"Is that a no to naked photos?"

I give him my best stern look. "Focus."

He pulls his hands back, crossing them behind his head. "I'm not really model material, you know?"

I lift the camera in front of my face, looking through the viewfinder. Yeah, there's a screen right below it, but for whatever reason, I love looking at my model through the viewfinder. When I shoot, I rarely look over my photos before I'm done. It's like I'm in a zone, and I don't want any distractions or second-guessing. I seize the moment and take the shot.

"Did I hear a little bit of humility in your voice? You going soft on me?"

He raises one of his brows, and I quickly press my finger over the shutter, getting the perfect shot of that smug smile of his. "Do I feel soft to you?"

"You're not being serious about this," I chastise, snapping another photo.

"I'm never joking when I'm talking about my dick." Suddenly his smile falls, he pulls his hand from under his head and tries to get up, but I don't budge. "Wait, you're not really planning to submit those photos to your professor, are you?"

"Maybe I will, maybe I won't." I shrug.

"You can't do that."

"Says who?"

"Says me. If the guys were to find out..."

"Can you see any of your friends attending a gallery showing? And that is if I get it. Besides, chill. I had way better models than you, and I'm still not happy with the results. This is just for fun."

"I think I'm offended."

"Of course you are."

Prescott lets out a sigh, "Just for fun?"

"Or practice." I wink at him. "Now, will you stop wiggling and let me shoot?"

"I guess so."

"Great." Sliding my leg, I get off the bed and look at him. Prescott's leaning his chin against his palm as he watches me work.

Click.

"Lose the shirt."

He raises his brow but doesn't comment as he slowly sits upright and pulls his shirt over his head in that sexy way only guys know how.

Abs peeking under the material.

Click.

Bicep bulging as he grabs the back of his shirt.

Click.

The material sliding over his torso and revealing all the golden skin and wicked grin of his.

Click. Click. Click.

"Having fun?"

"Yup."

It's the truth. This whole gallery thing has been on my mind, and I haven't had a chance to do something just for the sake of it. I missed it.

Spotting the football peeking from under the bed, I crouch down and pull it out. "Catch."

The football slips easily from my fingers, and I raise my camera just in time to capture Prescott catching the ball.

"What should I do with this?" he asks, throwing it in the air.

"Just play with it for a bit."

I snap a few more photos before Prescott puts the ball on the bed and crooks his finger at me. "C'mere. I want to see."

Pulling the camera away, I switch to view mode and look over the photos. Nerves make my stomach tighten, but I force myself to get back on the bed and hand him the camera. I rarely ever let anyone look at the unedited photos. It's like letting somebody read a half-written essay or showing them an unfinished play. You just don't do it.

My teeth sink into my lower lip as I watch Prescott flip between the photos, an unreadable expression on his face.

"You don't like them."

He looks up, the corner of his mouth raised in a grin. "Those are really good, not that I'm surprised."

"You're not?"

Yes, he got a peek at that photo I was editing a few weeks

back, but I'm not sure how much he remembered since he passed out so quickly.

Prescott shrugs. "I've seen your photos online before."

"Oh, did you now? Stalking me, Wentworth?"

"It's hardly stalking when your social media is open to the public."

I tilt my head. "I guess there is that."

"But those are good. More than good. I'm sure you'll figure it out."

"Let's hop— Hey!"

Prescott turns the camera toward me, and I hear that familiar *click* as he presses the shutter.

"What do you think you're doing?" I lunge for the camera, but Prescott pulls it out of my reach, making me stumble onto him.

"What does it look like I'm doing? Taking photos."

Pressing my hand on his chest, I glare at him. "Gimmie that, Wentworth."

"Don't tell me you're one of those people that doesn't like her photo taken."

"What if I am?"

"But you're taking photos for a living!"

"Exactly the reason why I don't like my photos taken." Straddling his lap, I grab the camera. "Seriously, give it back. Do you know how much that thing costs?"

He looks at the camera in his hand and then at me. "Do I want to know?"

"You don't. Trust me."

I still remember my parents freaking out when I told them about it. In hindsight, it is quite pricey, but it was the best of the best, and I had to have it if I was serious about pursuing photography. In the end, it was Mom who caved and got it for me.

"Hey," Prescott places the camera on the nightstand, his hand cupping my cheek. "You okay?"

"I'm fine. I just remembered something."

"Something?"

I tug the collar of my shirt down. "My mom."

I try to look away, but Prescott doesn't let me. "What about her?"

"She loved my photography. She was the only reason I got this camera in the first place. My dad thought it was a dumb hobby I'd grow out of, but not my mom."

"She could see the beauty in your art."

"She most definitely could. She was my biggest cheerleader, even when..." My throat tightens as that day on the beach flashes in my mind.

"Even when?"

"Even when I gave up on it, she never did. She never gave up on me."

Prescott's finger slides over my cheekbones, and only then do I realize I'm crying. Looking down, I brush the tears away. "Sorry. Thinking about her... it's just hard."

Gently, he nudges my chin up. "There is nothing to be sorry for. You miss her."

"I do. I miss her every single day. Especially now."

Now that I need her to tell me what to do, but she's not here. If she were here, she would know what to do. How to deal with this. How to stay strong when all I want to do is break.

"Why now?"

I graze my teeth over my lower lip. The words are on the tip of my tongue. It would be so easy for them to come out. But I can't. I can't say it because if I do, nothing will ever be the same again.

I'll never be the same again.

And I'm not ready.

I'm not ready to lose the little bit I have left of the person that makes me, me.

So I shove the words back into that dark, hidden place inside of me.

"It doesn't matter." I shake my head. My fingers graze Prescott's chin, my eyes falling to his lips. "I don't want to talk any longer."

Prescott watches me silently for a moment before letting his hands drop down, those strong fingers gripping my thighs. "What do you want?"

I lean closer, my mouth brushing against his. "You. I want you."

Chapter 33

JADE

Hotshot: What are you up to?
Me: Netflix and chill.
Hotshot: Is that an invitation?

I roll my eyes because, of course, he had to go there—typical guy behavior.

Me: No, that's what I'm doing.
Me: Lying in bed, watching Netflix and hibernating.
Hotshot: What are you watching?
Me: Reruns of Criminal Minds.
Hotshot: Didn't take you for that kind of girl.
Me: What kind of girl do you think I am?
Hotshot: Not sure.
Me: Well, I love to watch shows about serial killers. Keeps things interesting.
Hotshot: Should I be worried?
Me: You should always be worried.
Hotshot: Your roommates there?
Me: Date night.

Hotshot: What if I came by?

My heart pitter-patters in my chest, my stomach clenching in excitement at his words.

In the last couple of weeks, we've been hanging out more. Yes, our hanging out always ended up with us naked in one of our beds, but it was more than that.

I liked it.

I was starting to like *him*.

Liked spending time with him.

Although it might not seem that way at first, Prescott was a good listener. And he was wicked smart. I've seen how hard he works, not just out on the field but also when it comes to his degree. He was dedicated, and I was sure one day he'd make a good doctor.

And I wasn't sure what to think about that.

Me: My stomach hurts, I think I might get my period soon.

Hotshot: Okay so?

Me: So we can't have sex. No point in you coming. Just sex, remember?

Hotshot: Well, if you want to be technical about it, we could have sex.

He can't be serious, right? That's his reasoning? Technically?

Me: You're joking, right?

Hotshot: I'm just saying it as it is.

Hotshot: You know, technically.

Me: Well, when you technically have your ovaries explode inside your body once a month, let me know so we can talk about technicalities.

Hotshot: Touchy.

Hotshot: I didn't take you for one of those ultra

hormonal girls, but I guess I got one more thing wrong. Oh well...

Me: You want me to put my tv show watching skills to use?

Hotshot: Not particularly. No.

Me: Good.

Me: Don't you have anything better to do?

Hotshot: Not right now.

Me: You should go out. It's Friday night. I'm sure some of your teammates are out partying.

I shoot off the message and watch, waiting for those three little dots to appear on the screen, but they never do.

Gunshots sound from the speaker, reminding me that I've completely spaced out while I was texting with Prescott.

Okay then.

I shift in my bed, feeling that familiar stabbing in my stomach. Turning to the side, I move my laptop and curl my finger under the pillow, pulling my legs all the way to my chest as I curl in on myself and continue watching the show. But every so often, my gaze darts to my phone and that unanswered message.

I don't understand what's going on between Prescott and me. The sex is as good as ever, but somehow, it's not the only thing that's connecting us. Not any longer.

I talk with him probably more than with anybody else in my life right now. I'm not sure when or how it happened. Maybe it was that night in the gym, or maybe it was when he found me walking on the side of the road at night and took me to that lookout where he goes when he needs time to think.

Either way, somehow, along the way, he has turned into something more than a casual hookup, and it scares me.

It scares me shitless.

Because I know just how easy it is to lose somebody you care about.

Not that I care about Prescott. Not in that way. He drives me insane. Like right now. Completely and utterly insane.

Letting out a sigh, I pause the show when the credits roll and push myself upright. My stomach still hurts, but the pain has dulled slightly thanks to the painkillers I took earlier. Grabbing a change of clothes, I go to the bathroom and turn on the shower as I take off my clothes. I make sure the water is warm enough before sliding under the spray and letting the water warm me up.

I slowly wash my body and then just stand under the shower for a good five minutes before I'm finally ready to leave. Grabbing the towel, I dry myself before slipping into the comfiest pair of boxer shorts and an oversized tee.

Pulling open the bathroom door, I come to a stop when I see Prescott sitting on my bed. "What are you doing here?"

"You really need to start closing your window."

"You really need to stop climbing through my window."

Prescott grins at me. "Where would be the fun in that?"

"Oh, I don't know? Not breaking your neck in the process?"

"Still intact." He slides his hand at the back of his neck, rubbing at the muscles. "Although it's sweet that you worry."

"Worry?" I huff, moving closer to the bed. "I'm just thinking of all the possible consequences of your actions and how they might disrupt my life." I sniff softly. "Is that pizza?"

"Maybe." Prescott lifts the box off the bedside table. "I figured I'd bring the bribe in case you go serial killer on me."

"If I went serial killer on you, you wouldn't get a chance to open your mouth."

I try to grab the box from him, but the asshole he is, he lifts it out of my reach. "I think what you wanted to say is thank you, Prescott, for bringing my grumpy ass some carbs."

"What I want is pizza, so gimmie."

"What if I want something in return?"

"I haven't thrown you out yet or murdered you. That's as good as you'll get."

"But..."

I jab my finger into his chest. "Hand it over."

He rolls his eyes. "Fine."

The moment the box is in my reach, I grab it from his hands and open the top, the smell of cheese hitting me in the face all at once, making my stomach rumble.

I look up at Prescott. "How did you know cheese is my favorite?"

"Lucky guess?" Prescott shrugs.

"Lucky guess, huh?" I narrow my eyes at him as I sit down on the bed, placing the box on the mattress. Prescott sits on the other side. "Okay, maybe it's my favorite too."

"I'd have taken you for a pepperoni guy."

"Well, I guess you don't know everything about me either, now, do you?" he asks, grabbing a slice of pizza.

No, I guess not.

Shaking my head, I start the next episode before grabbing a slice of my own. I bring it to my mouth and take a big bite. My eyes fall shut at the first taste of the melted cheese on my tongue, a moan slipping past my lips.

"Damn, you didn't even sound like that when I made you come."

I glare at him. "You're lucky my hands are full, or I'd throw a pillow at you."

"You're violent when you're PMSing. And here I was trying to be nice and bring you some food."

"I'm not having sex with you, so you don't need to try to get into my good graces."

Prescott lets his head fall back as he lets out a loud groan. "For fuck's sake. It's not all about sex."

There's a beat of silence as his words ring between us.

I lower my hands, my tongue darting out to slide over my lips. "Well, that's what we agreed on."

"I don't fucking care what we agreed on." Prescott stuffs the rest of his pizza into his mouth.

He doesn't care? Is he for real now? How can he not care?

"Well, I care." I let out a sigh. "Why are you here, Prescott?"

"I was bored and figured we could hang out. Is that so bad?"

"It's strange. We don't just hang out for the sake of hanging out."

"We do."

"Tell me once that we hung out just for the sake of it."

"Are you serious right now?"

"Humor me."

"Fine." He grabs another slice from the box and leans against the wall. "We hung out that night at the gym."

I shake my head. "Doesn't count."

"Why the hell not?"

"We met at the gym by coincidence and then proceeded to have sex, that's why."

"Okay, how about that time you took photos of me for that article?"

"That was work."

Prescott groans. "I don't see how it matters anyhow. Can we just eat pizza and watch your murder shows?"

"Fine." I roll my eyes. "This is my favorite episode, anyhow."

We finish the rest of the pizza by the time the episode is done. I kind of expect Prescott to get up and leave, but he doesn't give me any indication he'll do it. Instead, he lies down, and one episode turns into two.

A shiver runs through my body, but before I can slip under the covers, Prescott pulls the blanket from the foot of the bed and covers us both with it, his arm sliding around my waist as he pulls me to him.

Snuggled under the blanket, I look over my shoulder, my eyes meeting his.

"What? You were cold."

"I didn't say anything."

"But you were thinking it." He tweaks my nose. "I can see it on your face."

I frown and shove his hand away. "There is nothing on my face." I turn back to the laptop. "Shouldn't you go home?"

"Nope, I just settled down. Plus, the show is getting interesting."

"See? I told you this is fun."

"As much as a bunch of psychopaths can be fun," he scoffs. "Now, shush and let me watch."

I shove my elbow back, connecting it to Prescott's gut.

"Ouch, what was that for?"

"For bossing me around."

"You know that only means I'll have to hold you tighter, so you won't be able to do it again, right?"

"Prescott!" I protest as he squeezes me, making it hard to breathe.

I try to squirm out of his hold, but he's relentless. I look over my shoulder, only to find his face just inches away from mine. I suck in a breath, the spicy scent of his cologne filling my lungs. My gaze falls to his mouth, those full lips slightly parted, his warm breath touching my lips.

Those damn lips that tempt me so badly.

It would be so easy, so damn easy, to lean in and close the distance between us.

So. Damn. Easy.

I graze my teeth over my lower lip and slowly raise my gaze.

All the amusement is gone from those chocolate irises, and there is only raw aching need left there.

My tummy clenches in anticipation, and I can feel that familiar pulse between my thighs.

"What?" he asks, his voice rough.

I inhale a shaky breath. "Just watch the tv show."

"No."

I shift, pulling the blanket closer around me, as I snuggle deeper into the warmth. I'm just about to drift back to sleep when the soft sound comes again, louder this time, more desperate.

"No. No. *No*! Gabriel..."

Gabriel?

Before my brain can connect what's going on, an elbow connects with my side, knocking the air out of my lungs.

The warmth surrounding me? It's not just blankets.

It's Prescott.

He's sleeping with me.

He came over, we watched Netflix, and, at some point, we fell asleep.

"No!" Prescott shifts in bed, pulling the blanket from me. "Gabriel, don't go. Don't leave me."

I scramble out of his way, switching the bedside lamp on. The dim light illuminates Prescott's thrashing form as he shifts this way and that. Sweat coats his forehead as he shakes his head; his brows are pulled together in a tight line.

"No, no, no..."

"Prescott," I whisper, moving closer. I try to cup his cheek, but he turns away.

"You can't leave me."

"Prescott," I repeat, this time my voice sharper. I place my hands against his chest, trying to hold him still. "It's just a bad dream. You need to wake—"

"It's too soon! You can't leave me, dammit. You can't leave me." His voice breaks and one tear slips down his cheek. "You. Can't. Leave. Me. It's all my f-fault."

Prescott. Crying.

I bite the inside of my cheek to hold back any emotions and just stare at him. I've never seen Prescott like this. So... broken.

"Gabriel, wake up."

"Prescott." My throat bobs as I swallow, forcing the words out. "You're just dreaming, please... Come back." I cup his face, letting my thumb skim over the scruffy cheek. "Just come back to me."

Before I can react, Prescott's fingers grip my hand tightly. He shakes his head violently as more tears stream down his cheeks.

"No! You hear me, Gabriel? You don't get to leave. It should have been me. All along. It should have been me."

Tears prickle my eyes, partly in pain, partly because of the desperation in Prescott's voice.

"Shh..." I lean down, pressing my forehead against his. With my free hand, I stroke his hair back gently. "It's okay. I have you. It's okay. It's just a bad dream."

I repeat those words over and over. My body is completely plastered to his as I continue soothing my palm up and down his side until his body finally stops thrashing and his breathing slows down.

"Jade?" Prescott asks, his voice hoarse from all the talking.

My eyes fall shut for a split second. Inhaling deeply, I pull back so I can see his face. A strand of hair is stuck to his forehead, wet with sweat.

"I'm here," I say, brushing it away gently. "You're okay. I've got you."

He blinks his eyes open and looks around, confusion written all over his face as if he, too, is trying to figure out how he ended up here. "W-What... What happened?"

"You were having a bad dream. I tried to wake you, but..."

"Shit, I'm so so—"

"It's fine." I tighten my grip on his face, not letting him pull away. I can't let him pull away, not after I've witnessed this. "You're awake. That's the only thing that matters."

"Did I hurt you?"

I shake my head. "I'm fine."

His Adam's apple bobs, and he nods. "Maybe I should just g—"

"No, stay." I caress his cheek, waiting for his answer. "Please?"

Prescott watches me for a moment before he lets out a shaky breath. "Sure. I can stay."

"Are you okay?" I ask, laying my head on the pillow next to him.

Prescott just nods, so I keep brushing his hair, my hand gentle as I stare at those brown eyes. For a while, we just lay like that, in silence, neither of us saying anything.

What demons are you fighting, Prescott?

The words are on the tip of my tongue. I can see the darkness swirling in his eyes. It's etched into every line of his face. Whatever it is, it has to be pretty bad in order to upset him so much. No, not just upset him. Break him. Because the man lying next to me is broken, his spirit is completely shattered.

Like calls to like.

Isn't that what people say?

Is that what this feeling inside me is? Recognition of somebody who's more like me than I'd ever imagine?

Pushing away those thoughts, I concentrate on here and now. "Prescott?"

"Hmm?"

"Do you have nightmares often?"

There's a beat of silence, and then, "Sometimes."

I nod absentmindedly. His skin is warm under my touch, his heart beating wildly. No matter how calm he pretends to be, whatever he dreamed about unsettled him. "Do you remember what you were dreaming about?"

"Past," he clips, his voice distant.

Okay then.

My throat bobs as I swallow. His arms tighten around me, pulling me closer. We just lay like that for God only knows how long. But no matter how much I try to convince myself I should go to sleep, I can't.

I let the words hang in the air between us. I don't want to pressure him to tell me about it, but damn, I want to help him.

What must have happened to make Prescott Wentworth have nightmares like this? I thought his injury was the cause of the demons hiding in his gaze but after tonight... After tonight, I'm not so sure.

Prescott just stares forward, his face completely devoid of any emotion. His body is here, but his mind? It's gone. Lost to whatever happened in the past.

What happened to you, Prescott?

"Prescott?" I whisper softly, unsure if he's even listening to me.

"Hmm?" he murmurs sleepily, his hand sliding down my back.

I nibble at my lip, debating if I should ask it, but curiosity gets the best of me. "Who's Gabriel?"

At first, I couldn't remember why the name sounded so familiar, but then it hit me.

The night when his father punched him after the game.

He mentioned Gabriel too.

Prescott goes completely still under me. The hairs at the back of my neck raise as I wait for an answer, unsure of how he'll react or what to expect.

The silence stretches between us, making me uneasy for some reason. It's like I've just entered a cage with one very pissed-off lion.

Why couldn't I just leave it alone? But of course, I had to be nosy...

"How do you know about Gabriel?" he asks slowly, his voice pure ice.

"You mentioned him when you were sleeping."

Begging him to stay.

I don't say that last tidbit. I don't want to make him uncomfortable if this is a sensitive subject which it most likely is. Otherwise, he wouldn't have nightmares like the one he just had.

The room is so quiet I swear I can hear the sound of my own heart beating. I know I've crossed an invisible line, but there was no going back now. I just wasn't sure what to expect at this point.

"Gabriel was my brother," Prescott says softly, so softly at first I think I misheard him.

"He was..." my words trail off as I try to wrap my head around it.

Brother?

Prescott had a brother?

Out of every possibility, I'm not sure why I'm surprised by this revelation. I don't think I've ever heard Prescott mention having a sibling. And I'd probably remember if Nixon said anything. And if somebody would know, it's my brother.

He was my brother.

Wait... "Was?"

I tilt my head back, looking up at Prescott. He still hasn't shaved off his stubble, and with his lips pressed together in a hard line, it makes him look even harsher.

"He... He died when we were thirteen."

"Oh..."

I don't know what to say. I'm sorry or, God forbid, my condolences don't feel like enough. I despise those words. Hate them to my very core. Everybody kept saying them when Mom died. How sorry they were, and what a wonderful person she was, but it was all a load of bullshit because those people didn't know her the way I did. They didn't understand my pain. They couldn't.

But Prescott does.

"*We* were?" I push up from his chest, so I can look at his face. "You were twins?"

"Irish twins. He was eleven months older." The corner of his mouth lifts in a wistful smile. "Never let me live it down. Until..." His voice trails off, hollow. "Until he was no longer older."

His Adam's apple bobs as he swallows, the pain in his voice almost palpable. I lie back down on his chest, wrapping my arms tightly around him. It's the best thing I can offer him. The only thing I know *how*.

"I'm so sorry, Prescott. I wouldn't have pried if I knew."

"It's fine. You didn't know." He lets out a humorless chuckle. "Nobody knows."

My eyes widen. "Nobody?"

"Not a single soul," he confirms. "Back home, I was always that guy who lost his brother, so when I came here..." He shakes his head. "I just wanted a clean slate, you know? I just wanted to be me. Selfish, I kn—"

I push off his chest and glare at him. "You're not selfish."

Prescott just watches me for a moment, a pain I haven't even seen until that moment reflected in his dark eyes. "Sometimes I feel selfish."

"Well, you're not. When Mom was sick..." I lick my lips, a little bit of that sadness that I keep safely stashed away slipping out of its confines and wrapping around my heart. "People look at you differently when they know somebody close to you is dying. Nobody can blame you for wanting to separate yourself from that part of your past. From wanting to dissociate from it. Least of all me."

Not with the secret I've been keeping.

"I know." Prescott's hand falls over mine, giving it a firm squeeze. "Doesn't make me feel less guilty, though. It's like I'm ashamed of him or trying to hide him when it couldn't be further away from the truth."

I look down at our clasped hands. Slowly, I turn mine around, and his fingers intertwine with mine before meeting my gaze.

"Survivor's guilt is a real thing. And I can't even begin to imagine how it was for you to lose somebody so close."

I was close with my mom, but to lose a *twin*? How do you recover from that?

Prescott's gaze grows distant. Physically, he's in bed with me, but mentally, he's far, far away. "He was the best. It was never supposed to be him. God knows my parents would have preferred it was me."

"Don't you dare say that."

I try to remember the couple from the restaurant. I didn't pay them much attention that day, but I clearly remembered Prescott storming out of the restaurant mid-dinner. I remembered his dad punching him and the ugly words he said.

How does somebody, *a parent,* say something like that to their child?

I couldn't understand what they were dealing with when they lost a son, but that didn't excuse their behavior toward Prescott. I wanted to punch them for hurting him the way they did, even more now.

"Jade..."

"No," I shake my head, refusing to listen to this. "What happened was a shitty thing, but it's not your fault."

"But what if it is?"

"It isn't," I say sharply. Letting out a shaky breath, I change the subject.

"What was he like?" I ask softly. "Gabriel?"

"Funny," Prescott chuckles, and this time it even reaches his eyes. "He had the stupidest jokes, but he made everybody smile. I swear he could charm everybody. It was so natural for him. People loved him." Prescott glances at me. "You'd have liked him way more than you do me."

"As if that's hard." I nudge him with my elbow. "What else?"

"He was brave and resilient. He never let anybody bully him, or me for that matter, regardless of the fact that he was the smallest out of all the people in our year. He was always so optimistic and cheerful, making sure to make us smile." The smile that was growing on his face as he recalled his brother, slowly slips away. "Until cancer took him."

Cancer.

My eyes fall shut as his words echo in the quiet room so loud I can hear them ringing in my ears.

"C-cancer?" I repeat, my voice breaking at that one word.

"Leukemia. He got it for the first time when we were seven. He was in and out of the hospital for years, and when we finally thought things were getting better..." He shakes his head and shrugs. "Yeah."

This can't be happening. It just can't. Out of all the people...

"Jade?" His fingers slip under my chin, nudging my head up. Those dark eyes fixing on me. I swear it's like he can see to my very core. He sees all of me. All the shattered pieces, and he isn't afraid. "Are you okay?"

No, I'm not okay.

"Sure," I blink a few times, pushing back the tears. "Talking about cancer... it's just hard."

Prescott nods in understanding. His palm cups my cheek, thumb sliding over the cheekbone and wiping away the tear. "I'm sorry if I upset you."

"You didn't. I'm glad you shared Gabriel with me."

"It felt good. Talking about him. Remembering him. Good, not just the bad. It still hurts, but..."

"It's dulled?" I suggest.

"Yeah, a little."

I knew that feeling well. I don't think the pain will ever completely go away, but somehow, it's not as intense as it used to be before.

Prescott stares at me, neither of us saying anything. His finger traces the curve of my lower lip, his gaze falling to my mouth.

My lips part on an exhale.

I'm not sure which one of us makes the first move, but then his mouth is on mine, and I'm pulled into his lap. I shift so I'm straddling his hips, feeling his hard erection pressed against my pussy as we devour one another.

"I don't want to talk anymore, Jade," he breathes against my mouth. "I don't want to remember. Not now."

I run my fingers through his hair, tugging his head back. "Then let's forget. Together."

Tonight.

And that's exactly what we do.

Chapter 34

JADE

Hotshot: Having N quiz me isn't half as fun as when you do it.

Me: Did you tell him that?

Hotshot: Hell no. You want me to return in one piece, right?

Me: Depends on which piece we're talking about *smirk*

Hotshot: You'd seriously take me in pieces?

I'd take you any way I can get you.

The words ring in my mind as my fingers hover over the keyboard. Not like I can say that to him. Not when I know that Prescott and I don't have a future.

Borrowed time.

That's all this could ever be.

Borrowed time.

The front door opens, snapping me out of my thoughts as Yasmin marches into the room.

"I hate football." Yasmin sits down on the couch next to me, crosses her arms over her chest, and lets out a loud huff.

"Well, hello, to you, too."

Yasmin completely ignores me and continues on. "Like, who got to decide that football will take over all of our lives for six months straight?"

Letting out a sigh, I close my laptop and lean back. "Somebody who likes to torture us?"

"Damn right! I swear if I had that person in front of me, I'd give them a piece of my mind."

I press my lips together, trying to hold back my laughter as I nod. "I'm sure you would."

"Of course I would. They're so—" She turns to me, her eyes narrowed. "Jade Devney Cole, are you laughing at me?"

"I would never."

"You're laughing at me." She lets her head fall back against the couch and covers her face with her palms, letting out a loud groan.

"Okay, maybe just a teeny, tiny bit." I grab her hand and tug it back. "But seriously, what did football do to you?"

Yasmin pouts, "It took away Nixon."

"I'm sorry, babe, but that's nothing new."

"It's his birthday tomorrow."

I go over the dates in my head, and shit, she's right.

Yasmin gives me a knowing look. "You forgot about it, didn't you?"

"Who? Me? No way."

"You totally did."

"Okay, maybe. But there's been a lot going on." I wave her off. "Seriously, though, you know that this is just the beginning, right? Next year when he goes pro, things will be even more intense."

"I know. That's why I planned this whole thing. It's our first year that we've been married, and with everything awaiting us... I just wanted to make it count, you know?"

"You can still do it when he gets home."

"That's the plan," she lets out a sigh. "I guess I'm just bummed that Nixon had to have an away game tomorrow of all days. And here I was hoping to do something special for his birthday."

"Like what?"

"I was planning to bake him a cake, and then..." She bites her lip, and it takes my mind a moment to register where she's going with this.

"Okay, I don't want to know the rest. Thank you very much."

Yasmin chuckles, "I figured as much. What have you been up to? Any boys grabbing your attention?"

The image of Prescott sprawled over my bed, shirtless, a book in his hand, pops into my mind. If only she knew.

"Nope," I lie. "No boys."

"You're no fun."

"At least I don't have to think about when a guy's birthday is and how to make it special for him." I switch the channel, and ESPN pops on the screen. They're doing a recap of a football game, and an idea pops into my mind. "Although..."

Yasmin shifts on the couch. "What?"

I bite the inside of my cheek as I mull it over. It's slightly crazy, but... "What if you could still surprise him? No cake, but... the rest of it?"

She pulls her brows together. "What do you mean?"

"I mean, we could drive there and surprise Nixon."

And Prescott. But I keep that last part to myself.

"But they're away for a game..."

"So?" I shrug. "We'll book a hotel room and go to the game. Have breakfast together. His birthday isn't until tomorrow." I check my watch, calculating the time. "Hell, I'm pretty sure we could make it there before midnight if we tried."

Yasmin shakes her head. "This is crazy, Jade. We can't—"

"Is it?" I wiggle my brows at her. "What do you say, Yas? Are you in?"

It takes us a good five hours, but we finally make it to the hotel. While I was driving Nixon's car, Yasmin booked our rooms at the same hotel the team was staying at.

"Which is the guy's room again?" I nonchalantly ask as we go to the elevators to head to our floor.

"367. Nixon's rooming with Prescott, but he texted me saying the guys are at the hotel bar until curfew."

"You going to meet him there?"

"That's the plan. I just want to drop the bag off first," Yasmin smiles at me. "You wanna come?"

"Oh, no. I'll stay in my room. I want to do some editing on the photos for my class."

"You sure?"

"Yes." The elevator pings, and we walk onto our floor and go to our rooms, which are next to each other. Not ideal, but it'll have to do. "Hey, Yas?"

She presses her key against the door lock, there is a soft buzzing sound, and the door opens. "Yes?"

"Don't tell him I'm here. I'll surprise him tomorrow at breakfast."

"Okay, sure. I'll see you tomorrow?"

"See you in the morning. Don't have too much fun."

Unlocking my door, I push inside and flick the light switch on. Dropping my bag on the bed, I look around the simple room and wait to hear the door next door open. It doesn't take long before I hear Yasmin's footsteps walk toward the elevators.

I wait five minutes, and then another five just to be sure, before grabbing my essentials and leaving the room.

The hallway is empty as I make my way to the reception. The same guy that checked us in is still working. Perfect.

Plastering a smile on my face, I walk up to him. "Hey there."

He looks up and smiles back. "Good evening, miss. Is there something I can help you with?"

"As a matter of fact..." I lean closer, biting my lip. "So my friend and I came to surprise my brother. He's on the Raven's team. It's his birthday, and I wanted to leave a present in his room, but I don't have a key."

His smile falls. "Miss, I'm sorry, but I can't..."

"Look," I shuffle through my bag until I find my driver's license and pull it out. "His name is Nixon Cole. He's in room 367. I really am his sister and not some crazy fan or anything."

The guy looks at the photo and then at me, giving me an apologetic smile. "I'm sorry, but it really is against the hotel's policy."

"Damn, and I really hoped to surprise him. It's his first birthday with just the two of us. Our mom died last year, and well..." I tap my fingers against the counter. "But I understand you have to follow your hotel's policy." I give him a sad smile. "Thanks anyway."

I start to walk away.

"Miss!"

Biting the inside of my cheek to stop myself from smiling, I turn around. "Yes?"

Chapter 35

PRESCOTT

"Dude, it's not fair that we can't get you drunk on your birthday!" Gregory says as he throws a dart at the board and groans when it barely hits one of the outer circles.

"It's not like I haven't been drunk before."

"But today's your *birthday*," Phillip adds as he shoves Gregory out of his way. "It's different."

His tongue peeks from the corner of his mouth, his eyes squinting at the board as he tests the darts in his hand.

"Dude, just shut up and throw. You look like a damn dog," Gregory says, joining us back at the table and taking a sip of his Red Bull. "But seriously, we should throw a party or something when we get back to campus."

"I don't want a party, and no, I don't want to drink. Or get drunk. I definitely don't want that. Been there, done that."

"You've turned into such a wuss, Cole."

Nixon laughs, "Why? Because I don't want to get drunk?"

"Because of everything. There are only three things you're currently doing." He lifts a finger as he ticks off the statements. "Go to practice. Go to class. And talk about your wife. Like I said, wuss."

"And I'd rather go straight home tomorrow to my wife than go out with you assholes and get drunk at some party to the point I have to go and have my stomach pumped." Nixon turns to me. "Remember that party our freshman year?"

"Which one exactly?" My brows pull together. "There were a lot of them."

The first couple of years, we were partying like crazy. Thursday through Sunday, if there wasn't a game, we were out partying, drinking, and hooking up. Hell, sometimes, even if we had a game, we'd do the same. But somewhere over the last year and a half, that has changed.

"True," Nixon chuckles. "But there was that one when seniors issued a challenge."

"What kind of challenge?" Phillip asks.

"Shit, now I remember."

"They told us if we manage to sneak booze into the dorms for a party, they'd fake to be injured so we could play."

"Did you?" Sullivan asks as he and a couple of sophomores join the table.

"Of course we did," Nixon smirks.

"At that time, any of us would have given our left nut if it meant that we could get some playing time. So Nixon, Hayden, and I made a plan. We found a guy who'd buy some booze for us and meet us at the dorm in the middle of the night. Then I snuck out of the window to make the exchange. The next day we threw the party in my room. The booze was shitty, not that anybody cared that much, but then one of the sophomores got so drunk he passed out, and we had to call the ambulance. So everybody found out about the party and booze."

"And then, on top of everything else, the coach found out, and he made us run suicides until we were all throwing up on the field."

"True."

"So no, I have had enough of drinking to last me a lifetime. What I crave now is calm. Which means you assholes better not get yourselves into a hospital because that'll be my problem, and I don't like problems." He pulls out his phone, a frown appearing between his brows.

"What?" Phillip smirks. "No message from Mrs. Cole? Maybe *she's* out partying when you're not home. Ever think of that?"

"Dude, have you met my wife?" Nixon shakes his head. "Her idea of fun is ordering tacos and tequila and snuggling on the couch to rewatch her favorite TV show."

"That's what you think. For all you know, she could..." His eyes dart to the door, mouth falling open. "Be entering the bar right at this moment."

"What?" Nixon pulls his brows together. "What are you talking about?"

"No, seriously, dude. She's here." He points at the door.

I look up over Nixon's shoulder, and sure enough, Yasmin is standing right there. She places her finger over her mouth in a keep-quiet motion as she crosses the bar toward us.

"Dude, I'm not falling for..." His words die when small hands cover his face.

My best friend's whole body stiffens, and a few guys start chuckling.

"It's not funny, you assholes. I'm not sure who you paid..." He covers Yasmin's hands with his, pushes them away, and turns around, only to come to a halt when he realizes Phillip had been telling the truth. "Yas?"

"Surprise!"

"They weren't joking."

"No, they weren't." She looks up at us, shaking her head. "For somebody who relies on imperceptible cues to play, you guys suck at playing along."

"You're really here."

"I'm really here."

"Fuck, you're really here."

The guy pushes out of the chair so suddenly that it falls down on the floor with a loud *bang*, making other people turn toward us, not that the asshole cares. He's wrapping his arms around his wife and lifts her in the air, his mouth crashing against hers.

"You'd think he didn't see her for the past ten years," Gregory shakes his head, taking a sip from his drink. "Anybody wants to play pool?"

I signal the waitress to bring us another round of drinks when Nixon finally puts his girl down. He picks up the chair, sits down, and pulls her onto his lap.

Yasmin notices the empty table. "Sorry, I made them all scurry away."

"You came just in time. They were starting to annoy us anyhow," I say, just as the waitress comes and brings us our drinks and takes Yasmin's order.

"But seriously, what are you doing here?"

"It's your birthday tomorrow." Yasmin gently caresses his cheek. "I didn't want you to spend it alone."

"Well, you won't hear me complain." His hand goes to her neck, pulling her down...

"Okay, I'm out." I finish my drink and get to my feet. "Do you guys need me to make scarce?"

There is no way I'm staying in our room and listening to the two of them have sex all night long. Thank you very much.

Color creeps up Yasmin's cheeks. "Umm... no need. I got a room."

"Perfect. I'll see you in the morning." I pat Nixon on the shoulder. "Try not to fall asleep."

"Fuck off, Wentworth."

"Happy birthday, bro."

With another slap, I make my way to the bar, where I cover the tab before going to the elevators. The hallway is quiet, but that's to be expected since there's about an hour left before curfew.

Pulling the key card out of my wallet, I unlock the door and slide into the room. Flicking the switch on, I turn around only to come to a stop when I see a person in the room.

"What..."

The words die on my lips as Jade leans against her palms and smiles at me from the bed. "Surprise."

My heart is beating frantically in my chest as I just stare at her, neither of us saying a word.

Jade slowly slides her legs off the mattress and gets to her feet. She's dressed in my jersey that falls to mid-thigh and leaves all that smooth skin of her legs out in the open. Her hair is loose, the corner of her mouth curling upward.

"I figured you'd be surprised. That was the whole point. What I didn't realize was that I'd leave you shellshocked," she whispers as she moves closer, her fingers slowly tracing my chest.

I grab her wrist and blink, but she's still here.

Real.

"Jade?"

She arches her brow. "Prescott?"

"What are you doing here? *How* did you get here?"

"Didn't you see Yasmin?"

"I did. She just came—" The understanding flashes in my mind.

A grin spreads over Jade's mouth. "Now, you're getting it. I drove her here. She came to me all sad about not being with Nixon for his birthday, so I figured if he can't be at Blairwood, why shouldn't she just drive here?"

"So you decided to come with?"

"It's my big brother's birthday," she shrugs.

"And that's the only reason you came here?"

She looks up at me, those big blue eyes shining with mischief. "I might have had my own reasons."

"I bet you did." I brush a strand of her hair behind her ear, leaning closer so I can breathe her in. The scent of lavender and something else, something intoxicating and potent, enters my lungs and calms me. "Still doesn't explain how you got here. What if Nixon…"

"I might have told my sob story to the guy at the front desk to get the key. And I knew Nixon would be otherwise… occupied. There is no way he'd come back here once he saw Yasmin. Can we stop talking about my brother now? I didn't come all the way here to discuss him."

"Then why did you come here?" I ask, my voice turning rough.

Her hand goes to my nape, and she pulls me closer, so close her lips brush against mine as she whispers: "I came here to wish you good luck for tomorrow."

"Oh?"

"Mhmm…"

Rising to the tips of her toes, she closes the distance between us, her lips meeting mine. That familiar jolt of energy goes through me as she coaxes my mouth open, her tongue sliding inside.

Letting out a groan, I lower my hands to her waist, grabbing the material of her shirt and pulling her flat against me. Those soft curves press against me, and any restraint that I hold onto snaps.

My mouth devours hers, lips gliding, teeth crashing, tongues swirling together.

Jade grabs the hem of my shirt, her chilly fingers making

goosebumps appear on my skin as she lifts my shirt. We break the kiss as Jade pulls the shirt over my head and tosses it to the floor.

My breathing is ragged as I reach for her, but she falls on her knees, her fingers quickly working the button of my pants. She tugs them down, along with my briefs, her fingers wrapping around my aching length. She looks up at me, that wicked smile on her face, and before I can even blink, she sucks me into her mouth.

"Fuck," I hiss.

My fingers slide into her hair as she takes me into her warm mouth, my eyes falling closed at the sensation of pure ecstasy. Jade pulls back, leaving just the tip of my dick between her lips. Her tongue swirls around the head, and a shudder runs down my spine as her head lowers once again, pulling me in deeper.

"Jade," I groan in warning. "Stop, I'm going to come."

Jade hums, her tongue licking the underside of my cock, and I can feel that familiar pressure building at the back of my spine. Cursing softly, I tighten my grip on her head and tug her back. My dick pops out of her mouth, glistening in the dim light.

"Why did you stop me? I want…"

I help hoist her to her feet. My finger slips under her chin as I rub my thumb over her pink lips. "And I want to be inside you when I come."

Leaning down, I seal my mouth over hers. Shoving my pants all the way down, I push her back until her legs meet the mattress, and we both fall on the bed, mouths still clashing together.

"I want to be inside you when I come. Just like you are now. Naked except for my jersey on your body, and my dick in that hot pussy. Nothing else," I murmur, brushing my lips against the side of her neck.

Jade.

In my jersey.

My number on her back.

My name.

Mine.

Wholly and utterly mine.

Letting out a groan, I press my mouth against hers in a crushing kiss. Jade arches her back off the mattress, her hand moving mine lower to her bare pussy.

I don't need to be told twice. I slide my finger between her lower lips, letting her wetness coat my fingers as I rub her clit in hard circles.

Kissing the column of her neck, I make my way back to her lips, and as my tongue meets hers, I plunge two of my fingers inside her.

I swallow her moan with my mouth as I move my fingers inside her. I can feel her walls tightening around me, pulling me deeper, needing to be filled. I curl my fingers the way I know she likes it, finding just the right spot.

"Prescott..." she breaks the kiss, her head falling back as she comes.

I watch her, in awe of the woman in my arms.

Makes me wish her camera was here so I could capture her like this. So she can see herself just like I see her.

She's always beautiful, but damn, there is something about her open and unbound as she is in this very moment that's mesmerizing.

She is mesmerizing.

I kiss every inch of naked skin I can find until she turns her head to me, her lips meeting mine.

Turning to my back, I pull her over me as we continue kissing. With my free hand, I grab the wallet from the nightstand, pulling out the condom.

Jade grabs it from my hand. Throwing one leg over mine,

she straddles my lap and opens the condom. Her teeth sink into her lower lip as she grips my length. She gives me a few pumps, my hands gripping the covers underneath me.

"Jade..." I growl, done with playing games.

She laughs, her grip tightening. "Somebody is getting nervous."

"What I'm getting is impatient."

"Fine," She tsks, but finally, she puts the condom on.

Loosening my grip on the sheet, I grab her shirt and pull her to me. My mouth crashes with hers, hard and bruising.

She rolls her hips over me, my cock falling in line with her pussy. She grinds against my length, and I can feel my dick twitch in need.

Breaking the kiss, I cup her cheek, rubbing at the soft skin. "Ride me, baby."

Those blue eyes turn the color of the stormy sky. Bracing her hands against my shoulders, she moves up, once, twice, and just when I'm ready to shove her on her back and have my way with her teasing ass, she slides over me, taking me in.

Groaning, my fingers dig into her hips, pulling her to me. She's so fucking tight, so warm and inviting. But then she starts moving, and I'm in heaven, or maybe it's hell. Not like it matters because she's right there with me, and as long as I have her, I know I can withstand everything that's thrown our way.

"Prescott," she pants, burrowing her head in the crook of my neck. Her warm breath teases my skin as her movements become hurried.

"Come for me, doll," I breathe, my finger slipping between our bodies and finding her clit. I rub the sensitive bud, feeling it pulse under my fingertips. Her walls grip me tight, and then she's falling, hard and fast.

Groaning, I turn us so she's lying on her back as I chase my own release.

My hips thrust inside of her, deeper and deeper. There's only her and me and this moment, and then I'm coming.

Calling out her name, I bury my head in the crook of her neck, inhaling her scent. The orgasm hits me like a wave, pulling me under until there's nothing else, nothing except her.

Jade.

She's everywhere, she's mine, and I can't get enough of it.

Enough of her.

And that's how I know I'm screwed.

Chapter 36

JADE

Stifling a yawn, I step into the elevator, only to be greeted by my tired reflection. Not even the makeup could help hide the dark circles under my eyes.

I had to set the alarm at three in the morning because I didn't want to risk my brother sneaking in at the crack of dawn and finding me sleeping in Prescott's bed. Talk about awkward. And just as I was falling asleep in my own hotel room, I got the message from Yas that they were going down for breakfast, and I should join them.

The temptation to turn around and go back to bed is strong, but instead, I press the button to close the door.

Maybe I'll get some sleep before the game. That sounds nice. I'll grab something to eat and hop right in—

"Hold the elevator!"

I look up, my hand slipping between the closing door just as Prescott and Sullivan appear in the hallway.

"Jade?" Sullivan's eyes narrow at me. "What are you doing here?"

My gaze meets Prescott's, and I feel my tummy tighten. He looks gorgeous, all sleepy and disheveled like this. My eyes fall to his mouth, remembering the feel of it on my skin as he worshiped my body last night. As if he could read my mind, his eyes darkened, making me wish we were alone. Preferably back in the room. Naked.

Screw sleep. It's definitely overrated.

Forcing a smile out, I shift my attention to Sullivan. "Being the best sister Nixon could ever ask for."

They join me in the elevator making the small space seem even tighter with their hulking height.

"Wait, you came here last night with Yasmin?"

"Yeah, she came to me all sad that they had to spend Nixon's birthday apart because of football. I couldn't watch her mope for days, now could I?"

A hand brushes against mine, making me suck in a breath.

What the hell is he doing?

My heart speeds up, and I bite the inside of my cheek, keeping my gaze straight ahead, hoping Sullivan hasn't noticed it.

"Why didn't you come to the bar with her last night?"

Because I was preparing a surprise of my own?

"I was..." Fingers brush against mine once again. This time the movement is more intent. The hairs at the back of my neck rise as a pinky links with mine. "T-tired." *Damn. Get a grip, Jade.* I tuck a strand of my hair behind my ear. "From the ride."

Prescott lets out a soft snort next to me, his other hand rising so he can rub his nose and cover his laughter.

Asshole.

I'm going to kill him for this.

"I guess there's that," Sullivan agrees. If he notices something is strange, he doesn't let it show.

Thank God for small mercies.

"You ready for the game?" I ask, needing to change the subject.

Sullivan grunts, "It's not like I'm going to play, so I guess it doesn't matter."

The elevator chimes, and Prescott lets go of my finger. Sullivan's eyes meet mine. "I guess I'll see you later?"

"Sure."

I watch him walk down the hallway and toward the dining room, feeling shitty for bringing it up, when I knew from earlier how upset he was over losing his spot.

"Shit. I wasn't even thinking."

"Don't worry about it. He'll get over it."

"He'll get over it?" I look up at Prescott, crossing my arms over my chest. "He wants to play!"

"And so do all the other backup players. But there is a reason why they're just that, *backup*."

"He's a good player." I'm not even sure why we're discussing this, but I can't seem to let it go.

"I didn't say they're *bad* players, I said they're backup. Every team needs them in case something unexpected occurs, and you never know when that might be. He got cocky and greedy last year when he was one of the lucky few. He has two years of his college career left; he'll get his turn. Not a lot of guys who are in his spot can say the same, Jade."

I know he's right. I've listened to the statistics of it my whole life. The hurdles Nixon will have to overcome to get to where he wants to be is a road only a select few travel. Because the truth is, there are so many talented young players out there, tens of thousands, but only the best of the best will ever be able to play pro.

"Well, you're the first person who should be more sensitive about it since you tasted just how shitty it is to sit on the sidelines and watch your teammates play."

I start to walk to the dining room, but Prescott grabs my hand and tugs me to him, his eyes ice cold. "You're right. I know exactly what it feels like to sit on the sidelines, that's why I'm fighting tooth and nail to keep my spot. We all have dreams and promises we have to keep, but some of us don't have time."

Shit.

He doesn't have to explain who he's talking about. I already know—Gabriel. He made a promise to his dead brother that he was trying to keep.

And now, I feel even more shitty than before.

"Prescott, I..."

"It's fine," he tilts his chin toward the restaurant. "Let's go inside. I have practice soon."

"Okay," I nod, giving in.

He places his hand on the small of my back, and we make our way to the restaurant. The moment we reach the threshold, his touch falls away.

I look around the busy space until my eyes finally land on my brother's. He laughs at something Yasmin said, and I'm glad that I got to do this for him.

Yasmin notices me first, and she tips her head toward me. I watch as Nixon turns in confusion, his brows pulling together when he sees me standing there.

"Smalls?" Nixon looks to Yasmin before returning his attention to me. "What are you doing here?"

"What does it look like I'm doing?" I ask, joining them at the table. "Somebody had to deliver your birthday gift and save your team from a possible loss because their quarterback is too heartbroken to play. So happy birthday, big brother."

"What?"

"It was her idea to come," Yasmin chimes in.

"She came to me moping yesterday, and it was either bring her to you or risk her committing a crime."

"I wasn't moping!" Yasmin protests.

I just raise my brow.

"I wasn't!"

"Keep telling yourself that."

"Here," Prescott says, handing me a mug of coffee.

I take it instinctively, taking a long sip of the black gold as he sits next to me.

When I look up, I find Yasmin and Nixon watching us, matching dumbfounded expressions on their faces.

"Since when are you two friends?" Nixon asks, his eyes narrowing suspiciously.

There is a beat of silence as I process his words before my heart kicks up a notch as the panic spreads through my body.

Shit.

Shit, shit, shit.

"We're not friends," I say quickly.

"I saw her in the elevator, and she looked grumpy so I figured I might as well get her coffee if I don't want her to bite my head off."

I turn my head toward him, glaring at him, but he's already digging into his food, not looking the least bit worried about the whole situation. "Grumpy? I'm not grumpy."

He looks at me, and I can see the amusement dancing in his irises before he shifts his attention to Nixon. "See?"

"I'm not grumpy." I bump my leg with his under the table hard, but he places his hand over my knee, making me freeze.

Is he serious right now? Does he want us to get caught?

Nixon just shakes his head. "I don't know why I even try with you two."

"Because I bring your wife to you as a birthday present? By the way, you're welcome."

"There is that, I guess."

"So generous."

Coach enters along with the rest of the staff. He comes to a stop when he sees Yasmin and me sitting at the table with the boys and just stares for a heartbeat before shaking his head.

"I'm not even going to ask," he mutters before going to grab his breakfast.

"And on that note..." I get up, Prescott's hand dropping from my leg. "I'm going to grab something to eat. You know," I look pointedly at Prescott. "Before I bite somebody's head off."

"You said it, not me." He cuts a piece of a waffle. Not able to resist it, I lean down, wrapping my mouth around the fork before he can move it to his mouth. "Hey, that's mine."

I lick the syrup from my lip. "Better that than your head, right?"

And with that, I turn on the balls of my feet and make my way to the table to grab something to eat.

"You'll pay for that!" Prescott calls after me.

Chuckling, I look over my shoulder. "You can always try, Wentworth. You can always try."

As I start to turn around, I notice Yasmin's gaze is still on me, watching.

Chapter 37

JADE

"Look who finally got home!" Grace says the moment I enter the apartment. "Where have you been?"

"Out. Trying to figure out what I want to shoot for this damn competition we have going on."

The whole thing was starting to drive me crazy. I wanted this. I wanted this so badly, but nothing was good enough.

I enter the living room, letting my backpack drop on the floor, and then, more carefully, placing my camera bag on the coffee table before I slouch onto the couch next to her.

Grace closes her book and sits up. "No luck so far?"

I shake my head. "Nothing that I'd even consider submitting."

Grace hums, grabbing my camera from the table and pulling it out. If it was anybody else, I'd tackle them to the ground, but Grace has seen my work in their early stages before, so I don't try to stop her. Maybe if she looks at it, she can help me figure this shit out.

"What's the theme again?"

"Raw beauty." I roll my eyes. "I honestly don't know what

she was thinking when she gave us that theme. She could have easily said to submit a photo of despair."

"Despair?" Grace chuckles. "Seriously?"

"What? It's true. The concept is just too broad, and it means different things to different people. What I can see as raw beauty she can consider trash."

"I guess you're right when it comes to that." Grace keeps sliding over the photos in the gallery. "These are all good. When did you wake up, though? At the crack of dawn?"

More like I didn't even go to sleep. I barely got a couple of hours of sleep before I was awoken by another nightmare. I knew there was no chance I'd fall asleep, so instead, I put on some clothes, grabbed my camera, and went out. The best part is I managed to stop at Prescott's since—

"Well, damn, that's some raw beauty right here," Grace says, her teeth sinking into her lower lip as she gets to the photo of a half-naked Prescott. Thankfully his face isn't showing on the image. One slide to the right though…

"Gimmie that," I mutter, grabbing the camera from her.

"Who's that? You keeping secrets from me, Jade?"

"Nobody important." I turn off the camera before I put it back into the case and close it.

"Maybe you should shoot him. I'm sure your professor would be happy about that."

Oh, I didn't doubt that for one second, but there is no way I'm sharing Prescott's photos with anybody else. Nope, they were just for me.

"But seriously, who's the guy?"

"Nobody you know." I push to my feet. "I'm going to take a shower."

Grabbing my backpack, I toss it over my shoulder, Grace's laughter follows me all the way down the hall. "You know you can't keep that secret forever!" she yells after me.

Maybe. But I'm going to give it my best to hide it for as long as I can.

Slipping into my room, I place my bag on the bed and pull my shirt over my head. Shower first, then I'm going to deal with everything else.

I make my way to the bathroom, dropping the shirt into the hamper. Then I do the same with the rest of my clothes as I make my way to the shower. I turn on the water to the hottest setting, waiting for it to warm up before sliding under the spray.

The hot water trickles down my naked body, relaxing my muscles. Damn, this was exactly what I needed. Maybe I can even try to take a nap after I'm done here. I don't know how long I will be able to keep on like this. If I didn't have nightmares, I was with Prescott, and the last thing we had on our minds was sleeping.

Grabbing my shampoo from the shelf, I squeeze some into my palm. I rub them together before smearing the shampoo over my skin, the scent of lavender filling the bathroom. I glide my hands over my body, my sides, and down my legs before making my way up my stomach, cupping my full breasts. I'm about to move them to my arms when I feel it—the bump just on the underside of my breast.

"No," I whisper.

My whole body freezes, my finger stuck on that bump that wasn't there before.

So you wanted to believe.

The hot water keeps cascading over my body, the sound echoing in my eardrums as my heart starts to beat faster. My throat bobs as I swallow. I force my fingers to move. The round motion is familiar, but is it even strange considering everything I've been through?

Calm the fuck down, Jade, I chastise. *It's probably just in your he—*

Then I feel it again.

A thickening of the skin the size of a coin just on the underside of my right breast. Too big to be one of those annoying pimples or ingrown hairs.

No, this one is definitely a bump.

My hand drops down, almost like I've burned myself. I clench my fingers into fists by my sides. My breathing is ragged, my heart is beating a mile a minute.

Calm down.

I inhale a shaky breath.

Get out of the shower.

Exhale.

You might be wrong.

Inhale.

Maybe it's just a pimple.

Exhale.

Or a cyst.

Inhale.

It doesn't have to be anything.

Exhale.

Slightly calmer, I finish rinsing and turn off the water. I grab the towel and wrap it around myself before I get out of the shower.

The mirror above the sink beckons me. I've been trying to avoid it for weeks.

No more.

I place one foot in front of the other, forcing myself to move closer. My throat bobs as I swallow, my knuckles white from the force with which I'm clinging onto the towel. Slowly, I unclench my fingers, the towel dropping to the floor as I look at my reflection.

Really looking at my reflection for the first time in weeks.

Searching for any other signs that I have brushed off.

My right breast is a little tender and slightly red, but then again, I was just in the shower, so it could be from the burning hot water. That one is also just a tad larger. Maybe? I narrow my eyes at my reflection. But honestly, how many women out there have a pair of real, completely symmetrical boobs? That one bruise I had on my side, just under my armpit, is still there, surrounded by a couple more smaller ones. Some are faint yellowish green; some are vivid purple. And then there are the bumps under my armpit. I'm still pretty sure those are due to the lymph node inflammation, but instead of disappearing like they usually do, they've multiplied and grown bigger. The little bumps are an angry red color and hurt like a bitch.

My tongue darts out, sliding over my lower lip as I continue with the self-examination process. My hand trembles slightly as I lift it, pressing three fingers against my skin, just on top of my nipple. With slow circular motions, I make sure to pass every inch of the flesh, feeling for any thickening of the skin, lumps, or irritations.

I suck in a breath, my teeth sinking into my lower lip as time drags by, until I feel it again.

I let out a breath, my eyes shutting.

I didn't imagine it.

Just on the underside, an inch to the right there is a lump. About an inch wide. It isn't necessarily painful, but definitely tender.

It could be a pimple or cyst or a...

I brace my hands against the sink, my vision growing blurry as I try to suck in a breath.

"This can't be happening."

Not again.

Not so soon.

My knees feel weak, so I sit down on the toilet seat. My

breathing is ragged, and no matter how much I try to inhale, it's like the air isn't reaching my lungs.

The image of Nixon and Yasmin, my friends, and *Prescott* all laughing and happy flashes in front of my eyes.

This can't *be happening!*

How am I supposed to tell them? How am I supposed to tell my brother that we might be back to where we were two years ago?

No, I just can't. If he were to find out, he'd be devastated.

He was broken after Mom died.

Completely and utterly broken.

If I tell him...

I shake my head, brushing away the tears that have spilled down my cheeks as I struggle to breathe in.

Calm down. Just calm down.

Pressing my hand over my mouth, I force myself to inhale through my nose. I repeat the motion over and over again until my lungs finally open, and I'm not gulping for air.

I can't deal with this.

Not now.

Not yet.

Pushing to my feet, I enter my room and go straight for the closet. Bypassing the clothes, I look at the back of my closet until I find the half-empty bottle of tequila. Unscrewing the cap, I bring the bottle to my lips and take a pull.

Forget.

That's what I need. To forget this has happened. To forget that my body is betraying me. To forget this new reality, I'm not ready to confront.

A reality I'll have to face, but not just yet.

Not tonight.

Tequila burns as it slides down my throat, warming my

belly. Grabbing my phone, I find a message from Prescott waiting for me.

Hotshot: How about I come to your place after practice tonight?

I stare at his message for a moment, my teeth grazing over my lower lip.

What will he think when he finds out? After everything that has happened to his brother...

My chest tightens, making it hard to breathe. Why does it hurt? It shouldn't hurt so much. It's just sex, for God's sake. Just sex.

Keep telling yourself that.

Exiting the message, I sit down on the floor, pressing my back against the bed. I bring the bottle to my lips and take a sip, my gaze fixed on the mess that's my closet. Prescott's hoodie is safely stashed inside, a couple of basketball shorts peeking from one of the drawers where he left them a few weeks ago.

Then the bright pink of my gloves catches my attention, and an idea forms in my mind. I pull up a browser, quickly typing until I find the info I need before opening my inbox once again.

Me: What are you doing tonight?

Hitting send, I grab the bottle and take another sip. I'm not sure if it's the alcohol or my resolve, but whatever it is, I'm finally calming down. Only one thing on my mind—erase this pain.

Marcus: Studying. Always studying.
Me: How about you take a break?

I don't have to wait long for his reply.

Marcus: What did you have in mind?
Me: There is this one bar I wanted to check out.
Me: Pick me up in thirty?

Chapter 38

PRESCOTT

I look at the message only to find one word written underneath. *Seen.* That's it. Just seen. No reply. No call. Nothing.

Maybe Jade fell asleep?

I didn't see another reason why she wouldn't answer. Jade isn't one of those girls who likes to play games. If she has an issue, she damn well makes sure everybody knows it.

"Damn, I think I overdid it."

Locking my phone, I let it drop into my bag before turning to face my best friend.

"Or maybe you're just getting old."

"Shut up. I'm in the best shape of my life."

"Mhmm… so you keep saying."

Nixon chuckles, "You're such an asshole, Wentworth."

"Yeah, well… I'm going to grab a shower."

"Hey, I wanted to thank you."

"For what?" I pull my brows together, not knowing where he's going with this.

"For giving Jade a break. I know she's a lot to deal with sometimes, but she's not a bad person."

My stomach clenches at his words, the guilt slamming into

me. Me giving Jade a break had nothing to do with him and all to do with her. And the fact that we've been hooking up for weeks now. Although, was it just hooking up? What started off just as sex turned into something more. I don't remember the last time Jade threw me out of her bed, and when we slept together, I could actually fall asleep. Most nights having her with me kept the nightmares at bay.

"I know that," I say lamely, rubbing the back of my head.

I need to get out of here before I do something stupid. Like, tell him exactly what's been going on. If he were ever to find out, I'd be a dead man. And I can't even blame him.

You don't mess with your best friend's little sister, even if she wants you to. And you especially don't do it behind his back.

My feet pound against the ground as I turn the corner. I check the stats on my watch, speeding up—one more block. I have one more block left. I try to keep breathing deeply as I push my body to its limits. I can feel that familiar ache in my knee, but I don't let it slow me down.

One more block.

I chant those words as the familiar buildings come into view. I look up, my eyes going straight to Jade's window, but the damn light is off, and the window closed like it was when I left my apartment earlier this evening.

Where the hell is she?

I texted her when I got home once again, but I haven't heard anything from her.

Coming to a stop in front of my building, I lean forward and press my palms against my knees, trying to get my breathing under control.

Maybe she went out with the girls? But still, she would have gotten back to me by now. She always got back to me.

The sound of an engine has me straightening. Bright lights blind me as the car comes closer. I raise my hand to shield my gaze and find a black Honda pulling up in front of the building. The driver turns off the car and steps out. "Prescott?"

I move closer, narrowing my eyes. "Marcus?" I vaguely remember the tall guy from around campus since we have some classes in the same building, and I'm pretty sure I saw him hang out with Jade a time or two. "What's going on? What are you doing here?"

It was almost close to midnight, and Jade wasn't home. Maybe he was coming to meet somebody else?

"I..." His throat bobs as he swallows, and for the first time, I notice that his face is completely pale. "I need your help."

The hairs on my body stand to attention. *Help? Help with what exactly?* "I... sure."

"I swear, I don't know what happened." Marcus runs his hand through his hair as he walks around the car and opens the passenger door. He shakes his head, his voice faster with every word he says until it's all just a blur. "One moment she was with me, and the next..."

I step closer, my heart slows down, and I suck in a breath, bracing myself as I look inside the car.

Somebody is lying on the passenger seat, and it takes me a moment to recognize the person.

"Jade?" My heart starts beating faster as rage courses through me.

Hot, boiling rage.

I shove Marcus out of my way as I bend down so I can get a better look at her.

"Doll?" My fingers tremble as I reach for her, unsure of

where to even touch her to not hurt her, but at the same time, knowing that I can't *not* touch her.

She's lying on the seat, almost like she's sleeping, if there wasn't blood covering her face. So much fucking blood. Her eyes are closed, one dark, angry bruise coloring her eyelid.

"What the hell happened?" I yell at Marcus, my eyes still taking her in. Still assessing. "Who did this to you?"

Who do I have to kill?

Ripped clothes.

Busted lip.

Blood.

Scratches.

More fucking blood.

Why is there so much blood?

"Apparently, the bar she wanted to visit has pit fights. And she applied. She won against two chicks before one beat her."

Pit fight? She was in a fucking pit fight?

"Why didn't you take her to the hospital?"

I lean closer, pressing my fingers to the side of her neck and let out a shaky breath when I feel the steady thrum of her heartbeat.

"She didn't—"

"N-no... h-hospital," Jade groans, her fingers wrapping around mine. She tries to blink her eyes open but only manages to squint through one.

"You need a hospital, Jade. You could have internal bleeding, and you most likely have a concussion."

More possible complications cross my mind, but I shove them back. She's alive. She's talking. That's good. Focus on the good.

"No h-hospitals..." she repeats, this time her voice coming out steadier. "Nobody... know."

"She's being stubborn, as you can see," Marcus mutters. "I swear to you, Jade. If you weren't lying inside that car already bloodied, I'd strangle you myself. What the hell were you thinking?"

"Pain... G-go... a-away..."

"Fuck..." I run my fingers through my hair, looking around the empty parking lot. "Is anybody home at your place?"

She gives her head a shake.

"Okay."

Okay, I repeat. *She's not Gabriel. She's not dying. I can do this.*

Nodding more to myself than to them, I unbuckle her seatbelt and pull her into my arms. Jade rests her head against my chest, her fingers holding onto my sweaty shirt as I turn to Marcus, who's watching us silently. "I'll take her upstairs and take care of her. Thanks for bringing her home to me."

"Sure thing." He nods at Jade. "You need help?"

I shake my head. "I've got her. Thanks, man."

"No problem. And I mean it. Tell her I'm going to strangle her once she gets better."

"You'll have to get in line."

With Jade safely in my arms, I make my way to the building. Marcus helps me pull the door open and finds the key to Jade's place in her bag before going back to his car. I climb the stairs, my leg protesting at the additional weight, but I grit my teeth and push through.

It takes me a moment to unlock the door, but somehow, I manage to do it. Hooking the door with my foot, I shut it behind us and continue straight down the hall into Jade's room and bathroom.

I gently place her on the toilet, my hand cupping her cheek. "Doll, I need your help now."

She murmurs something incoherently.

"I'm going to take your clothes off, and then we're going to wash the blood off of you."

I didn't even want to know what the hell I would find once she was clean again. What kind of damage.

You kill everyone you love. My dad's words echo in my head, but I shove them back.

As gently as possible, I slide her ripped shirt over her head. Jade lets out a soft whimper.

"Shhh... Just a little bit longer," I whisper, working the button of her pants. "I've gotcha. Can you stand up?" Jade nods slowly, so I help her stand, making sure to place her hands on my shoulders. "Lean on me, okay? Just like that."

Her fingers dig into my shoulders as I tug the jeans down along with her panties before helping her sit once again.

"I'll turn on the water and fill the bathtub—" I start to get up, but Jade grabs my hand and pulls me back.

"No." Her grip turns stronger than it was before. One eye is fully open. Her pupil is dilated, hiding the bright blue of her irises, but it's not that that feels like a kick to my gut. It's the horror in her eyes. "No, bathtub."

"Jade, I can't..."

She shakes her head. "No, p-please... no."

Tears shimmer in her eyes. She blinks and lets them fall, the liquid turning pink as they trail down her cheeks.

I just watch her completely terrified. I don't know this girl. I've never seen her before, and I don't know what to do to help her.

I *need* to help her.

What the fuck happened to you, Jade? And how did I miss it so far?

But I can't ask. Not now. Not when she's like this and needs my help. Needs me to take care of her.

Gripping the back of my shirt, I pull it over my head and let it drop on the floor before shoving down my pants and underwear. Finally naked, I pick her up in my arms.

"Together, okay?" I whisper as I somehow get us both in the bathtub and sit down, Jade in my arms. "I'm here, the whole time. I'm here. Okay?"

She nods as she squeezes herself against me. I grab the showerhead and turn on the water, making sure the temperature is good before I start to wash her.

The sound of the water is the only thing filling an otherwise quiet room. I watch as pink water trickles down the drain as I wash the blood away. Only when I'm completely sure that I got all of it, do I grab her shampoo from the shelf.

The scent of lavender fills the room as I squeeze some on my hand and start washing her hair. It doesn't seem like she has any injuries on her scalp. In reality, her face took the worst of it. There are some bruises and scrapes on her hand and torso, and one of her knees is scraped, too, probably from a fall, but it seems like she's okay.

She's okay.

Rinsing out her hair, I grab the body wash and place some on my hands, sliding them gently over her body. My movements are methodical as I wash her, and then wash myself before rinsing us both off.

Grabbing the towel from the hook, I wrap it around Jade's shoulders and help dry her off the best I can before picking her up and getting out of the bathtub. I place her on the toilet seat and grab a towel for myself. I quickly dry off and tie it around my hips before crouching before Jade once again to give her a good look. Her face still looks pretty bad, but all the bleeding seems to have stopped, so there is that.

As gently as I can, I cup her cheek and skim my finger over the tender flesh. "What happened out there, Jade? Pit fight? Seriously?"

"Can we... not?" She looks away, avoiding my gaze. "Not tonight, please?"

"Okay." I let out a sigh, "Not tonight."

But soon. We'll have to talk about what happened soon.

Helping Jade to her feet, I walk her to her bed. I rummage through her closet until I find a large t-shirt and help slide it over her head. Then, I go to the drawer in which I stashed a few of my clothes and pull out a pair of basketball shorts.

When I turn around, I find that Jade's already lying under the covers. I just stand there watching her, letting myself drink her in. Drink in this moment and the fact that she's okay. Sleeping in her bed.

Jade looks over her shoulder, that one blue eye meeting mine. "You should probably put ice on that. It might help—"

"Come here," Jade rasps, her voice low.

"What?"

My throat tightens, that knot that's been there ever since I saw her in that car growing bigger and making it hard to breathe.

"Hold me? Please? I need you to hold me tonight."

I don't need to be told twice. Pushing away the covers, I slide behind Jade, wrapping my arms around her and pulling her to my chest. She feels so small in my arms. So breakable.

She could have been seriously hurt tonight. She could have been seriously hurt, and I...

Jade lets out a soft sob, her body shaking.

"Shh..." I whisper, tightening my hold on her. "I've gotcha. You're safe."

I keep murmuring those words as I gently stroke her hair long after she stops crying. But even with Jade asleep, I don't let go. I hold her long after I've fallen asleep.

Chapter 39

JADE

A loud *bang* snaps me out of my dreamless sleep. I moan in protest, snuggling deeper into the warm body next to mine. Prescott. I know I probably shouldn't get used to this, after all, we've just agreed to sex, but at this moment, I don't really care. He's warm, and his arms are wrapped around me tightly.

"Where the hell is my sister?"

My eyes snap open at the sound of Nixon's voice.

Shit.

Shit, shit, shit.

I look at the still-sleeping Prescott next to me, completely unaware of the shitshow that's about to happen. There's a frown etched between his brows like even in his sleep, there's this weight hanging over him.

"Prescott," I whisper, giving his shoulder a little shake. "Wake up. You need—"

My door bursts open, banging against the wall. Prescott's eyes snap open just as the light is turned on.

I close my eyes, partly because of the headache that's booming behind my temples, partly because I don't want to be here and face this disaster.

"Jade, what the..." Nixon's voice dies down.

Maybe this is all just in my head. A bad dream. Maybe...

"Wentworth?" my big brother's voice has turned to ice.

My eyes snap open to find Nixon looking from Prescott to me and then back to Prescott. His hands ball into fists.

"I'm going to kill you," he growls, crossing the distance to the bed. He pulls Prescott out of the bed, his fist connecting to Prescott's face before I can even open my mouth. "That's for sleeping with my sister."

"Nixon!" I yell, jumping out of bed as Prescott staggers back from the impact.

"And this is for lying to me about it." This time his hand connects to Prescott's gut, and he does nothing to stop it. Of course, he wouldn't.

"And this..."

"Stop it!" I get in between the two of them, facing my brother. "You need to stop this, Nixon. Right now."

"He was sleeping with you behind my back!"

"Well, then you should punch me also because I've been sleeping with him too."

Nixon turns his glaring eyes to me. "I'm not punching you. Him, on the other hand..."

He tries to reach for Prescott once again, but I press my hands against Nixon's chest and push him hard. "Stop this. You're acting like a jackass."

"Jackass?" Nixon lets out an unamused chuckle. "I'm acting like a jackass? What about you, Jade? Huh? What about you?"

"We're not talking about me. You need to calm do—"

"Calm down? You want *me* to calm down? You're drinking and partying like you're never going to do it again. You're sleeping behind my back with my best friend. You're entering *pit fights* that leave you all beaten and bruised. And you want *me* to calm down?" Nixon shakes his head, the disappointment clear on his face. "What were you thinking, Jade?"

"Nixon..." Prescott tries to push me behind him, but I stay put. This is between my brother and me.

Nixon shifts his attention over my shoulder. If looks could kill, I'm pretty sure Prescott would be dead.

"Shut up, Wentworth. Just shut the fuck up. Fucking my little sister behind my back, seriously, dude? This whole situation has you written all over it. Was it your idea?" Nixon tries to grab Prescott, but I shove him away. "Was—"

"He didn't do anything!"

"It doesn't seem like that to me. You were never like this before. Now you've become reckless. Drinking, partying, fighting... Do you have a death wish or something? Seriously, Jade, give me one good reason why you'd be so reckless to..."

"Because I'm dying!" I yell, the truth slipping off my lips before I can think twice about it.

I cover my mouth, but it's already too late; the words are out in the open. The silence that falls over the room is deafening.

My brother's eyes, the ones that perfectly match my own, widen in shock.

And Prescott...

I'm grateful I can't see his face right this moment, but I can feel his body go utterly still behind me.

"What..." Nixon takes a step back, his throat bobbing as he swallows. "What are you talking about? You're not dying. That's bullshit."

Oh, Nixon.

The way he says it, with utmost certainty, like if he can say it out loud, it'll make it so, breaks my heart.

"You're not dying! Tell me this is some kind of joke because I swear, Jade..."

If only it would be that easy.

But nothing is ever easy.

Not for us.

But I knew I couldn't keep hiding this for much longer, and I couldn't have Prescott take the blame for something he didn't do.

So I do the only thing I can. I say the truth, although, I know it'll shatter the world as we know it, and nothing will ever be the same again.

"I have cancer."

Does Jade really have cancer? What will happen now that Prescott knows the secret she's been hiding from him? Find out the end to their story in *Kiss To Salvage, Shattered and Salvaged book 2.*

New to Blairwood University? Most of Prescott and Jade's friends already have their story out: Kiss To Conquer (Hayden and Callie), Kiss To Forget (Nixon and Yasmin), Kiss To Defy (Zane and Rei), Kiss To Remember (Grace and Mason) and Kiss To Belong (Maddox and Alyssa)!

Bloggers, bookstagrammers and booktokers join Anna's share team to be the first to know about her upcoming releases and sales.

Want to stay in touch with Anna? Join her reader's group Anna's Bookmantics, or sign up for Anna's newsletter.

PLAYLIST

Beth Crowley - I Scare Myself
Faouzia - Born Without a Heart
Beth Crowley - Monster
Isak Danielson - Broken
Madilyn Paige - Bleed
Faouzia, John Legend - Minefields
Taylor Swift - willow
Ed Sheeran - Photograph
Zoe Wees - Control
Sam Smith - Fire On Fire
Tate McRae - bad ones
Dean Lewis - How Do I Say Goodbye
Julia Michaels - Little Did I Know
Beth Crowley - In The End
SIX, Natalie Paris - Heart of Stone
All Time Low - Monsters (feat. Demi Lovato and blackbear)
G-Eazy - Breakdown (feat. Demi Lovato)
Taylor Swift - illicit affairs
One Direction - Perfect
Avril Lavigne - Love It When You Hate Me (feat. blackbear)

PLAYLIST

Conor Maynard - Don't Let Me Down
Allie X - Devil I Know
Paloma Faith - Only Love Can Hurt Like This
Chase Wright - Lying With You
Tate McRae - uh oh
Blu Eyes - you'd never know

OTHER BOOKS BY ANNA B. DOE

New York Knights

NA/adult sports romance

Lost & Found

Until

Forever

Greyford High

YA/NA sports romance

Lines

Habits

Rules

The Penalty Box

The Stand-In Boyfriend

Blairwood University

College sports romance

Kiss Me First

Kiss To Conquer

Kiss To Forget

Kiss To Defy

Kiss Before Midnight

Kiss To Remember

Kiss To Belong

Kiss Me Forever

Kiss To Shatter

Kiss To Salvage

Standalone

YA modern fairytale retelling

Underwater

Box Set Editions

Greyford Wolves: The Complete Collection

The Anabel & William Duet

ABOUT THE AUTHOR

Anna B. Doe is a *USA Today* and international bestselling author of young adult and new adult sports romance. She writes real-life romance that is equal parts sweet and sexy. She's a coffee and chocolate addict. Like her characters, she loves those two things dark, sweet and with a little extra spice.

When she's not working for a living or writing her newest book you can find her reading books, binge-watching TV shows or listening to music while she walks her shi tsu puppy Tina. Originally from Croatia, she is always planning her next trip because wanderlust is in her blood.

She is currently working on various projects. Some more secret than others.

Find more about Anna on her website: www.annabdoe.com

Join Anna's Reader's Group Anna's Bookmantics on Facebook.

Printed in Great Britain
by Amazon